What Actually Happened to Isaac Moore

Samantha J. Rose

IMMORTAL WORKS
SALT LAKE CITY

Immortal Works LLC
1505 Glenrose Drive
Salt Lake City, Utah 84104
Tel: (385) 202-0116

Cover Art by Rebecca Barney
barneydesign.com

ISBN 978-1-953491-46-6 (Paperback)
ASIN B0BLMVWPBH (Kindle)

Prologue: The Question On Few People's Minds

"What ever happened to Isaac Moore?" a young lady asked. She had fancied him, what with his charm, sophisticated look, and magically smooth brown hair. Oh, and the successful business he'd inherited. There was no overlooking that.

A young man responded with pretend hesitance. "Well...I'm not sure how to tell you this,"—but he was actually very happy to tell her since he fancied her—"but he went out to sea and hasn't been heard of since. I reckon he and his crew got caught up in that big storm a few months back. Tragic, really. I'm so very, very sorry." He moved in closer, putting a comforting arm around her shoulders.

Yes, that was the word among anyone who cared enough to ask the question. They went on with their lives, assuming he, his crew, and his ship with her sails had drowned in the depths of the ocean.

But this is what *actually* happened to Isaac Moore.

The Great Arnaud

Isaac was a dreamer. He had been ever since he could dream because dreams were all he had. Well, *that*, and the beat of his heart. But these things were all he really needed. His mother had told him so.

Isaac held on to that truth long after she died. As he mopped the mud and filth-encrusted floors of the orphanage he grew up in, he would drift away in dreams of grandiose palaces on the tops of mountains that touched the stars, like in the storybook his mother used to read to him. He'd think about those times when he and his mother would look at the brilliant night sky and talk about those palaces, what they might look like, what kind of food they'd have, and what it might be like to live so close to the sky that they could catch the moon. They did that a lot before she died.

When he was older, Isaac realized that there was another thing he needed in life in order to survive. Something that his mother had not really mentioned, but of its necessity, the orphanage had taught him well: money. One cannot eat or sit in warmth—let alone build a palace in the mountains—without money.

Isaac began working at a young age with a merchant crew. He sailed the seas and traded goods between countries. It didn't take long before the captain, Benjamin Snow, took notice of Isaac's strong ambition and discipline, how he worked harder than anybody else. See, in Isaac's mind, in order to be true to one's own beating heart, one had to be willing to work hard and obey the rules. This was another wise thing his mother had taught him. "Sometimes you have to work hard and obey rules before you find freedom," she had said. "You have to be disciplined, always making sure you're doing your very best. Then, when the time is right, you break free."

This wisdom proved very beneficial. He quickly rose through the ranks, from the forecastle to third, second, and finally first officer, making quite a name for himself—a name which he'd back up with the many lies he'd tell about where he came from, such as his father being a wealthy duke from the north of England who owned a large estate in France. He spoke properly—as his mother had inspired him to do—and told these stories with such ease and arrogance that people couldn't help but believe him. He'd almost convinced himself. For all he knew of his father, it could've been true. When people asked, "Why, then, are you part of a merchant crew?" he would come back with, "For the adventure! Oh, it's *so boring* living in a mansion, having servants wait on you hand and foot—you haven't the faintest idea. It's just awful. I simply *had* to get away from it, make my own way and my own fortune."

Captain Snow was perfectly aware of Isaac's unfortunate origins. But when asked, he'd confirm Isaac's stories. "It's the truth," he'd say. Having no children of his own, he saw Isaac as a son. He wanted to be the sort of father that his child could rely on, one that would protect him and even uphold his harmless nonsense. And, as many loving fathers often do, he never judged Isaac too harshly.

The years passed. The captain became ill and died, leaving his ships and his business to Isaac. As the old sea captain had loved the boy as his only child, Isaac had loved him as any child would love their benevolent father. It wasn't easy for Isaac to accept how every important person in his life had found an exit out of it, leaving him alone with nothing but his beating heart and his dreams.

He had a profitable business. He had freedom. He'd sailed the world from the coasts of Sydney to Maine. But he was empty. What value was any of this without the people who had given life warmth and light? All he really had was a dark, festering void inside his chest that nothing could fill, that refused to heal. It was a pain that would choke him sometimes, completely stealing his breath and his mind. It usually happened with an unexpected reminder, like seeing a mother embrace a small boy with a loving smile or meeting a woman named Christine—the name of Captain Snow's favorite ship and of the girl from his stories. He'd freeze, blinking back tears and pushing away scars. He heard nothing and saw no one, not until someone brought him back to the present.

The most important people in his life were gone.

Earning money was a rush, however. He'd throw it at the void and silence its cries for a time. He reasoned that maybe if he had more money, he'd feel better—less empty.

And there was Arnaud.

Among the crew Isaac had grown up with was an old man whose hair, beard, and long mustache ranged from white to a little less white and was missing patches in random places. He was also missing one of his eyes. This was Arnaud.

Arnaud had been in the background of Isaac's life since he'd joined the merchant crew, telling strange stories that raised eyebrows. His presence made everyone a little uneasy, no matter how nice he tried to be, and he did try. He had been there for Isaac through the loss of Captain Snow. He never judged the tears he shed in the quiet of his cabin and always looked upon him with a genuine understanding and sympathy, never saying a hollow or patronizing word. On top of this, he was an expert at negotiation and spotting crooks.

So whenever any of Isaac's crew spoke ill of the old man, whether Arnaud was present or not, Isaac went out of his way to defend him. No one was allowed to mock the weird gurgle in his voice or speak about his bad smell. Yes, Arnaud needed to take better care of himself, but he deserved respect. Anything less wasn't tolerated on Isaac's ship.

Business went well enough for a while. He started to make plenty of money and was able to purchase another ship.

But it didn't last.

What really marked the beginning of the end for Isaac was the loss of his ships through a series of misfortunes, one to pirates and another to a storm. He was forced to sell another to pay off debt. It had all happened so fast. He'd managed to fool some into thinking he still had money to his name, but the reality was that Isaac was about to lose his business. He was down to his last ship. He'd be penniless, homeless, a despised and nameless beggar left to die on a cold winter night.

The thought frightened him, chilling the marrow in his bones every time it crossed his mind. He could almost see the snow falling from the dark sky.

He'd die and be forgotten. Left to the dogs.

They returned home from a business venture early one morning, Isaac slightly drunk and discussing his hopeless plight with the one person on the ship he trusted not to tell the world: Arnaud.

He even told Arnaud about the book his mother used to read to him.

"In this book," he said, with his handsome yet sad smile, "There was this prince. I believe his name was...was it Sky? Something. Anyway, his sister was kidnapped and taken to this enchanted river. Each of the River's branches led to a completely different world. Worlds that were colorful, and others where gold was as plentiful as sand. And there was one that was all fire and rock—so of course you had to be careful of which route you chose. He went to all these different worlds in search of her." He sighed, his eyes glittering with nostalgia. "I used to dream of traveling up that river, of finding a world that was better than this one. I'd build a castle there on a mountaintop that touched the stars—just like he did."

Isaac looked at the rising sun, lost in his memories. Arnaud smiled. He glanced around the deck as if to make sure they were alone.

"What if I told you," Arnaud said, his voice sounding like gurgling sewage trying to find an outlet to the ocean, "that the River is real?"

Isaac laughed. "Then I would trade you my ship for directions to it." After a thoughtful moment, he added, "And for a lift, of course. I'd probably need a lift since I'd no longer have a ship." He returned his attention to the dawn, taking a drink.

Out of his dirty inner coat pocket, Arnaud pulled out a battered, old book and placed it against the railing in front of Isaac. Isaac's brown eyes grew wide. He asked with reverence, "Where did you get that?"

It was the book. The book from his childhood. He hadn't seen it since his first month in the orphanage. He had returned to his room one day to discover, with tremendous heartbreak, that it was gone. He'd assumed it'd been taken by John One or John Two, since they'd given him grief over the title, telling him it was a book for girls. What did they know? They hadn't read it. He told them they were primitive apes doomed to live sad lives, just as his mother would've said. Then they beat him up.

"It's mine, ya?" said Arnaud with a gargle. "It doesn't matter how I got it."

Arnaud handed it to Isaac, and he took it carefully as if it was the most sacred object in existence. It had seemed so much bigger when he was little, but it was small enough to fit comfortably in the palms of his hands. He ran his fingertips over the letters of the faded title: *Princess Song and the River.*

"You keep it, Captain," Arnaud told him.

Isaac's eyes couldn't contain his surprise and gratitude. "I couldn't possibly—" he began, only to be polite.

"Stop it," growled the old man with a small wave of his hand.

Isaac opened the book and looked over the old pictures. His head spun with the flood of memories, emotions, and wine, but he managed to hold himself together. He would not allow himself to fall apart right there on the deck. Maybe when he was back in his quarters alone, he'd let himself sob like a woman gifted her dream wedding gown, but not there. Although, when he managed to finally say, "Thank you, Arnaud," some of the emotion slipped out in spite of himself. He cleared his throat and pretended it didn't happen.

He turned to a drawing of the River. It mapped out the tributaries leading off to other worlds.

Arnaud placed a finger on the picture and said, "The River is real."

Isaac raised his eyebrows and studied Arnaud, looking for any sign that he had a secret side to his sense of humor that he had never noticed before. He'd thought it possible earlier. Seeing that he was serious, Isaac decided that he would play along. He returned his attention to the book and asked nicely, "Is that so, Arnaud? So where is it? South America?" He perked up and said with a sly smile, "Perhaps it's how you actually get to that city of gold you hear about, eh? Like, maybe it's not a city of gold, but an entire *planet* of gold!"

Arnaud reached into another pocket of his coat and then held out his hand.

Isaac had never seen anything like these gems before in all his life. They looked like pieces of the sun contained in perfect diamonds, but their surface was round and smooth like pearls. They looked as though they should be burning right through Arnaud's palm.

Where had he gotten them? Arnaud had always appeared to be the *opposite* of a wealthy man. He wore the same outfit every single day and seemed to spend each dollar he received before it ever reached his hand. Isaac never would've imagined him as someone who had a secret hoard of treasure.

Before Isaac could ask, Arnaud stated, "These came from the River." He pointed to a world toward the upper middle-but-slightly-left of the map, and when he spoke, his voice cracked with sorrow. "From this world."

"So...you're saying you've been there before?"

Arnaud looked longingly at the page, seeming to hold back tears as he nodded. "It has been...my greatest dream to return. And a few years ago, I found the way back."

Was Isaac really supposed to believe that? Arnaud had disappeared for two or so years after Captain Snow died, but he'd said it was for family reasons.

Isaac studied him. He looked completely serious. But it was impossible.

Wasn't it?

But then there were those gems, those absolutely magnificent gems.

But it was impossible!

But those gems...

They couldn't be genuine. Because it was ridiculous!

They sure appeared to be genuine. They certainly weren't glass. They held a brilliant sheen that made them glow ever so subtly.

But they couldn't be real because it was all nonsense. He couldn't even believe that they were having this conversation. Everything about this was impossible.

Wasn't it?

Isaac closed the book and tucked it protectively under his arm. "You really expect me to believe this?"

Arnaud raised his patchy eyebrows. "I really thought the gemstones would convince you. But perhaps you're not looking at them closely enough."

He held them out a little farther and Isaac, looking skeptically at Arnaud, took a step closer. He studied the gems a little more carefully. Under the smooth, diamond-like surface, the bright orange color seemed to swirl like clouds and change in intensity.

They were indeed genuine.

An array of possibilities flooded his mind like a vivid dream. The gemstones arranged as pearls, strung around the slender necks of the world's most beautiful women—an item sure to be so popular that he would become one of the wealthiest men in the world. He'd be able to travel upriver to a world far better than this one. He would live in a mansion at the top of the mountains, garbed in fancy clothes, smoking a pipe, surrounded by gold, with a gorgeous wife. She'd be safe there.

They'd both be safe there. He'd never be destitute or alone again. All he needed was those gems and to find the River. He just needed to reach out and—

Arnaud closed his hand and returned the gemstones to his pocket. Anger burned through Isaac, and his chest constricted as though he were drowning. He had to stop himself from throwing the man overboard. It was as if his inner self had taken a step in between the two of them before Isaac could lay a hand on Arnaud, yelling, "What are you doing, man? Get a hold of yourself!"

Isaac put his outstretched hand to his spinning head like he'd been shaken awake from a deep sleep.

But Arnaud looked happy. "What do you think about it now?"

Think? Could he still think? He thought about that for a moment and realized that he could, apparently. Then he considered what he'd just seen. Everything he'd ever wanted—it had felt so real and so close. He just needed to find that river, that world. "Where is this river?"

"You're holding the map to it," Arnaud said.

Curious, Isaac took the book and opened it. Arnaud guided him to the very end, to the picture that covered the back of the last page and the inside of the back cover. It was a crude, elaborate drawing of the known world. In great emphasis, mapped out over Southern Asia above the Indian Ocean, was the tributary leading out of the planet Earth and to the River. He studied it. Though he had never been to that particular coast of Asia, he knew it had been sailed to plenty of times, and no one had ever mentioned having accidentally ventured off to a completely different planet before.

Of course, perhaps that was because no one had ever returned.

No one except Arnaud.

"I have a proposition for you," Arnaud said, with that gurgle that he would never, ever clear away. "A proposition that will save your business and will make you richer than you can imagine. Something I would like to propose to you and the crew."

"All right, let's hear it," Isaac said, trying not to sound too eager.

"I have been saving money, waiting most of my life for this opportunity. I will fund the entire expedition to this river, and you can have all the treasure found if you will take me with you and name the ship after me."

"Name it *Arnaud?*"

He nodded.

Isaac raised an eyebrow. "I fail to see how that benefits you at all."

"You don't have to see it. Those are my terms."

This ship had been Captain Snow's most beloved: *Christine*. Isaac was not about to name it after Arnaud. What kind of name was that anyway? *Arnaud.* Granted, he had a great deal of respect for the man, but in comparison to Captain Snow...well, there was no comparison. To change the ship's name from the one he'd chosen to *Arnaud* would be cursing it to smell like armpits and bad breath for all eternity. It would make a gurgling noise everywhere it went.

No. This would not do. It didn't matter that he had passed away to unseen shores; this was Captain Benjamin Snow's ship. It was the last possession of his that Isaac could touch. His presence accompanied Isaac when he stood on the bow and breathed in the salty sea air. If he changed its name, would it still be Captain Snow's ship? Would his presence vanish for good? Isaac's heart, his very soul, fled from the thought.

No. This was Isaac's business and about to be his expedition, and this was Captain Snow's ship. He was certain that they could come up with something better as far as terms went. Maybe Isaac could name his *next* ship *Arnaud.* Heavens, that could be the name of the next two or three—however many Arnaud wanted!

But not *this* ship.

But then again...treasure from another world was a sure way to save Captain Snow's business, his legacy. Perhaps if changing the name of his ship was essential to the cause...

No. He didn't like it. Considering it made his skin crawl. It couldn't be that important to Arnaud. There had to be something better they could both agree to.

Isaac asked, "Why now, Arnaud? If you've known about this for so long, why be sitting on it all this time?"

Arnaud looked at the sky. "I wasn't ready. Now I am. The time is right."

That really didn't answer anything. In fact, it added questions.

A voice of reason crept its way into Isaac's mind, telling him he wasn't making intelligent decisions and something was clearly wrong, but those vivid visions of wealth and cured loneliness quickly silenced it. His hopeless prayers had been answered. Did it really matter if Arnaud's motives made any sense?

Isaac shrugged. "All right then! That's good enough for me. Wake the crew. We have important matters to discuss."

Maybe Not the Smartest Thing He's Ever Done

I saac gathered his faithful crewmates around a splintered table in the ship's bowels—the few men who had sailed multiple voyages with him throughout the years—leaving the rest to their duties on deck. Isaac paced in front of them, bubbly and important-like.

"Gentlemen," he said, "I have a matter of great importance that I ask you to ponder on our journey home. I haven't wanted to worry anyone with just how dire circumstances are, but," he hesitated, hating what he had to say next. "This could be our final voyage on this great ship. I am very nearly out of business."

A few murmurs and whispers rippled through the men. Most of them weren't surprised.

He brightened, quickly moving on. "But! I have discovered something that could save this business! Even more than save it. It could launch us far into the future! We could make our mark on history and be remembered forever."

He looked around the room. He had their attention—sort of. Some of them were still waking up, but he wasn't deterred. "Arnaud has discovered a map to an unknown, unexplored land."

There was a groan among a few of the crew. A big man, his second officer, Grundy, said, "With all due respect, Cap'n, It's the nineteenth century. There really ain't nothin' left to explore."

"Now, now," an older gentleman chided, "there's always somethin' that's been overlooked. The world is vaster and more mysterious than we can imagine." He eyed Arnaud and then looked at Isaac. "But with all due respect, Captain, we're not explorers. We always know where we're goin', and we always know the way home."

"This is merely a proposition," explained Isaac. "See, I'm not just talking about an unknown land, but a whole other world."

Someone else asked hesitantly, "You mean, whole 'nother world, like how the Americas were?"

"No, my good sir," Isaac said, smiling. "I'm talking about," he turned and gestured dramatically to the sky that they couldn't see from the belly of the ship, "the stars!"

No one said anything. They looked at each other and back at him as if he'd finally cracked and gone mad. Even the older gentleman's eyes watched Isaac with deep pity. Grundy considered Isaac with a hint of concern, then laid his head on the table, ready to go back to bed.

Isaac was well aware that they all thought he'd fallen off his rocker—frankly, he wondered this himself—but he was not about to let this hurt his fantastic mood. "Look, no one has to join me. But I wanted you men to be the first to have a chance at this fantastic opportunity. Arnaud," he looked at him, "if you would, please."

With an unsettling smile, Arnaud removed the gemstones from his pocket and set them in the center of the table. The crew let out *ooohs* and *aaahs*, their forms leaning into the pile of precious stones as if drawn in by a magnet. Silence fell over them as their mouths gaped open and their eyes dimmed. Their expressions turned empty; their minds clearly lost as though they'd suddenly come down with severe dementia. Arnaud's smile grew twisted, and his gaze found Isaac's from across the room.

Isaac's stomach turned to lead with a darkness that spread through his limbs, making them heavy. He shuddered and looked away. A feeling in his bones told him there was something horribly, horribly wrong, and he should put a stop to all of it immediately.

But he trusted Arnaud, mostly—less now than yesterday, but he did. He imagined those gems having that same effect on thousands of people. He would be filthy rich in no time. Filthy rich. Captain Snow's legacy would be saved, he could build a mansion on a mountaintop, and perhaps the pain in his chest would finally cease.

His blood frosted over when he watched each member of the crew, with perfect synchronization, reach out for the gems. Arnaud snatched them up, snapping the men angrily out of their daydreams. Grundy stood, fists raised and ready to turn Arnaud into bow wow mutton. A few of the crew caught him by the arms. Isaac leapt over the table to help hold him back, yelling, "Get ahold of yourself! What is the matter with you?"

Although he'd narrowly avoided being beaten to death, Arnaud continued smiling as if everything were going according to plan.

Grundy shook everyone off him, composing himself and demanding, "Where'd you get those?"

Isaac straightened out his coat. "If you will just sit down," he looked around, "—all of you—I will tell you."

They did. Isaac showed them the map and told them some of his grand ideas. Each of them ignored every major problem that presented itself, thrilled with the thought of finding the River that led to the world where those magnificent, precious stones were to be found.

"I will fund your entire voyage," announced Arnaud, his voice its standard, bubbling syrup. "I have here," he dragged a large chest from the shadows, "my entire life's savings."

Isaac noticed something. "Wait, where did that chest come from?"

"It was all I brought with me," explained Arnaud. "Some of you brought clothes; I brought my life's savings."

Everyone was satisfied with this explanation, especially once Arnaud opened the chest and revealed a mountain of gold and precious jewels. He spoke as if only to Isaac. "You will never want for anything again. Not food, not clothing, not company. You'll have all the adventure your heart could ever desire, for I will guide you safely to the River. All I ask in return is that you take me with you and name the ship after me."

Isaac and the crew leaned in, not looking at Arnaud but at the vast contents of the chest. Someone asked, "How did you get all that on board without anybody noticin'? Someone had to have helped you, right?"

The crew looked at each other, confused. Arnaud continued to stare at Isaac with that one cold eye.

Isaac took a deep breath and grinned, feeling more optimistic than ever about his decisions and the future, throwing all his caution and doubts to the sea. He felt sick at the thought of changing the name of the ship, he simply couldn't go through with it, but Arnaud was reasonable. They could work this out. "Tell you what, my friend," he said, "I will accept your very generous offer. And *of course* you'll come with us; you always have a place among this crew. You'll remain first officer. But, um," he straightened his shoulders, "I will not name this ship after you. Maybe the next one. And the one after, if you like! But *this* ship, in honor of Captain Snow, must remain the same. Without him, none of this would even be possible. This ship is *Christine* and always will be *Christine*."

Arnaud's smile faded.

Grundy furrowed his brow and frowned. "What? Are you mad?"

"I have given this a lot of thought—"

"You're aware Captain Snow is dead, right? God rest him."

Isaac winced, narrowed his gaze at Grundy, and replied with venomous sarcasm, "You don't say? So that's where he's been all this time?"

Grundy's expression softened, compassion rising in his eyes. "This ain't his ship no more, Isaac. He don't care—"

"*Enough*, Grundy." One more word from him, and he'd be a bloody mess on the floor; Isaac would make sure of it. Grundy must've seen it on his face. He sat back, silent, his arms folded.

Isaac continued, "Yes, he's dead. That's *why* it matters." The older gentleman nodded his approval, as did many others. The rest were clearly on Grundy's side, but Isaac didn't care. "I'm sure we can come up with something—*anything*—else." Isaac turned to Arnaud, who wore a deep frown. "I'm sure you understand. Ask what you will, my friend."

Someone reached out to touch the gold in the chest when the lid slammed itself shut. The walls of the ship creaked and trembled. The men shifted in their chairs with nervous and confused glances as they listened to the wind pick up outside, and to the hollering of the crew on deck. They struggled to steady themselves as sudden waves heeled the ship violently. Before Isaac could shout orders, he looked at Arnaud, whose entire demeanor had darkened. Arnaud's brow furrowed, and his lips curled into a vicious scowl. Light emanated from his hands, and his once-dim eye glowed bright green.

Arnaud's body jolted, and he threw out his hands, letting out a high-pitched scream. A blast of light threw Isaac into the ocean. Something hard smacked his shoulder blade, stealing his breath as he sank beneath the waves.

Isaac couldn't breathe or move. He could only sink into the freezing depths as time slowed. His eyes stung with the water, and the ocean above him turned red.

His frantic mind forced his limbs to swim through the pain. When he broke the surface, each gulp he swallowed as he struggled to breathe was thick and tasted of metal. His ship was nothing but fragments floating on the waves. Gasping, he grabbed the closest piece of debris, likely the one that had hit him, holding onto it to keep his head above the angry waves.

All around him, the sea gushed upward in a flowing wall of water as angry storm clouds gathered above him, tearing apart the sky with lightning. He looked to where his ship had once been and saw a woman. Her eyes were a brilliant green, her hair thin vines with small leaves, her build one of strength. She wore a simple yet elegant gown with short sleeves, made of white silk and embroidered with white flowers. She floated in the air with gossamer wings that could've been made from spiderwebs, and her complexion was a very pale green. Was she some sort of goddess? He'd never believed in that nonsense, but unless he was dreaming—and the pain burning down his arm from his shoulder made him quite sure he wasn't—he couldn't deny the sight right in front of him. She was young, beautiful, and furious, and her fury was directed at him.

It was in that moment that whatever spell he had been under vanished, and his mind became clear. She had tricked him and destroyed *everything*—what very little he'd had left. The ship, his friends —they were gone. So, despite the horror of staring into the face of some supernatural being, he couldn't stop himself from screaming, "*What have you done?*"

There was no more gurgling when she spoke. Her voice was a sweet song on a summer breeze, yet as powerful as the mighty wind. "I offered you riches, everything you could ever want. All I asked was for you to give the ship my name!"

"That's what this is about? You're angry about that? 'Arnaud' that... that's not even your real name! I mean, I guess it could be your real name, and I'm sorry if it is, your parents should be punished, but—" What was he saying? His fingers trembled against the driftwood, and his voice cracked, but he was delirious and hopeless and had nothing more to lose. He let out a chuckle that was nigh-hysterical. "Y-you really expected me to name my ship *Arnaud*? Really? To go down in history with it written that, 'He sailed on the *Arnaud*'? That's a horrible, awful name!"

Her gaze narrowed even further. "There is absolutely nothing wrong with that name! It's a good, strong name!"

"*Christine* is much better. I would never change it. Especially not for you."

Her eyes burned like green flames. Isaac was going to die. He was sure of it.

However, instead of dissolving him into blood soup, she smiled cruelly. "Says the man who now has nothing, whose own name is about to be drowned in the depths of the sea and forgotten forever."

A horrible, sinking fear and ugly despair wove its way through his body, gripping his heart and stomach with their cold, cruel hands. She was right. Everyone who would have ever remembered him was gone, his name lost to the sea. He was nothing more than the driftwood he clung to.

He couldn't help himself. "You-you destroy my ship and murder my crew? All over the name of a ship? Was it worth the price?"

His stomach twisted with his own words: *Had I known the cost...*

She looked around as if she hadn't quite realized what she'd done. She had the look of a child who had been running carelessly through the house and broken her mother's favorite figurines. Guilt flashed across her delicate features, and the wall of water around them fell. Composing herself, she reassured Isaac. "When you understand life as I do, you won't find death such a terrible thing."

"Then I hope I never understand life as you do."

"It's not as bad as you think. See, we can travel upriver, find the world where spirits go to rest. We can bring them back. We can bring Captain Snow back, and your mother—"

"Stop!" he cried, "Stop it! *Get out of my head!*"

"I am not in your head!" she shouted. "I used the gems to show you what you wanted to see, but only to persuade you to take me to the River, nothing more. Whatever you saw in your head was what you wanted to see."

"Why?" he asked. "Why do you need me? Clearly, you are powerful enough; find the River yourself!"

"I have found it, but I can't get in. There is a force keeping me from it, from returning home. I need you to go ahead of me and break it."

"What? Why? Why *ME?*"

"Because..." She didn't answer right away. She looked around at the mess she'd made and then at her hands.

He'd seen that bashful look from girls trying to think of something forward to say to him—not too forward, of course, making them less of a lady. His eyes widened, and his stomach felt as though it were stewing in black tar as he suspected the sheer depth of his problems. He prayed that she wouldn't say what he thought she was about to say, hoping there was some greater god out there that could save him.

She floated closer, looking at him. "Have you not always wanted to find the River?"

It wasn't what he'd been dreading, but he didn't feel any better.

She went on. "Have you not always wanted a world better than this one? Free from the cold, cruel people within it? You and I want the same thing. I was your closest friend, remember?"

"I remember a creepy old man with horrible breath who was constantly ill."

Her full lips trembled into a frown, hurt and frustration reflecting in her eyes. "That is the curse I am forced to live with in this world. I can either appear like *this* or try to blend in. But when I try to blend in, I am perceived as an old, smelly, sick, dying man. I am either hated and feared or hated and ignored. And I am *tired* of being ignored." Her gaze fell. "You were the only one who was ever kind to me."

"And this is how you repay me?"

"I just wanted you to name the ship after me! Just once! Just once, I didn't want to be ignored. I didn't want to leave this world and be forgotten. I wanted you to *remember* me!"

He went to rest his head against the debris and realized that everything was covered in blood. He wanted to cry, to scream, to sink and disappear, but all he could do was cling to the debris and float there.

At his silence, she demanded, "You will go with me to the River."

It crossed his mind that he could go to the River and find another world and leave her trapped on Earth far, far away from him forever and ever.

She pulled out a strand of her ivy-like hair and wrapped it tightly around the wrist of his injured arm. He struggled as she held it painfully against him. She was so strong. She didn't look at him as she said, "I am sorry about this, but you leave me no choice."

She closed her eyes. He let out a cry of agony as the vine pierced his skin, stinging and tearing as it ripped flesh from muscle and muscle from bone, weaving its way through like a snake making its home in his body. It slithered its way up his arm and deep into his shoulder. Tears spurted to his eyes and down his cheeks. He slipped beneath the water as he let go of the debris and dug frantically at the vine, but it was no use. There was nothing he could do. The vine had become a part of him.

She pulled him back to the surface and whispered in his ear, "If you try to leave this world without me, this will continue to grow and grow until it consumes you and you are *dead*. If you want to live, you will take me home. Just so you know, this is not a pleasant way to die."

Isaac scoffed. "There's a pleasant way to die?" He closed his eyes, listening to the frantic and hopeless beat of his heart. His mother's words crossed his mind then as if it were a message sent through time that had always been meant for that exact moment. *Sometimes you have to work hard and obey rules before you find freedom. You have to be disciplined, always making sure you're doing your very best. Then, when the time is right, you break free.*

He looked up at the creature and asked, "What do I have to do?"

She smiled. "That's more like it."

So, Faeries Are Real, Then?

As Isaac floated in the water, a thought flickered through his head—a slightly obscure one where, if he'd have had more of a mind, he would've told himself how irrelevant it was in that moment. He wondered what the word of him would *really* be once his ship never returned home. Perhaps he had been too hard on himself before. Maybe he wouldn't be forgotten.

Unfortunately, he was more right the first time. While there were a treasured few who would remember him fondly, they didn't know his name, and he didn't know theirs. Those who did know it would gradually forget it, reducing it to, "Remember that one man? What was his name again?"

And little did he know just how quickly the lady named Jane, who had once fancied him, would move on. See, the man named Fredrick, whom she had been speaking to before, was some well-to-do manager of the banking industry—one who was a sort of king, at least in his own mind. In fact, Isaac's business was one of the many accounts under his reign. When no one could track down Isaac's wealthy relatives—since they didn't, in fact, exist—there was no one to inherit what was left of his business.

So, Fredrick took it. The lady Jane was very interested in becoming well-to-do herself, and she threw aside any feelings she'd had for Isaac the moment Fredrick told her he'd taken Isaac's business and how this was just a penny of his large fortune.

Soon after, there was a wedding, complete with rare flowers and church bells. The heavy, wooden doors of the cathedral opened upon the newlyweds. Rice was thrown as they looked adoringly into each other's eyes, and as they stepped into the carriage and rode away into the sunset, any lingering thoughts they had of Isaac were swept away with the wind.

But never mind any of them. They would have never believed what had actually happened to Isaac Moore.

Isaac watched as "Arnaud" grew pensive, making it clear that she hadn't thought anything through and wasn't sure, exactly, how to proceed. This did not fill Isaac with any confidence. They were in the middle of the ocean with no land in sight, surrounded by a violent storm, with no ship. Oh, and the blood would attract sharks. They were probably on their way already; the thought sent terror through him that his broken heart tripped over. He bitterly wondered how she planned to get them both out of this alive. Well, clearly, she wasn't going to have a problem helping herself, so it was more of, how was *he* going to get out of this alive?

He really didn't want to be eaten by a shark.

With a mournful, nervous look on her face, she reached out to him with her hand rotated upward. A strange, uncomfortable sensation filled every particle of his body, like at any moment they might each fly off in separate directions. Feeling a new surge of horror, he wondered if he should hand out apologies for everything he'd said to her before. Not just the insults, but everything. For speaking at all. Perhaps he would've if he could breathe, but his body was no longer in his control.

She lifted him out of the water until he was floating above it at her level. She smiled a little, looking relieved and filled with confidence. His vision blurred; he couldn't expand his lungs enough to really inhale.

He was going to suffocate while *floating in the air*. How ironic.

With her other hand, she pushed the storm away—literally, *pushed the storm away*—of course, he was too involved with the whole "I'm dying" thing to really care about that. An instant later, they were soaring through the sky at a remarkable speed. The world rushed by underneath him, quickly changing from ocean to farms and trees. The sun sank into the horizon, falling from early morning to afternoon. It seemed to him they were moving as fast as a falling star, passing above rivers and lakes in the time it took to blink.

And then he passed out.

His eyes opened to bright blue sky and the peaceful crash of waves along the shore. His lungs filled with air in panicked gasps as though he'd nearly drowned. He rolled onto his side, curling into a ball. He couldn't get enough air. He barely noticed the grains of sand sticking to his wet body.

Maybe it was the feeling of drowning or all the horridly contaminated ocean water he'd unintentionally drunk, or perhaps it was the fact that he'd crossed the world way too fast and had felt as though he might explode the whole way there, but with the next gulp of air, he retched all over the lovely sand.

Arnaud was excited. "I did it!" she exclaimed with glee. "I can't believe it! I did it!"

Isaac rolled away from his red vomit to face her. "W-what?" His whole body shook as he rose to his knees.

"I brought you all the way over here without killing you! You're still in one piece! This is wonderful!"

"What?" He stared at her, trying to comprehend. "Y-you mean...y-you've never...successfully...done that? Carried someone...w-without killing them?"

"Well, I've never tried with a person before, but you know, small animals. No, it's rarely...well, it's *never* ended well. Until now. I carried you safely! Look!"

Isaac's stomach gave another nasty turn at this information and what was left of its contents ended up on the beach. Seeing this, she added, "Well, you're not in perfect condition, but this gives me hope." She glanced at her hands. "It's like you said to me. 'It's amazing what you can accomplish with hard work and belief in yourself. Just look what I've done!'" She snorted. "You were referring to yourself when you said that, of course, but I took it to heart just the same."

He glared at her from under his matted, blood-soaked hair. How was she so chipper? Oh. That's right. She wasn't puking up the blood of his friends.

"Oh!" she exclaimed as if she'd just remembered to tell him about a party. "Right. You'll probably feel better if you're cleaner, ya? One moment. Just...don't move."

She took a step back and held out her arms. Her eyes glowed, and light radiated from her form. Clouds appeared just above Isaac, and with a clap of thunder, rain poured heavily upon him. He looked around. It was not raining anywhere else, just where he was, rinsing away the blood, vomit, and seawater.

"You should take off your coat," she shouted over the rain. "It'll help!"

Just because she'd suggested it, he didn't want to. But it had become ridiculously heavy, and his body was too weary to carry it. So, with his one good arm, he peeled it off and tossed it aside. It was then that Isaac remembered the book Arnaud had given him. It had been in his coat pocket.

There were no words in existence to describe what he felt. Until that moment, there had been a shield of numbness surrounding his mind, keeping him from feeling any of the recent events as deeply as he should've. A fragile shield, as though it were made of glass, but it had been there. And the state of that book, the thought of the condition it was in and how he'd probably never find another copy, well...it was the brick that had been thrown at that glass shield, shattering it.

His heart was imploding, sinking into black despair. His body tensed as if he were being shoved into quicksand. If he let himself fall, if he let himself sink, what would become of him then? He couldn't face where that pit, that void, might lead. His mind gripped the edges of whatever sanity he could hold onto, anything to keep himself from being consumed by that darkness. What he found was—

Rage.

It ignited in his veins, devouring his entire being like fire.

What could he do about it? Nothing. Nothing but narrow his glare as he watched her from underneath his rain cloud. At least, not yet. But he was patient. He'd stick to his plan. He'd wait for his moment.

"Is the rain warm enough?" Arnaud asked. She actually asked that. "I think I can make it warmer for you if you'd like."

He didn't answer. He would never admit it, but the rain was quite lovely and rather fitting.

"I'll just assume it's fine, then, ya?" she said. She turned her attention to the coat. She glided over to it and picked it up, letting it float in the air in front of her.

He wiped the rain out of his eyes and scooted forward to get a better look. He couldn't believe what he was seeing. Bubbles of filthy water separated themselves from the coat. She tossed them into the ocean as though she were simply throwing away an old rag, leaving the coat dry. She asked for his shirt and did the same for it, removing all the stains.

From there, she rummaged through his coat pockets until she found the book. It was a shriveled mess, as expected.

She took it and turned her back to him so he couldn't see what she was doing. A wave of desperation hit him. He attempted to rise to his feet with his wobbly legs but toppled back to his knees.

What was she doing to it?

He struggled to his feet again and managed to stay on them this time. He stumbled toward her, his boots making suction noises with each step and the raincloud following him as he moved. He looked up at the cloud, using his good arm to shield his face from the deluge, and then tried waving it away, as if it would actually work.

She turned. "Oh! You finished, then?" With a gentle wave of her hand, the rain stopped, and the clouds moved on, revealing the happy afternoon sun.

He glared at her with a new surge of contempt. *Sure. It works when she does it.*

"Feel a little better?" she asked.

He was sopping wet. *Do I look like I feel better?* he wanted to say but didn't. If he wanted to live through this, he thought it best to not say anything at all.

She gazed at his horrifically mangled arm, which he couldn't bring himself to look at too closely. Then she looked away, guilt and discomfort seeming to rise in her expression. She handed him his shirt and coat. "I dried these for you. I'd do the same for you, but I haven't quite been able to separate liquid from things that need it to live without...never mind. We'll just leave the drying to the wind and sun, ya?"

He took his clothing from her and tried not to ponder what she'd said too deeply. To his amazement, they were completely dry. With a great deal of pain, he put on his shirt. He held his coat in his good hand and blinked at it, finding himself wanting to cry. Not tears of joy over a dry overcoat, no. What a ridiculous notion. No, it was because of, well, all of it. His brain simply couldn't understand anything that was happening. These sorts of things happened in nightmares when he was stressed with the business or when he'd struggled to sleep after a good beating at the orphanage.

He didn't want to be awake. He wanted this to be a dream, the kind where he'd wake up and breathe a great sigh of relief and think, *Losing my business isn't so bad after all. It could be much worse.* Then he'd go on living his life, maybe always wondering, in the back of his mind, if Arnaud was really a woman.

But no. He was awake. Remnants of sand ground against his skin underneath his clothes. Vomit and blood coated his tongue. The salty sea air filled his lungs, and the warm sun baked his matted hair. And the vine...it made his arm heavy and useless, and he couldn't move it without blinding pain. It was an ache, an agony, that was unfortunately very real.

That was where the urge to cry was coming from. What was he supposed to do with this new, ridiculous, unbelievable reality? With *any* of it? *What was he supposed to do?*

"Here," she said, snapping him out of his maddening thoughts. She handed him the book. He draped his coat over his good arm and took it with his good hand. "I fixed it. It's not perfect, but I put it back together to the best of my memory."

He was skeptical. He winced as he awkwardly lifted his injured and vine-infected arm to open it. The water damage was still obvious as he flipped through the worn pages, but the excellent pictures and the letters —everything important—were in near-perfect condition. Perhaps even better than they had been before. *Remarkable.*

How about that? He'd gotten something back. One perfect, fragile little thing. In that moment, it was worth more than the mansion on the mountain and the piles of riches he'd seen in his dreams because it held something far more valuable: memories of the happiest moments of his life. It was the strength he needed to make it through this. He'd been thrown a fragile thread of hope to cling to. Relief and joy stung his eyes with tears, though he made sure they did not spill over, and he would never tell her so. There were so many other things he would rather say, things that she deserved and that would cut her into a thousand tiny pieces.

But there was a vine growing through his arm, so he didn't.

She glanced at the book and looked back at him. With a sense of deep sadness in her voice that surprised and resonated inside him, she said, "I am truly sorry. For everything." Tears lined her eyes, and she looked as if she were about to say more but changed her mind and turned away.

Sorry? She'd actually said sorry as if she really were. As if she hadn't shoved a vine in his arm and dragged him here on the threat of death. As if "sorry" had any power to change anything. As if it could bring back the lives she'd stolen, that she'd destroyed. How *sick*. How twisted and pathetic.

He balled his battered hand into a fist and, digging his nails into his palm, steadied his breathing. He closed his eyes. He needed to live through this.

There came a call from behind him. "Hello!"

Well, That's Not Helpful at All

Isaac furrowed his brow and turned around. An older man with graying hair and dark skin, wearing a white, long-sleeved shirt and tan trousers, crossed the sand toward them on his bare feet, holding his shoes in one hand.Isaac was torn between wanting to warn the man to flee for his life and running toward him screaming, pleading for him to save him. The conflict left Isaac frozen in place. He hid his book in the breast pocket of his coat, then draped the coat over his good arm again.

Isaac stared at the man's shoes as he approached. They appeared to be made of leather, but it wasn't any kind that Isaac had ever seen before. They were shiny and dyed a dark blackish red and stitched together in swirling patterns.

"I know," the man said, "I could've left them over there in the shade, but I didn't want any nasty surprises." The man spoke with a harsh drawl in an accent that seemed American, but he couldn't place it.

"Where, exactly, are we?" Isaac finally thought to ask, turning to Arnaud. Isaac gave a little start. Arnaud had changed back into the form of the gross old man. She was hiding in plain sight. This annoyed him more than he could adequately express.

"You're just outside the entrance to the River," said the man. Seeing their shocked expressions, he added, "You know, the one you're looking for? And," he looked at Arnaud, "there's no need to hide in front of me; I know who you are."

Isaac and Arnaud exchanged a look. Isaac blinked and said, "I beg your pardon?" Surely he hadn't heard him right. Because if he had, then that meant things might have just gotten much worse for him, and things were already terrible.

But wasn't that just how life was? Things couldn't get worse—until they did.

However, Arnaud grew very stern. Her gaze narrowed at the man in a way that made Isaac feel as though he'd stepped into an ice-filled ocean in bare feet. Her voice bubbled. "I believe you are mistaken, sir."

The man smiled. There was a light in his eyes that, on a normal day under normal circumstances, would've given him the appearance of someone who was kind and trustworthy. But today, it did the opposite.

Isaac didn't trust him for a second.

The man said, "Oh no, I assure you, I am not mistaken." He looked them each in the eyes, first Arnaud and then Isaac. The man's gaze pierced him. It was like looking at someone he'd known from childhood but forgotten, someone who knew his whole story: the beginning, middle —and the end. He nodded at Isaac. "I know exactly who I'm talking to."

Isaac did not like this man.

Arnaud took a step toward Isaac as if they were suddenly on the same team.

They were not on the same team.

The man studied Isaac, looking at him as if this thought had been spoken out loud. After a prolonged moment of silence, the man said, "She's standing close to you because she wants to protect you, just in case I'm not such a nice man."

Arnaud's and Isaac's eyes grew wide. Arnaud's face flushed. Not only had the man made a very good guess, but he had also called Arnaud a *she*. It was convincing enough that Isaac had to stop himself from screaming, *Protect me? She just blew up my ship! My crew!*

Arnaud's tone darkened. "I think it would be best for you if you left."

Isaac raised his eyebrows at the clear threat in her voice. His skin wanted to crawl right off his frozen body.

The man was unfazed. He took a step closer. "I should introduce myself. They call me The Prophet."

The Prophet? Where have I heard that before? Sure, it was a title given to all sorts of conmen, but for some reason, at this moment, the title struck him as unique and familiar, like he'd read this very scene out of a book.

The Prophet continued. "They say I have a gift. I say I'm simply a really good listener with a really good memory. You see, there are two forces at work in the universe. It is very simple. Light and Darkness. Light sees everything, every shadowed corner of the universe. It pierces through the darkness with such power that it can be seen from billions of miles away. I've discovered that the Power behind this light is a profound and peaceful teacher, but it speaks so gently that no one can hear it—unless they're really listening.

"And that's my job. I observe, I listen, and then I teach, help, and guide. It is astounding what Light will teach you if you're willing to listen."

Arnaud balled her hands into fists. "Well. Thank you for that. That was the longest, most *pointless* personal introduction I've ever heard."

The Prophet laughed. "You haven't met many celebrities, then."

"Is that what you are?" Isaac asked. Maybe that would explain why he seemed familiar.

"Nope." The Prophet smiled and pointed at Arnaud. "Elise. Elise is the name you prefer to be called because you think it's the most beautiful name that has ever been given to you. And I agree."

Arnaud grew pale as though she'd been struck dead.

If only Isaac was so lucky.

Her voice was ice. "How do you know that?"

The Prophet smiled, raising his hands and nodding his head in an I-told-you-so sort of way. "As I said, I'm a very good listener—"

Anger etched into Arnaud's face with each of her wrinkles, and her eye glowed. "No." She marched toward The Prophet with her shoulders rounded, clearly stating without words that she intended to tear off as many fingers as needed in order to get honest answers from him. "No, we all know someone must've told you—"

The Prophet raised a hand without flinching. Somehow, that was all it took to stop her. He turned to Isaac. "You must also be wondering how I know this, Captain Moore." Isaac's stomach dropped and shrunk three sizes at this stranger's use of his name. Had he met this man somewhere in his travels? Isaac's mind ripped open every cupboard and drawer in his memory, scanning through any documents that referred to his many journeys. He couldn't recall seeing him anywhere. Had he been watching them from the trees? Even if he had been, it wouldn't explain this. Arnaud—Elise—had never once said her real name; had never called him Captain Moore.

The Prophet continued. "I've been told some of these things by someone called Arnaud." The Prophet looked at Arnaud-Elise. "The *real* Arnaud. He, along with many others, are cheering for you."

Arnaud's face changed. More color drained from her skin—and she hadn't had much to spare. Her eyes froze wide.

Isaac's stomach, however, churned and twisted like he might be sick. Very, very sick. His face tingled. It was like he was back in the ocean and drowning. They were cheering for *her?* Really? Who were these wretched people?

The Prophet went on. "You are one of the most powerful creatures in the universe. There is no one quite like you. You can learn to control your gift and use it for good. I wish I could tell you more, but I can't. You are meant to learn on your own. But I have a message for Captain Moore."

Hope flickered like a dying candle in Isaac's hollow chest. He clung to it, desperate for anything that suggested this man was going to rescue him.

The Prophet stepped toward Isaac and put a hand on his shoulder, which Isaac didn't like but was too lost to do anything about. "Now, you need to remember this message. It is important."

Isaac was mentally on his toes, ready to hear the solution to all his problems, the key to getting the vine out of his arm and escaping.

The Prophet looked him square in the eye, deep into Isaac's soul—his very story—as he said, "Remember, Isaac, it is forgiveness and compassion that separates the monsters from the men, and the demons from the angels." Abruptly, he let go, saying, "Well, that's it. Good luck!" and walked away.

Isaac had been punched in the gut several times in his life, and this was remarkably similar. "Wait, that's it?"

"Yep!" The Prophet hollered over his shoulder. "That's all you need to know!"

Isaac was sure his heart had stopped beating. Stars fizzled in his vision as he chased after the Prophet. "But..." What was he doing? What did he plan to say? He didn't even know at this point. He wasn't really in control of himself anymore. "H-help," Yes, yes, that worked. "Help me."

The Prophet stopped, but he didn't turn around.

Isaac took courage. He spoke softly, trying to hide his words from Elise—as if he could. "If you know what she is, then please, help me."

The Prophet's strange, twinkling eyes looked up at the sky as though observing something that no one else could see, his expression that of someone focusing on a whisper. He grew thoughtful. "Well, there is one thing. It's actually why I came here, but then...then I had second thoughts. But then again...I see that time...time will still heal. It's just *enough* of a difference. So, that's good."

The Prophet turned and placed both hands on Isaac's head. A surge of energy ran through his brain, warping it with what sounded like thousands of voices talking all at once. The world around him spun until it faded into darkness—a darkness that was dotted with brilliant little stars.

After some terrible effort, Isaac dropped his coat, grabbed The Prophet's hands, and pushed them off him. "Don't touch me! What are you doing?"

Arnaud stepped between Isaac and The Prophet, looking ready to rip the man apart.

The Prophet smiled. "You'll do better with that."

He started to walk away again.

Isaac shouted, "What did you do to me? How does that help anything?" Isaac's vision was doing somersaults, but he refused to let himself fall over. He stumbled around Arnaud and seized The Prophet's shoulder.

The Prophet turned, giving Isaac a severe look that pierced his soul in a very strange way, making him let go as if he'd touched a hot iron. The look filled his head with images of a cavern, a river that glowed with an eerie light—and a universe with planets being consumed by fire. It all happened in an instant, throwing Isaac a step backward. As Isaac staggered away, a voice whispered in his mind, *There is so much more at stake, far beyond what you can see.*

Where that message came from, Isaac wasn't sure.

The Prophet smiled and said cheerfully, "Well, goodbye! And good luck."

As Isaac watched that one brief glimmer of hope walk away again, he couldn't stop himself. "No, no, no, no, no, you cannot do this to me! You have to help me. She's going to kill me!"

"She hasn't yet," The Prophet pointed out. "She killed everyone on that ship except for you."

How did he know that?

The Prophet looked at Elise. "By the way, have you given any thought as to how you did that? How you managed to save him? Because you might want to."

She mused over these words like she really hadn't thought about that before.

The Prophet seemed genuinely pleased. "I have faith in you two."

Isaac's eye twitched.

"Wait!" Elise's voice bubbled as she ran after The Prophet, grabbing his arm without any apparent adverse reaction. "You've been there? You've seen him?"

The Prophet's expression changed, his eyes filling with a sorrow that Isaac swore he could feel from where he stood. He put a hand on her shoulder. "You have so much to learn."

Then he left, disappearing into the trees. Isaac followed a mere few steps behind him, but there was no trace of him. The Prophet was gone.

Isaac blinked. Then blinked some more. With each blink, his rage crawled closer and closer to the surface until it found his voice box and squeezed. No longer caring what would become of him, he began yelling, screaming, kicking the sand, and throwing rocks. He whirled on Elise, who was back in her winged form with her white silk dress. "*You!* You destroyed my ship and killed all my friends! I—" He gagged on his next words as an image of the red water flooded into his mind. His vision spun again, and he lost all sense of place.

"That was an accident!" she exclaimed. "I didn't mean to! I just lost my temper! I'd been burying it and burying it—all this time—and I just broke."

That had been the nun's excuse, too. The one who'd beat him in the orphanage, Sister Maria. That darn *temper* had always been so easy to blame. He could hear her voice: *"Look at what you made me do!"*

"Oh, right," said Isaac, "and this vine in my arm, was this an accident, too?" He rolled up his sleeve to reveal his lumpy, deformed arm. It was black, purple, and splotched with red. A leaf had sprouted near his wrist. Isaac struggled to keep himself from retching as he looked at it. He couldn't believe that was his arm.

He tore off the leaf and, after a moment of shock at the completely unexpected amount of pain he felt, he cried out in agony. It was like he'd just ripped a limb from his body, and the blood that poured down his arm from the wound only added to the feeling. He threw more things, kicked more sand, and pulled his hair in frustration until he collapsed onto his knees, light-headed with a throbbing, horrible pain in his head.

"This is a nightmare," he said, putting his sweaty face in his hands. "A bad, bad dream. I just need to wake up."

He closed his eyes and let his breathing slow until it was in rhythm with the waves brushing against the shore. He inhaled the scent of the wet sand and the grass on the breeze and the salt of the ocean. The heat of the sunrise against the back of his neck and the pounding of his heart reminded him that he was still alive. When he'd calmed down, he told himself that when he opened his eyes, he'd be back on his ship, having passed out on the deck from drinking too much wine.

He opened his eyes. Elise stood in front of him. He groaned. "Oh. Oh no...you're still here."

She looked away, appearing hurt and annoyed. "Of course I am. What? You thought that you could just throw a fit and scream at me, and I'd disappear?"

"I really hoped so."

She kicked his hip. "Get up! Let's get this over with."

He didn't move right away. He'd barely noticed the kick. He debated staying there and dying on the beach but eventually concluded that this wouldn't be a very effective solution to the problem—since his goal was to *not* die, and the problem was that he might. Really, to do as she'd suggested and just "get this over with" was truly the best way to, well, get the whole thing over with.

"Fine." He lumbered to his feet, nearly falling over as he straightened his legs. His vision blurred with every beat of his pulse. "What do we do now?"

"Well, we go to the entrance of the River, and...and that's all you need to know. I don't feel like talking to you right now."

That annoyed him. *Well, I don't feel like talking to you, either!* was what he might've said if he hadn't felt horrible all over. He bent down to pick up his coat, thinking his head might pop off and roll away as he did so, then dragged his one-thousand-pound arm along the beach. Elise kept glancing back at him as he struggled to follow her. It took him a moment to be sure it wasn't a hallucination, but she was not walking in front of him—she floated with her feet relaxed, gliding just inches above the sand. He also could've sworn the trees turned to watch her as she passed, but he really wasn't entirely sure of that one. It could've just been the migraine he was getting with his sudden onset of madness.

Then again, it really looked like they were turning. He even swore he could hear them whispering.

He was so hypnotized by the trees, he didn't notice that she'd stopped, and he bumped into her.

"You look awful," she told him.

He was offended and irritated. How dare she point this out *now*. An unamused grin spread across his face, and he whispered, "I can't imagine why."

"No, really," she said very seriously.

Talking was nearly impossible. Every time he used his brain and breath to make words, his head screamed in pain, and his stomach threatened to turn itself inside out. He took deep breaths and said with great effort and care, "I think—I deserve some leniency—since you're the one who did this to me."

He winced and put a hand to his head. The harder his heart pounded, the more pain he was in. Then the sun! That bright, horrible specter that insisted on shining. He wished he could throw something and knock it right out of the sky. Where were the clouds? Hadn't they just been there?

"Isaac," he thought he heard Elise say, but it sounded distant, drowned out by babbling, like that of rushing water. It seemed to be coming closer and growing louder, and as it did, he realized it wasn't water. It was the sound of thousands upon thousands of voices speaking different languages all at once. He'd heard it when The Prophet had touched him, but this time it wasn't going away. He covered his ears, crying out in misery, but it didn't silence them. They were coming from inside his head.

He fell to his knees.

Elise's panicked shout came from under the weight of all the voices. "*Isaac!*"

A Perfectly Dull Cave

He was floating amid the stars in the dark of night. Despite being weightless out in the middle of nothing and having no pain, he was very uncomfortable. He had the unsettling feeling that someone was watching him.

But then the feeling changed. Whoever they were, they were no longer looking at him, but *past* him. An ugly thrill shook the universe.

They had found what they were looking for.

Way out there, in the midst of the black void, a voice spoke. It was deep and cold—so cold it could almost be felt. He searched for where it had come from. There, in the void, were two great eyes, their lids warped and their color covered in a white film. The voice sent electricity up his spine and into his heart as it spoke. *"It is time."*

Isaac jumped awake. His eyes opened wide to dancing shadows on a stone ceiling. He was covered in sweat, his clothes clinging to his body. His arm was still in agony, but he could move it better.

"Isaac!" Elise's voice chimed like a lovely, soft bell. She rushed to him and reached out as if she meant to touch him, but her hands remained a safe two feet away.

He would've liked it better if they were farther away.

He also would've been a fraction happier if he could blink away the image of those horrible eyes, but they were seared into his brain. He sat up and rubbed his own eyes. It did no good. Everywhere he looked he could see them—staring through the dark shadows, through the stone walls, from behind the stalagmites that were dimly illuminated by a few flames. Looking into the small fire was the worst of all because it was like they were staring out from Hell itself. But they were looking past him. Not interested in *him*, but whatever it was they saw beyond him.

Isaac wiped his face with his hand, which soon turned into more of a scrubbing of his face as if he could cleanse the image from his brain by doing so. It seemed to work. It faded enough that he could focus on seeing exactly where Evil Elise had taken him. Were they in a cave? Yes, they were in a cave. Why were they in a cave? How did he suddenly end up in a cave?

He looked at Elise. "Where are we?"

"We are in an air pocket a couple of miles underneath the ocean." Her gaze held deep concern like she wanted to ask him how he was feeling, maybe tell him how she'd been so worried. Instead, she finished answering his question. "It's the entrance to the River."

"Really? And how did we—" He stopped, pressing his palm against his temple. His head still hurt there, though not nearly as much. He answered his own question. "Because you're all-powerful and probably parted the waters like Moses to get here and whatnot." He wiped sweat from his forehead with his sleeve. "Right. You can do all that and yet you still need me?"

"Yes. I can travel about a mile in, but I can't go any farther because of the—"

"Why am I so sweaty?" He interrupted, thinking out loud and suddenly overwhelmed with concern for his health, thinking this probably had to do with the monstrous weed growing through his arm, which had sprouted another leaf. He pulled at his shirt and trousers that were sticking to his body. "At least, I hope it's sweat. Or maybe I don't. Or there's probably no good alternative. It's all bad. This is all bad."

She answered patiently. "Most of it is sweat. A lot of it is water. You were terribly dehydrated, and I had to make you drink it, and it went everywhere. You were delirious and muttering to yourself. I got you down here as quickly as I could since the sun was clearly not helping at all. Then you started shivering and...it was awful." She hid her face under the shadow of her vine-like hair. "I thought you were going to die."

He wanted to retch at her words. He looked at her warily. He was quite certain he'd never hated anything more than he hated her. Not even Sister Maria, and she was tough competition. This was a whole new level he'd never experienced before. "How long have I been out for?"

"I'm not sure. A few days, I'd say."

He raised his eyebrows. "Well! That's a new record for me." He snorted. "Not all that unusual, minus the whole I-nearly-died part. No, wait." He remembered that one time in New Orleans. "Actually, that has happened before."

Now she looked annoyed. "I can't believe you're not taking this more seriously."

"Oh yes. Please excuse me. I do apologize since I'm the one who stuck a vine in my arm and blew up my ship. Clearly, my life is in my own hands. I shall handle it with greater care from now on. Thank you." Oh dear. That was stupid. Why did he say that? He really needed to control himself better because, judging by her narrowing glare, not only was she about to blow him up with her mind, but he was about to die because of his stupidity. No one else would know, but his ghost would, and it would be disappointed in him forever.

"When you're strong enough, I will take you to the edge of the wall that is keeping me out of the River."

"How do you know I'll be able to get through?"

"I don't. I just... You wouldn't understand."

"I wouldn't understand," Isaac muttered. He shook his head. "You know, you're probably right."

Her bright green eyes flashed in the light of the flames. She folded her arms. "You're sure being awful for someone trying to get out of a death sentence."

Isaac really couldn't stop himself. "Yeah, well, you sure spout off a lot more words than *Arnaud*."

She groaned. "Ugh. I absolutely *hate* the way my voice sounds when I'm Arnaud." She grimaced. "It's disgusting."

"Well, that's something we can agree on." He'd done it again. He briefly wondered how he'd survived this long with such a lack of intelligence.

She laughed. Actually laughed, and far more heartily than the comment warranted. If he were to be completely honest with himself, his remark didn't even deserve a courtesy chuckle. He truly didn't understand why she laughed, but the sound was as sweet and lovely as sleigh bells on the morning of the first snow. He hated her for it.

She asked him if he could walk, and after a bit of effort, he discovered that he could. He put on his coat, patting the breast pocket to make sure the book was still there. She then led him through the dark cavern with a ball of fire hovering over the palm of her hand. He was certain she was doing this just to show off. She could've at least *pretended* to be semi-normal here. How hard was it to hold a torch? Or a lantern? But *noooo*, it had to be a glowing, floating orb of fire.

There was nothing spectacular to look at. After the initial feeling of walking into the nasty mouth of a very large worm with stale breath, the stalagmites and stalactites grew very boring very fast. He tried turning it into a game. *What's over there? Oooo! A rock. How about over there? More rocks. Oh look! There's water!*

It was a boring game.

His feet ached in his beat-up boots, but that wasn't as bad as the humid, musty, moldy air. It consumed all his senses, like walking through and eating a rotten cloud. Before this awful situation, if someone had asked him if he thought clouds could rot, he would've said, "Why, of course not! What a ridiculous notion." But he would've been wrong.

They reached a space where he couldn't see anything but darkness beyond the glowing orb. There were no walls to reflect the light, which was terrifying. He couldn't be sure there wasn't a cliff beside him somewhere that wouldn't swallow him up into oblivion if he didn't tread carefully. Other places had nothing but a small crevice that was wet and slimy to touch and that he could barely squeeze through. As he was wondering just how long they'd been traveling, she stopped. "We're here."

He wasn't sure what he had been expecting, but he knew it'd been—well, something different. But it looked the same as every other rocky cavern. There was nothing special about it at all. He furrowed his brow and almost asked, *Are you sure?* but thought better of it. He asked instead, "Really? How can you tell?"

She glanced ahead and then back at him. "You can't see it?"

"See what?"

She put the fire orb aside, leaving it floating in the air, and slowly reached out her hand. It hit something solid, like a thin wall made of glass—the clearest glass he had ever seen. Yet as she pressed against it, her hand divided in two. There was the mist-like hand resting against the glass and then another solid one on the other side of it, hanging lifeless. Had Isaac been holding anything, he would've dropped it the way his face dropped his jaw.

"How did you—?" He couldn't think of words to finish that question. He tried again, "Just what is—?" No, that wasn't working either. "What just—?"

She pulled her hand back through the glass, and it became whole again. She looked at her palm and touched it gently. "It's not a shield against my body, but a shield against the soul that powers it. If I were to try to go through it, I would lose my body." She looked at him. "I would die. I would be nothing more than a ghost. I need to get past this so I can go back to my own world, find the planet where the spirits rest, and bring everyone back. *Everyone*. Grundy, Pegleg the Second, Weird-Eye Jack...all of them. I will make everything right."

She said it with such conviction. It would've been nice if he could believe her. While there was nothing in her expression that said she was lying, he couldn't shake the images of the red water, the taste of blood and ocean that lingered like a wound on his tongue. He also couldn't ignore the voice of reason, a voice that pointed out that he'd never once seen a long-dead body return to life.

He would get through this moment. He would do what he had to do in order to survive and keep Elise from becoming a ghost. There was nothing more terrifying to Isaac than imagining her as a ghost. He was sure she'd follow him home and haunt him forever—that is, if he could even leave this cavern alive without her, which he probably couldn't.

"Well then, we can't let you become a ghost now, can we?" He glanced at the strange glass thing, sweat beading his brow and his face feeling as though it fit on him too tightly. "What makes you think I'll be able to go through there? The whole point of me doing this is so I don't die. If I walk through this thing and become a ghost, that will defeat the purpose, don't you think?"

She narrowed her gaze with a sneer. "I don't know if you've noticed, Captain, but the soul powering your body and the soul powering *my* body aren't quite the same. I believe that you'll make it through just fine. But of course," she gave a small, flippant shrug, "there's only one way to find out, isn't there?"

He gave a slow blink and sighed, then glared at the glass—or at least he thought he was glaring at it. He couldn't see it anymore.

He just had to touch it. That was all he had to do. He decided to use his damaged hand, just in case. No need to walk around with two mangled hands if he could avoid it. He used his good arm to support it, wincing. Sweat poured down his face as he tentatively reached out. He considered asking if it was going to hurt but shut down the idea. *How old are you, Isaac?* He scolded himself. *Five?* He felt as small and helpless as a five-year-old, but she didn't need to know that.

Sooner than he expected, he hit something solid. He flattened his palm against it. It did not feel like glass at all, and really, he had known it wouldn't because it couldn't be glass. No one could go through glass without shattering it, and glass certainly didn't separate souls from bodies. So *of course* it wasn't glass. It was warm and left his entire arm feeling strange and tingly, like how he imagined touching a storm cloud might feel just before lightning was about to strike. It was unlike anything he had ever experienced before.

What on Earth was it?

He looked over his shoulder at Elise, who watched him with hopeful curiosity. He took a deep breath and pushed his hand through. The strangest sensation rippled through his fingertips and up his arm as though he were sticking his hand in a bucket of warm water full of dull needles—not sharp enough to really cause pain, but enough to make one nervous. His entire hand remained intact to wiggle his fingers on the other side.

That, or he had no soul, which was also a possibility.

Elise's face lit up with delight. "I knew it!"

Isaac pulled his hand back through, staring at his fingers. He shifted his feet. "So, what now? I just go through there and...and then what?"

She disappeared into the darkness and returned a moment later with a helmet, thick leather armor, and a shield and a sword. Isaac was almost more surprised at the sight of these than he had been at Elise's duplicate hand. "You might want these," she explained. "Whatever the shield is attached to, it moves."

He froze. "What do you mean 'it moves'?"

"I mean, it *moves*."

That was completely unenlightening. "If it moves, then how did you know it was here?"

"Because I can see it," she snapped.

Isaac threw up his one good arm. "So, what, I'm supposed to go in there and hope for the best?"

She gave him the world's most irritated, venom-filled smile. "That's the plan."

"Why am I doing this? I'm not a soldier! Why can't you just make a —a—a puppet out of rocks or something and send it in there to smash whatever is holding up this barrier?"

"I wouldn't be able to see what I'm doing! I can't just take my eyes out of my head and attach them to it, now, can I?"

"It really wouldn't surprise me if you could."

"Besides, I doubt my ability to control the thing would get past that barrier. The rock puppet would go through and then crumble back into nothing but a big pile of rocks."

Isaac put on the armor and scabbard. He examined the sword, and when he couldn't complain about it, he sheathed it. He asked, "Do you have something against pistols and rifles?"

"I wanted the latest models, and it took some time to gather them all, and um, well," she folded her arms and looked away, "they may have gone down with the ship."

Of course they did. He winced as he put the shield over his vine-eaten arm, really wishing he had something strong to drink. He turned toward the barrier, his heart pounding in his head again. Elise materialized a stick of wood from somewhere and used her fire orb to light it, handing it to Isaac.

A torch, of course. Where had it been earlier?

"Do you just make these things from nothing? The armor, the torch?"

"It only looks that way to you," she told him. "It all comes from something, Isaac. And I can't just create anything, either; there're some things that I don't know how to make yet. It's easier to collect what I can and move it with my mind. I've been planning this for a long time. Of course, with how wrong everything went, you wouldn't think so, but I've been collecting supplies. I had enough of everything here for the entire crew. I...I honestly had planned on everyone making it."

Anger swelled in Isaac's gut at the reminder. She seemed to be telling the truth, but it didn't matter. A lot of murders were unplanned. The victims were still dead.

As if she'd read his thoughts, her gaze hardened. "They were my friends, too."

Was that really supposed to make it better? If anything, it made it worse.

"I don't know how to control it," she blurted, much to Isaac's surprise. "I have this *curse*. My father used to call it a gift, but it's a curse. I can see so much, every particle of everything, and they listen to me. They do whatever I tell them. And sometimes, they just *react* to me. I get emotional or lose my temper, and they scatter." Her green eyes filled with deep pain. "I spent so long trying not to break, to control my emotions so the elements around me would hold their peace, and I just..." She took a long, slow breath, and tears rolled down her cheeks. Her voice wavered. "Isaac, it was an accident. I loved those jolly seadogs. I didn't mean to. I didn't mean to." She turned away, covering her face. "I'm so sorry."

Her words pierced his heart like a hot blade into ice, causing his eyes to brim with tears. But then Isaac's brain packed up and moved somewhere far away. It was simply too much. Too much of *what*, he wasn't sure. His mind wasn't willing to examine it close enough to figure it out.

What if he let himself believe her? What if he let himself feel sorry for her? Forgive her? He might as well tell her that he condoned everything she'd done, that it was all right that his friends were dead, their voices and laughter forever lost to the old sea, and that he'd nearly drowned in their blood. And that putting a vine in his arm, hovering death over him, and forcing him into this cave to fight an unknown monster was all perfectly reasonable to do.

He couldn't do that. He would *never* do that.

What could he do about any of it? Nothing. Nothing but turn, push through the dull-needle barrier, and hope that soon this nightmare would be over—which he did.

As he meandered through the cavern, visions of his warm bed back home filled his mind. Memories of the smell of roasted turkey, potatoes, and gravy made their way through the musty air as shadows danced like raging monsters against the teeth of the cave. It didn't take him long to realize that these were the things he was looking forward to coming home to. No person or fortune. Turkey, potatoes, and gravy. That was it.

Wow. His life was very sad.

But then he thought, *Right, well, maybe it's a simple life, but it's mine. And I'm going to fight for it. I'm going to fight for roast turkey dinners and a good night's sleep.*

For Turkey Dinners
and a Good Night's Sleep

Isaac journeyed through the cavern, his vine-infected arm shaking as he struggled to hold the shield in front of him, wondering if the weight would cause it to fall off. He moved in such a slow, forceful way that to look at him, one would think he was fighting against a heavy wind, even though the air was stagnant and moist and tasted like it had been there for centuries. No, Isaac was simply dreading what lay ahead of him. His imagination reeled with the worst of possibilities. If the last day had taught him anything, it was that nothing was truly impossible. Indeed, the word *impossible* was always accompanied by a little footnote in fine print at the bottom of the page that read: *Destined to expire eventually.*

Which was terrible. It really was. He had no idea what he should be preparing himself for, and the merciless darkness ahead of him gave no clues. He wondered what would be worse, being eaten by a plant growing in his arm or being burned to death by a dragon. But what if whatever lay ahead was worse than a simple dragon? Maybe it would be a creature with a whole bunch of heads, like a hydra. Then he could be ripped apart instead.

At this thought, it took everything Isaac had not to embrace his looming madness and run back through the cavern screaming. The torch trembled in his hand. All his irrational thinking made him extra aware of the rushing blood in his veins, of the sweat pouring down his back, and the throbbing agony in his arm. He followed the cave through a narrow turn to the right, expecting to find more darkness.

Light reflected off the dark rock.

Singing echoed in the chamber.

The tune was eerie, high-pitched, and slightly off. It was shockingly cheery for being sung by something hanging out in a cave miles beneath the surface of the planet. Perhaps that was what unnerved him so much. It was too happy.

He was doomed.

Isaac wedged his torch in a crevice and then unsheathed his sword as he drew closer to the opening. He pressed his back firmly against the wall, wishing he could be absorbed into it and somehow crawl up through the earth and escape. With great control, he forced himself to peer around and see what creature was singing the freakishly high-pitched, happy song. There was a large room lit by strange balls of light, like the one Elise had made. And in the middle of the room, was...there was...

A little old man. Well, he wasn't a human man. He didn't recall ever seeing a human that looked like *that*. The man couldn't have been much taller than four feet. He had long, yellowing grass for hair that grew thinly from the top of his head. An old, elegant tree grew out of a hump on his back, and a tiny yellow bird, the likes of which Isaac had never seen before, lodged in the branches. The man faced away from Isaac, dressed in robes made of bark and moss, and waddled a little when he walked.

Isaac looked back at the wall in front of him and blinked a couple of times, then gazed back at the little figure just to be sure, part of him expecting him to disappear, but no. He was still there.

It was a little old tree-man. Not a dragon, not a monster, just a little old man. The stress that had been building up in Isaac deflated, and he couldn't help but release a sigh of relief.

The singing stopped, and so did the little old man. A pointed, wrinkly ear that looked like a withered leaf twitched. He turned to look directly at the cavern entrance where Isaac lurked. The skin on his face looked like moss-covered leather and was shriveled and sunken. His eyes were bright green like Elise's, but they were dimming in their luster. It was impossible to say for sure, but the creature could've been hundreds of years old.

"I know you're there," said the creature. It wasn't English that he spoke, yet somehow, Isaac understood it—which was bizarre and hurt his head, like using a very, very sore muscle. The language was so strange, like French and gibberish mixed with the creaking of wood and the whistling songs of birds, yet he knew every word.

He didn't like that. It shouldn't be possible. How was it possible?

The little old tree-man sounded like he hadn't spoken in a very long time. He reached out with his two hands, his long fingers like branches from the tree growing on his back. He motioned toward Isaac, saying like any kindly grandfather, "Come out from over there. I know you're there. No need to linger in the shadows."

Despite the situation, Isaac was comforted. This was clearly a kind, reasonable old man. He could've wept as the weight of a thousand heavy shadows lifted from his body. He was almost ashamed that he was wearing armor; he didn't want to frighten him.

But then he remembered how he'd thought Arnaud was just some sad, loony old man, and something told him that it might be too soon to cry those tears or remove any armor.

Still, there was no need to go in there brandishing his sword. He sheathed it before entering the cavern.

"Ah," said the creature knowingly as he saw Isaac. "That's how you got through my shield. You're a creature of Earth. A human. Very little energy, you creatures. I never thought I'd see one of you here. There is no way any of you could combat the sea." He studied him. "How did you get down here?"

Isaac wasn't sure what to say, partly because he wasn't sure if it was safe to admit that he'd had help, but mostly because he wasn't sure he could speak the language.

"Hmm," mused the little man as he slowly waddled up to Isaac, the tiny bird fluttering from one branch to another. He lowered his shield as the creature strode within a generously close distance. Isaac's breathing caught on the sudden stench of rotting things as the tree-man sniffed him with his pointed nose, then gripped his sore arm that wore the shield. Isaac winced and let out a suppressed "Owww" as he did. The creature rolled up Isaac's sleeve, revealing the vine and the leaf sprouting near his wrist. He then concluded in a tone that made Isaac very uneasy, "I know how you got down here. She is ruthless and clever, indeed."

"Wait," Isaac somehow managed to say in the creature's language, surprising himself. He didn't know he could whistle so well. "This is not what it looks like. I don't want to hurt you; I'm dressed like this because, I just, I didn't know what to expect—"

The creature laughed darkly as he shook his head and backed away. "You still don't know what to expect, not from me. I have no desire to reason with you, you self-serving creature. A creature so small, so weak, so pathetic that you would slaughter whole worlds to gain power."

Isaac was confused. "I think you have me mistaken for someone else."

The tree-man chuckled. "In some dark part of me, yes, a dark part of my heart, I had hoped that there would be nothing left of you monsters by now."

Isaac was now terribly confused and a little insulted. He gripped the hilt of his sword. "What do you mean by that?"

"Slaughtered so many of ours, she did. Shame she didn't slaughter those who deserved it."

Isaac's mind whirled. "Wait. Did you—did you send her to kill us and then..." He looked around, "and then build some sort of wall to keep her in until she finished the job?"

"Ha, you think yourselves so important. Destroying you, that would be a pleasant side effect. No, not so simple at all. It was built to keep her *out*." The tree-man spread his hands, and the little bird flew away as if sensing danger. The stagnant air swirled around them, whipping out bits of dust that circled above his outstretched arms. "And I'm not about to fail."

The wisps of air and dust expanded and twisted above the little creature's head, rising as they weaved together to create a snake-like body with claws and a long snout with large, sharp teeth. Isaac's heart sank at the sight of it, crushing whatever hope he'd had.

It was a dragon.

A dragon made of air.

"*Really?*" Isaac lamented. A voice in the back of his mind shouted at him before he realized what was happening. *Shield, SHIELD!*

He raised the shield and a blast of blisteringly hot air threw him back against the wall, the heat threatening to boil the skin off his body. Sweat streamed from his pores, the metal of the shield turned white-hot, burning the leather lining and frying the skin of his arm. He cried out in agony, unable to move, sure that if he did, he'd be vaporized.

The vine slithered beneath his skin, then ripped through his flesh and his shirt sleeve, forcing tears to Isaac's eyes. Thick green cords covered in leaves grew in between his burning arm and the shield, shriveling up and dying again and again as the vine created a layer of protection from the searing hot metal.

At a break in the onslaught of scorching air, Isaac peered around the shield. The misty-white beast swiped at him, throwing him like a discarded doll. He leaped to his feet and jabbed at the air dragon with his sword, which did nothing. He might as well have been trying to murder a cloud.

The monster opened its mouth again, and Isaac dove behind a pile of rocks. The air all around him simmered, reaching oven-like temperatures.

He was going to be cooked alive by a cloud. What a ridiculous end. And there was no way to stop it.

Unless he could somehow get to the evil old man behind it.

At the edge of the shield, Elise paced like a caged tiger. When Isaac screamed out streams of profanities, the walls of the cave around her trembled. She slammed her fists against the barrier. It was not supposed to happen this way. He was not meant to be alone. Now he was going to die, and it was all her fault.

A stalagmite ripped from the floor of the cave and flew into the shield. It did almost nothing to it—which was strange, as it shouldn't have done anything at all. But the shield had bowed ever so slightly as the stalagmite soared through.

The intensity of the barrier had changed. The creature controlling it was growing weary. She stretched out her hand and told the stalagmite to roll over.

It did.

She could send things through.

She turned to the cave wall and, at the risk of collapsing the entire structure, ripped away a layer of stone.

The Scary Snowman

The ground rumbled in rhythmic beats, growing louder and louder until the cracking of the earth that followed each thud resounded through the cavern like fireworks. The cloud dragon mimicked the old man, turning its head to watch as something burst through the cavern opening—a large, eyeless rock monster. A voice floated down through the cavern on an unnatural breeze. "I need you to be my eyes."

Isaac's heart took courage. He shouted back, "Gladly!" He and the old tree-man eyed each other before Isaac instructed, "Go straight! And just pummel as you go!"

The rock monster lurched forward, knuckles dragging along the floor. The tree-man jumped out of the way with surprising gusto and used the dragon to throw a mighty swipe at the rock monster, crumbling it to pieces.

Isaac's heart sank.

With a rumble, the rocks rolled on top of one another as the thing rebuilt itself. Isaac could've wept as he cheered, *"Yes!"*

The dragon turned toward him, letting out a blast of hot air. Isaac ran, shield in place. "Left!" he shouted. "Go left. LEFT!"

The rock monster lurched to the right.

"OTHER LEFT!"

From the air Elise said, "What are *you* doing to help? Are you just standing there?"

Isaac yelled, "I'm trying *not* to die!"

The dragon stopped following Isaac. The tree-man was cornered by the rock monster, and the dragon attacked it with renewed vigor, shattering it over and over. The air in the room made Isaac weak. Not only did he feel as though his insides were boiling, but it was difficult to breathe. Each inhalation was devoid of oxygen and burned his lungs.

With every bit of strength he had left, Isaac lunged at the little tree-man with his sword. The tree-man dodged him, Isaac's sword severing only a few branches from the tree on his back. Isaac collapsed on the hot stone floor, trying to hold himself up as best as he could.

A puddle of water rose into the air just ahead of him, which was odd. He must've been hallucinating, probably because he was dying.

His gaze followed the flying puddle as it floated toward a man standing at the opposite end of the cavern. The man held a wickedly happy grin as all the water in the room gathered into the palms of his hands. He was perhaps in his early-to-mid-twenties, and his skin, hair, and goatee were as white as fresh sparkling snow, except for where his eyes *should* have been white. Instead, they were as black as the midnight sky. His irises were cold and blue as ice. He had on a long coat that appeared to be woven from shiny black and gray leather and lined with silver, with matching silver boots.

Isaac blinked, expecting the man and the ball of water to disappear. They didn't. Instead, the ball of water increased in size as moisture was torn from the cracks in the rocks, puddles, and air until it was nearly as big as the man himself. He threw it, sending it across the room and drenching the tree-man. The temperature plunged, making the room feel like a winter night in the far northern seas. The air dragon vanished as the man advanced, forcing gallons of water upon the tree-man, water that began to freeze. The tree-man tried to crawl away, but his movements slowed until they stopped altogether. Ice hung from his chin and the branches of the tree on his back, and he sat still, frozen solid.

The little balls of light throughout the room vanished, throwing Isaac into darkness that was only broken by the flicker of his torch outside. What looked like a sunbeam rose from the tree-man and disappeared, and as it did, Isaac swore he could hear the same cheerful singing that had echoed through the cavern when he'd first arrived.

Isaac was numb, but not from the sudden cold. His whole body felt distant from him as if he wasn't quite connected to it anymore. Still gripping his sword—he was sure he'd never let it go again—he lifted a trembling hand to his face, just to see if he could still feel it or if it was even there. He could, and it was.

The water-man straightened his coat, switched on some strange, flameless light that he held in his hand, and turned to Isaac. He smiled when he looked at him, his eyes studying Isaac's face with interest, and said in a voice that was deep and rough like large grinding rocks, "No need to thank me." He adjusted his black glove. "I only just saved your life. No, really, it was my pleasure; I'm happy to help. You're welcome."

Isaac shakily rose to his feet, listening. The water-man was speaking a language that was like the tree-man's but held a distinct accent where some of the whistling sounded more like a hiss. Once again, he somehow knew what he was saying, and the understanding hurt his head. The man—Snowman, Isaac decided to call him since that was what he looked like—continued, "I'm assuming that's my end of the conversation we're mentally having."

Isaac said nothing.

"Isaac!" Elise stood at the entryway to the cavern with her ball of light, and the rock monster tumbled back into a simple pile of rocks. At the sight of her, the man dropped his hands to his sides and watched as she glided toward Isaac. This time she didn't hesitate to throw her arms around him, and he had slipped far enough into some strange, psychological limbo that he let her. She hugged him so tightly it hurt. A lot. It probably wouldn't have hurt so much if he didn't feel like his insides were all very badly burned.

She jumped away as though he'd suddenly turned into a dead cactus and asked his boots in a sad tone, "Are you all right?"

Isaac nodded, though he wasn't, really.

She turned to Snowman; she was in about as equal awe to see him as Isaac had been. She went to speak but then stopped, perhaps realizing the futility of saying anything since he likely didn't speak any language she knew. Snowman raised a hand and spoke in English with a thick accent, "There is no need to thank me. I heard a commotion, so I decided to check it out. I'm only happy that I got here in time."

"You speak English?" she asked, surprised.

He smiled charmingly—well, maybe it was charming. Isaac wasn't sure since the man was terrifying to look at. But he was well-built with a strong jaw and humanoid features that would've probably been considered pleasant. He also had straight, brilliantly white teeth, and his smile worked, turning at the corner of his mouth in an almost flirtatious way. "I've studied many worlds along the River—"

Of course you have.

"—and am a very fast learner."

Of course you are. Isaac wasn't sure if he was bitter about it or fascinated. Possibly both. All he really knew was that this scary Snowman seemed to be made of nothing but pure magic, and it just wasn't fair.

"My goodness, where are my manners?" said Snowman, "I haven't properly introduced myself." He bowed a little. "My name is Asael."

"Really?" coughed Isaac, tasting blood. "Not some weird, other-worldly name like Sherman?" Every word he spoke caused agony.

Worth it.

Elise hurried to explain. "He's trying to make a joke."

Snowman stared at Isaac with his inhuman eyes. "Well, my name is spelled in a manner very unfamiliar with your world's languages, but it sounds like Asael. So, let's just keep it simple, shall we?"

Isaac decided he hated this man. And he also decided that, no matter what he *thought* his name was, it was, and always would be, *Snowman.*

Elise mimicked his bow. "It's a pleasure to meet you, Asael. I'm Elise, and..." She gave Isaac a look that suggested a debate in her mind— probably whether or not she should pretend he wasn't there. Finally, she said with a tone of resignation, "This is Isaac."

"I assure you," Snowman said with a small smile, gazing at her with those eyes that surely haunted the dreams of children, "the pleasure is mine."

Isaac's stomach turned at that smile and the tone of his voice and choice of words. "Ugh." The groan escaped involuntarily.

Elise gave Snowman an apologetic smile and excused Isaac. "He's not feeling well." She cleared her throat and floated over to the ice statue of the little tree-man. Her expression grew sorrowful. "He was just a little old man."

"A vicious little old man." Isaac choked, his airway stinging as he spoke. He coughed, blood splattering his sleeve. He cringed as he pried his hand from his sword and sheathed it, then pulled off the armor and shield and let them clang onto the ground, ripping dead vines out of his arm. His coat and shirt were torn, bloody, and burned where the shield had been, but the book was still in his breast pocket. "Really, the dragon was unnecessary. I swear he only used it because he was made of pure evil."

She glanced at Isaac. "A dragon?" She looked at Snowman for confirmation, then turned back to the frozen tree-man. "Goodness." She reached out and touched the branches on the creature's back. After a moment, she said with a deeply unsettled expression on her face, "He sort of looks like me."

She wasn't wrong. They'd both had glowing, green eyes, were merciless, and appeared to have been made from trees.

Elise eyed Snowman, her expression nearly unreadable—at least to anyone who hadn't known Arnaud. But Isaac knew the look. It was the one Arnaud would give clients when he felt they were trying to cheat them. It was a subtle, studious look, one meant to give off an air of innocence and friendliness while scrutinizing and measuring their character. Honestly, Isaac was glad to see it. Arnaud had always had a knack for sniffing out crooks. She said, "We were certainly fortunate that you arrived when you did. I can't bear to imagine what would've happened."

Snowman smiled and bowed, not flinching or showing any sign that he saw the strangeness of the coincidence. "Only doing my duty, miss. It is the code of my ancestors to aid fellow travelers."

She nodded as if he were clearly being honest, just as Arnaud would've done. "Of course. If only all the universe abided by such a code."

"Indeed," agreed Snowman. "Imagine it."

Isaac narrowed his gaze. Snowman didn't seem to notice.

Elise smiled. "So, what brings you all the way to the depths of Earth? To our obscure little world?"

"Your beautiful world is anything but obscure. I love Earth with all my heart. I spend as much time on it as I can. I know it must seem strange, but I actually do come through this cavern rather often. And as you can see—and not to boast—"

No, never to boast.

"—I am fluent in English. I also speak a bit of Spanish, Hindi, German, Italian, and am currently learning Mandarin—those are just a few that you're probably familiar with. Oh, and I'm also fluent in French."

Elise asked him a question in French, which was simply, "Ah! You speak French?"

He replied in French—very good French, much to Isaac's annoyance. "Yes, I do. I lived in Marseille for a time and spent many years in Paris."

On his own, Isaac only understood a word or two in French. He'd never really gotten the hang of it. But now he understood what they were saying for the same bizarre reason he understood the tree-man's language. And imagining Snowman spending any time in France without stirring up riots over his appearance was so absurd, Isaac blurted out—right in the middle of their conversation—"Like *that*?"

To his surprise, Elise didn't chide him for his outburst.

Snowman gave him an of-course-not sort of look. "No, absolutely not. Can you imagine?"

With a simple swipe of his hand, Snowman changed his appearance to that of a perfectly respectable gentleman with sandy-blond hair, normal blue eyes, normal trousers, a leather coat, and a black suit. With another swipe, scary Snowman reappeared.

Elise dropped her hands to her side, her expression replaced with shock and a flare of anger. "How did you do that?"

"It's an illusion," he stated. "Surely you must know how to create an illusion. You can't be living on Earth floating around with wings."

"Yes, of course I do," snapped Elise, narrowing her gaze, "but how do you choose how you'll appear?"

He seemed to find this question puzzling. "Just like I would an outfit, I suppose. I think about it, piece it together in my mind, and then I put it on."

Elise looked as though someone had just rudely pointed out that she had only one outfit in her closet. She folded her arms, her brow furrowed. "I see."

As *interesting* as this all was, Isaac had never felt more horrible in all his life and was sure he was dying. With every breath he took, the air ripped through his lungs as if it were made of broken glass. His knees buckled under the weight of his body, and his vision spun and sparked with stars.

It wasn't pleasant.

He lumbered a short distance to the cavern wall and leaned against it. Before they could venture off on another *fascinating* topic that he cared deeply about, he had to ask, "What's next, then?"

"Right," Elise said. She asked Snowman, "So you were just passing through, you say?"

"Yes," said Snowman. "I've made plans to stay in Barcelona for a time."

"You've stayed on Earth often, ya? Have you ever had trouble passing through here before?"

"Sometimes the old man would give me some trouble, but he always let me through. Nothing ever like this time. It was obvious your friend's situation was dire."

"And the solution was to kill the old man." Elise's friendly demeanor had faded, just as Arnaud's would've done when he'd decided he was talking to a crook.

"Eh, I never liked him. And there was clearly no reasoning with him, he was trying very hard to kill your friend," said Snowman. "He also kept bringing birds down here, and they'd always die."

Isaac felt the need to point out, "Birds do that a lot." Then he erupted into a coughing fit.

Snowman paid as much attention to Isaac as he did his conscience. "And when I saw him attacking your friend here, I'd just had enough of it."

He said it with such ease. It didn't sit right with Isaac. Isaac certainly despised the tree-man and was relieved he was dead, since he'd pretty much succeeded in cooking him alive. Isaac had also tried his best to kill him in self-defense, but had he succeeded, he would've felt sick. There was something very wrong with Snowman's cold casualness toward it all.

He would've made a great executioner. Maybe that was his job when he lived on Earth.

Elise said, "Well, we shouldn't be keeping you any longer. Could you point the way out for us? We're new to this area, obviously."

"Nonsense," said Snowman. "There's no need for that. I'll take you through it."

"No, that's unnecessary."

"I assure you it is necessary. It's a labyrinth out. If you've never been through before, you're going to get lost."

Elise studied him for a long moment.

Isaac's frame shook with exhaustion, and his breathing had turned into a wheeze. *I can't believe it. This is it. This is how I die. Cooked to death by a little old tree-man and his cloud-dragon.*

"All right," said Elise finally. "We'll follow you out."

Something in Isaac cracked at this. "*What?*" He wobbled over to Elise and pulled her aside by the elbow. "*Excuse* me." He paused to cough, blood spurting into his mouth. He wiped his lips on his bloodied sleeve and gathered himself. "Are we really going to listen to some random *man*-creature—who just *happened* to show up and just *happens* to speak English—how is that not odd to you? Just because he looks like a Snowman doesn't mean he's some lovable winter fairy. He just killed a little old man!"

Elise murmured, "A horrible old man."

"Who just kills a little old man?"

She whisper-shouted, "The little old man just tried to kill you!"

"And he probably succeeded and I'm glad he's dead, but that's beside the point. The point is, that man over there is a *terrifying* Snowman. He is the monster that lurked in Sister Catherine's pantry. He made it very difficult to steal cookies."

She folded her arms, furrowing her brow in thought. "He is obviously a crook of some sort. He'd probably shortchange us if he were to hire us. He's after something." She looked at Isaac. "Because of that, I think he'll take us to the River."

"Yes. To rob us and feed us to his Snowman children." The image made Isaac shudder inside.

"We'll be ready for him—" She looked Isaac over. "*I'll* be ready for him."

Isaac backed away, shaking his head. "No. Nope. I'm not doing it—"

"What choice do we have?"

"—I'm not following him—"

"Do *you* know the way out of here?"

Isaac announced to everyone, "I'm just going to lie down right here." And he did, wincing and unwilling to admit that despite the cold, the rock was somehow still uncomfortably hot, and he wouldn't be able to lie there for long. "And not move. Ever again. I'm never moving again."

Snowman, while holding a magical device that lit up the cave with a bright white light without a flame, and that was apparently too special to let Isaac inspect, led Elise and a hobbling, wheezing Isaac through narrow corridors that took them deeper and deeper into the Earth. Isaac's vision faded in and out with fizzling lights, and his head spun as he fought to breathe. Snowman turned to them. "We're not far now."

The remaining tunnel turned sharply upward, not quite a sheer wall, but enough that it would be a challenge to accomplish with only three fully functioning limbs. Isaac groaned and seriously considered curling into a ball and crying at the sight of it. Climbing it would surely be the end of him. But instead, for reasons he wasn't sure of anymore, he began the climb. He gripped onto rocks and, farther up, strange blue and green vines. Elise had already floated to the top and reached to pull him up the rest of the way. They stumbled out of the hole and into a peculiar, dark, open void.

The air had changed. It wasn't stagnant and old anymore, but fresh and clean, like after rain. Isaac swore he could see stars in the darkness and hear rushing water. His heart gave a little leap at the sound.

It was so dark. Elise lit a ball of fire, and Isaac looked to see where Snowman and his magic light had gone. Isaac and Elise stepped forward into the darkness as she shouted, "Asael?"

Who was Asael? *Oh right. That's Snowman's name.*

After a few more steps, their feet touched water. Isaac cried out as he was pulled into it. A warm, glowing liquid flowed all around him that tasted like mud, weeds, and salt. He dropped into a pool. Frantic and sure his lungs couldn't take any more stress, he flailed his limbs in what he hoped were swimming motions until his head broke the surface, where he was dragged to the shore by Elise. He coughed and sputtered, wiping the weird liquid from his eyes, and looked.

The rocks and water had changed into bright colors and glistened as if he'd slipped into a dream. All around him was a sky painted with cosmic colors and littered with stars. Looming behind him was the Earth, a beautiful green and blue gem swirling with white clouds. He grasped onto bizarre glowing plants to pull himself up. As he stood on his feet, he forgot all his pain. He'd even forgotten how to breathe.

Tears filled his eyes as he drank in his surroundings. Planet after bright, glorious planet stretched beyond him into the stars as far as he could see, connected by a flowing force that started right at his feet.

It was real. He was standing where the impossible met reality, on the bank of the River.

Just Another Day

Meanwhile, among the planets they gazed upon was the planet of Thera. In fact, it was the closest one to Earth, just a little way down the River. A branch of the River led to it like a winding pathway to a house.

On Thera, there was a creature by the name of Rhaenmeinnah (Rain for short). He wasn't having a good day. No, not at all. Because it was just another day.

And that was a problem.

It was another day haunted by memories. Memories that didn't have the decency to fade away, no matter how much time passed. Memories that washed over him like waves as though he were caught in a current and couldn't reach the safety of the shore, no matter how hard he fought against it. His limbs were heavy. His heart was broken and weary, and the shore was fading farther and farther away.

What was left to do but surrender and drown?

Rain had tried so hard to be strong for the ones he loved. He'd told them to be brave, that this darkness could not last forever, for surely one day, they would see dawn. Things would be different if only they held on. The future was full of hope, of freedom, of bright possibilities.

Many had believed him, too.

But instead, Rain had watched the light of that hope drain out of their bodies with their blood, making his words empty. They were born into a world of misery and despair, and were murdered to cheers and laughter, their cries turning to gargles as they died. He couldn't escape that sound nor the sight of their heartbreak as life vanished from their eyes.

Neither could he escape what had been done to him, not even in his sleep. Though Rain was now a free creature, there were moments when he swore he could still feel the shackles around his wrists, when he was consumed with fear as if the torture and violation he'd once endured nearly every day were still impending, still happening. Sure, his brother had found him, had rescued him from that nightmare, but the shadows of it still followed him every day. They haunted him in his every move, in every dream.

Day after day, he'd watch the sun rise and set. Rain remembered a time when that had meant something, back when he had expected things to change. But day after day, his mind, the memories, the nightmares—they all remained the same. He now knew that the movement of the planet, the passage of time, was full of nothing but empty promises.

He was tired. So very tired.

So, no. He couldn't endure just another day.

Little did he know, he would never endure *just* another day.

He was determined to use a military training exercise to seize the one thread of control he had over his fate in a very unfortunate way, as many of his fellow Hassune had done. Tears streamed down his aged, wrinkled features as he flew his ship up into the atmosphere of Thera, something he'd been planning to do ever since his brother had taught him how to fly it.

Humans dominated Thera, and though Rain and his people were not human, his brother had taught him how to disguise himself as one. There in the cockpit of his ship, he looked perfectly human in his black, red, and gold embroidered military uniform. It was tight-fitting enough that he had full mobility and could wear it under his armor, which he was. The armor was designed to fill their enemies with terror. The helmet looked like a warped, demonic skull, patterned in black and gold with red strategically painted to look as though he were covered in blood. With a vocal command, it would retract and fold itself away in a pack that extended the length of his back. Underneath the armor, Rain's once-youthful dark skin and strong features were now withered and gray. This was because, in his final moments, he had chosen to let go and no longer bury how broken he felt, and the emotions had aged his form. It was how creatures like him grew old. Therefore, although he'd only been alive for twenty-four years, he appeared to be in his eighties.

He gave the command to remove his armor. His mind flooded with memories he'd almost forgotten, of a life so foreign now that he almost wondered if he'd made it up in some attempt to convince himself he'd once been happy. They were memories of him playing with his brother along the seashore, their laughter innocent and genuine, as his mother watched them from their home that was carefully hidden in the trees nearby. His mind clung to these visions like a treasured childhood toy. It filled his soul with a long-forgotten peace, a feeling he wanted to die with as if death could somehow seal it in his heart and make it last forever.

Nothe, who was another Hassune in disguise, monitored his movements and vitals from the ground. "Rain..."

Rain took down his ship's shields. Nothe's deep and perpetually hoarse voice grew nervous and stern. "Rain, what are you doing?"

He was sure his friend already knew the answer. "Forgive me, Nothe."

"No—"

"I...I have lost the battle."

Nothe's voice grew angry and desperate. "No, don't you do this to me. Don't you *dare*."

"I'm sorry."

"No! Don't you—"

Rain shut down his communications. He used his ship's navigation system to aim it at the jagged rocks of the seashore and locked it into place. At the speed he was flying, and from that distance, not even a Hassune like him could survive the collision.

He took a deep breath and closed his eyes, his mind swept up in wonderful memories, his expression serene.

Within a very frantic, curse-filled matter of seconds, Nothe hacked into the ship's computer from the ground and threw the shield back up. He also hacked into the navigation system and altered its course by a crucial three hundred feet, something he was able to do simply because he was *that* good.

Instead of crashing into the rocky shore and bursting into flames, Rain hit the water. Without his helmet, he smacked his head, cracking his skull. Without his armor, his body was shattered here and there, twisted and mangled, and indeed, had he been anything other than a Hassune, he would've certainly died.

Unbeknownst to anyone, deep under the surface of the ocean at that precise spot many years before, a rather large hole had been opened.

This hole created a rather powerful current, which Rain's rather small ship sank into. The current carried his ship away, pulling him into the rather large hole, setting him up to wake in a rather strange place.

Needless to say, Rain was severely disappointed when he opened his eyes and found that he was not dead. He couldn't move very well—as he couldn't feel much below his neck, which meant it was likely broken—but from his very uncomfortable, slumped position, stars twinkled happily at him through the blood-stained, cracked window of his ship, and the sight was infuriating. How had his ship not been obliterated?

A name came to mind: Nothe.

It had been Nothe. He was sure of it. How could he do this to him? How could he be so cruel?

He closed his eyes, consumed with nausea and a blinding headache. As furious as he was at Nothe, a light flickered on inside his heart because of him, a light that caused his whole chest to ache as it writhed in hope and confusion against chains of despair. He couldn't be angry. Nothe cared. He cared enough to try to save him.

He didn't know how he felt about that or about anything stirring around in his chest. His headache wasn't going to let him figure it out. But whatever he felt, and however faint the light was, it was enough for the healing process to begin as he drifted back out of consciousness.

He didn't know how long he was out or how long it took for his body to heal itself, but it had to have been a very long time. He woke up dehydrated with a mouth that tasted like old blood, smoke, and sand. He sat in his ship long after his body was healed enough to be able to leave it, exhausted from the energy that had been spent to repair it and thoroughly drained at the thought of facing the world outside. Though his arms were whole, they felt heavy when he lifted them to open the cockpit, like they'd been filled with rocks.

He first noticed the smell of mud and the sound of babbling water. Dazed, he pulled his body out of the ship and dropped down onto soft, murky soil. Being Hassune, he could see the energy of living things. The more powerful a thing was, the brighter its energy. Here, he had to squint to look around as his eyes adjusted. Everything around him was so bright it was almost excruciating, which meant everything was alive and powerful, even the mud at his feet. His gaze darted to the sky.

He forgot all his dread, his inner pain. He even forgot how to breathe.

Stars and cosmic swirls of color surrounded him. They reached far into the unknown above him and fell deep into the oblivion below. Patches of the scene were obstructed by the most exhilarating of sights: planets, connected by an eerie, glowing thread that weaved from world to world. As he studied them, he noted that each planet appeared to hold water, which meant that each one could harbor life.

There were so many, stretching above and below him as far as he could see. He only recognized one: Thera, the planet closest to where he stood, looming over him like his deepest regrets. But none of the others were of his solar system.

His gaze followed the glowing thread until it ended at the marsh by his feet. It was made of a water-like substance, and the only source of actual light in this strange void came from its purplish glow and the strange plants that grew alongside it. He couldn't be sure (though he was quite certain) but judging by how the glow seemed to bleed into the marsh, it appeared that this massive, flowing "river" had somehow created it, allowing solid, endless ground to float throughout the oblivion. Perhaps it was why everything there held living energy.

He marveled at how he wasn't dead.

He took several deep breaths. How was there oxygen? And warmth? The strange river not only had life but somehow had its own atmosphere.

Really, there was no way he should've been standing there, and no way the thing he stood on should exist. It was impossible. *Perhaps I'm dead after all.*

He tentatively approached the River, noting the fluffy, purplish-pink mist that hovered and sparkled above the gentle waves. As he studied it, his heart drummed with a new purpose and thrill, and a few of the wrinkles in his aged face faded away.

He knelt and studied the waves that absorbed his reflection. He cupped some of the liquid in his hand and watched it drip from his fingers. It was warm like bathwater, and yet too thick to actually *be* water. It reminded him of soup that had been sitting too long. Purplish, glowing soup.

Several feet away from him, the "soup" began to bubble. Rain's heart leapt, bringing him to his feet. Fire bit his veins in panic as he stumbled backward, waiting for what might emerge. He was terrified, and yet some twisted part of him was excited. He could be meeting his demise at the hands and hunger of something completely unknown, some monster of space he was sure no one had ever encountered and lived to tell the tale. His death was going to be so much more impressive than he had ever imagined.

But what emerged was a small submarine made by the Theran military. It looked like a short, black bullet, slightly larger than a kyriki—the large, fluffy animals that he had lived with for a time as a child. All enthusiasm drained out of him as he watched it career out of control and crash upon the riverbank.

He sighed and looked down at the marsh, concluding that this was all life was: a series of tragic disappointments.

He returned his attention to the ship, approaching it carefully. *Someone must've followed me. Why?* His stomach sank. *Is this river a Theran creation? A secret military operation?*

Anger surged through him. He might've wanted to die, but he wasn't about to give the honor of taking his life to any Theran. He ran back to his own ship, climbed upon the wing, and reached into the cockpit for his double-bladed ax. As the hatch to the submarine opened, Rain leapt down and swung it expertly, bracing himself for the monster that was sure to emerge.

The individual slowly rose out of the ship, his military helmet turned toward the sky, clearly distracted. His energy was surprisingly bright, with flickers of shadow here and there. Usually, Therans held no light in their energy but were made of shadows darker than the voids of space.

No matter. A Theran was still a Theran.

Rain contemplated a quick decapitation, but where was the fun in that?

He was glad for this decision when the Theran removed his helmet. It was someone with messy, dark blond hair, pale skin, and a strong jawline, wearing a military uniform with the armor retracted. He was well-built with striking features and eyes that glowed with the dark, golden colors of the setting sun—and he also wasn't really human.

It was Nothe.

Rain's heart did a somersault. Any feelings of gladness and relief were swept away with guilt, warping them into a solid rock of dread that sat in his gut, making him want to vomit. Rain shifted his stance and glanced at the weird bushes behind him and thought about hiding. Nothe hadn't noticed him yet. He hadn't even left the ship. His gaze was fixed on the planets and stars with his mouth hanging open. He watched Nothe stumble out, which was rather amusing. Nothe was very gruff and dignified and never stumbled, but Rain could tell he was struggling to keep his knees from giving out.

Rain fixed his attention on a moss-covered twig and kicked at it with the tip of his boot. It was the wave of emotion that erupted from Nothe that made him look up, hitting him like the aftershock of a bomb. The Hassune were not only capable of feeling emotion as though it were its own kind of language, their emotions—if unrestrained—were powerful and could overwhelm anything capable of feeling them. Nothe's emotions were a complicated mess, a tangled whirlwind of relief, confusion, unspeakable joy, and fury. But burning underneath it all was something Nothe fought to repress, something bright that Rain couldn't define.

All of this was reflected in Nothe's eyes as his gaze fixed on Rain as if the strange and beautiful scenery had suddenly vanished. This made Rain feel worse. He was pretty much fungi—fungi growing on the rock that had formed in his gut. Tears stung his eyes as he felt all that his friend was going through. To be the cause of such torment... He was certain he was something worse than fungi, something that shouldn't even exist.

With tears in his eyes, Nothe threw his arms around Rain, embracing him so tightly that he thought his ribs might collapse. Rain hesitated before he returned it, the act and emotion breaking down his walls until all the pain rushed through. "I'm sorry."

Nothe hugged him tighter. Once the hug had gone on for too long, they broke apart with a series of awkward throat clearings. Nothe had a sudden interest in the mud at his feet as he discreetly wiped away tears, then quickly cleared his throat again. "Now that's out of the way..."

Nothe punched him in the face like it was the next line in his sentence. Rain fell on his back, staring up at planets and stars, feeling as though Nothe had dropped a house on the side of his head. Rain's first instinct was to try and cradle his face, but he knew better than to touch it, and the conflict left his hands hovering a few inches over it as he writhed in agony. He tried to shout curses at Nothe but couldn't move his jaw.

Nothe's footsteps drew closer. Rain looked up at him with his one good eye, proud to see that his face had broken Nothe's hand, bending it where it wasn't supposed to be bent. Nothe glared down at him, saying with a brightness that clashed unnervingly with the fire in his eyes, "Well, you're bleeding, so I guess we're not dead."

With several sharp, painful jolts, the bones in Rain's face slowly popped and ground themselves back into place. His ability to heal was waning with the blood he had lost and the energy he had spent recovering from the massive bodily damage inflicted earlier. He spat out blood as he shakily pushed himself to his feet. Nothe squared his shoulders and set his fury-filled face mere inches from Rain, making him flinch. Nothe pointed accusingly at him with a finger on his good hand, his words now dripping with anger and pain. "Don't you *ever* put me through that again."

Rain's stomach gave another nasty twist of guilt at the words, but he said nothing. He brushed it all aside and, with weary eyes, turned his attention to the cosmic sky. "So, if neither of us are dead, where—or what—where—no, let's start with, *what* do you think this thing is?"

He looked over at Nothe, whose stern expression made it perfectly clear that he was not about to let Rain dismiss everything that'd just happened so easily.

Rain went on as though he hadn't noticed. "Or perhaps we *are* dead, and death is not at all what we expected. We still," he sighed, "we still feel pain, bleed, break, and it's, overall, magnificently disappointing. Just like life." He gave a cheery shrug. "I don't know. What do you think?"

Nothe folded his arms and mused with the same cheeriness, "Ya know, I think...I think..." His gaze narrowed. "I think I can punch harder."

"I'm sure you can."

Nothe put a hand to his forehead. "I just—I don't even know what to say to you right now."

"Nothing! There's nothing to say. Just help me figure out where we are." Rain ran a hand through his hair, his fingers catching on multiple blood clots. "It's like you've never seen someone try to kill themselves before."

"Yeah, well, not someone I actually—" Nothe paused. Rain knew he'd used up all the points on his sentimental card with the hug. "*Tolerate.* What am I supposed to do when the only creature I can tolerate up and dies? How dare you leave me behind." He swallowed. "I might as well follow right behind you."

Rain threw up his hands. "Oh, c'mon! Don't—I said I was sorry; what more do you want from me?"

"I want you to promise me that you won't ever be stupid like this again."

He rolled his eyes and let out a series of dark guffaws that expressed the absurdity of Nothe's request. "Oh, so you want me to lie to you, then?" He rubbed his wrists. "How are we arguing about this when we're standing out here, on this—this impossible..." He couldn't think of an adequate word for it. "*Thing?*"

"Because this thing—this—" Nothe also seemed to be at a loss for words, "this...*river* thing and anything that might follow after—none of it even matters if you're not alive to *see* it. What's even the point, Rhaenmeinnah?"

Rain wanted to yell at him. Nothe was being entirely unfair. How did he not understand? Had he not suffered as much—if not *more*—than himself? How had Nothe found any amount of peace to quell his pain? How was he not just *tired?*

There really wasn't a point in yelling. It would just be exhausting and upsetting, and for nothing, because Nothe had clearly already made up his mind on the matter and would never understand.

He wasn't bitter about that, though. He was glad Nothe didn't understand; it meant he still had hope for better days. Nothe deserved hope and better days.

Rain drew a pace away from him, looking out over the expanse, studying the strange river. Each of its branches led from a planet to one main vein—the one at his feet.

All rivers flow somewhere. His curiosity burned at this thought, sparking something within him that made a few more wrinkles fade away.

He turned to Nothe. "I can promise you this. I will not die until we figure out where this river thing goes."

Nothe sighed and rubbed his eyes.

"Is that enough?"

Nothe shrugged, then threw up a hand. "Fine. I guess I'll take it."

Rain flashed him the most genuine grin his face had displayed in a very long time. "Then let's begin."

We Speak the Same Language?
What are the Odds?

Isaac wiped away a few tears, trying his best to be discreet about it. He was so overwhelmed by what lay before him that he was sure he was dreaming—or dead. Was he dead? Maybe he'd died back at the ship, and the cavern had been Purgatory. That would make sense. In fact, that would actually make far more sense than being alive and experiencing this exact moment.

Yes. He was quite sure of it. He was very dead.

But then, what was this? Was this Heaven? If it was, then it was much different than he'd expected. It was much darker and far more terrifying. And yet, it was absolutely... Was there even a word for it? It was so wondrous, so stunning and magnificent that there simply were no words. Words could only diminish its glory and beauty.

A sniffle came from near his right shoulder. He looked over and remembered that Elise existed, which made him sad. Her cheeks were wet with tears, and her large green eyes mirrored the childlike wonder and hope he'd imagined were in his own only a moment before.

Then he remembered he was covered in a soup-like slime and there was a vine in his arm. And it hurt. A lot. And the book in his coat had probably been destroyed again by the soup.

And he'd been burned and boiled alive.

And he was dehydrated and starving. And had a migraine. And was probably dying. Could you die in Heaven?

Probably not. Actually, he probably wouldn't even *make* it to Heaven if he had died, no matter how much Purgatory he went through —or however Purgatory worked.

So then, was this real? Existing alongside his beating heart? He put a hand to his chest just to check. There it was, beating away. He was alive, and he was in too much pain to be dreaming. It must've been real.

But how? How could it possibly *be?*

As Isaac and Elise sat goggling over the magnificent river, a loud hum washed over them with a gust of swampy, moss-smelling wind.

Pink mist and shimmering bits of dirt swirled over them violently enough that they both felt the need to raise their arms over their faces to shield themselves from it. Isaac gazed in the direction of the wind, confused to see a bright light coming from upriver. He'd never seen anything like it. It was whiter than the sun.

The light rose into the starlit sky, shining out of a...of a massive bug? Was that what it was? It was the size of a small cutter ship, black as night, and looked somewhat like a fat beetle, but it flew with small, set wings. Where eyes should've been, Isaac swore he saw a large window, and through the window, he *swore* there was—

Snowman.

That simply wasn't possible. He was sure of it.

But then Elise floated after the giant bug, shouting, "Wait! Wait!" and frantically waved her arms as if Snowman were actually in the bug and flying away. With a flutter of her wings, she rose in the air, but the bug was too fast and was long gone in only a matter of thirty seconds or so. "You can't just leave us!" She landed and stomped her foot, shaking the ground beneath her. "We could've used a lift, you pigeon-livered, hornswoggler!"

A little way down river, Rain and Nothe saw the bug, too. Only, unlike Isaac, they knew exactly what it was, though it wasn't from their world. It was a small spaceship from that one planet the queen of Thera had once attacked, but a clearly more updated version. Many years after the attack, the people of that planet had sought revenge on Thera from the sea but had failed so spectacularly that neither Rain nor Nothe could even remember the name of the planet anymore. It had become a mere blip on their history. No one had even bothered to figure out how they'd snuck all their ships into the ocean, although Rain and Nothe were pretty sure they'd now figured it out. They watched it fly by, awestruck. Rain asked, "Where do you think he's going?"

Nothe thought about shrugging but was too baffled. "Who's to say?"

"Should we follow him?"

He glanced at Rain. "Well, I guess we can follow him with our eyes."

They watched as the little black ship turned into a little black dot and then disappeared around the next branch down from them. Once it was out of sight, their gazes turned to the direction from where it had come.

They thought they could hear some faint shouting coming from a couple of barely discernible little spots along the riverbank.

THEY *WERE* HEARING SHOUTING from those spots, as those spots were Isaac and Elise, and now Isaac was shouting at Elise. Not because he was angry at her—though he was, and always would be—but because he was, completely and most assuredly, losing his mind.

"*What was that?*" This was what he was shouting. Not necessarily because he thought she knew, but more because he really needed to shout something. "What was that? *What!*" He made nonsensical flapping gestures with his hands. "Was that?!"

"Stop yelling at me!" Elise shouted back.

Isaac didn't know how the giant bug was her fault, but she'd blown up his ship and his crew and put a vine in his arm, so he was sure she'd done it somehow, and he'd had quite enough of it all, thank you very much. He threw his arms out in the direction the bug had gone and shouted again, "*What was that?!*"

"I. DON'T. KNOW!" Elise plopped on the ground like a disgruntled child, folding her arms. "I think it was some kind of ship."

Isaac smirked at how stupid that idea was. He was a sailor. A captain. He knew ships. That was no ship. There had been no quarterdeck or bowsprit, no spars, no sails—what could've possibly made that ridiculous, sorry contraption a ship? Nothing, that's what. "No. No, that was not a ship. That was a...a..." When he couldn't think of anything, he landed on "*not* a ship!"

"It was too a ship!" Elise snapped, "It just wasn't a sea-ship—"

Preposterous. That was what ships *were*. And how long had this person, as Arnaud, served as first officer on his "sea-ship?" "*I beg your pardon?*"

"—I rode in one when I was little. It didn't float in the sea; it floated through the air."

"That's...that's..." He wanted to say "impossible." He really wanted to say it. He swore that it was just yesterday when he could use that word to shut down any obnoxious, inconceivable ideas he didn't like.

But in that moment, it hit him—yes, it'd taken until then to truly hit him and sink in. He'd been too frightened or too upset or too so many other things for his mind to absorb his day right away, but something about the giant bug with Snowman and this conversation with Elise had finally made it permeable. He couldn't really use that word anymore, ever. The whole fabric of what was and wasn't, of what could be and couldn't be, had been officially and completely torn to shreds. The foundation of everything he'd once been sure of had crumbled away. He knew nothing. Absolutely nothing.

Something dark and cold ripped through Isaac's stomach then, spreading through his limbs and filling him with dread. His mind grew numb yet alert. His chest burned in intense, inescapable agony. The bubbling noise of the River was so loud, growing to the level of a thousand drunks shouting at each other in a cathedral. The rustling of the strange plants and leaves sounded as though they were turning to each other, whispering. And the smells—the old water, moss and mud, and strange, floral scent—were so strong, they threatened to split his skull with each breath.

He was helpless. Useless. Frozen.

Broken.

Just like when he was a child, sitting in the cold alleyway, his toes and fingers numb, watching the snow drift down from the sky. He tried not to think about that moment, ever. Yet when it entered his mind, it was vivid and clear, as if it were occurring right at that moment. He could feel the hopelessness, the fear.

Isaac went into a coughing fit, blood spattering with each cough. He couldn't breathe. His vision spun, and he found himself stumbling—though he hadn't been walking—and falling to his knees. His head, once again, was trying to split itself in two with a white, blinding pain. He crumpled into a ball with his head in his hands and then fell to his side.

At least he stopped coughing.

Elise let out an annoyed, "Isaac?" When he didn't respond, she groaned and pushed herself to her feet. "Not again."

She knelt beside him and shook his sore shoulder. "Isaac?"

Isaac swatted at her with his good hand as if she were a bug and grunted, "Go away."

She tried again. His words slurred as he spat, "I'm dead. Go away."

"Stop this. You're being ridiculous."

It was so hard to talk. *Stop hassling the dead*, he wanted to say but couldn't. His tongue, his face, he couldn't feel them anymore. They wouldn't move.

"Get up! Isaac—"

He closed his eyes and kept them closed.

HE HEARD voices he didn't recognize. They were speaking a language he swore he didn't know—yet he understood every word. Elise said in this language, "You speak Theran?" Her accent was thick, and the words clearly didn't come to her easily. How did she even know the language?

There was so much Isaac didn't know about his former first officer.

A voice answered, one that was rough and raspy, making Isaac picture sunbaked sand, "We do. And so do you! Isn't that just the strangest coincidence? I mean, what are the odds?"

"I can't even fathom it," said a very deep voice, serene and almost musical, like the ocean depths.

"Me neither," said the raspy voice. "We're from there, unfortunately."

Elise said, "We were at war with you."

"Oh no, that wasn't *our* war," said the voice. "We just live there. Well, technically, we're soldiers now, but our war isn't with you people."

The dark voice told her, "It's with the Therans."

"But that's a secret, so shhh." There was a long silence. "It's a long story."

Isaac didn't care about any of this, but he couldn't help listening since they were so loud, which was rude. He had a migraine. Couldn't they see he was trying to sleep?

He drifted out of consciousness again and was awoken by the two unfamiliar voices. The raspy voice spoke first: "It *does* look like a pretty easy fix."

"It's really not. Why are you still talking about it?" said the dark voice.

"It seems very important to her."

"That really doesn't matter."

"And his energy has light. I've never seen a human with light before. It's got shadows, too, but look at how much light there is! It's fascinating. Most Hassune don't even have that much light."

"Doesn't matter. He is what he is."

"Listen to you."

"What?"

"You've become so cruel."

"Oh, *please*."

"You're one of those people who'd kill an adorable, furry, baby shookenkerg just because it was a shookenkerg, with their four, adorable, big black eyes—"

"Oh I would not!"

"—looking up at you with trust and adoration and no plans to eat you yet."

"This isn't a baby anything! It's a grown *man!*"

A grown man? Isaac wondered, trying to pay attention now through the pain in his head—a pain that seemed to sever the bones in his neck and stick in his chest like a dull sword. *What grown man? Is there a grown man out here?*

"We could raise it as one of our own," the raspy voice insisted.

"No, Nothe. We couldn't. You know why? Because it's a *grown man!* It's already been raised! Let it die. It'll be a win for the universe. There'll be one less monster in it."

Wait. Isaac grew more concerned now. *What monster? Is there a monster nearby?*

There was a little voice in his head that suggested that perhaps, maybe, they were talking about him.

What a ridiculous thought that was. *I'm not a monster!*

Then that same little voice reminded him of his promise to marry Marie while he was courting Florence, and then Alice found out and told them both. Marie joined a convent after that.

But did he really have to die for it? Alice would certainly think so, but wasn't there somebody he could talk to about this? Make some sort of deal? Maybe if he could wake up. *Wake up, man!*

His head screamed in agony. His eyes fluttered, but they wouldn't stay open, and his whole face was still numb. He felt horrible and sick all over.

There was a moment of grave silence, a moment where Isaac's heart started pounding against his skull, the pressure and agony building in his head as though his heart were chipping away at it with a chisel and a hammer.

The raspy voice finally spoke. "Look, I hate humans as much as you do. So very, very much. I've killed more than you have—"

"One hundred and two to my meager fifty-three." He sounded disappointed in himself.

"Right. But who's counting? Anyway, the point is, you know I do. But she's in pain. Desperate pain. Can't you feel it?"

"Like many others and their masters."

"Does she *look* like a slave, Rain?"

Wait, did they just say "humans?" What did he mean by one hundred and two to fifty-three? What are they talking about? What slave? She isn't a slave, I'm a slave! Me! I'm the one with the vine in my arm! His lips moved a little in an attempt to say this. A whimper slipped through, but nothing more.

"Did *I* look like a slave?" The dark voice roared—and at this, something strange rushed over Isaac's body, seeping through his skin and into his heart, like an intense heat from a blazing fire, though it wasn't heat. It was an emotion—if emotions could radiate in such a way. It was vivid and clear.

Rage.

The other voice was silenced, and the dark voice continued. "I won't do it. All it takes is *one* of them, Nothe. You know that."

Isaac was panicking now. *One of* what? *What do they think I am?* He had to say something. Anything. Preferably something simple that he could get out in one painful breath. He worked all his strength into his stomach muscles and forced them to release enough air for him to make a sound as his numb tongue and lips attempted to form the word "help."

It came out as more of a loud groan with very little structure. It was a truly awful sound, something he couldn't believe had come from him.

This was far from his proudest moment.

He tried to move his fingers, his toes. They didn't want to listen. He didn't know what had happened to him, but he knew it had something to do with the pain in his head. It seemed to be a wall of thorns, unreasonably standing in the way of his body's ability to do anything productive at all.

"Why are you two still arguing?" Elise said, but not in English. It was in the strange sounds that the other voices were speaking in, though it sounded terrible. Her accent was so severe, he wondered if they'd understand her. "What's there to argue about? He needs help!"

Isaac totally agreed with her, which was something he hadn't thought possible.

Dark voice said, with little kindness, "I know this is hard to understand now, but once he's dead, he won't be able to hurt you or anyone else ever again."

"What? He hasn't hurt me! Well, he's an idiot—"

Rude.

"—but, actually, he's one of the few creatures that have ever been kind to me."

Isaac didn't know how to feel about that.

Dark voice wasn't convinced. "Once you're free, the pain will fade."

"Free?" Elise sounded confused. "But I *am* free."

At this, raspy voice asked, "He is not your master?"

She was clearly disgusted. "No! Absolutely not!" At this, her tone grew enthusiastic, as if she'd been drowning and had grasped a lifeline, something that could work to her advantage. "In fact, I am *his* master. You see the vine in his arm?"

Raspy voice said, "I do. It's hard to miss it."

"I put that there. It's how I get him to do what I want."

"Really?" The two voices gave small hums of approval, and raspy voice added, "I like that."

"Yes," said Elise. "Yes, he is my servant. I need him to get me home."

Dark voice said, "He can't be that useful. All humans ever do is sit, drink, and complain."

He and the other voice laughed at this. Elise chimed in, her laugh sounding forced. Then she exclaimed, "Too true! Yes. Whining is the only thing he's done all day."

Isaac wanted to know how much *she'd* complain if she were to switch places with him.

Elise pressed on. "But, he is useful enough. So, please, help me get home by helping my servant. I need my servant."

Isaac felt so much in the silence that followed this plea. There was a soft-yet-not-soft kick to his back as if whoever owned the foot were a child, checking to see if he were really, truly deathly unwell or just faking it. But worse than this kick was the complicated, angry, and desperate ball of tangled knots in his stomach. He really didn't want to die. How perfectly horrible would it be to die on the starting line of the greatest adventure of his life? And oh, how he hated Elise. He hated her so much for this day, yet she had brought him here and was pleading for his life. He hated that, too. Yet he was grateful to her.

He despised being grateful to her.

Raspy voice said cheerfully, "Well, she's won me over." His tone changed to one of a banker who felt very good about a business decision. "I don't care what you think, Rain. I'm going to heal this creature. It'll be my good deed for the day. In fact, I think this good deed will count for the rest of the month!"

"Whatever," said dark voice, kicking him again—at least, Isaac assumed he was the one who was doing the kicking. "I suppose it'll lengthen out his overall suffering."

"That's why I like you, Rain. Somehow, you manage to see the good in every situation."

Elise exclaimed, "Wonderful! What are we waiting for, then? How, uh, how do we do this?"

"I'm not doing it," said the dark voice—this Rain fellow—though no one asked him. "I'm not shedding another drop of blood for a human. If you want him to live so much, then you do it."

"I kinda felt that went without saying," said the other one, "but if you feel better driving that point home, then—"

"Just get it over with, will you?"

"You're the one who keeps talking."

Elise said what Isaac was thinking—although much more politely. "Will you please help him? Now? Please?" She quickly added, "Sorry if that came off as rude, I'm a little—you know—'let's just do this!' Because he's sort of dying, ya?"

"Oh, he totally is," said raspy voice.

Isaac knew this, yet the words still sent another wave of panic through him, one blackened with despair.

"Definitely," agreed Rain.

"He's very dehydrated, and there are quite a few burns on the outside—and some pretty severe ones on the inside—of his body."

"His brain is bleeding. I'm shocked he's not dead already."

"He's developing a pretty bad infection. I mean, he's a human, and you put a vine in his arm. What'd you think was going to happen?"

All of Elise's composure disappeared. *"Will you fix him already?"*

Her words seemed to echo off the very stars, resonating through the soil and making it tremble. A rush of waves crashed against the shore, and, as the sounds faded, the silence that fell in their place was as deep and unsettled as the darkness between stars. Isaac's heart tripped terribly over the scene, though he couldn't open his eyes to see it.

Rain said, "I think you'd better get started, Nothe."

"Yes, I do think so."

There was some shuffling. Isaac was rolled onto his back, his head then tilted upward, and his mouth pried open. He tried again to open his eyes to see what was happening. It almost worked. They fluttered and rolled so he thought he saw a flash of black and red clothing and the brilliant sky.

Elise exclaimed, "What are you doing?!" This made Isaac even more nervous than he'd been when he heard he was dying, which he hadn't thought possible. So nervous, in fact, that he thought he might faint, which was utterly ridiculous since he was already on his back and completely helpless.

Elise sounded horrified. "Stop! *What are you doing?!*" The ground trembled again.

Rain said in a soothing voice, "Just wait." A rush of inexplicable comfort and light seemed to fill every particle in Isaac's body. It was in the air he breathed. Elise must've felt it also because she instantly fell silent.

Isaac coughed and sputtered as a horrible, metallic liquid coated his mouth—a taste he'd experienced when he'd bit his tongue, and when he'd bit one of the Johns on the playground, and when he'd been drowning earlier in a nightmare.

It was blood.

His fingers twitched. His left arm flailed as he tried to push away whoever was doing this, but his movements were wild and uncontrolled. Warm, sweaty hands were placed over his eyes and forehead, and all at once, a light flooded throughout his whole body. He could feel its warmth and see its brightness flash behind his eyelids, like sunlight reflecting off snow.

It rushed to the burns along his arms and back, to the vine along his right arm, relieving the pain and making the wounds itch as they closed. It rushed to his chest, removing the pressure there, soothing the burns so he could breathe easily, and lifting a heartbreak he hadn't realized he'd been carrying—it was a massive old wound, deep, triggering visions of two funerals, one on an uncharacteristically bright morning, the other gray. Of freezing on a dark street as snow fell, and of a girl at a party. Tears sprang to his eyes as this balm of light made the pain fade.

While it did this, it lingered in his head, refusing to fade until the pain there was gone—not a trace of it left behind. Darkness lifted from his shoulders, and he let out a sigh at the relief of its absence—he hadn't realized how heavy it had been. Indeed, if he were to sleep now, it would be the deepest, most wonderful sleep he'd had since he was a small child, back when his mother had been alive. In fact, he could almost see the room he used to sleep in. He could almost see the stars in the window and the lamp on his bedside table. He could almost feel his mother's arm around him and hear her voice as she read to him about the princess and the River.

He could also still feel the vine in his arm.

"There," said raspy voice—Nothe. "Your servant is all better."

Ugh. Servant. The disgust and anger at this were fleeting. His mind was too busy drifting away into a peaceful slumber.

HE WAS in his childhood bedroom again, held by his mother. She'd just finished reading his favorite book, and he was busy flipping back through the pages, looking at the pictures. There, in the comfort and magic of that moment, he was whole again.

But then, an old wound opened up in his heart. Tears filled his eyes, and his little voice trembled as he gazed up at his beautiful, kind mother and asked, "Why did you leave? Why?"

She held him tightly. She was warm and radiant and smelled of lilacs, butter, and flour. "I didn't want to. I tried so hard to stay."

Tears streamed down his round cheeks. "Nothing's been the same. I can't do this without you."

He felt her tears fall into his hair—actually felt them, as if this weren't a dream. "But I'm still with you. Everywhere you go, I'll go, too. I can't wait to see you stand on the moon and live in your castle on the mountaintop."

In that moment, with all his heart, he believed her. He knew she was there. He wasn't alone.

A light illuminated the floor. It came from the crack beneath the bedroom door.

"What is that?" he asked, sniffing and wiping his face. He looked to his mother for answers, but she was gone. The room was different. Empty. Dark. He wasn't a child anymore or even sitting on a bed but standing in the darkness.

But he was okay. Because he wasn't alone. Not really. He could feel it in the beat of his heart.

His mother's voice whispered, "Freedom is on the other side of the darkness."

Isaac stared at the door, at the light.

He slowly approached, turned the knob. The door creaked as he opened it.

The Prophet looked up into the cosmos, the light from the swirling stars illuminating his face. "It's a tangled mess now, but I will fix it," he said. The language wasn't English. "I *am* fixing it."

Who was he talking to?

The Prophet glanced at a ball of light at his shoulder. "And I can still save a few. I just—" He shook his head. "I have to do what I can."

A voice whispered through the room. It was so soft that Isaac couldn't distinguish what it said, but it came from the ball of light.

"Yes, yes, I know," said The Prophet. "I've learned from my mistakes. It's very delicate, but I'm going to get it right this time. And Thipka—"

He stopped. There was more whispering.

The Prophet turned and looked right into Isaac's eyes. He appeared about as startled as Isaac felt—actually, that was impossible. Isaac's stomach leapt into his chest as if he'd just been caught snooping through Sister Maria's liquor cabinet.

The Prophet asked, "What are you doing here?"

The Prophet's face melted away until all that was in its place was a great nothing, a hole that opened to the center of the universe.

He remembered then why The Prophet's name sounded so familiar. The Prophet had been a character in the story his mother used to read to him. He'd guided the prince to his sister, down the great river. How had he forgotten?

It was real.

It was all real.

Isaac slammed the door, and his eyes opened.

WHEN WORLDS COLLIDE

He wasn't sure what he'd been expecting. Frankly, part of him was hoping he'd open his eyes and find that all of this had been nothing more than a vicious, fever-induced nightmare.

But instead, once his eyes opened, his body decided—without his permission, seeing as he didn't really understand what was going on at all—to leap up and scramble away from everyone, gasping for air as if he'd been holding his breath underwater for a particularly long period of time. Despite its own opinions, his body wasn't quite ready to be on its feet, and when he tried to stand, he stumbled forward and collapsed on his knees, trembling all over.

His panicked gaze fell on the bright eyes of two strange-looking men. One was old with blue eyes, black hair, and dark skin. The other looked to be about Isaac's age, maybe a bit younger, with golden eyes and dark-ish blond hair and a light tan. Both had thick, black lines drawn artfully around their eyes and tight black clothing lined with gold and splashed with red as if they'd had blood thrown on them. Their outfits were shiny and looked almost like pajamas but much tighter. They were absurd. Perhaps they were costumes? *Were* they costumes?

Elise was with them. He let out an involuntary groan at the sight of her. It didn't help that, for some reason, she was glowing now. They all were.

Heaven help me.

He blinked several times and wiped his eyes. Everything had changed. The world around him looked so *bright*. There was a vivid glow around everything: the beach, the moss, the plants, the River—oh, the River! He had to squint to look at it.

Each individual in the group was surrounded by light—various degrees of broken light, but light. The blue-eyed one was a bit more shadow than light, like sunlight blocked by clouds. The sun-eyed one had a deep, dark shadow here and there but was far brighter, more like midday light filtering through falling leaves. Elise, however, was the brightest of all, almost like staring at the sun through cracked glass.

He swore he could still taste blood in his mouth. He vaguely remembered the moment and Elise shouting, *"What are you doing?"* Had it been a nightmare?

No. They'd done something.

He wasn't in pain anymore. At all. And his mind—it was clear. And he had...hope. He thought he'd had hope before, but nothing like this. It was so strange.

He didn't understand any of it, and it made him angry. Why was everyone and everything *glowing*? Had he really nearly died? What had they done to him? Why was he tasting blood? Why did his brain feel...*better*?

"Isaac!" Elise reached out to help him up. "Isaac, are you—"

He swatted her hand away. "I'm fine." He was not fine. He was the opposite of fine.

The men gasped. The one with bright blue eyes—were they also glowing? They looked like they were glowing—growled in his melodically deep voice, "How *dare* you."

That one must've been Rain.

"Wow," said the other—he had to be Nothe—who had the raspy voice and golden eyes that seemed to glow like the setting sun, "I lost my eyes for less than that."

Isaac frowned. Was that a joke? If it was, he didn't get it.

Rain turned to Elise, the look on his face clearly asking, *You're not going to let him get away with that, are you?*

She started a little as if remembering her obligation to compliment the duchess' croquet set. "Oh!" She furrowed her brow at Isaac and shook her finger in his face, chiding him like a dog that had pooped on the porch. "No, no! *Bad* Isaac. Bad!"

She and Isaac both glanced at Rain and Nothe's confused faces. Their expressions remained that way for several glances more. Then Nothe said, "That'll show him."

"Yes," agreed Rain, seeming to struggle against far more irritating thoughts. "I'm sure he's fully reformed."

"Problem solved."

Isaac demanded of the men in their language, "What did you do to me?" He spoke it better than Elise did.

Elise appeared shocked, almost lost. Isaac realized this was the first time she'd witnessed his new, bizarre ability to speak and understand random languages.

Nothe looked at him as if he were an ungrateful, heathen child at a birthday party. "I healed you." He then looked at Rain as if to say, *And this is the thanks I get.* Rain returned his look with one that clearly stated, *I told you so.*

Isaac hissed, "Then why is everything glowing?"

Nothe seemed confused. "Glowing?"

"Yes! Glowing! You're glowing, she's glowing, he's glowing, that's glowing, they're glowing."

Nothe appeared concerned now, which Isaac didn't like at all. Rain asked, "You charged him? Why?"

Isaac asked, "What does that mean?" It sounded bad.

Nothe waved it away. "It's just a little energy boost. It affects everyone differently. It'll wear off. It's a good thing! It's all good." Before Isaac even knew how to respond, Nothe brightened. "He seems fine."

"Does he?" asked Elise.

Nothe ignored her. "Shall we move along?"

"No," said Isaac. "What did you do to me? I demand an answer!"

"And I gave you the answer!" said Nothe, clearly annoyed. "I healed you! You're better!"

"Everything's glowing!"

"Yes, but that will go away—probably—and you're not dead." He looked at Rain, gesturing to Isaac as if to say, *Can you believe this guy?* Rain shook his head disapprovingly in response.

Ignoring Isaac now, Nothe gestured to Elise, "Where are you headed off to? Do you have any idea at all? Because we haven't any idea at all."

"Nor do we know what we're even doing here," Rain added.

"We thought about figuring out where this whole river thing goes but got distracted by the whole, we-can-go-to-other-planets-now thing. Honestly, I thought I was dead for a moment. But then I punched Rain in the face and broke it."

"Completely unfair."

"*Excuse* me?"

"You caught me totally by surprise."

"Who knew your face was so fragile?"

"You're going to be telling everyone about this until the day I die, aren't you?"

"Nah, just for the next hundred years or so. Seems fair since you tried to ditch me. It was very rude."

Isaac and Elise had stopped listening. Elise pointed emphatically at Isaac, which Isaac had to squint to see since she was so bright. Although the gesture was completely obscure, he somehow knew that it meant *get the map*. And so, with his hands still shaking and his head feeling as though someone had lit a thousand candles inside it, he did, hoping she'd fix the book again.

She did. It was difficult to see, but she went from page to page, hovering her hand over each one. It was like watching the water damage happen but in reverse. She pulled liquid from the paper, and the ink bled back into place. When she was finished, she tossed the soup-water into the bushes. It all happened so quickly that Rain and Nothe didn't see what she was doing until she was done.

"What have you got there?" asked Nothe.

Isaac blinked some more, hoping to blink the light away and blink some reasoning and comprehension back into his brain. He knew he'd love to ask some questions. What were those questions again?

Elise turned to the page with the map and handed the book over to Nothe.

Nothe's brilliant eyes widened as he gazed down at it, and so did Rain's. Rain stole the book from Nothe as Nothe stared at Elise and asked, "Where did you two say you were from again?"

Of All the Times
to Be Honest...

"We're from Earth," Elise said. She pointed to the large blue planet looming over them and shrugged. "Well, *he's* from Earth. I suppose I simply lived there for a while. I'm trying to get back home to my world—it's there on that map, ya? I need to visit the Wise Man from my city so he can guide me to the Planet of the Dead."

This was the first Isaac had heard these details.

Nothe raised an eyebrow. "The Planet...of the Dead?"

"Yes." Her hair fell into her face for a moment, but then she straightened her shoulders. "So I can bring back souls that have been lost."

Rain looked up from the book and furrowed his brow. "Uuuhhh..."

Nothe, with a face that clearly said, *I regret to inform you that you don't know what you're talking about*, added a profound, "Naaah..."

Rain's expression mirrored Nothe's, "No..."

"I don't think that's how death works..."

Rain shook his head. "No."

"At least, not from what I've experienced," said Nothe.

"At least, not on our world."

Nothe gave a small, thoughtful shrug. "I suppose it could be different—I guess—organized differently, on different worlds."

Rain shook his head again. "But, I *really* don't think so. Death—it's made up of completely alternate dimensions."

"True."

"*Completely* different planes of existence against our current plane, regardless of the planet, right?"

Nothe nodded. "Right. Yeah."

"Would it not, like—"

"—totally cover the whole universe—"

"Yeah. That."

"Probably. That's probably how universes work, I imagine."

"I would think that's probably right."

Isaac wasn't sure what to think of anything he'd just heard. *Alternate dimensions* were apparently *different planes of existence against our current plane* and were what Death was made up of. If it were a different plane of existence, then it could live right alongside this plane of existence, correct? Isaac was trying to understand. He thought it made sense. Maybe.

To everyone's great surprise, Elise did not seem to care for their reasoning and said in a tone that silenced even the grass, "You're wrong."

Isaac looked at the two men, amused to see someone else unsettled by Elise. Their lips fused together, and their glances met each other. Then Rain said with a shrug, "Well, what do we know?"

"Right, yeah. We're just, ya know, healers and things."

"I'm sure time will—will show us all the, uh...the truth. And that."

"Indeed."

"Which is," said Elise, "that there is a world of spirits. And I'm going to go there."

Nothe cleared his throat and took the book from Rain, returning his attention to the map. "Right."

"Very good," said Rain.

"So which planet did you say was yours?"

Elise fluttered toward them. They stepped back. Her hands were in fists, and the ground trembled. Isaac grew concerned. He really didn't want to end up covered in blood again. One time was plenty, thank you.

"I *will* find that planet," Elise said, clearly and ridiculously upset. Her eyes were cold like glass and alight as if a green fire blazed within them. Her fists shook, and the soupy substance of the River seemed to bubble in frightened anticipation of what her next move would be.

Why was she being like this? Why did she keep saying *that*? What did she want from them? Applause? A "yes, ma'am, everything you've said is perfectly reasonable, and of course you will"?

Probably.

But as silence passed, it became clear that she wasn't going to get that answer from these men. Judging by their unshakable confidence on the subject, Isaac thought they might know more about what Elise was talking about than she did, and they weren't about to give her any answers she wanted. He worried that they might literally explode over it

—just as his ship and crew had done. Inside, he was cheering for them to throw aside their integrity and not die.

Not that he really cared since they were awful.

But he did. A little.

Isaac certainly wasn't above throwing out his integrity for life's sake. Perhaps he ought to intervene.

But they hated him. Why should he—?

"Of course you will," Isaac found himself saying as he struggled to his feet. "Of course you'll find that planet. Everything you've said..." His leg gave out a little, but he righted himself. His mind spun but in an oddly chipper way. "Yes." He closed his eyes for a moment and focused. "We will find your world, and we'll find your Wise Man." He gazed into her terrifying eyes. He didn't think anything he said was true or certain. Frankly, the only thing he was sure of was that he didn't know anything at all. "We'll find those lost souls, Elise. All right?"

Elise blinked, and a bit of that upset-ness faded. She folded her arms. "Good. I'm glad we understand each other."

She whirled back on the men, and they recoiled a little as if expecting sparks to fly from her eyes. "Right," she said. "So you guys are lost, then, ya?"

They hesitated, then Nothe said with as much confidence as ever, "Yep. We sure are."

"Well," disagreed Rain, "I suppose we could try to find our way back home. We just have no desire to."

"We are happily lost. But food and drinkable water would be good to find. For some strange reason—maybe I'm crazy, but—I just don't think that river water is drinkable."

"We did see that spaceship earlier, and we thought about following it."

"But then we heard screaming and came over here instead."

"I...regret nothing...I suppose," Rain said.

Oh, now he chooses to lie, thought Isaac as he watched Nothe elbow Rain.

Elise asked, "Did you see where the spaceship went?"

These so-called "spaceships" were still such weird, eerie things to Isaac. He would've been happy to never see one again.

Nothe gazed down at the map and pointed to a branch in the River about two branches away. "I believe he went this way—wouldn't you agree, Rain?"

"Yes. I would."

"Which means he went to *this* world."

Elise's eyes widened. "That's my home."

"Oh!" exclaimed both men. Rain added in a tone that was less than enthusiastic, "How about that?"

Nothe nodded. "I guess we're headed to the same place, then."

Isaac couldn't decide how he felt about this. He thought he despised it. Really, with the way his brain was growing more and more muddled, optimistic, and inexplicably tired, he really didn't feel much of anything about anything anymore.

Isaac rubbed his eyes with the palms of his hands. He hoped it would make the glow around everything finally go away. It didn't.

What had those men given him?

Elise then asked, "Can you give us a lift?"

Sure, she was asking. At least, the intonations of her voice made it seem like she was asking. But the look in her eyes and the way the leaves trembled suggested she wasn't really asking. Isaac remembered how intimidating Arnaud had been when he'd done this, but he was nothing compared to Elise.

Rain and Nothe looked at each other, clearly realizing their lack of options, before cheerfully saying, "Sure!"

"Of course!" said Nothe.

Rain shrugged. "Why not?"

Isaac furrowed his brow. "A lift? On what?" His tone grew hopeful, "Do you have a ship?"

What About Snowman?

Asael—known as Snowman to Isaac—had flown through the portal to Elise's home planet, Ethra. He had been rather confident and happy when he'd first emerged out of the boisterous sea. He'd found the powerful creature his father had been looking for, and he'd brought her to the River, just as his father had asked.

Honestly, though, a small hole had formed in his stomach, one that made him sick. He hadn't noticed it until he'd hopped out of the ship and began his walk toward the small, unassuming house of stone. He had to do a bit of soul searching before he knew what the source of this sudden discomfort was, and it hit him with a wave of nausea and despair.

Oh. That's right. I killed that old man.

And yet he'd spared the human, and humans were monsters. It just didn't feel right.

But when he'd seen the rock creature fighting on the human's behalf, Asael knew he was with her. He needed to be spared in order to win her trust. Besides, the human would likely die anyway. For all their awfulness, they were fragile creatures.

What had been the old man's name, again? He'd spoken to him many times. *Egre,* that's right. *Egre.* He had been far from a pleasant fellow—anything but; in fact, he was too old and a little insane—but hardly an evil one.

Asael stopped at the door and leaned against the entryway, holding his stomach. He was going to be sick. He really was. He took deep breaths. The old man *had* been in the way. He had kept the creature, Elise, from getting to the River, and she needed to get to the River. And Egre certainly had no intention of being reasonable. He'd given him that chance many times. So what other option had he had? None. It was the old man's fault, not his. Egre made his choice.

And besides, once his father had accomplished his plan, it wouldn't even matter anymore. It'd be like it never happened. Everything would be made right. *Everything.*

Some part of him wished he was more like his father. He didn't have a problem with things like this. He knew there were certain things that simply *had* to be done, no matter what. That was how important his plan was. It would make everything right, and therefore, there was no need or room for guilt. This was written in his father's heart.

It was not written in Asael's heart.

He didn't like to take the life of *anything*. He never had. His father didn't seem to understand it. His father never had to say anything for Asael to know how much he loved the power he felt when he stole a life, and even more when he made Asael do the same. It was clear in the small smile that creased the corner of his scarred lips, in the way he straightened his shoulders and briefly turned his blind gaze to the stars as if to challenge them. His father was determined to never be powerless again. Instead, he'd take power from everyone else.

After all the battles Asael had won, the lives he'd taken in the name of the cause, this was perhaps the first time he'd felt the same. He'd thrown up during his first battle, crumbling to a shaking mess, haunted by the faces of those he'd fought and beaten, and after that, he'd become sort of numb, a robot following orders. But he'd felt powerful fighting Egre. Egre was a force to be reckoned with. That was why he'd been standing guard in the first place. And yet, Asael had beaten him with ease. At this point, he knew no one stood a chance against him. He could've taken them all, including Elise, but he'd *chosen* who lived and who died. And for a moment, he felt that power, that *thrill.*

That was what truly sickened him.

The first time his father had made him take a life, it'd been a luvoloo, which was like a rabbit from Earth but with more intelligence. They repeated things their owners said sometimes and could hold little conversations. They were a great pet for lonely people and were frequently found in the homes of the elderly. They had a larger head than rabbits, big paws, big eyes, spots, little horns, and fangs.

He'd only been nine-years-old. He was forced to turn it to ice. When he'd wept, his father had told him it was his own fault he had to do it. If he hadn't let his family die, he wouldn't have to learn how to use his powers for "strategic attacks," although there was no real strategy to killing a luvoloo. They weren't violent creatures, despite their little fangs. Asael didn't see it then, but he knew it now: this had been about punishing Asael and letting him know who was in control. The more he wept, the more he was beaten and burned, and the more luvoloos—his mother's favorite animal; *his* favorite animal—his father made him kill. The only way it'd stop was if he quit crying about it.

So he didn't cry about it.

He'd wanted his father to forgive him, to love him again. So he stopped fighting him and did what he asked. He'd do the best he could, even if it broke him.

And if his father succeeded with his plan, it'd all be taken back. All of it. Right?

No.

Asael took deep breaths, trying to steady his heart.

What was he becoming?

He'd felt so powerful in that battle with Egre, just like his father seemed to feel. Egre, in that moment, had become nothing more than an obstacle in his way. Asael had forgotten he was a creature, someone with a soul who was now gone forever. He'd never forgotten before. Tears burned his eyes.

What am I becoming?

He slipped back into the mind of that nine-year-old boy, the boy he had once been. *I should've stood up to him more. I shouldn't have let him win. I should have let him kill me that day. Then I wouldn't be the monster I've become.*

He pushed the thoughts away, just as he always did when they bubbled to the front of his mind. Because of the plan, his father was in the right, wasn't he?

Why did Egre have to be such an obstinate old man?

Why were there so many evil creatures out there? Why was it so difficult for them to just be decent? And why was it so hard for creatures like Egre to understand what he and his father were trying to do?

That's right. Remember all of this. Remember it. You're going to fix everything.

He was still nauseated. He'd need to wash these horrible feelings away with a very strong drink later.

The stone house wasn't large at all, but the stone it was carved out of sure was. It was one large, smooth slab with a small chimney in the back that billowed smoke. It sat beside a hillside surrounded by thin, white trees with small, pale green leaves. It was far from any other civilization. Many didn't even know it was there. That was how his father wanted it.

The beating of his heart grew frantic as he stepped through the door. He could only vaguely remember not being afraid of him. His father had changed long ago, after the attack.

That was what Asael remembered. He had been kind and gentle before then. Full of light and laughter. He remembered his father's laughter. *Their* laughter. The games they'd play. There had been more to his family back in those days. The chemicals hadn't just taken his father's eyes; it'd taken his mother, his brothers, his sister, and all the goodness and joy they'd once had.

All their people had been peaceful in those days before the attack. The attack was how they'd learned there were other worlds out there. Other worlds with lifeforms not as kind and good as their own. It had been a harsh lesson. So many of their people—their cities, their livestock, their farms, their *lives*—had been destroyed, burned to the ground, their bodies turned to ash that fluttered in the breeze like snow. As with so many others, his father had never been the same. Though the invading forces had been driven back to the stars, it was as though they had never left. They were in the whispers of the trees, in the creak of the wood, in every shadow, waiting to return.

His father wanted to change that.

The creatures that had invaded their world had relied on a technology that could fall apart. He'd seen it as a child when his father and kindred used their powers against their airships. Their technology was lifeless, completely devoid of energy.

So his father, even without his eyes, conducted the creation of weapons and machines that were built from energy. Energy that could be pulled from wind, from fire and darkness, from bodies. Energy that was not easily destroyed. With it, he wiped out a neighboring planet, leaving nothing but fire and ash in his wake. It hadn't been the one that'd attacked them, but they might have down the road. Sure, they had been a more primitive people whose primary source of joy was to cook various foods, but no one knew what vicious creatures they could blossom into. Asael couldn't see it, but his father was wiser than him.

That was what he'd believed back then, anyway.

He only causes pain. His mind is failing him, failing me, failing us all. He pushed the thoughts away, grateful his father couldn't read his mind. He could put images in his head, but he couldn't see the secrets he kept inside it.

His father knew those monsters had to be stopped. They all had to be stopped. It was for the greater good. To his father, it was for the safety of the people, of his *son*. This was what Asael had to tell himself, today and well, regularly. His father did this because he loved him. He loved his mother, his brothers, his sister. His father pushed him because he loved them.

His father was able to do all this without his eyes because, when they had been stolen from him, he had been gifted greater sight.

He could see energy.

His father's first attempts hadn't satisfied him. Once he found the planet that had attacked them, even with all his abilities, he still couldn't beat them. Asael's people had gone to war and had been slaughtered. There was hardly anyone left in the world now.

His father knew if he really wanted to change things, greater measures needed to be taken.

And Asael knew that once his father succeeded with this, everything would be better. His father would be better. The gods knew that this was all Asael wanted, for his father to be better—to stop tormenting him and everyone else.

Asael's footsteps sounded against the stone floor, careful, calm, as if he were approaching a sleeping beast. There in the quaint, white rocked living room, in a chair near the fire, sat his father.

Asael's stomach tightened. It always did when he saw him. He almost didn't notice it anymore. Today he did because he already felt like vomiting. Yes, he would definitely need a drink later.

His father's broken, hoarse voice chilled the air, as it always did when he spoke, though it was deep and crackled like fire. "She's not with you."

Asael hesitated. "No, sir. You asked me to bring her to the River, not here." His skin prickled as if it were going numb. His mind raced. He'd done exactly what his father had asked, yet it was wrong. Again.

Of course it was.

Asael knew it made more sense to bring her, but it wasn't what was asked. He also knew that, had he actually brought her, it still would've been wrong somehow. Very wrong. His father would've said, "That's not what I told you to do," and then punished him, burned him for disobeying.

There was no winning, but he had a better chance of not meeting physical or mental anguish by obeying and making his father unhappy than by trying to exceed his expectations.

These days, Asael was numb to most everything. Just a machine of fear and orders. But sometimes, he remembered his mother, how she'd loved him. Made him feel safe. He'd remember playing in the garden with his siblings, out on adventures. The treehouse was their fortress; the colorful insects and the luvoloos within the stones along the garden wall were their beloved kingdom. He remembered being loved.

He liked to believe they knew he'd tried so hard to save them. Sometimes he swore he could still feel their love from an unseen world and hear their voices telling him they knew how hard he'd tried.

"Why would you come to me empty handed?" his father asked.

Asael didn't have an answer that'd make him happy. His father knew it.

The figure in the chair didn't move, didn't speak. It sat as though it were long dead. Asael waited, saying nothing, a pain growing in his chest. Panic. The air grew still. Eerily still. Asael watched the tiny leaves of the thin trees dance in the breeze through the window. It was as though he were in a completely different dimension, where time stood still, and worms crawled under his skin.

Finally, his father spoke again. "Go get her."

Not a Ship

I saac had never seen anything like it before. He didn't understand it at all, and that was just downright upsetting. When did human beings begin traveling in giant bugs? Or perhaps the better question was, *why? Why* did they travel in giant bugs?

It was a perfectly relevant question. Because what he was looking at—well, it looked like a giant, carriage-sized bug. Not quite like the bug Snowman flew off in earlier—that one had looked more like a beetle from the deserts of Africa. No, this one was much less friendly in appearance. It looked more like a nasty, pointy-headed mosquito, black with one large, bulbous eye. He hated it immediately. He wanted to smash it with a giant boot. Where could he find one of those? *If these giant bugs exist, then surely a giant boot must be somewhere.*

At least it didn't glow like everything else.

Rain and Nothe scurried about the bug, cleaning blood from the cracked glass—clearly there'd been a collision of some sort—and fiddling about inside it and underneath a fierce, unbending wing. They prattled off to each other in their weird language, going on about how surprised they were that there wasn't more damage, what a great fortune that was, and how Rain was an idiot.

"So that's supposed to fly, then?" Isaac muttered to Elise, his arms folded and his expression one of perfect disgust as if what he was looking at was indeed a giant mosquito, and they were expected to crawl into its smelly, hollowed-out insides.

Elise gave a curt nod, reminding him of the Arnaud she used to be. "Yes. Like the ship you saw before."

"That is *not* a ship," Isaac insisted.

"Yes. It is."

"No, it's not."

"It *is*."

"It has bloody *wings!*"

"Well, obviously," she gestured to the mosquito, "some ships have wings!"

"No, they don't. They have *sails*."

"What's the difference?"

"You can't be serious."

"They both use air—"

"Just stop. Stop right now." He said this as firmly as he could muster while rubbing his forehead. He felt he should've been getting a headache, but he wasn't. He was just tired. *Very* tired. He needed a nap. A very serious one. "This is ridiculous. You're ridiculous. They're ridiculous. This entire situation is ridiculous, and I hate everyone."

Elise scoffed, but her voice cracked a little as if she took this statement personally but didn't want him to know it, "Oh, right. *Everyone?*"

"Yes! *Everyone.*"

Isaac was about to sit down, and he had plans to lie down after that, right there on the mossy, muddy ground. Before he could do this, Nothe hollered cheerfully from under the wing. "Hey! She's ready to go!"

Next thing Isaac knew, he was ushered on top of the giant mosquito.

"All right, just *squeeeeze* on in," said Nothe with a gentle shove as Isaac wondered exactly where he was supposed to *squeeeeze* into, seeing as Rain was in the only chair and didn't look the least bit interested in sharing. He wore a frown that matched Isaac's personal feelings about the whole situation.

"Right back there," Nothe said, pointing to the tiny bit of empty space behind the chair that was surrounded by a wall of...things. Things that glowed, showing large maps and, well, other things. He was smart enough to know it was probably all important, and, like with the statues in Sister Rosa's office at the orphanage, he knew he probably wasn't supposed to touch any of it.

Which was why he had the strongest urge to smash his hands against the end closest to him and run them all the way across to the other side, touching everything he possibly could in the seconds before they could stop him.

But he didn't because he planned to live through this. He planned to go home, eat roasted turkey and potatoes with a ton of butter—*ooooh, yes, butter!*—and then snuggle down into his bed and sleep this whole nightmare off.

He let Elise step down into the compartment first as Nothe said, "Yep. There you go." She moved awkwardly to the end, wrapping her creepy wings around herself as best as she could as Isaac uneasily stepped down, right onto her foot. She let out a restrained "Ow," and Isaac instinctively said, "Sorry," not that he meant it.

Maybe he did a little. Her feet were bare, and his boots were thick soled and merciless.

If only he could use them on this giant mosquito.

Nothe said as he followed behind Isaac, "Yeah, kind of a tight squeeze."

That was an understatement. He was shoulder-to-wing in between Nothe and Elise. He tried to touch them both less by squishing his arms together, causing him to grit his teeth in pain, what with that horrible vine in his arm. Even with all the healing he'd had, it still hurt because it simply wasn't supposed to be there. When the eye closed over them, the three of them had to crouch down so as not to bang their heads against it. It was officially impossible for the smells of old sweat, leather, feet, mud, dried blood, and grass to go anywhere.

He hated the mosquito so much more now.

Rain smirked as he looked at them from over his shoulder. "Everyone comfy?"

"Oh, you know it!" Nothe said, his breath right in Isaac's ear and smelling very much like breakfast had been a long time ago. "My only regret is that I'm not in the middle."

Rain laughed. So did Isaac with one very hearty, "Ha! Well, we can certainly trade."

Rain said, "Nope," and quickly flipped a flat, metal switch above all the dials and levers and bobbles and whatnots on the desk-thing in front of him, and then pushed a black button next to it.

The entire mosquito shivered to life. A soft humming sounded from behind them. Isaac's heart picked up speed. The thought fluttered through his head, *You know, you fellows can just leave me here. I'll be fine.*

However, if he were to be perfectly honest, he was curious about this. About flight. He used to watch birds soar above him as a child with great envy. It hadn't seemed fair that God had given such brainless creatures one of the greatest gifts imaginable while he, a battered, intelligent, exhausted, and lonely child, was stuck mopping Sister Sarah's kitchen and scraping bird droppings off the balcony. He couldn't fly away somewhere where people were kind—if there even was such a place. He couldn't fly away to the top of the mountains like his mother had once dreamed.

But then he grew up. He knew that humans would never fly. It wasn't the least bit possible. But God had given man oceans to sail. That was the closest thing humans would ever get to flying. He *knew* it.

But of course, now...

Nothe asked Isaac, "How's the whole glowing thing?"

Isaac, holding his breath a little, admitted, "Slightly better."

It really was. He could look at things without squinting so much now. Elise was still fairly bright, however, like a full moon on a particularly clear night at sea.

Isaac was very aware of the sweat lining his brow, of the blood flowing in his veins, of the feeling of his feet on the floor and his hand on the back of Rain's chair as he watched Rain push another button. Rain then turned a wheel with one hand while slowly pressing a lever with another. The humming grew from quiet to less quiet, and the mosquito jolted. Isaac's knees buckled, and he hit his face on the back of Rain's chair as the bug rose from the ground, which he immediately recovered from and set about to pretend that no such thing had happened.

At the gentle twist of the wheel, the mosquito turned, sending Isaac into Elise. Again, he apologized, hating himself for it immediately.

With the mosquito aimed in the proper direction, Rain's lips curled into a mischievous grin as he said, almost to himself, "Get ready for some fun."

The punch of another lever threw Isaac backward as the mosquito sailed forward. A moment later, all three of them were holding the backs of their heads in pain, having smacked them against the eye. Nothe punched Rain's shoulder. "What was that for?"

Rain laughed, apparently finding the whole thing hilarious. Isaac was thinking about how lovely it'd be to whop him in the back of the head—surely Rain would be feeling left out later, being the only one not wearing a goose egg-sized lump—when he finally looked out of the mosquito at the scene that surrounded them. He gazed with his eyes and mouth wide open as if his eyes couldn't quite capture enough of the sight so his mouth had to make up the difference.

The stars—they'd never been so close. Isaac had never climbed any large mountains, but he imagined this was what it might've looked like if he had. He watched the blue, white, and green Earth and its branch of the River disappear behind them as they passed the nearby purplish, white, and red-green planet. Nothe pointed at it and said, "That's our home."

Isaac acknowledged this with a nod, as he had no idea what to say. It was too much for his mind. He'd never been taught what to say when someone pointed out their home planet and said, "That's mine!"

Elise exclaimed with breathless wonder. "Wow. It's beautiful."

It most certainly was. Why hadn't he thought to say that?

Rain playfully bobbed the mosquito up and down a little, making Isaac's heart flutter in the most terrifying and wonderful way. As the fear left him, he found himself laughing, his stomach flitting about at the feeling of weightlessness.

Elise laughed as well, and as they looked at each other with pure delight, he almost forgot—for a fleeting second—that she'd blown up his ship and that he was at her mercy. They were simply two individuals enjoying the magic of an impossible adventure.

They turned with the River, falling into each other again, but it was no longer annoying. It was actually fun. They all giggled like children and said "Whoa!" as they fought to hold onto the back of Rain's seat, all of them friends on equal ground for a moment. In fact, Isaac could've sworn that Rain looked a bit younger, full of the light and life of the universe around them.

The purplish planet faded into the background, and Elise's world rose. It was still some distance away, but he could see that it was brilliantly green, not unlike Elise's eyes and hair.

Rain was the first to fall silent. Isaac followed his gaze and looked ahead of them.

The soup of the River was rising, like a wall of mist and pink, shifting and swirling in forms that appeared and disappeared. Isaac squinted at them, studying them.

They were faces. Faces yawning in sorrow with empty eye sockets.

His stomach shriveled, creating a numbness that spread to his limbs. He seemed to have swallowed his tongue.

They were approaching the wall of faces rather quickly.

Nothe said, "Uh, Rain, do you see that thing?"

"I do," Rain said, as though he was acknowledging the existence of a particularly interesting rock.

"Then why are you still flying at it? Are you hoping it'll move? Because I don't think it's going to move."

Nothe, Isaac, and Elise cried out as, for a moment, they all thought they were about to crash into the wall and be devoured by the purple faces. Rain turned the wheel, throwing Isaac into Nothe as the ship veered left.

Nothe blurted, "*Finally* you're turning!"

Rain snapped, "What, is that not good enough for you? Would you have liked me to turn later?"

"*Earlier* would've been preferred—"

It was clear then that Rain wasn't turning completely around as Isaac had hoped, but rather, he was flying uncomfortably close to the wall of sorrowful, yawning faces, each about the size of the ship itself. Isaac studied the details—they had human features, but they weren't human at all. There were men, women, and even children among them. As the mosquito passed by, they reached out with hands of mist as if to try and stop them. Isaac had an urge to weep, but he didn't quite know why.

Nothe asked in a warning tone, "What are you doing?"

Rain threw up a frustrated hand. "I'm trying to find a way around!"

"What? Are you kidding me right now?"

"What else are we supposed to do?"

"Are you seriously not a little bit deterred by this? I mean, I know they *seem* friendly and all, what with them reaching out to us like that, but—"

Isaac couldn't help himself. "My mother always taught me not to trust strangers."

Nothe pointed at him approvingly. "Right. Yes. Especially when they're so eager to meet you."

"Yes. I think those were her exact words," he said, though they weren't.

Elise then suggested, "Perhaps we should land, ya? See if there's another way?"

Nothe added, "Make some sort of plan."

Rain's face changed at this. His lips thinned into a stern line and his eyes narrowed with grim determination. He pushed on a lever, accelerating the mosquito to a speed that threw Isaac backward, hitting his head again and tossing his stomach up into his chest.

Nothe declared, "That's it. It's official. I'm never letting you drive again."

They were speeding to the end of the wall—no, they were racing it. It was moving alongside them. Isaac's heart leaped into his brain. They were flying to the edge, toward the vast nothing of space.

Elise screamed, *"What are you doing?"*

There was an opening. They were ahead of the wall.

Rain abruptly turned the wheel. Nothe's elbow landed on Isaac's forehead, and Isaac fell onto Elise's hip as she crumpled to the bottom of the compartment. Isaac blinked away the stars, far too worried about dying to notice just how much his vine-infected arm and that elbow-to-the-forehead hurt. He gazed out of the roof of the eye just in time to see the wall of mourning and worried faces, with their outstretched hands, collapse on top of them.

A Whole New World

Everyone on the mosquito was certain they were about to die. And Rain, who, deep down, was actually a very good soul, had a moment of clarity as he watched the wall of nightmares fall upon them. Time slowed, but it was completely ineffective as his ability to do anything had slowed with it. It was more as if Time were out to torment him, to show him exactly what he'd done without the ability to do anything to change it. He was frozen, forced to watch as his reckless behavior took not only his own life but the lives of those who were with him.

It wasn't something he'd done intentionally. He hadn't thought to himself, "I think I'll kill all of us right now." No, he'd really thought he could make it. Or, rather, he'd *had* to make it. There hadn't been another option. He'd been consumed with a sort of madness, a panic, that if he couldn't get around this wall of faces, he'd die—although he hadn't thought it with any sort of words. It was a feeling, something without real structure, something that'd gripped his heart, his lungs, making him feel as though at any second, he might drown. It was the thought that he might lose hope again. There wasn't real logic to it, and he didn't quite see it in himself.

He'd finally fled Thera—something he'd thought he'd never be able to do. He could discover a new world. He could follow a strange creature down a strange river on a fantastic adventure, and that gave him hope, something that he could actually *live* for.

He couldn't quit. Not for anything, not even for a nightmare wall. He couldn't go back. What might happen then? What if—?

No. No, his mind wouldn't even entertain the idea. They were flying *now*. They were almost there. He needed this. He needed to make it through.

But now, in his desperation to save himself, he'd killed Nothe. He'd killed all of them, but he didn't care about the others. Nothe didn't deserve this. He'd let him down. Again.

No, he hadn't just let him down. Rain had let his madness, his pain, his self-destruction drag his best—and only—friend, the one living creature he loved most, to his death. This was the worst, most horrific thing he had ever done.

OF COURSE, unbeknownst to any of them, the River had no intention of devouring them. It simply wanted them to go somewhere else. So, it took them to the planet Lolaar.

On Lolaar, there was another creature who was thinking deeply about his life.

He was a worm. A giant worm, the size of a small boat, with yellowish white skin that resembled glue and paper mâché. His face had a large mouth that opened with five triangular flaps, above which were several black, olive-like eyes. He lived with his fellow worms, burrowed inside a large, volcanic island, each inside their own cavern as if the whole island were an apartment complex. They spent their days leaping out at birds or travelers unfortunate enough to pass by.

It wasn't something he liked to do, though, which was why he found himself in such melancholy thought. He was far more of a forward thinker compared to his brethren.

See, a few years before, he'd found a book that had been left behind by an unfortunate group of travelers, and the beautiful pictures in it had changed his whole world. Now, he observed everything his people did from a new perspective and couldn't help but question their ways of handling things. Did they really have to destroy everyone and everything that passed by? What did it profit them? What if these creatures that wandered too closely had something to teach them? What a tragedy to chase away another point of view—to chase away wisdom and knowledge.

He swore his relatives knew what they were doing was wrong. Many guards and politicians had nightmares of the dead returning from their graves to torment them. There was no other reason for them to be haunted by such dreams unless, of course, they knew they were in the wrong.

Yes, he had grown up and older, living in his own hot and dark burrow in the volcanic island, and was rather sad. He didn't want to live in the volcanic mountain with his ignorant relatives anymore.

But was there a place out there in the beautiful world...for him?

He wasn't sure there was. He was a giant worm, after all.

The Story Held in a Look

Isaac had passed out. Again.

He seemed to be doing that a lot lately.

Once this happened, the strange methods Nothe had used to heal him completely overcame him. It was as if those methods had seen the opportunity to power his body down in order to apply the rest of the healing he needed and said to themselves, "Hey, he's out anyway. Might as well take advantage of it."

So, when the others reached the shores of Lolaar—which were lined with obscenely large trees that obscured much of the sky, the likes of which none of them had ever seen before—they were quite unsettled when they couldn't wake him. Well, mostly, it was Elise who was unsettled. Rain couldn't have cared less, and Nothe knew what was going on, insisting that they just give him some time because his body hadn't had a chance to fully recover yet.

Once the yellowish-orange sun set behind the massive trees and the world around them grew cold, Rain and Nothe built a fire along the beach. Elise sat next to Isaac, waiting.

Meanwhile, Isaac felt better than he had in a *very* long time. In his mind, he was docking his ship at the wharf after discovering a heap of treasure. Clumsy Grundy, who was now a giant, talking bulldog—which was perfectly normal—had knocked over a lamp, setting an old house on fire, and there it was! A mountain of gold lying in the rubble.

Grundy hauled the gold onto the ship on his back, and when they docked, he promised to guard it while Isaac went into town and ate a massive plate of roasted turkey, potatoes, and gravy.

While there, a very serious-looking banker informed him that a distant relative had died and left him a vast fortune, which made perfect sense. Of course he had a rich distant relative who'd died! Goodness, how had he forgotten?

When he left, he floated over to an inn where Grundy was now a vulture and had filled an entire room with the treasure. Sitting on top of the treasure, in an almost scandalously low-cut gown, was the long-lost Alice. She'd never really hated him. Neither of them needed to say it; it was simply known. She glided down the pile of gold, cradled the back of his neck in her palm, and said, looking deep into his eyes, "Oh, Isaac, I've missed you."

Isaac smiled. "I knew it. I knew you missed me."

She laughed, then said, "Has the worm flown south yet?"

He had to think about this. *Had* the worm flown south yet? He shook his head at this perfectly logical question. "No, I don't think so."

She frowned at his answer. "He will soon."

That was probably a good thing for the worm, Isaac assumed. "Well that's nice."

My, her green eyes are stunning tonight. He didn't remember her having green eyes. He was pretty certain they'd been a dark brown, but clearly, he had been wrong. Actually, her face no longer looked like Alice's face at all. Her features were soft and perfect, her lips full, her skin pale green, and her expression warm, wonderful, and familiar, like the girl from that masquerade party he'd fought so hard to forget. He was absolutely going to kiss her in about three seconds. Who knew where the night might go from there? He was pretty excited about it. He just had to shoo Grundy away. He was being creepy, staring at them both with those vulture eyes from over there.

A gust of wind rushed over Isaac from above, filling the room with a bitter cold. He turned to look at the ceiling from whence the wind had come, but there was no ceiling. There were only two large eyes staring at him from a vast darkness. They looked as though they had melted and were covered in a white film so that whatever color they might've been was completely obscured.

No, it wasn't a film. It was scar tissue.

These eyes—they'd been burned. He didn't know how he knew it; he just did. It spoke to his very bones. Something about these eyes filled his heart with a fear that spread through his veins until it had consumed his entire soul.

A growl resonated through the room, shaking the floor at his feet. The eyes rushed at him.

Isaac startled awake. He was on his back, covered in sweat, staring up at a dark, cloud-covered sky dusted here and there with unfamiliar stars. Smoke billowed from a fire that was smoldering not too far from him. He was warmed by its crackling flames as the waves of the sea crashed gently against the beach. He took a deep breath, inhaling the scent of smoke, distant rain, the salt of the ocean, and something muddy and floral that was unfamiliar. Closing his eyes, he saw those two burned eyes staring at him from behind his eyelids.

Ugh. Every time he blinked, there they were, watching him. What, was he not allowed to have normal dreams anymore? He rolled onto his side and rubbed his face.

How about that? He wasn't dead. He supposed this was a good thing —at least he hoped so.

But seriously, it was very rude of those eyes. He'd been having such a lovely dream.

Wait, why wasn't anyone rushing to rescue him? Where was scary Elise with her, "Isaac! Oh, Isaac! La-la-la, I truly care about you, even though I blew up all your friends and your ship and am threatening to kill you, la-de-dah!"

Maybe she was gone. He brightened a little and sat up on his elbows.

Nope. There she was, sleeping on a bed of leaves next to him, using her wings as a sort of blanket and a massive leaf as a pillow. His heart went right back to its new irritated norm. A vast, dark ocean was to his left, and to his right, the tallest, widest trees he had ever seen, even taller than the castles in Spain. The darkness they created beneath them seemed to crawl with shadows. It was one thing for darkness to be empty and another entirely to know that it was *full* of *things* you simply couldn't see. Pits you could fall into. Animals that could maul you. Or even the spirits of those who'd never made it out.

Or bugs. Just—bugs.

Isaac was sure that if he walked into that forest, he'd leave it a haunted man—that is, if he left it at all.

He looked around the campfire, seeing Nothe asleep at his right, facing the forest. Directly across from Isaac were two glowing blue eyes glaring at him. Rain's eyes. They were very, very glow-y there, in the dark. He didn't glow in any other way, which Isaac was relieved to see. Neither did Elise. It'd finally worn off.

His stomach knotted with anger at the sight of Rain. He had the urge to leap up and scream in Rain's face, *What's the matter with you? Were you* trying *to kill us all?* with spit flying and everything.

But he didn't. He knew better. He'd miraculously survived thus far; he wasn't about to kill himself in such a foolish way now.

He took a deep breath, letting all that steam go, then said calmly, "So, we didn't die, then?"

Rain looked away and didn't answer. If Isaac didn't know better, he would've said he looked ashamed. In fact—he didn't know how, but—he swore he somehow *felt* Rain's shame, regret, and remorse.

Regardless of if it was real or just in his head, it made Isaac feel a little better. Perhaps screaming in his face hadn't been necessary after all.

Isaac moved on. "Where are we?"

Mock curiosity took over those blue eyes as Rain looked at the sky. "Well, gee. I've just plum forgot the name of the place. You'd think I'd know it by heart now since I travel here so often."

Isaac couldn't suppress his glare. Silence fell between them, and Isaac's gaze landed on Elise, who was surprisingly far more pleasant to look at than those menacing blue eyes or the cursed forest. She did look rather peaceful, lying there asleep. He was forced to admit that her features were probably the most perfect he'd ever seen. She was much prettier than Alice, greenish skin and all. And nicer—minus the whole vine-in-the-arm and killing-everyone things. Alice would've probably done worse if she'd had Elise's powers.

Alice did have brown eyes. So why had he dreamed she had green eyes? And Elise's face?

Oh heavens. Ugh. What was the matter with him? He was going mad. It was official. He was ill. His mind was crumbling. This was the beginning of the end.

He sat up fully and saw that he had been carefully wrapped in giant leaves, which was absurdly nice. Ignoring Rain's look of death, Isaac gestured to the leaves and asked, "Did Elise do this?"

Rain grew mock-thoughtful and grumbled, "Well, let's think here— let's do some *deduction* if you will. Hmm...the only individual here that doesn't want you left in a desert, or the middle of the ocean—that would be..."

Isaac nodded. "Right."

"Well, *you*. But you were unconscious. My, that is a mystery..."

Isaac was unamused. "Indeed."

"I'm sorry I couldn't solve it for you. I know how difficult it is for you humans to *think*."

Isaac nodded with a hum. "Yes, many of us do struggle with that."

Isaac thought he saw Rain suppress a smile. He couldn't help but feel a little proud of that, despite his intense dislike of the man. Rain then said, "I've never heard a human admit it."

"That must be incredibly frustrating for you."

"It is."

"Yes. But..." *Dare I ask the question?* That was what he would've asked himself had he thought to, but he didn't. "Is that reason enough to hate *all* the humans? Everywhere?"

Rain looked at the sand and chuckled. It was perhaps the darkest, scariest, most bitter chuckle Isaac had ever heard, and that was when Isaac finally thought, *Dare I ask the question?* But by then, of course, it was too late.

The fire reflected on Rain's face in the most menacing way, showing anger there—and a deep pain, a pain even greater than Isaac could begin to relate to. It was the sort of agony he'd tried to ignore in some of his travels, seen in too many faces. However, it was the thin face of a widow that really stood out in Isaac's mind. She'd been left to the mercy of the streets, living in a town of crumbling buildings that smelled like feces and rotting fish.

He'd tried to ignore her—not because he didn't care, but because the sight of her hurt Isaac in a way that made him uncomfortable, and he simply didn't know what to do about it. Amid his trading, he passed her again and again, her faded red dress attempting to hide her fading health and entice the sailors into her chambers for a price. Her two children peered out of a window, only for her to shoo them out of sight. They were thin but in far better condition than their mother.

Isaac imagined her evenings spent with strange, merciless men, only for her to go hungry so her children could eat.

It was cold the day they were to set sail again, and that was the day she'd caught Isaac trying to slip money into the pocket of her dress. This was back when the business wasn't in ruin, and he knew the amount he was giving her would feed her and her family for a while, maybe give her a chance to move on, do something different, even if it meant he might not eat much until his next business deal. The anger in her face when she first saw him, not knowing what he was up to—it pierced him. He took a step back, holding up his hands and then showing her the money. "I just—I just wanted to give you this." Tentatively, he handed it to her.

He intended to dash away after she took it, but he was frozen in place by the look of shock on her face, followed by unease. He knew she must be wondering what, exactly, he expected her to do or let him do. She glanced up at him, and then, looking at the dirt behind Isaac, she invited him inside.

Isaac held up his hands. "No. Nope. I'm not—no. I just..." He didn't know what to say. He looked into her eyes. That pain...oh, how profound that pain and darkness was. It tore his heart into a thousand bleeding pieces, and he didn't even know who she was.

He fished in his pockets for the last coin he had on his person and handed it to her, blinking back tears. "I just want you to take care of yourself and your children."

She seemed utterly confused. Baffled. Lost. Isaac turned and began to cross the street, but something told him to look back.

The widow held her hand over her mouth as she wept. She looked up at him, and in her eyes was a gratitude that words could've never done justice to.

Yes. Her face had always haunted him. He'd always hoped everything had turned out okay for her, that her pain had been eased, that her children were well and happy.

That was the kind of pain in Rain's face.

Isaac wondered what he'd been through. He had a strange urge to throw money at him and tell him to feel better because everyone knew that money made everything better.

His question had been stupid. In his way, he'd been trying to ask why Rain hated humans. But this was a question that didn't really need answering.

And Rain didn't answer it.

The Little Girl in the Woods

Almost uncomfortable silence fell between Rain and Isaac after that. To end it, Isaac announced that he was tired and was going to "turn in." When Rain asked, "Turn in where?" He explained that he was going back to sleep.

However, despite being sure that he could sleep for centuries and still be tired, his eyes had a lot of trouble shutting. Rain seemed to have no intention of sleeping, and Isaac couldn't help worrying that, at any moment, Rain would sneak over and murder him.

He wondered why they were on that world. Well, obviously, they'd crashed there, but that wasn't a permanent thing, was it? The mosquito wasn't *broken*, was it? Isaac thought about asking Rain this but decided he'd rather ask someone else and continued to stare, wide-eyed, at the sky above him. Where dark clouds broke apart, he thought he saw the largest sliver of moon he'd ever seen. It seemed to start at the top of the sky and then disappear under the sea. But it was so covered by clouds, he couldn't tell for sure. Perhaps it was a different sort of light, something otherworldly—which would make sense, as they were, in fact, on another world.

Very curious, indeed.

He watched the clouds for a long time, waiting for them to disperse enough that he could get a better look.

Isaac's eyes hadn't been as frozen open as he'd thought because the next thing he knew, Elise was shaking him awake, and it was dawn. He'd been about to ask her what all the fuss was about, but at the look on her face and shushy-finger to her lips, he stopped and followed her gaze.

At the edge of their camp, just outside the trees, stood a *thing*. A very large thing. Isaac let out a startled, *"Eeeugh!"* which made everything worse because it drew the thing's attention to him.

It just *stared* at him.

It didn't move. Its gigantic, black eyes didn't blink; they simply *stared*.

The beast stood as tall as a small house. It had a roundish body, covered in fluffy fur that was the color of forget-me-not flowers. Its arms hung to its knees, which were connected to short, furry tree-trunk-like legs. Its head and neck were so wide that Isaac couldn't tell where its shoulders ended and its jaw began so the whole creature truly looked like one big ball of fur. It probably would've been considered adorable, maybe, possibly, had it been much, much smaller because it had massive black eyes and a little black nose that reminded him of a cat. It also had ears that were tall and wide and two small horns growing out of its head.

What ruined the cuteness for Isaac was that it had the widest mouth he had ever seen. It hung slightly open, never shutting, like a sleep-deprived guest that'd been at a party for far too long and had forgotten everything they'd wanted to say and why they'd gone to the party in the first place. It was such a wide mouth that Isaac was sure he could comfortably take a nap in it. But of course, he wouldn't want to do that because it was full of pointy teeth. The thing could eat him very quickly with little trouble.

In front of the monster stood a little girl. Only, she wasn't quite a little girl because she had large, animal-like eyes and tall, deer-like ears. She had wavy brown hair that went past her shoulders and wore a simple gray dress that went just passed her knee. Her tan skin seemed to sparkle in the sunlight that filtered through the trees. Only, it wasn't sparkling skin; it was fur. She stood with her hands in the pockets of her dress, her gaze drifting from Isaac, to Elise, to Nothe, and then settling on Rain.

Through these several moments of silence, the thing never stopped staring at Isaac, and its mouth never closed. At least it finally blinked, not that this made him feel better.

The little girl muttered to the thing in a bizarre tongue in a darling little voice, "They are a weird-looking bunch, aren't they?"

The thing let out a long grunt.

"Yes, I *know* they kinda look like Thipka when he changes his form. I told *you* that. That's why we're here."

Isaac had to blink at what she said. He wondered if the translator in his brain was broken because while he understood the words, he couldn't make sense of them, which was irritating.

Nothe tore his gaze away from the guests and turned to Rain, saying as though he'd just come face to face with a lion in the forest and hoped that if he didn't move too much, it would go away, "Should we say something? I feel like we should say something."

Rain said, "I don't know what good that would do. I imagine they don't speak Theran or Hassune."

Though Isaac couldn't see the mosquito anywhere—it must've been in the trees—he suggested, "What if we run for it? Jump in the"—he forced himself to call it what they called it, though he still disagreed with the term—"the *spaceship* and leave?"

"The ship won't start," snapped Rain. "The battery is fried and the acid damaged the engine."

What acid? What did he mean by "battery"? He wasn't making any sense at all, but rather than get into it—there clearly wasn't time for an explanation—Isaac blurted, "Then what are we supposed to do?"

"I don't know what we're supposed to do. I've never been in this situation before." Rain looked at Nothe. "Maybe we should feed them Isaac."

Isaac's stomach shrunk to the size of the most minuscule ball in the entire universe. He whisper-shouted, "*What?*"

At this whisper-shout, the thing turned its whole body toward him.

Nothe said, "That's not very nice, Rain."

Rain shrugged. "Just look at the way that thing is staring at him! I'm just saying, maybe if we give them Isaac, they'll go away."

Nothe looked like he was actually considering it. That was upsetting.

The whole world froze as Elise rose to her feet. The little girl's eyes fell on her. With great caution, as if she were approaching a snake, Elise stepped toward her.

Finally, the thing quit staring at Isaac. Instead, it turned its attention to Elise, even going so far as to let out a low growl, sounding like distant thunder. Elise, quite wisely, stopped. The little girl took a hand from her pocket, touched the arm of the beast, and spoke to Elise. "What is your name?"

Elise blinked. When she didn't answer, the little girl asked the same question again but in English. Both Elise and Isaac's jaws dropped. Elise gestured to herself and stammered, "M-my name?"

"Yes, *your* name. I'm looking at you, aren't I?"

Elise was taken aback. Isaac stifled a laugh. He wasn't sure if it was nerves or what, but that comment was hilarious. However, his snickering was short-lived as it brought the beast-thing's attention back to him.

Elise managed a smile. "My name is Elise. What is your—"

The little girl cut her off, gesturing to the rest of the group, "What are their names?"

With perfect patience, Elise pointed to each person as she said, "That is Rain, Nothe, and the jumpy one over there is Isaac."

"Isaac what?"

Elise looked confused. "What do you mean?"

The little girl let out a frustrated groan as if Elise was the dumbest living thing in the history of the entire universe. "What's his *other* name? Thipka says the Isaac he's looking for has two names."

Isaac and Elise wore identical concerned furrowed brows. Rain and Nothe looked awestruck and lost as if Elise had just turned into a penguin.

"Moore," said Elise. "His name is Isaac Moore."

The little girl's face lit up with excitement, and she let out a laugh. The beast-thing looked at her and nodded with a grunt as she hugged its arm and said to it, "It's them! Oh, he's going to be so happy. I can't even believe it!" Then she hissed, "This'll show those jerks." She shouted at the trees, "Who's crazy now, huh?"

The beast-thing grunted, probably in agreement.

None of this made Isaac feel warm and fuzzy inside. At all. Not even a little bit. In fact, his insides were more like a fireplace in winter, filled with snow-covered logs in a cabin with a hole in the roof. The odds of starting any sort of warm, crackling fire in there were not good.

The little girl grabbed Elise's wrist and pulled her toward the trees. "All of you have to come with me."

Elise pressed her heels into the ground and would not be moved. "But—wait. What? Where?"

The little girl turned to the rest of the group and hollered, not letting go of Elise's wrist, "All of you! Come with me!"

Unable to understand the little girl at all, Rain asked, "What's going on?"

Isaac said, "She wants us to come with her. She wants to show us to someone."

Nothe and Isaac turned their baffled stares onto Isaac as if Isaac had also turned into a penguin. Nothe asked, "You can understand her, too?"

Isaac gave a hesitant I-don't-understand-how-this-is-possible-either shrug. "Yeah. She's speaking English. It's a language from our planet."

It was clear on their faces that they didn't know how to feel about that.

When none of them moved, the little girl stomped a little, furry foot on the ground. "Come *on!* Let's go!"

Elise explained, "I-I think they're afraid. They don't know where you want us to go."

The little girl snorted as if Elise had said they were afraid of kittens. "Nobody's going to hurt you guys. C'mon!" She pulled on Elise's wrist.

Elise didn't move. "Yes. You say that, but how can we know for sure?"

The little girl gazed over every worried face, then shrugged. "I guess you can't know right *now*. You'll just have to see for yourself. Look, all I know is, my friend has been waiting for you people for a really long time. He says you're the only ones who can help him. Everyone thinks he's crazy, but he's actually really nice, and he's not going to hurt you—I don't think. Okay?"

Elise stared at her and then looked at Isaac. Isaac imagined they were wearing the same stunned and terrified expression as if they'd just discovered that some stranger on another planet had predicted their arrival and needed their help.

Nothe asked Isaac, "What did she say?"

Isaac summed up the message for them, and their expressions changed as if they'd also just discovered that some stranger on another planet had predicted their arrival and needed their help.

Frankly, Isaac didn't know what to do. He thought the moment should've come by now where nothing surprised him anymore, where he could take on absurd surprises with grace and a fast-thinking mind. But instead, he felt as though his brain had been struck by lightning. He could do nothing but sit there and wonder what had just happened.

Rain said, "I suppose the ship needs parts..."

Nothe nodded. "True."

"We don't know this planet at all."

"Not at all. And things might go better with a guide, if this creepy individual might be willing to point us in some helpful direction or something."

"That is also true."

Isaac couldn't stop himself from blurting, "Or they might go horribly wrong. She might just want to feed us to that monster."

Rain said, "I'd be worried about that, too, if I were you."

The little girl shouted, "What's taking you guys so long? Let's *go!*"

Rain hollered to Elise, "Tell the girl we're bringing our weapons."

The little girl guffawed. "Fine. It won't do you any good against him, but if it makes you feel better, sure. Knock yourselves out."

Isaac and Elise were even more stunned at this, and when Isaac translated her words, so were the others. She understood Rain and Nothe's language, too? How? Did she have the same gift Isaac had?

Also, Isaac didn't see how *knocking themselves out* would make any of them feel better. Why would she say that?

He didn't like this situation at all.

A Stroll Through a Dark Forest on an Alien Planet

Isaac didn't *want* to go into the woods.

Frankly, he thought all of them—yes, *all* of them—were downright mad for following these creatures into the forest. Yes, even he was mad for letting this happen. Rain and Nothe were less mad since they had scary helmets and magical armor that could magically cover their bodies at will. Not to mention how they could magically heal things. They could probably survive about anything.

It just wasn't fair.

He asked himself why, exactly, he'd agreed to follow everyone into the woods, where the trees were so tall and took up so much of the sky that they had to carry torches to light their way. Not torches as Isaac knew torches. No, these were sticks that held no flame. Their light shone through a small, oval glass, and was activated by the push of a button near the handle, which was padded by some squishy, comfortable, and slip-resistant material. It was the most magnificent thing. There were only two of these torches, so of course, it was Rain and Elise who got to have them, which Isaac resented. It was the orphanage all over again, and Jack, Madeline, John One, and John Two had gotten to the playground first and stolen all the balls. Typical.

Anyway, he decided his answer as to why he was doing this was very simple. It came down to would it be better for him to die a slow, painful death from thirst, starvation, and the vine in his arm, or would it be better to be eaten by some monster?

He'd been severely dehydrated quite a few times in his life, and the migraine it caused—it was torture. Pure torture. One *wished* for death in that sort of pain. The monster would be faster. At least, that's what he hoped.

But there was more to it than this—a strange pull in his chest wouldn't let him turn away. However, he was too bitter and angry to take a closer look at it or even fully acknowledge it was there.

The forest smelled sweet, like apple blossoms and vanilla. Even though Isaac hadn't seen any rain, the air was rich with moisture, and the scent of mud and rain mingled with the sweetness. It was as though the entire forest had captured the rain in a bottle, and they were walking through it. Droplets fell from Isaac's face, but he was certain he couldn't be sweating that much because it wasn't that warm. Even Elise was wiping water from her face, as were Rain and Nothe, lifting their helmets to wipe their foreheads with their gloves, until Rain removed his helmet altogether with an irritated growl. No, this was just a very weird, moisture-hoarding forest.

His body seemed lighter here, like he'd lost a substantial amount of weight. It was also easier to breathe as if there was more air somehow. Although it didn't make any sense, he was sure that, if given the opportunity, he could absolutely outrun and out-jump John One and John Two.

Nothe nudged Rain. "Hey, have you noticed what I've noticed?"

Rain's expression suggested that he'd been thinking very little about anything at all.

Nothe jumped, soaring a good ten feet into the air. He held his hands out to steady himself as he landed, a delighted grin spreading across his face. Both he and Rain giggled as if they'd just overheard self-righteous Sister Maria curse. Rain jumped after that, flying up into the air as if he'd become weightless. This turned into a competition to see which one of them could jump the highest. After Rain disappeared into the dark foliage above them for about a second too long, it was agreed that he'd won.

Isaac knew he'd regret it forever if he didn't try this, so he leapt. He watched the ground sink beneath him, the faces of his comrades turning completely upward and shrinking as he soared higher and higher without any sign of stopping. The light faded below him as he was swallowed by the darkness of the trees above, his stomach somersaulting as it filled with a sense of dread and terror.

Then he fell back toward the ground. His stomach leapt into his throat, stifling his scream. The ground rushed toward him. He was sure he was about to break his ankles.

He landed with a normal thud as if he'd done a regular, old jump on the playground back on Earth.

Well. He hated that.

But he most certainly could out-jump John One and John Two.

Nothe applauded, and Rain laughed. "The look on his face!" Rain said to Nothe.

Nothe laughed, then said, clearly impressed by Isaac's jump, "Hey, that was pretty good! You know, it's close, but Rain still won. It's the hollow bones."

Then Elise jumped. Isaac counted to seven before she reappeared, laughing.

"Nope," Rain corrected. "She won."

"She has wings," Nothe protested. "And she must weigh next to nothing. There is no way that counts."

"What do you mean, it doesn't count?" argued Elise. "Of course it counts!"

As the argument continued toward Elise winning, the little girl shook her head at all of them, clearly thinking they were all ridiculous.

As they continued their journey—Nothe taking larger, flightier strides than normal—it sank in that Isaac was on a completely different world, countless miles from home. His stomach twisted and fell in a strange way. It was a feeling that was somewhere between getting caught stealing a ball from John One and knowing that he was in very serious trouble and the feeling of falling through the Earth while talking to that shy, beautiful girl at the first masquerade he'd ever gone to. Grundy had dragged him there. What had that girl's name been?

That's right. She'd never told him. But he remembered her face. Yes, that warm, kind, radiant face behind the black and silver mask over her brilliant, green eyes.

He stopped.

Wait.

No.

It couldn't have been.

She'd had the most elaborate costume of all. She'd worn a beautiful, black gown with bell sleeves that extended to her wrists. It was gothic and the most elegant one there. Her hair was pinned up and covered in a lace veil, and her black and silver mask sparkled in the light, highlighting her vivid green eyes.

Could she possibly have been...

Elise.

Elise prodded him forward and he stumbled along. He just had to think...he couldn't think...

Elise whispered, "How do you know Theran?"

Isaac jumped a little at the sound of her voice. His heart was lodged somewhere in his throat. "Theran? Who's Theran?"

"Theran. The language Rain and Nothe speak."

Isaac rubbed his eyes. *Come back, Isaac. Come back to the present.* "I don't know. I, uh. I don't know. It's strange. I knew what the little girl was saying, too, before she started speaking English. And Snowman—"

Elise was clearly confused. "Snowman?"

"You know, the scary guy with the black eyes."

"You mean Asael?"

"Sure. I know them all. I think The Prophet did this to me. I don't know how he did it, but I swear he did. I was fine until—"

"Until he put his hands on your head. At the beach."

"Yes. Then." Isaac was suddenly bitter. "No one bothered to ask *me* if-if I wanted to speak a million languages—I always have, but I've never been good enough at it—but that's not the point. Is it too much for me to ask for some polite consideration and maybe an explanation, like a simple, 'Just so you're aware, Isaac,' or a 'How would you feel about'—"

"This is it!" announced the little girl. The beast-thing let out a higher-pitched grunt right in line with the tone of her voice as if it were repeating what she'd said.

Isaac peered up at the "it" she was talking about.

"It" was a cave. Not a monstrous sort of cave, just a person-sized fissure in a rocky mountainside. Not that it was really a mountainside—Isaac had seen mountains, and this wasn't big enough to really be a mountain—but a good-sized hill that would take a solid forty-five minutes to climb. Every bit of dirt was covered in grass, massive flowers, and bushes. The hill itself was surrounded by the biggest splash of light within sight and a soft blanket of fog. It was actually pretty, almost heavenly.

Still, Isaac didn't think he'd survive if he went into that cave.

The girl turned to the group. "You might be a little...*surprised* by his appearance. But don't do anything stupid. He will win."

"Annabel," a most dark and terrifying voice called out from the cave. It made Isaac think of ink. If ink could talk, he was sure this was what it would sound like. It growled, bubbled, and slurred as it asked in the little girl's language, "Is that you?"

Her face brightened. "Yes!" She laid her hand against the cave opening and hollered, "You've got to get out here! You'll never believe what I found!"

The giant, fluffy beast grunted in an indignant sort of way.

The little girl gave him a look. "And Gof. Gof helped me."

The beast—Gof—grunted again as if to say, "That's right."

Isaac translated. Rain, Nothe, Isaac, and Elise gave each other wary looks. The question was on all their faces: what, exactly, should they be bracing themselves for?

They heard the scratching of claws against rock and the clang of metal. *Scratch. Clang. Scratch. Clang. Scratch. Clang.*

Nothe raised a weapon that looked like a very fat, orange rifle, having grabbed it from the pack on his back. Rain raised his absurdly large double-bladed ax. It had blue veins throughout that seemed to flow like melted metal. Isaac bitterly wondered what the point of that flashy look-at-me-I'm-so-fancy feature was. The little girl looked at them both, smirked, and shook her head.

The noise grew louder. *Scratch. Clang.* The fog billowed away from the cave as a metal, skeletal hand caught the edge of the light and pressed against the cave wall, followed by a tall hat, and a hunched back covered in a black coat.

Scratch.

A scarred, violet claw—a foot that almost looked like a hand—stepped into the sun.

Clang.

A metal version of that claw brought the whole creature into view.

This is Fine

Underneath the hat was a smiling face, which should've been fine.

But this wasn't fine.

Because the flesh on the left side of the face was missing, freezing it in a permanent grin. There was a metal plate over the side of his eye, cheekbone, and along the jaw, and the eye in the socket was a bright glowing red.

Isaac was sure he'd probably seen this face in a nightmare from his childhood.

The part of the face that had a nose and skin was violet and scarred and covered with what appeared to be bits of shrapnel. The cracked, dry lips were curled into a grin that one might see on the face of a very troubled person, something that was unwelcoming and made you want to cross the street when you saw it. The eye on that side was a bright, glowing blue, like Rain's eyes. One thin, horse-like ear stuck out from underneath the hat on that side, and behind him was a very battered tail extending to his knee. He had a hump on his back and was dressed in black trousers, a black dress coat, and a white button up shirt—very Earth-like attire, which, when Isaac thought about it, was odd.

The little girl had been right. He was very surprising. In fact, there wasn't anything about him that *wasn't* surprising.

Rain and Nothe seemed more surprised and upset than Isaac was.

When this creature's gaze fell on them, his grin became inhumanly wide, seeming to stretch to the base of his ear. "They're here!" His inky voice bubbled and slurred in Theran, and a strange wave of indescribable joy and relief rushed over Isaac as though the emotions were carried in the mist. "They're finally here. It is time." The creature's good eye filled with tears, and as it did, tears spilled down Isaac's own face—tears of perfect joy, though Isaac was sure it couldn't be *his* joy. No, his heart was screaming in fear, though these feelings softened that fear. Isaac glanced over at Elise, Nothe, and Rain, who were also wiping away tears and wearing similar looks of bafflement.

Where was this coming from?

The creature continued, "I have been waiting for you for so long. So very long."

"He really has," the little girl said in Theran with a smile and tears in her eyes. "For my whole life!"

How did she know so many languages?

"And longer," said the creature. He reached his non-metal hand toward them. It was covered in scars. Some fresh, some faded, and all of them reading, *Save Them*. In English.

That was unsettling.

He said, "Won't you join me inside?"

Isaac was about to say 'No, thank you,' when Rain said, looking rather pale, "How? It can't be..."

Nothe blurted, "He's a Hassune."

Isaac furrowed his brow. "A Hassune?" It was his way of asking, *What is that?* But no one seemed to catch this.

Rain shook his head. "No. It can't be."

Nothe asked, "How did you get here? Where are your wings? And your tail—it's...well, it seems you're missing...quite a lot of it."

The creature raised the one eyebrow it still had, though its grin didn't waver. "You don't say? I hadn't noticed. Hadn't noticed at all. But now that you mention it, I am having trouble feeling," he gestured to the side of his face that was missing, "*this* side of my face." He patted the metal cheekbone. "I don't have a mirror. Does it look okay to you?"

No one answered him.

The little girl doubled over in laughter. Gof, the beast, let out a very clear *hah-hah-hah*, and the scary, red-eyed creature tossed his head back in a rich, hearty chuckle, which had a pleasant tone to it. It was something Isaac would expect to hear from Father Christmas, which somehow made him feel worse about everything.

The red-eye creature let out an end-of-laugh sigh. "I should introduce myself. I am Thipka. There. Now, join me inside. I'm in a hurry, and I need my boots."

That statement only added to Isaac's confusion, and his face said so as he glanced at Elise.

Rain and Nothe followed Thipka with little hesitation, but Isaac couldn't convince his feet to move. Elise seemed to be having the same trouble. She whispered to Isaac, "He's speaking the same language as Nothe and Rain. Did you notice?"

Isaac had other concerns. "Did you see his hand? Not the metal one, the other one."

"Yes, that was disturbing."

"Yes, it was."

"I don't want to go in there."

"Neither do I."

"You're going," the little girl hollered, making them jump. Her ears were turned toward them, eavesdropping on everything. "He's been waiting for you for forever, and you're not standing him up now."

Elise asked, "But, what do you mean, *waiting*? What—how—just, *how*?"

She shrugged impatiently as if this were an inane question that only a stupid person would ask. "I don't know!" She gestured toward the door. "Why don't you go in and ask *him*?"

Did she not understand how unreasonable that sounded? *Yes, I'll just let myself get trapped in a cave with a monster that's absurdly happy to see us and seems to know exactly who we are, even though we're from a completely different* planet. *Can no one see what's wrong here?*

How were they expected to go in there?

Gof the beast seemed to grow a foot in size. He let out a bellowing growl that shook the ground, his mouth opening to a width that took over the whole middle of his body. Isaac and Elise rushed inside the cave to get away, the laughter of the little girl following behind them.

That laughter...it reawakened his rage, causing it to spread like wildfire through his veins. He shouldn't have been here like this—no, not like this. Not a prisoner pushed around by everyone else's whims. He swore to himself that the moment the opportunity presented itself, he would break free of this—of Elise, of *all* of them. He would find a way.

He would *never* be a prisoner again.

They were ushered into a room that was surprisingly large and lit with flameless lanterns along the walls. On one side was a kitchen with a stove, and a square basin with a faucet inside a counter. Next to that was a man-sized black box that looked like an upright, oversized coffin, which was disturbing. At the far end, the cavern narrowed into a hallway that led to another room. In front of where Isaac stood was a small, round table with the words *Save Them* carved into every visible space, which really wasn't all right.

When his gaze fell on the group sitting around the table, he wondered if he'd said all his I'll-never-be-a-prisoner-again thoughts out loud. Nothe, Rain, and Thipka stared directly at him, wearing different looks on their faces. Rain had an eyebrow raised while Nothe appeared concerned, and Thipka—well, Isaac caught a glimpse of heavy sadness behind his good eye. His expression was full of what Isaac could only label as *empathy*. He couldn't quite believe it. The creature was looking at him with sorrow as if he actually felt sorry for him.

While part of him hated this—he never wanted anyone to pity him, ever—he'd thrown out his pride in favor of not-dying when his ship was blown up. He couldn't help his relief at the sight, and the hope that pierced his heart, hope that he might finally have found an ally.

But he didn't let himself get carried away by these feelings. He knew they made no sense. He'd never met Thipka before, and Thipka shouldn't have any knowledge of his situation. How would he have any real empathy for him? The idea was absurd.

"What?" Isaac asked the room, looking over at Elise, who seemed equally confused. He asked her, "Did I say something out loud?"

She gave a small shrug. "I didn't hear anything."

The little girl trotted into the room, clutching her stomach as she laughed. "You should've seen the looks on your faces!"

Gof was peering in through the door, far too big to fit inside, which was nice.

Thipka gave the little girl a stern look like a mother would give her beastly child at the playground. "Annabel, Annabel," he said in a sing-song way, "you ought to be kind to these people. They're not from here."

Isaac was very confused by her name. He was sure that she shouldn't be named Annabel as it was an Earth name. An English name, even.

A feeling filled the room. Isaac couldn't put his finger on what it was exactly, but it made it clear that Thipka was very serious. He rose to his feet and guided her away from the group. He crouched to her level and said so softly that Isaac had to strain to eavesdrop, "Annabel, Annabel, they're frightened. How would you feel if you were them?"

Annabel's ears fell back. She glanced at the group, who looked around as if they weren't listening to every word, then looked at the ground.

"Hmm?" prompted Thipka.

For the first time since Isaac had first seen her, she truly looked like a little girl, not more than eight or nine. Her voice grew so small it was barely audible. "Sad."

Thipka nodded. "What can we do about this?"

She sighed, then approached the group. Her eyes were so large and her face so adorable as she said, "Sorry." She looked down, turning back to Thipka, looking like she might cry. "I just really wanted them to see you."

The rage in Isaac's heart ebbed ever-so-slightly

Thipka smiled and stood. "I know, I know." He held out his arms. "Come here."

She ran to him. This little girl ran to the world's most frightening monster, threw her arms around his neck, and hugged him as if he were a giant plush doll, and he held her tightly, as if she were the purest, sweetest angel of hope and light in the universe, not a brat.

At least Isaac was less sure he was going to die right then. It was nice to feel a little better about things, however minutely.

"Now," said Thipka, setting the girl on his knee as he sat back down at the table. She wiped her face a little. "It's okay, it's okay."

She glanced at Rain. "You're so different. It's hard to believe that you two are—"

Thipka shushed her, his eye was very serious. "Remember? We're not supposed to talk about *before*."

"Oh. Right."

He whispered, "We can't change too much."

She nodded as though she was a soldier given orders for a very special mission. "Of course."

Rain had grown pale.

She gazed over the group again, looking disappointed. "I wish Emily were here."

He shushed her again. Isaac swore he could somehow feel Thipka's gut twisting, though his expression was full of patience.

Her ears twitched a little, and she looked at him, apologetic, her voice falling to a whisper, "Sorry."

Isaac didn't understand what was going on, but he was sure she wasn't really sorry.

Nothe sat back. "Okay. All right. Let's get back to the question, shall we? *How* do you two know who we are?"

Annabel said, "I know from Thipka's stories."

Rain folded his arms. Nothe glanced at Rain in obvious frustration before he continued, "Great. So, that answers that question..." He made a gesture with his hands, attempting to encourage Thipka to follow the girl's example.

Thipka's gaze drifted away as though he'd just caught sight of a distant memory. "I remember from before." He added in his sing-song voice, "Before, before, before." He shook his head, his expression lost and solemn. "Time is a strange, strange thing."

There was silence for an uncomfortable period of time. Isaac rocked on his heels, his pulse rising in annoyance, then he prompted, "And?"

Thipka looked surprised. Isaac wondered why until he realized he'd spoken in Theran. Thipka leaned back in his chair, looking at him curiously as if he were an ancient artifact that had suddenly appeared. "That's different."

Isaac glanced around at everyone as if hoping an answer as to *why* Thipka had said this would be written on someone's forehead. It wasn't. Isaac asked, "What's different? What do you mean by that?"

Nothe said, "Yes, and what do you mean by 'before?'"

Thipka shook his head and sighed. "Time, time, time." He looked at Annabel and smiled.

Everyone looked at Annabel as if maybe she could somehow explain things. She just shrugged. "He does that sometimes. Time is weird, I guess."

Rain leaned forward. "Let's try again. *How* do you know who we are? We," he gestured to the group, "are from different worlds. There is no way that you can *possibly* know who we are."

Elise had grown thoughtful. "There was that one man on the beach. Remember, Isaac?"

He frowned. Of course he remembered. "Yeah."

"The Prophet. That's what he called himself. He knew who we were."

Thipka nodded and hummed in a dark, knowing sort of way. "I'm familiar with The Prophet."

Isaac hated that he'd said that. It was just one maddening thing after another. He wasn't answering any questions. On the contrary. He was creating *more* questions. "Of course you are."

Nothe asked, "Who's The Prophet?"

Isaac grumbled, "He's someone we bumped into back on Earth. He also knew things he shouldn't. It seemed really odd at the time, but anymore..."

Thipka said, "The Prophet can see the future, among other things." Thipka didn't sound like he much cared for The Prophet, which Isaac approved of.

Rain asked, "And...is that what you do? See the future?"

Thipka shook his head. "I know the future. Well," he gazed at Isaac as if he were an interesting fruit at a market, making him uncomfortable, "most of it."

With the narrowing of Rain's gaze and baring of his teeth, frustration and annoyance seemed to erupt from him. Isaac wasn't sure how he did it, but he swore these emotions flooded the room like a fog. It was something he hadn't consciously thought emotions were capable of, but when he thought of the grief that permeated every particle of the room at Captain Snow's funeral, it was clear he'd always taken their power for granted. Rain's rage only compounded his own feelings, making his heart beat in such an irregular way that he thought he might collapse.

Rain took a deep breath and the emotions faded. He forced a smile. "And the difference is...?"

Annabel intervened. "Does it matter?"

Rain snapped, "Apparently he thinks so! Why else would he have said it?"

Nothe rubbed Rain's shoulder in a there-there manner and said, "All right, all right. Settle down—"

Rain plunked his elbows onto the table and held his face in his hands.

"There ya go," Nothe said, "that's better."

Rain shook his head and mumbled, "No, it's not better." He took a deep breath and rubbed his wrists.

"That's better."

"No."

"I think we're all just a little tense here. Tired. Hungry. Thirsty. Stinky. All of those things."

Annabel jumped down from Thipka's knee and passed behind Isaac and Elise to the other side of the room. Isaac watched her approach the large, black box that looked like a coffin. It was made of some sort of smooth material that he wasn't familiar with. On one side, there was a hole carved into the box and what looked like a spout. She grabbed a cup from a wooden cupboard, pushed a button on the box, and *water* came out of the *spout*.

Isaac's jaw dropped. He wasn't paying attention to Nothe's ramblings anymore; the girl had pushed a button on a big, black box, and *water* had come out of a *spout*, like when Moses hit the rock in the desert with his staff and gave water to the children of Israel.

And here he thought he'd seen everything.

He meandered over to the black box as Elise asked, "What is a Hassune?"

"It's what our people are called," explained Nothe.

Isaac reached out and touched the box. It was cold and smooth.

"But wait," Elise said. She sounded very confused.

Everything was confusing. But not as confusing as that box.

Annabel got a large tray out of a lower cabinet and placed the cup of water on it, then got out another cup and pressed the button.

Water came out of the *spout*.

Rain said, "He is clearly a broken Hassune, but he is a Hassune."

Nothe asked Thipka, "Why haven't you healed?" He added, "We can heal, quickly and completely."

Meanwhile, as Annabel placed the cup of water onto the tray, Isaac whispered, "What is this thing?"

She gave him a look, like he was from another planet or something. "It's a refrigerator."

Isaac had never seen a refrigerator like this. They were typical ice boxes that didn't look like coffins or hummed, or had *water* that came from a *spout* at the push of a button. He whispered, "Curiouser and curiouser." There was a pocket made from the smooth material near the center of the *refrigerator* that he could slip his hand into. He did so and pulled. The box opened. A flameless light spilled across the floor, followed by a rush of cold air.

Then Thipka said something that chilled him more than the refrigerator. "Why would I want to forget what they did to me?"

The room fell silent.

But then Isaac gazed inside the refrigerator and gasped. "There's so much food in here!"

That Thipka, Always in a Hurry

They each drank glass after glass of water from the refrigerator. Isaac kept expecting it to run out, but it never did. They ate two loaves of tough bread that tasted like cake, cold meat that wasn't beef but tasted quite similar, and an entire bowl of bizarre purple and blue fruit. The purple fruit was gigantic and bumpy in texture and bitter in taste, like grapefruit. The blue one was about apple-sized, and the flavor reminded him of kiwis, but with less taste. Isaac didn't care. He was starving and ate it all anyway, all the while casting nervous glances toward Gof, who was still staring at them from the cave entrance and wouldn't move. At all.

Thipka seemed to be letting them eat everything rather begrudgingly. After Elise apologized for everyone devouring all his food —because they pretty much did—he said, "Just be quick about it. I'm in a hurry. I only meant to get my boots." He had his boots on and was tapping one foot in a quick, anxious sort of way.

Rain asked, "What are you in a hurry for?"

There was silence. Annabel said, finally, "He's got lots of things to fix from before, and he's been waiting a long time to fix them."

Thipka cast her a glance that made her turn her attention to the slice of bread she was eating.

Thipka straightened. "You need metal. To repair the battery and engine of your ship."

Nothe and Rain's eyes widened. Food fell from Nothe's mouth.

Thipka continued, "A very particular kind of metal, right? Found around volcanoes? I can't remember what it's called anymore, but I know where you can find it. Exactly where. If you hurry and finish, I'll take you to it."

Isaac hated that idea. The fuller his stomach got, the more exhausted he was. And the longer he sat, the more he realized his feet hurt. His body was telling him to nap for an indefinite period of time, not hike an indefinite distance.

He didn't notice Elise studying him with concern.

Rain leaned forward. "All right. Tell me—what's in it for you?"

The sadness that lingered in Thipka's eye surfaced. "I need Time to move faster." He rubbed his wrist and looked away, muttering, "faster, faster."

There was silence once again. Silence seemed to be all that could answer many of Thipka's bizarre comments.

But then he added, "And maybe a ride." Annabel's ears twitched, and her eyes darted to him, full of surprise and sorrow, twisting Isaac's heart a little. He didn't even like her, but she looked so sad.

Rain's eyes widened briefly in annoyance. "A ride to where?"

Thipka didn't answer.

Nothe held up a finger. "One moment, please."

Rain and Nothe huddled together. Their voices fell so low that there was no chance that anyone else would be able to catch a word. Isaac and Elise looked at each other, their expressions confused and concerned. It was clear that neither of them was fond of staying on this dark and creepy planet nor of the idea of dying—although Elise could easily obliterate Thipka with her mind if she felt the need to. Hopefully she wouldn't because she might end up obliterating the rest of them as well, which would be sad for Isaac and the little girl. Annabel might've been odd-looking and a brat, but she was still a little girl.

Rain and Nothe whirled to face Thipka. Nothe said, "We will take you up on your offer and maybe give you a ride to...wherever."

Thipka gave one curt shake of his head. "No. If I decide I need a ride, you will give me a ride."

Rain furrowed his brow. "How are we supposed to know if we can give you a ride somewhere if we don't know where you want to go?"

Thipka's face didn't flinch. There was a certainty there that was clear and yet impossible to grasp. "You will be able to."

Rain and Nothe's shoulders slumped, and they huddled again, whispering. They turned back to Thipka. Rain said in a bitter tone, "All right."

He Just Has to Change

Thipka rose from his chair immediately after Rain and Nothe agreed to his terms. He had an enthusiasm about all this that was troubling.

"It's not far from here," Thipka said. He marched toward Gof the beast, who was still peering into the cave. Gof moved out of the way, and then Thipka was out of sight.

Annabel turned to the baffled group and said, "Well, what are you waiting for?" and went out the door after Thipka.

They exchanged uneasy looks before rising from their chairs. They followed Thipka and Annabel to a little shack against the hillside, a shack that was covered in green moss. In fact, it was so covered that one could hardly distinguish it from the hill. Thipka rummaged around inside it, gathering strange tools and what appeared to be fancy guns. Isaac couldn't help but glare at them, conflicted with a desire to know exactly how those weapons worked and become an expert, and a bitter resentment that they existed at all. He hated feeling so...so *small*. The world he'd known, that he'd thought was so advanced, with ships, guns, and locomotives, it was all nothing in comparison to where he stood now. It was maddening, really.

Thipka loaded everything up into a large knapsack and heaved it onto his shoulder, banging it against the hump on his back. He flinched a little and set it back down. "I suppose I ought to change first."

Annabel's ears fell back. "Are you sure you should do that? Your energy—"

He waved this away. "It's fine, it's fine." He sounded impatient.

Annabel's ears remained back. She didn't seem convinced that it'd be "fine."

Isaac didn't understand what the big issue was. What was so distressing about changing your clothes? He imagined Thipka changing his shirt and collapsing into a chair, saying, "Oh my, that about did me in!"

Well, if that happened, at least Isaac would get to rest. He liked that idea. *Yes, Thipka should most certainly change his clothes.*

Annabel took a huge step back, which seemed a bit dramatic since Thipka was simply standing there with his eyes closed. Isaac folded his arms, expecting him to reach into that little shed and pull out a clean shirt.

But then Thipka's skin began to glow.

No, it wasn't just glowing. It was outright *shining*. It illuminated the dark forest around them as though a piece of the sun had dropped from the sky. Isaac shielded his face with his hand as he struggled to see him, to understand what was going on. If he squinted very hard, he could see that Thipka had basically turned to sand, and the light came from the sand-like bits that had once been his skin, his metal face, arms, and legs. It was almost as if he were being consumed by tiny fireflies. They were shifting and moving, changing his form. Thipka's back straightened. His face filled out.

The sand settled, and the glowing dimmed until it was gone, and a completely different person stood where Thipka had been. He was wearing Thipka's clothes and top hat, but it wasn't Thipka. No, this person had red hair, pale skin, and—most different of all—a whole face.

Isaac's heartbeat resounded inside his ears. There were so many emotions swimming around in his chest that, for a moment, he couldn't feel any of them at all. Panic broke through, rising to the surface as he realized he'd been holding his breath. He took deep breaths, steadying his heart and mind.

The new person's eyes opened. One was blue, and the other very distinctly red. He smiled, and his smile stretched to his ears.

Oh. So maybe it was still Thipka.

But no, that didn't make sense.

Of course, neither did the thought of Thipka being eaten by tiny fireflies and then leaving someone else in his place, like some elaborate magic trick.

"There," said this strange, red-haired man, his voice deep but not repulsive and slurred like it had been before. "This will be better. Much better."

Right. That was weird. It was like this man knew exactly what Thipka had said before he was eaten by a bunch of fireflies.

The man then hoisted the pack of supplies onto his hump-less back, grabbed his walking stick from the shed, and strode away as if he were leading a jaunt through a park. Annabel followed close behind him, her ears still down and shaking her head with deep concern etched in her fuzzy features.

Elise leaned toward Nothe and asked, "So...can you guys do that?"

"Do what?" asked Isaac, surprised that his thoughts were finding his voice. "What even was that? What did I just see?"

Nothe and Rain stared after the man, their mouths agape. Nothe said, "Well, yeah, but...not..."

Rain finished his sentence for him, his tone dark, "Not like that."

"You don't just walk away from that," Nothe suddenly blurted. "*I* can't anyway. It's very difficult."

"It's so painful."

Nothe looked at Rain. "How did he do that? Practice, maybe?"

"Perhaps."

Isaac wanted to shake them. "What did he even do? What just happened? *What was that?*"

Elise said, "He...changed."

Was he supposed to understand that? "*What?*"

"You know—" she said with a small shrug.

"*No!* I don't!"

She went on as if he was silent and invisible, "—he, er. He changed his form."

Nothe explained, "We can pretty much make ourselves look however we want. Pretty much."

"Like through an illusion?" asked Isaac.

"No. Literally. We can physically change how we look."

Isaac struggled to comprehend this—to believe his own eyes. Sure, Elise had changed her whole appearance, as had Snowman, but Snowman had explained it to be some sort of illusion. To imagine the ability to physically change one's body, that was a thing of folklore and myth. "L-like in Greek mythology? Like Zeus? And the swan?" He wasn't sure he was right. He didn't know a lot of Greek mythology, but he thought he remembered some horrible story about Zeus turning into a swan and attacking a lady, which was absurd and wrong on so many levels—and for the first time in his life, he truly hoped it wasn't true.

Really, it was a ridiculous, terrible story, and no one should have to worry that it was true, but who was to say anymore?

Nothe shook his head, clearly puzzled, "I don't know. Maybe? What's Greek mythology?"

Isaac hated this place.

They hurried after Thipka and Annabel. Nothe caught up to Thipka and asked, "You know, if that's so much better, then, why don't you look more like *this* and less, er...*mangled* all the time?"

Annabel exclaimed cheerfully, "That's what his name means in my language! Like, the really old-school version, though. It means 'mangled.' That's what we named him."

Rain raised an eyebrow. "How very thoughtful of you." He looked at Thipka. "So what was your Theran name, then?"

Annabel said, as though he were talking to her, "He never told us, so we had to name him."

New-Thipka stopped and narrowed his gaze at them, apparently pretending not to have heard Rain's question and saying to Nothe, "Why would I want to forget what they did to me? Keeping every wound ensures I will always remember. *Always.*"

Isaac wanted to say, *Right, but it also ensures your life never moves on.* He didn't, however. He wanted to live to see where this journey took him next.

Thipka continued, "I return to my true form as often as I can, so I can remember *everything* as often as I can."

That really didn't seem healthy.

Thipka turned and walked away, shouting at them from over his shoulder, "C'mon, then! What's taking so long? I'm in a hurry!"

Ever Have the Feeling You're Being Watched?

Elise held a ball of light in front of her as they trudged through the jungle. Annabel and Rain held flameless torches. Isaac held nothing, having been left out of that deal yet again.

He couldn't help throwing glances at Gof the beast. Gof had a perfectly fine nose—it might've been a runny one, but it was fine—and yet he never closed his mouth.

Isaac didn't like it.

He decided to break the silence with a question to Annabel, "Why doesn't he close his mouth?"

She glanced up at Gof. "He's sick."

"Oh." Now he was concerned, though there was no logical reason for it. It wasn't as if he liked Gof, but Annabel clearly did. Of course, he didn't really like Annabel, either, but she was just a little girl. Isaac knew that one of the most traumatizing things in the world was losing your pet as a child. He'd once had a pet spider in the orphanage. His name was Harry. It was one of those fuzzy, twitchy ones with big eyes and chunky legs. Then Sister Maria smashed it with her heel on purpose, right in front of him. He was sure he'd never fully recovered from it. So he asked, "It's nothing serious, is it?"

"No. He'll get over it."

"Oh good."

She looked up at him, her eyes sparkling in the light. He thought she looked pleasantly surprised by his comment.

A flicker of white mist-like light in the trees caught Isaac's attention. He thought it might've been the flames against the darkness, causing his eyes to play tricks on him. But then he saw it again. A quick flash of heavenly mist dancing through the trees before disappearing again. He blurted, "What was that?"

In the tone of a parent brushing aside their child's fear of thunder, Annabel said, "That's just the ghosts."

"What?" Isaac looked at her incredulously. "Are you joking?"

"Of course not." She was very matter-of-fact about it, as if she felt her child were silly to be so afraid of thunder. "They won't hurt you. They're just annoying. Which I guess makes sense. Being dead must get boring. You can't really touch anything, or talk, or eat good food—like being in a museum."

Isaac had heard of museums, of course. He'd never had time to visit one—or rather, he'd never *made* the time because who would want to?

What an insightful observation.

He looked back at the forest, thinking of the ghost in the orphanage. It had liked the pantry, the ceiling, under his bed. It was always moving objects around, and it occasionally broke things. Isaac had sometimes wondered if it had been the one who'd stolen his book—which he now kept in his pocket close to his heart—since the Johns were so rudely adamant that they were innocent.

But he did love it when the ghost would terrorize John One and John Two, and when it broke Sister Maria's favorite statue while she was alone in her office.

Thinking about it now, Isaac realized that the ghost must've been very bored, indeed. Like being in a museum. Trapped in one of those for long enough, who wouldn't start moving figures around and breaking things?

Annabel scurried up to Thipka and asked him, "Don't you think you should rest?"

"I've been waiting so long for this moment, so very long," said Thipka.

"And you can't wait a little longer—?"

"No." This was a very fierce, final "no."

Elise coaxed Isaac into falling behind the rest aways and asked in a whisper, "What do you think he's in a hurry for?"

Isaac sighed, resigning himself a little more to all the things he did not know. "Who's to say? He is clearly... I don't know. *Something.* I want to say 'unwell,' but who's to say?"

Elise chewed her lip for a moment before she said, "So, um, did you see a...a light in the trees?"

"The glowing mist thing?"

"Yes! That. What do you think that was?"

"Annabel says it was a ghost."

Elise stared at him. "A ghost?"

"Yes. A ghost."

"And she wasn't spinning a yarn?"

"She seemed sincere."

"A ghost. A real ghost."

"That's right."

Elise blinked and looked away, appearing troubled. "Well, that's fine then, ya?"

"Yes, that's precisely what I was thinking."

There was silence for a moment. Rain and Nothe started whispering amongst themselves about things. Isaac overheard Nothe say, "Don't be so focused on-on the dirt and-and the clouds. That stuff just gets in the way, you know? It keeps you from realizing that you're on the adventure of a *lifetime*. It's all there. It's right in front of your face. You'd see it if you just changed where you were looking a little bit. Just a *little* bit."

Isaac could've strained to hear more, but he didn't want to. In fact, he slowed his pace ever so slightly in order to fall even farther behind. Judging by the amount of heart he heard in Nothe's tone, it was clear that this was the sort of sacred conversation where eavesdropping felt very much like trespassing.

Also, he didn't care much for Nothe's logic. It inadvertently asked Isaac to examine that pull in his chest a little more, the one that kept him moving forward on this journey, and he didn't want to.

But he did think about asking Elise about the masquerade he'd gone to long ago, the one with the girl who had bright green eyes and an elaborate costume. But how was he supposed to go about that? *Say, do you remember that one party? You know, the masquerade one that you may or may not have gone to? Were you there?*

Elise broke the silence. "This all must be very difficult for you."

Isaac looked at her for a moment, with her stupid ball of energy-light as she floated through the shrubbery with her stupid wings. Then he said, "*No*. Not at all. I'm taking this quite well, I think."

She hung her head and looked away.

He hadn't really been expecting that.

She said, "It really wasn't supposed to be like this."

"Yes. You keep saying that."

She grabbed his arm, stopping him. "Look at me. Please."

He did while raising an I'm-reluctantly-and-skeptically-listening eyebrow, as though she were a doctor telling him he ought to drink less alcohol.

She looked into his eyes, her own intense, lovely, and bright—he hated that they were lovely. "I will make this right. I will bring them back."

His gaze softened. Not because he thought she could really do what she said, but because he could see how much she meant it—how much she *wanted* it. Underneath her confidence, he could sense a terrible desperation, the kind that held no alternative, the kind that broke people limb from limb. Yet, he seriously doubted that what she said was possible. Rain and Nothe didn't think it was, and frankly, he trusted their judgment more than hers.

But what would happen to her if they were right? What would happen if she found out that she couldn't take anything back? Sure, maybe she could take the vine out of his arm, but the rest?

But what did he know? Clearly, not a lot.

He gave a curt nod. "Okay."

What else was there to say?

MEANWHILE, Nothe and Rain were in the middle of their own conversation.

Nothe glanced over at Rain. Rain had been controlling his emotions a little too well since they'd arrived on this planet, and he didn't like it. He was sure that Rain was imploding after nearly killing them all. It didn't help that they were in a dark forest, one that was so dark it was like being shut in a room with no windows. There was something about darkness like this that was suffocating for them. It broke the walls that held back memories of unlit cement cells, of basements, of chains. Nothe found it difficult to stay present, to breathe. Like Rain, he'd eventually had to take off his helmet just to breathe a little better, to feel the air against his skin, and to drink in as much light as possible. He had to focus on the different smells, on the scent of sweet flowers and rain, on the near-weightlessness, and on the feeling of the soft, mossy ground under his boots. He wasn't in a cell, he wasn't in chains, and he was fully clothed.

Once he'd composed himself enough, he hoped to guide Rain's mind to more pleasant and hopeful ideas also.

"I mean, look at this place," said Nothe with a smile.

"I am looking at it," grumbled Rain. "I can't really *not* look at it."

Nothe went on cheerfully as though Rain had clapped his hands together and said, *Yes! Isn't this dark nightmare of a place just delightful?* "Isn't it fantastic? I mean, not necessarily *this* place, this is more like walking through a black hole, but the *idea* of it. The idea that there are other worlds that we can actually live on. Once we can get the ship running again—"

"*If* we can get the ship running again."

"—we can go somewhere else. And not just somewhere else, but a whole different planet! It's not doing something dumb and boring like moving to a different city or-or continent, no. No, it's *waaay* more fabulous." He leaned into him, his eyes alight with all the possibilities. "We're moving to a different *planet!*"

While he hadn't expected Rain to start skipping at the thought, he'd been sure he'd react in some sort of positive way. Instead, he simply continued his elegant-yet-hopeless trudge forward, like a soldier on the front line of a losing battle.

Nothe felt the need to state the obvious just in case Rain had missed it, "We never have to return to Thera, Rain. It's behind us. Forever."

Nothe knew this wasn't true. Maybe the planet was behind them, but he knew the memories of Thera were attached to them like a shadow, and no one could ever fully escape their shadow. It was a shadow that was heavy, with claws and teeth, that would rise at the most unexpected times and devour them, tearing open old wounds and shrouding them in cold, bitter darkness, just as it had when they'd first entered this forest. Nothe had managed to wrestle it this time and win, but he wasn't always that lucky. Sometimes...sometimes he just couldn't beat the shadow.

He knew that Rain knew this, too. Rain knew the shadow all too well and had lost to it at least once when he drove his ship into the ocean. Nothe knew this was likely why there was no hope-fueled, near-weightless bounce in his step.

So Nothe added, "They can't hurt us anymore. Wherever we go, the Therans can't follow."

Rain's shoulders relaxed, and he held his head a little higher. "That is a very pleasant thought."

Ahead of them, Thipka stopped and parted a curtain of vines. Light spilled into the forest and, for a moment, all of them had to shield their eyes. "Come on, then," he said, grinning that unsettling grin—it was unsettling even with a whole face. "Come and see."

Nothe and Rain stepped through into the light. Nothe gripped his chest as if he were one million years old and having his eleventh heart attack. He turned to look for Isaac and Elise, who had fallen behind for some reason. "Guys!" He hollered, "What are you doing? Get up here! You need to see this."

Isaac and Elise rushed forward and stepped into the sunlight.

It was Isaac's turn to have an eleventh heart attack.

The giant trees were out of sight. All that lay before them was luscious green grass and white flowers the size of dinner plates. A few trees stood here and there, but they were more like regular, boring Earth-maple trees. In the distance were rolling hills and something that was absolutely wonderful and terrible and incredible. At first, all Isaac could do was point.

In front of him was a crescent, the misty moon-kind seen from the Earth in the early morning, only this one started at the top of the blue sky and then sank behind the horizon. Instead of being pockmarked with craters, it was woven with swirls that faded into the blue.

Thipka read Isaac's stunned silence and explained, "That is a gas giant, the planet Sam."

Isaac looked around, trying to see who he was talking to. "Who's Sam?"

"No, the *planet* is called Sam," Thipka clarified.

Nothe said, "So, wait—that's a planet?"

But Isaac's immediate reaction to this was, "*Sam?*"

Thipka nodded, but Isaac wasn't sure to whom. "Yes."

Nothe continued as if he clearly was the important one with the important question and the one who Thipka was talking to. "So...this isn't a planet."

"Not technically, no."

"No—no," Isaac blurted definitively, as if he knew better than any of them, "That is not a planet. *This*," he pointed to the ground, "this is a planet."

Nothe turned to him. "But it's not."

"Of *course* it is!" Isaac shouted like a mad man. "Of course it's a planet! What else would it be?"

Thipka said, "It's a moon."

"A moon?"

Thipka nodded again, still smiling. "A moon. Called Lolaar."

"This is a moon? We're on a moon?"

"Yes. Called Lolaar."

"But...but w-why? That doesn't make any sense! Why aren't we on *that*?" He pointed to the planet in the distance.

"It's a big ball of toxic gas. You can't very well live on it."

Annabel snorted with laughter. "Toxic gas. It'd be like living with my grandma!" She let out an after-laughter sigh, and then shouted into the trees, "Just kidding, Grandma!"

Thipka beamed at her, chuckling his hearty laugh.

Isaac could only stand there and stare. His mother's voice whispered in his mind, "You made it. You're standing on the moon."

Tears spilled down his face.

He had to sit down.

For the first time since they'd crashed onto this moon, Rain smiled a small yet genuine, *real* smile. "That is truly magnificent, indeed."

Isn't Camping Such a Delight?

They crossed the field and hiked beyond the hills until Isaac stood on a beach, staring out toward an old wharf. It was a surprisingly ordinary beach, with white sand and smooth stones and perfectly ordinary waves crashing against it. It smelled like an ordinary, salty ocean and moss. He felt like he was back at his ordinary weight again—he'd felt that shift near where the forest ended, like stepping out of a pool of water. He could've been back in New York or over in Brighton if it wasn't for planet Sam sitting in the sky, and the trees in the distant forest behind him looking like a mountain skyline, and the volcanic island resting about four miles from shore. Thipka had just informed everyone that this island was where the metal was and that it was mined by worms.

Had he heard him right? Yes, of course he had.

Worms.

They were very protective of the metal, as it worked as a sort of medicine for them. They also liked how it looked, and how everyone wanted it but couldn't have it. And since the worms jumped out of their caves full of hatred and on beds of fire at anyone who wasn't a worm who got too close—because worms were the superior race—they couldn't simply trade them for it.

No.

They would have to steal it.

This sounded *wonderful* to Isaac. "I can't see how any of this can go wrong!" he said. "When do we start?"

"That's the spirit!" said Thipka with a smile, his eyelids red and looking as though they might start bleeding as he slapped Isaac on his vine-infected shoulder. Isaac let out a dull, monotone "ow" but hardly noticed the pain. He was too hypnotized by Thipka's eyes.

Thipka turned to the rest of the crew. "See? Why can't you guys be more like Isaac?"

Rain and Nothe glared at Isaac, but he said nothing. He didn't feel like explaining himself. It should've been obvious that he wasn't serious, but perhaps his face was betraying him somehow. While he didn't think he had lost his mind quite yet, he was sure he was about to, and he was aware that his dawning madness might've seeped into his expression. Elise seemed to think so. She appeared concerned for him.

Thipka, unfazed, said cheerfully, "Well, here we are." He nodded. "Here we are. Getting here was the first step." He looked up at the setting sky. "I wish we could've gotten here sooner, sooner would've been better." His good eye twitched a little at this, but he kept his smile. "But now, the next step will be to camp here for the night. After that, we will take a boat out to the island when the sun is bright. They sleep during the day."

"Many creatures are like that here, at least on these islands," added Annabel.

They set up "camp," which was a small upgrade from their first night there and consisted of a campfire and thin blankets for beds. The only one that had any real bedding was the little princess, Annabel. She had a blanket and a cot, so she didn't have to lay on the ground. Thipka had managed to pack these things with the guns and whatever other mysterious things he had in his bag. Isaac wondered how he managed to fit it all in there.

Of course, even if he'd had something close to a real bed, Isaac was sure he wouldn't have been able to sleep, despite how horribly exhausted he was. It didn't help that the swirls of planet Sam had taken on orange hues with hints of blue. They were so bright, lighting the area as if it were early dawn, and they were so very *there*.

"Isaac," his name was whispered through the dark from his right. Apparently, Elise wasn't sleeping either. "Are you awake?"

Isaac didn't look away from Sam. "I wish I wasn't." Oh, how he meant that.

"Yeah," said Elise. "So do I."

The image of Elise at the masquerade—or perhaps an Elise-look-alike—drifted through the silence and into Isaac's mind. It hovered right at the forefront, taunting him to *just ask her*. He tried to brush it aside, to think of something else. But much to his dismay, he didn't want to think of anything else.

Without knowing how to say what he wanted to, he asked, "Have you ever been to a party?"

Elise shot him an annoyed look. "I wasn't a nun, Isaac."

"No, you were a gross old man."

"Gross old men go to parties."

"Do they?"

"I went *with* you to one. As Arnaud."

"You did?" He struggled to conjure up the memory.

She was indignant. "Yes!"

"Huh." His mind came up with nothing. "I don't remember that."

"Probably because you deserted me the second we arrived."

"Probably because you were a gross old man."

"We were friends! It was rude!"

He couldn't argue with that. "I didn't say it wasn't, it's just—"

"I'm glad we agree."

"—it's really difficult to meet girls with a gross old man—"

Elise covered her eyes with her arm. "Oh heavens, the girls."

"*Yes*, the girls! Why else do you go to a party?"

"You are just...so..."

Terrible? Selfish? He already knew this and didn't want to hear it. "That's harsh but fair," he said before she could finish. He could easily counter her mean thoughts about him with the reminder that she did blow up his ship and his crew, but then she would stop talking to him—or murder him, one of those—and he wouldn't find out about the party, and he really needed to know about the party. "But what I mean is, have you ever been to a party as *not* Arnaud?"

Elise fell silent.

"Elise?" Isaac looked over at her. Her eyes sparkled in the campfire light, staring at the stars without blinking. He wondered for a moment if she'd died. "Elise?"

She blinked. Isaac was surprised by his own reaction. *How about that? I'm nearly relieved.*

He tried again. "Did you hear my question?"

"I don't want to talk about it."

He was baffled. "Talk about what? The party?"

She rolled onto her side, awkwardly, what with her wings and all. With her back to him, she said, "Goodnight, Isaac."

"HEY!" A voice whisper-shouted, adjacent to them. Nothe was on his elbows, glaring at him. "You two need to stop chatting in your weird little language. If you're going to be talking, you might as well speak a language we can all understand."

Isaac hadn't even realized they'd been speaking in English.

In a voice that was far more awake than Isaac expected, Rain asked Nothe, "Why do you even care what they're saying?"

"Because I can't sleep, and I'm bored."

Thipka said, "They were talking about a party and how Elise used to be a gross old man."

Nothe looked surprised. "Really? Wow! You would never know." He looked over at Elise. "You are absolutely stunning!"

Isaac explained, "She only *looked* like a gross old man. It was a curse someone put on her or something."

Nothe raised his eyebrows. "Curses are real?"

Rain sat up now, his brow furrowed at Thipka. "How do you know what they said?"

"I learned English long ago," Thipka explained. "One day, you will learn it, too."

An unsettling silence fell over the camp.

Nothe said to Rain, "I should ask him something fun, like—will I be a king someday?"

ALL THE THINGS
THAT MIGHT'VE BEEN

It had been an evening in winter when Isaac had met the woman in the mask, an evening that was quiet and still, with only a few dancing snowflakes falling here and there from the frozen sky. What had it been—three years now? No. More than that. It had been exactly four years, one-hundred-eighty-six days, and...well, Isaac had no idea what hour it was on Earth, but he guessed it was somewhere around one hour. Maybe two.

He wasn't proud that he knew that. In fact, it both surprised and irritated him. He'd tried very hard to forget, to stop looking for her in the faces he passed by. He'd shoved it down deep into the cellar of his mind, stashing it in the very back of the tallest shelf in the farthest corner. And one day, it had successfully faded away until it was forgotten—or so he'd thought.

But here it was again, as though nothing had changed, rushing back to his mind as if he had only just left the scene.

He'd broken off his engagement with his fiancée, Alice—or rather, Alice had discarded him the way a farmer dumps a bag of old, moldy apples into a trough for pigs. He'd come home from a voyage to discover she had moved away. He tracked her to her hometown, thinking it'd come off as some grand, romantic gesture.

It didn't.

There wasn't even a hint of a smile in her dark brown eyes when she saw him.

Instead, she folded her arms. "Isaac," she'd said, "we just don't work. You keep saying you'll be better, but you never change."

"Change what?" Isaac had asked.

That was the wrong question. Apparently, he was supposed to know. Apparently, it was a conversation they'd had many times.

Alice said, "When something keeps happening, when a person just keeps doing something over and over—all the daydreaming, constantly drinking, not *listening*, just doing whatever they want, running away to the ocean instead of to the person he's supposed to love—"

Well, it is my profession, he wanted to say, and wished he had, *I'm not really running to it, it's all I really know how to do, and it makes me happy.*

"—It's clear it's just a part of who they are. So there I was, just tolerating life. Then I realized I don't want to just tolerate life, Isaac. I want to be *happy*."

There were very few moments in his life that had hurt more than that one. Only four, in fact, and two of those included someone dying.

He supposed, on the bright side, he could keep the money he'd been saving for their wedding.

After a few months of misery and despair, Isaac's shipmates—minus Arnaud, Captain Snow, who had not yet passed away, and a few faithful older seadogs—dragged him to a masquerade, forcing him to "get back out there." He thought it was a foolish idea. *Yes, let me just lay my heart back out on the chopping block. I'd just love to have another butcher take a knife to it.*

They tricked him into the carriage. They'd said they were going to a tavern, but instead, they pulled up to some enormous mansion with white columns. Grundy handed him a black mask with gold embroidery. Grundy's woman-friend—it was really unclear what sort of relationship they had—handed him a long, black coat with fancy gold stitching.

Isaac got out of the carriage, threw on the coat, and put a mask over his eyes. He informed Grundy, "This is stupid. I look ridiculous." He looked at Grundy's red mask that covered most of his face. "And you look like Satan."

"That's the fun of it," Grundy said with a smile. He offered his arm to his woman-friend, who wore a matching mask. Two other shipmates clapped their hands on Isaac's shoulders and escorted him up the front steps.

The moment he set foot inside, he was bored. He grew more and more bitter with every step as his friends pushed him through the entryway and into the ballroom. The chandeliers were too ornate, the walls too colorful, the floor too polished. How did anyone ever get their floors that clean? And how did they *stay* clean with so many people stomping around on them with their wet shoes? Witchcraft. That was how. He was sure of it. It was the only explanation.

And yes, that was another problem. There were too many people and not enough alcohol. Who was even hosting this? Who was hoarding the wine? It wasn't twenty minutes before Isaac decided to leave and walk to a tavern, where he was *supposed* to be.

Isaac crossed the room toward the entryway, and he saw her.

Her bright green eyes pierced him through her black and silver mask, her eyelashes thick and dark. Her lips were full and bright red, her features the epitome of grace. Her skin had a hint, a whisper, of pale green tinge to it, but that had to be a trick of the light. And she was wearing wings. Her costume was the most elaborate in the room. But that didn't annoy him like everything else there. In fact, he found it rather brave and endearing.

Her hair was tied back and covered in a black lace scarf that draped over her shoulders. Her dress was elegant and black, and she wore black gloves. One would've thought she was in mourning.

If that's the case, that's one thing we already have in common.

When his gaze caught hers, she looked away nervously. She took a noticeable deep breath and straightened her shoulders, fidgeting with her fingers.

He knew right then that if he didn't talk to her, he'd regret it forever.

But then again, he also knew he shouldn't. She seemed far too special of a person for a man like him. He knew what he was, and she deserved better.

He took another step toward the entryway when he heard a fit of giggles. It came from a group of fancy ladies with masks made of elaborate feathers, whispering not-so-quietly about the "green woman" and her "sad costume" and "those ridiculous wings." One of them approached the poor girl and said, "Tell me, who made your costume?"

She opened her mouth to respond but before she could say a word, another woman, wearing an awful lot of yellow with a yellow-feathered mask, said, "Surely it must've been the Grim Reaper. I feel overwhelmed with grief just looking at it."

The women laughed. She bit her lips, as if this might help hold back the tears.

A burning ball of rage burst in Isaac's chest. He approached the yellow-dressed woman and said with perfect matter-of-factness, "Well, surely you would know. By the way, your scythe is by the front door. You'd better grab it quickly if you're going to make your next appointment." Isaac pointed to an old man across the room who was falling asleep in his chair, his sickly, yellowing skin hanging from his face.

The young woman with wings burst into laughter. It was the loveliest sound: sweet, like the song of sleigh bells on Christmas morning.

He gave a slight bow and held his hand out to her. "May I have the next dance?"

Her response to this was the most beautiful smile Isaac had ever seen before and a far more joyful one than he deserved. It made his heart skip a little as she said, "I'd be delighted."

She took his hand, and he escorted her to the dance floor. One of the women behind them snickered, "Aren't they the perfect match?"

He took that as a compliment.

As she stood at his side, waiting for the next song to play, he could smell the soft scent of her perfume. It reminded him of the rose garden at the orphanage that the sisters made him prune. He used to hate the work, but over time it became an act of love. The garden became his sanctuary, a place he could run to. He would often hide there with a book and escape the dark world around him. It was the only place where he felt any peace.

This made him uncomfortably aware of how terrible he must've smelled. He'd begun the night thinking he was going to a tavern, not a fancy party. He could only hope the clean coat he was wearing covered the worst of his I-have-not-bathed-recently stench.

The waltz began. It had been a while since Isaac had danced with anyone, and he was quite rusty, but not near as much as this girl. They found themselves tripping over the other dancers and turning the wrong way with many a "Sorry!" "Oops!" "Oh dear, I'm so sorry!" "Pardon." "Excuse me, sorry," all followed by fits of laughter that many in their company shook their heads at with great disapproval.

Once the song ended, they escaped the dance floor, going off into a corner as she said, "That was a disaster."

"Well, at least everyone saw."

She laughed. It was wonderful. Like music.

He added, "And at least we know how to have fun."

"Indeed! My, how drab and dull their souls must be."

"Perhaps they have no souls."

"Do you think so?"

"Yes. Yes, I do. I mean, look at them."

They scanned the room. The next group of dancers twirled in perfect harmony with colorful dresses while the rest stood to the side discussing nonsense in muted voices.

"I think you might be right," she said. "I believe propriety has stolen their souls."

Isaac looked at her with mock concern. "Do you think we should tell them?"

She studied the crowd and sighed. "I think we're too late. They're too far gone."

Isaac hung his head with sorrow. "Drat. It's just as I feared." He brightened. "At least there's still hope for us."

"Yes. But only if we leave now."

Isaac raised his eyebrows. "What do you propose?"

She smiled. "Perhaps you can walk me through the garden, ya? Out back?"

"Are we allowed back there?"

She shrugged. "I don't know."

He smiled. "Yeah, all right."

He helped her with her coat, which was awkward to put on since she had to fold her wings down like a butterfly in order to get it over her shoulders. He never figured out how she attached them or moved them as if with a thought. These wings were so well thought out that they could've been real. What was more impressive, she said she made them herself. Unfortunately, she was surrounded by people who would never appreciate such creativity. He was more than happy to help her escape them all.

Together, they slipped out the back door to the large garden, which was frosted with snow. Isaac offered his arm, and she took it. He asked, "Do you have any idea who lives here?"

"Not really. I came here with some friends who left me."

He nodded. "I can relate. What fine friends we have."

"Well, they did bring us here."

"As I said, 'What *fine* friends we have.'" She laughed as he continued, "They bring us to this house full of people with no souls and then abandon us. It's like being left on a deserted island. It's cruel, I tell you."

Her smile was radiant as she said, "Well, if I were to be left on a deserted island with anyone, I'm glad it's you."

Isaac looked at her, his stomach dancing a little at her words. Her vivid green eyes seemed to glow in the moonlight through her mask. He didn't know how to respond. His tongue had lost all function. But he had to say something. "Thank you. S-same. Same to you." He cleared his throat and added, "Tonight has turned out to be a surprisingly..." He kicked his brain, *Word! I need a word!* "F-fun adventure."

"I do love adventure."

Isaac liked hearing that. "You do?"

"Oh, absolutely. Can you imagine being cooped up all day? Where the best part of your year is going to some dreadful party where all anyone can talk about is politics and what Anne wore on Sunday?"

"Right? Exactly!" *Finally! A woman who gets it!*

"I just can't imagine staying in one place my whole life. I should hope to see the whole world or die trying."

"Yes! I would travel the stars if I could."

She stopped and looked at him curiously. "You would?"

"I would."

She smiled, making his wretched, broken heart trip over itself again. But as it did so, he realized that since the moment he'd asked her to dance, he'd somehow forgotten it was broken.

He really wished she'd remove her mask. He wanted to see the whole face of the woman who'd made him forget his pain.

She bashfully looked down toward the hem of her dress. "Tell me. Have you ever been to Sydney?"

Isaac hadn't been expecting that question. "Australia?" He had to think about it. "It's been a while."

"That's somewhere I'd love to go to."

At this fine opportunity, Isaac launched into his stories of Sydney, which weren't many as he'd only been there twice, back when Captain Snow had a wealthy client who was willing to pay top dollar for products from Sydney. It was an arduous journey, with a high risk of piracy and storms, that someone always died on, so Captain Snow always charged a large amount of money for it. Isaac did his best to make each story sound as interesting as possible.

They sat on a bench not far from where they were standing and took turns telling stories from their travels. She'd lived in India briefly when she was very small until her father returned to France. After that, she was sent to live with relatives in Maine, which was when Isaac erupted with enthusiasm, "That's where I'm from!"

He listened to her dreams of travel. Actually listened. He hung on her every word. He loved the sound of her voice and the way her eyes lit up when she talked about something that made her happy.

It grew colder as the night wore on. His fingers were going numb, but he chose to ignore it. He didn't want to risk losing this moment. As a sailor who often traversed cold waters, he'd become fairly expert at ignoring the demons that sometimes arose when his fingers were frozen, reminding him too much of another cold night—one where he was abandoned to the snow. Occasionally he'd have to go indoors to warm up if it got bad enough.

But this time—he didn't know how she did it, but without even realizing it, she helped him keep those demons away. It was as if he were back in the rose garden or on his ship at sea on a calm, sunny day, safe from the world. He could almost feel his heart stitching itself back together.

Going back inside could wait a little longer. He didn't want to risk losing this moment.

"I think I would like a house of my own someday," she said. "And a horse. I've loved horses ever since I was a little girl. But I definitely need to see the world first, ya? And maybe visit the stars."

Isaac decided he could have a house one day, too, and sit still for a while with something simple, like a plot of land to farm and a few horses. He didn't *have* to live in a castle on a mountain, although he did tell her about that and about the book he'd lost. He told her a lot of things that he'd never told anyone, not even Alice, but that was because she never once reacted to anything he said with condemnation, as Alice would have done. She was the opposite of Alice. She was genuinely kind, listening with compassion and care, and in the process, something shifted inside of him, as if a piece of a puzzle had been fit into place. He was sure that everything—his courting one girl after another, his inability to truly and completely run to the woman he thought he loved, his traveling from one place to another on a continuous loop—was all because he had been in search of something. He'd thought it was more money, more freedom.

No. He *knew* right in that moment what it was, and it was her.

She was what he'd been looking for.

He took off his mask. He didn't know how he'd kept it on for so long, it was so unpleasant. But he hoped it'd prompt her to remove hers.

It didn't.

The door burst open. A maid shouted, "Who's out there? No one's supposed to be out here!"

Isaac and the woman-who-refused-to-take-off-her-mask jumped to their feet. He hollered, "Sorry!"

The maid yelled, "Everybody's supposed to leave now!"

Isaac's stomach dropped. "All right! Just—we'll be right there, we're just—" The maid turned around in the middle of his sentence and went back into the house. Isaac's shouting died with, "Oh. She's gone. I guess we'd better—"

The woman-who-refused-to-take-off-her-mask grabbed Isaac's coat and kissed him. His stomach leapt into his chest as though he were falling through the earth. She cradled his neck in her hand and slid her fingers through his hair as he wrapped an arm around her waist.

Then she let him go, dashing back toward the house as she called back to him, "It was nice to meet you, Isaac!"

It took him a moment to return to reality. She reached the door before he found his feet. He raced after her, doing his best not to slip on any ice. "Wait, wait, wait." He darted through the door. She was already in the entryway. "Wait—" He tried to think of her name but realized she'd never said it. Had he even told her his name? He didn't think he had, but how else would she have known it? "Excuse me, um, miss!"

He caught up to her, and she finally turned toward him as he said, "I'm sorry. I just—I didn't catch your name." *Or where you live, or when I might see you again.*

Her eyes filled with tears. Why? "I—"

Grundy and his woman-friend burst into the entryway, throwing themselves directly in front of Isaac. "Hey! Isaac! There you are," Grundy said, smiling, "We've been looking all over for you. I thought you'd left."

Isaac tried to look around him, but whenever he stepped to the side, Grundy moved right in front of him, clueless and rambling on. "I can't believe you're still here. Where've you been? Does this mean you actually enjoyed yourself?"

"Grundy, please, I'll tell you everything later." Isaac moved around him, pressing through the exiting crowd, out the door and down the steps to the street, his eyes searching every face for hers.

She was gone.

He'd never fully forgiven Grundy for that.

It'd taken Isaac until that party to get over Alice. And although he may have buried her memory in his desperation to forget, it was clear to him now that he had never gotten over the nameless woman in the mask. She had become the ghost of all the things he longed for but would never know, a girl that only existed in his dreams.

Going for a Ride in a Boat

Isaac's sleep was shallow and restless, full of dreams of the nameless girl at the party and of The Prophet in that strange room asking him, "How do you keep getting in here?" He also kept seeing the burned eyes watching him. Unintelligible whispers rushed by him as if connected to an invisible force and spoken to someone he couldn't see.

He missed sleep—the kind where he didn't dream.

Later the next morning, Thipka—whose eyes looked completely better, thankfully; my, they'd been difficult to look at—led them down the beach to a small wharf with multiple little boats. Isaac was almost excited to see it, except none of the vessels had spars or sails and none of them were much bigger than a lifeboat. He assumed Thipka must have oars hidden in his magic bag of random things. They were parked in five smallish stalls, leaving one stall empty.

Annabel cheerfully pushed her way through the group and approached the second, battered little boat on the left as Thipka threw the protective cover off it, tossing it onto the dock for some reason instead of storing it on board. She was about to get in when Thipka shouted, "NO!"

She glanced up at him, jumping a bit with wide eyes, but then proceeded to get into the boat and sit down as if Thipka's voice had been nothing more than an odd noise made by a passing bird.

"Annabel..."

She scooted to the far end of the boat, clearly interpreting Thipka's stern "Annabel" as, "Okay, darling, now be sure to make room for everyone."

Thipka, with the patience of the most angelic saint to have never walked planet Earth (at least to Isaac's knowledge), stepped onto the boat, picked up Annabel, and placed her back onto the dock. "Wait for us here with Gof."

She looked deeply offended. "No!" One look at Thipka turned her defiance into a heartbroken frown, her ears falling back. "But I can help—"

The sadness he held poured through his gaze. It was something everyone around him could feel, causing them to shift their stances and stinging Isaac's eyes with tears. Tears streamed down Elise's face, and she quickly wiped them away, looking confused. Thipka told Annabel, "I can't lose you."

She gave him a similar look but then gazed down at her feet.

He smiled, then patted her shoulder. "Stay with Gof. We'll be back soon. Very soon."

Isaac sat with the others inside of the battered little boat that had no sails. While there were oars, Thipka said that they wouldn't be using them. Isaac wondered, *What, are we supposed to just float along with the current and hope for the best?*

The boat had a rig on the back that was about the size of a knapsack, with a pole that extended down into the water and a handle that allowed it to be turned this way and that. Thipka explained that this was a small engine, and the pole was attached to a propeller. This was why the vessel needed no oars or sails.

Isaac had heard of engines. In fact, back on Earth, he'd heard they were working on creating maritime steam engines that were sure to make crossing the ocean faster and more convenient. It had been both an exciting and depressing prospect to him. Exciting because it sounded impressive; he'd always believed that he and his men were capable of learning to work with such machinery, and it would be *very* nice to sail across the ocean faster. Also, sails were a bit painful to work with, and the wind wasn't always cooperative. Depressing because he loved those canvas sails. And there was something wonderful and romantic about learning to work with the wind.

It was also terrifying because what if the engine decided not to work and you found yourself stuck in the middle of the ocean without oars or sails?

Anyway, of course this little boat had an engine. Really, he should've known it would. In all honesty, he was a little *less* surprised by it and therefore had made progress in adjusting to his absurd, new reality. He was almost proud of himself.

The boat propelled them through the water at speeds that made him feel as though he were flying. His stomach leapt into his chest with delight as they soared over a particularly large wave, the little boat jumping farther than he ever thought possible. Cool water crashed over the bow onto his face and clothes, and he couldn't help but laugh. It was wonderful. Absolutely wonderful. How he'd missed the sea!

He stopped feeling cheerful once the volcanic island loomed in the distance, surrounded by haze. It grew more foreboding as they drew nearer, with the black, rocky cone emitting steam and the little bits of greenery growing along the very edge of the shore as if longing to cross the ocean to safety.

They were a couple of kilometers out when Thipka shut off the engine. "We'll have to row from here. They're very sensitive to noise."

Elise glanced around. "I have a better idea."

It took Isaac approximately three seconds to figure out her idea. "Wait! No, no. I don't think that's a good idea."

She looked offended. "What would you know? You don't even know what my idea is!"

"I have an idea of what your idea is, and I really don't think it's a good idea."

Nothe and Rain looked from Isaac to Elise. Thipka studied the island as if he were alone on the boat.

Elise folded her arms with a frown. "Tell me, genius, what is my idea?"

Nothe leaned forward. "Yes. Tell us. I'm feeling left out."

Isaac straightened his shoulders and glared at Elise. "She plans to carry us to the island with her magic."

Nothe's lips squished into a thoughtful line, and he concluded, "I see nothing wrong with that."

"Right," said Isaac, "it's a great idea until she loses control and turns us all into puddles."

"Ew," said Nothe, looking disgusted. Rain appeared to silently share this opinion on the matter.

"I've seen it done."

"I won't lose control!" shouted Elise. Thipka shushed her as if they'd all suddenly appeared in the boat with him. She repeated calmly, "I won't lose control. I didn't lose control when I carried you halfway across the world."

"Right, but you said that was your first successful attempt. There are a lot more of us this time."

"No, no. I'd focus on the boat! One thing, not on everyone." She turned to the rest of the crew. "It's the best way to get us there without making any sound, ya?"

Thipka thought about this for a moment, his gaze drifting away again. "It worked out fine before."

"There's that 'before' again," Nothe muttered to Rain.

Thipka nodded, clearly not at Nothe's comment—Nothe could've been an invisible mute for all the attention Thipka gave him—but at his own thoughts. "Do it."

WORMS HAVE HOPES
AND DREAMS, TOO, YOU KNOW

Meanwhile, over on the island, the worm sat with his book full of pictures, turning the pages with his large tail for the one-hundred-thousand-and-thirteenth time. It looked abnormally small in contrast to his massive frame. It was how he spent most of his time when it was his turn for guard duty. He'd been great at guard duty once. It had been years ago, and it wasn't something he was proud of anymore. No, now he was ashamed of it. He was haunted by the faces of those he'd taken down, wondering where they'd come from, what their stories had been, what they might have taught him. Thankfully—and regretfully—no one really attempted to pass by the island anymore, so he hadn't had to go after anyone, not on his watch, not since the days when he was good at it.

So, he spent his guard days admiring his book. He couldn't read the language the book was written in, but the pictures were bright and rich with color, colors he'd never seen before, having lived in a volcano all his life, and depicting a world he had only ever imagined existing. But with these pictures, he could finally *see* it—sort of—and it was wonderful.

He leaned against the rock wall of the cavern. Pictures were nice, but oh, how would it be to see it with his own eyes!

There was a strange sound. It wasn't quite the rushing of wind. Wind was empty, hollow. This was heavy, the sound of something flowing swiftly *within* the wind.

He peered through a hole in the rock wall. He didn't see anything there.

He slithered down the dark cavern and peered out of the next hole. Ah. There it was. He'd found the source of the noise—and what a peculiar sight it was. Rather remarkable, really. A boat carrying a small group of people was floating in the air toward the island. A green woman, with wings and vines for hair, was following behind them with her arms outstretched, as though she were somehow lifting them through the air—or chasing after them for a hug, which he could understand. He'd seen hugs in the book of pictures. He'd also observed the phenomenon in individuals who were about to die when his comrades attacked them. His brethren thought themselves far too superior for hugs, but he thought they seemed like nice things.

There was a door next to the window and a thick, rocky platform atop a hidden bed of lava, all ready to launch him at the invaders with the press of a button. He should jump on it, shoot himself out there, and eat them. That was his job, after all, he and his comrade, Foar.

He turned and looked at Foar. He was asleep, and when Foar was asleep, not even a volcanic eruption could wake him. He knew this from experience. My, Foar was a terrible guard. He never should've been hired for the job. It was all politics.

Politics that were working on this worm's behalf today, seeing as he liked the look of these strange people. He couldn't explain why. They stirred something curious inside him, an unfamiliar hope that maybe... maybe if he did things different right *now*, then maybe things could be different tomorrow.

He closed his book and decided to let Foar sleep. He would let the invaders do their invading. Perhaps he'd get to redeem himself somehow today.

Into the Volcano

As thrilling as floating in the air was, Isaac really, truly, despised it. He didn't trust Elise for one second. The metallic frame of the boat creaked and popped. He was waiting for it to crumple like a piece of paper with all of them inside it and then drop from the sky into the depths of the ocean with their writhing, twitching remains.

To make matters worse, he could see the volcanic island draw nearer through the mist, casting a cold shadow and letting Isaac know that it was something he'd underestimated. It was much more horrible than he'd anticipated. It was gothic and skeletal as if a massive spider had woven it together with a web of lava that had then dried and blackened, leaving misshapen, yawning holes. It was out of one of these holes Isaac swore something very large was watching them. It didn't move, either. It just sat there. But it was so large, so pale, and so unmoving, Isaac wondered if it was simply some sort of rock.

He knew better, though. There was no way he'd be lucky enough for it to just be a rock.

Elise sat the boat down on the beach as gently as a seven-year-old child tripping over their shoes and dropping their basket of apples. They all tumbled out onto the ground with startled cries.

Every muscle in Isaac's body tensed, freezing him in his sprawled-out position, staring up at the massive figure in the window. A silence struck the air that was so thick he swore he could taste it. No one moved.

How about that? They didn't die. What a pleasant surprise.

But he *did* think the figure in the hole-window moved as if it had turned to look behind itself. Isaac was quite sure of this. It wasn't just a trick of the eye, though he certainly wanted it to be. He had seen the thing in the window *move.*

Was it one of the giant worms? It had to be.

He didn't like it. Not at all. Visions flooded his mind of helplessly swinging his arms while being devoured by a drooling, monstrous worm, making him want to weep quietly.

Someone tapped Isaac's shoulder. Elise placed a shushing-finger to her lips, making Isaac want to strangle her with a scarf woven from her hypocrisy. She moved to them, one by one, getting them on their feet. Isaac noticed that Nothe looked rather pale. A light wave of concern and profound frustration seemed to be emanating from him as if Nothe felt like yelling at someone. Rain looked at Elise like he was seriously considering tossing her into the ocean with the rest of the sharks.

Thipka led them, carrying the knapsack over one shoulder and limping slightly on his walking stick, guiding them through what little foliage there was on the island until their feet crunched across scorched dirt and volcanic rock. Every so often, Thipka muttered under his breath, "Save them. Save them. Save them." Isaac turned to his comrades with a terrified look that asked, *Are you hearing this?* And judging by their wide-eyed and pale faces, they were.

The smell of soot, moss, and pleasant floral aromas was all overpowered by the scent of sulfur. The closer they got to the volcano apartments, the worse the smell got. Isaac could barely breathe. Honestly, how could anything live there?

Elise floated behind Thipka along a rather wide trail studded here and there with large, black boulders. Aside from these, there was nowhere to hide. They were perfectly visible to anything watching from windows, and the figure had moved from its window to another one much closer.

Nothe swatted Isaac's shoulder and pointed toward the windows, his eyes wide. Rain looked nervous as well. Instinctively, the three of them looked ahead at Thipka since he was supposed to know the future and all that. Thipka didn't appear worried at all.

Why didn't that make Isaac feel better?

It didn't seem to make Nothe or Rain feel better, either. In fact, Isaac thought Rain looked downright furious as if he knew for a fact they'd just been led into a trap and they were going to die a terrible, terrible death.

Up the winding path they went, each crunch of black dirt resounding in Isaac's ears like shattered bells and breaking bones. They drew deeper and deeper into the shadow of the mountain, the loss of sunlight chilling him. When Isaac realized where the path was leading, he instinctively turned and headed back down toward the beach. Rain stopped him with a hand on his chest.

Isaac whispered, "I'm just saying," though he hadn't spoken until that moment, "is this really the best way to go about this? Do we need this metal, *really?*"

Rain and Nothe nodded.

"Sure, right—"

They shushed him. His voice was rising, apparently. At the ruckus, Thipka stopped and turned toward them.

"—but is this the *only* place where we can get this metal? It can't be the only place."

Nothe and Rain appeared to think Isaac had made a good point and looked to Thipka for an answer.

Thipka whispered, "It's the only place I know about."

Rain smirked. "How shocking. The human is a coward."

"I am not—!"

They all shushed him again.

"—I am not a coward. I am—" he pointed to his temple, "—*thinking* things through. How do you think I've lived as long as I have? It's by not being *foolish!* By not taking stupid, unnecessary risks for stupid reasons!"

Nothe looked confused. "How old are you?"

Isaac squished his lips into a line. "I'm twenty-eight. But I'll have you know, not many people live that long on my planet."

Nothe nodded as if he were making a mental note of this. He turned to Rain. "Honestly, Rain. I think you could learn a thing or two here about thinking things through."

"Shut up, Nothe," Rain growled.

Elise floated down toward them. "What are you doing? You're being too loud."

They shushed her.

Isaac snapped quietly, "What is wrong with you? Are you trying to get us all killed? You'll let them all know we're here with that tone."

"Oh, stop it," said Elise, "What's wrong with you people? There are only so many hours in the day, you know."

Before Rain could tell Elise that Isaac was being a coward—which was an outright lie!—Isaac rolled up his sleeves and marched up the path toward his worst nightmare—a massive cave in the volcanic mountain. A cave that looked like the mouth of a monster, waiting to digest the next helpless, unsuspecting victim that had the audacity to seek shelter from the rain. And it wasn't just massive; it was *outrageously massive*—large enough to swallow the country's best battleship. But what disturbed Isaac most of all about this cave was the thought of what *made* the cave—of what came and went *from* the cave.

Worms.

Giant worms.

Isaac did not like worms. At all. Not even a little bit. In fact, he detested them. He loathed them with the deepest loathing a person could loathe.

Because one time, when Isaac was living at the orphanage, he actually did get to the ball before John Two. But this made John One and John Two very angry. And the Johns had friends. Isaac did not. The Johns convinced their friends to hold him down on the playground while they attempted to force Isaac to eat worms. In the process, Isaac bit one of the Johns with everything he had, breaking skin and getting blood in his mouth. The other one punched Isaac hard in the face, the sound resounding in his head and sending his dazed brain spinning in his skull. In this state, one of them managed to shove a clump of dirt with squirming worms into Isaac's mouth.

There was nothing quite like that feeling, of something so alien wriggling over his tongue, fighting not to die. Isaac's jaw was forced shut, causing him to bite his tongue and his teeth to crunch over a worm's muscular form, spilling forth blood and sour-yet-sickly-bitter slime. His stomach lurched. His eyes scanned all around him, desperate for help.

Sister Maria stood nearby, the one who'd smashed his pet spider. She was watching, arms folded, smiling as if she were overhearing an amusing conversation.

Something snapped inside of Isaac then. He didn't understand it— not even later in his adult life—but whatever it was, it unleashed a strength he didn't know he had, strength fueled by every shred of pain, disappointment, and unbearable loss he had felt up until that moment, and it was set on fire with his seething anger.

He spat the mud, worms, and blood into John One's face and threw the boys off him. He leaped to his feet and kicked the still-crouching John Two in the head. One of their minions grabbed him from behind, and Isaac bit his arm. He kicked, clawed, and punched in a blind rage, barely noticing when someone got a hit in. It wasn't until Sister Sarah wrapped her arms around his, restraining him, that his mind began to settle, and he saw what he'd done.

Both Johns sobbed while Sister Maria inspected John Two's head. Another boy folded himself into a ball on the ground. Two others, bleeding from their faces, looked at Isaac as though he'd lost his mind, and he had. He'd lost it completely. And the look Sister Maria gave him turned his insides to ice.

He was in for the beating of a lifetime.

There was no hope.

No one was coming to his rescue.

Because anyone who could help him peered at him with accusing eyes as if *he* were the monster.

He allowed Sister Sarah to lead him into the orphanage. He waited for her to turn toward her office, then he bolted for the front doors. She didn't try to stop him. She let him leave.

Once he was far, far away from that place, he threw up.

That had been a dark day. Almost as dark as the cave Isaac now stared into.

"Here," Thipka whispered, making him jump. Thipka handed him a large, heavy sword. "This will make you feel better."

Good grief, does he have every possible thing in that bag?

Rain and Nothe gave each other a nod. They put on their helmets, assembled their armor, and readied their weapons, then walked into the darkness of the cave.

They didn't make it far before a scraping sound started, like a shovel —a very large shovel—being dragged heavily through the mud. A bitter stench of old decaying moss, dust, and mud filled the air, and the shadows ahead of them seemed to thicken. Elise lit a ball of fire and let it float above them. Isaac shielded his eyes at the sudden brightness.

Before them, the light glittered in the many eyes of a monstrous worm.

Can't We Be Friends?

Isaac would've screamed if he could, but his body wouldn't let him. He froze in place as if he had been turned to stone.

The worm was positioned much like a curious snake, its neck bent and its face peering down at them. Its entire form filled the cave. It made noises through five flaps underneath its many eyes, which Isaac assumed was its mouth—low rumbling sounds not unlike the songs of whales. Air, thick with the smell of mud and rotting things, rushed through Isaac's hair and clothing. Isaac willed his head to turn and gaze at Elise in shock.

He could understand the sounds.

It was a language. The worm was speaking to them. He had said, "Hello. My name is," and he emitted a noise that sounded like a very drawn-out, "*Booooooooaaar.*"

Silence followed. No one moved. Boar, the worm, looked with his many eyes—one, two, three, four, *eight* eyes, to be precise—from one person to the next as if expecting some sort of response. Finally, Boar added, "And you fellows are...?"

Isaac and Elise exchanged another look. Elise whispered, "What is it saying?"

There was a clatter of rocks to his right. Nothe had thrown a large stone against the cave wall.

It was a diversion.

Rain flew at the worm from the left with his ax raised. Isaac shouted, "No! Wait!" but it was too late. Rain was steady, aiming right for Boar's throat.

His ax hit the worm's hide and bounced off it, flinging Rain onto the cave floor.

The worm was entirely unharmed. In fact, he appeared to have no idea Rain had any intention of harming him at all. He said delightedly, "Oh! Why, hello there! I didn't see you." The worm lowered his head toward him to get a better look, "My, aren't you a strange one? Did you know your eyes glow?"

Nothe cried out, "NOOO!" He raised his gun. Isaac dropped his sword and grabbed the barrel just as it fired a molten bolt of light. It hit the ceiling instead of the worm, and small rocks rained down upon them. Rage and panic lit up Nothe's eyes and poured from his body. Isaac fought to separate these emotions from his own as they twisted his stomach and weakened his resolve. Nothe was so strong. Isaac was sure Nothe could easily kill him and the worm. "Nothe, I know what it's saying! It doesn't want to hurt us!" Nothe ripped the barrel from Isaac, and Isaac miraculously dodged Nothe's elbow. "Elise, help!"

Elise raised her hands, and Nothe froze, unable to move.

The worm studied the smoldering hole in the ceiling curiously, sniffed it, then turned toward them. "My, what a fun toy you have there. But you know, I think it could really hurt someone if you're not careful." He looked at Nothe. "Oh! Such marvelous eyes. And you, too!" he said to Elise.

Thipka hollered, "Isaac, talk to it!"

Nothe's eyes darted to Thipka. Isaac couldn't focus enough to talk to the worm, not when Nothe and Rain were bent on killing it. What if the worm figured out they wanted it dead? Someone would be eaten for sure —probably Isaac, and maybe somebody else, and then the worm would certainly die. Isaac quickly told Nothe, Elise, and Rain, "Look, he said his name is Boar, and right now, he thinks that weapon is a toy, and-and he said, if you're not careful, you could really hurt someone with it. A-and he thinks you have pretty eyes. You, Rain, and Elise all have pretty eyes. That's what he said."

Rain and Nothe exchanged a look of confusion, but Elise appeared flattered.

Isaac pleaded, "Give him a chance." He couldn't believe he was pleading on behalf of a giant worm.

Nothe looked at Elise and gave a stiff nod. Hesitantly, she let him go, and he ran to help an injured Rain. Rain told him, "That's probably the most ridiculous way I've ever broken my legs."

Isaac looked up at Boar and opened his mouth, making the same strange noises that had been coming from the worm earlier, though they made perfect sense to Isaac, "Hello, Boar."

Isaac couldn't be sure, but he swore the worm gave the smallest, gleeful jump. "Oh, you *do* talk! Hello!"

"H-hello."

"Hello!" Boar said delightedly.

"Hello. I'm Isaac." He gestured to Elise. "This is Elise. Rain and Nothe are over there, and Thipka is over there."

"Oooh, he also has glowing eyes. One red, one blue. How lovely. The only one of you that doesn't is you, Izzzzaaaaac." It shook its head at Isaac. "I'm afraid your eyes are a bit dull and boring. Like mine! How wonderful."

Rain asked, "How are you doing that?"

Elise whispered, "Some man—he did something to him, and now he can understand all sorts of languages."

"What's it saying?" asked Nothe. He and Rain still looked terrified.

Isaac hesitated, annoyed he had to repeat this again. "He thinks Thipka has lovely eyes."

Rain and Nothe shared the same confused expression. Even Thipka looked puzzled, and he was supposed to know everything already. Nothe said, "Really? What—that—that's not what I was expecting."

Boar flapped his tail. "Aren't you folks fun, with these weird little noises you make!"

Isaac nodded. "Yes. Yes, we are so much fun." *Please don't eat us.* He turned to the others and said, "He says we're fun."

Elise leapt all over this. "Oh yes! We are so fun, ya?"

"Yes, absolutely," said Nothe.

"So fun."

Rain added, "Such a delight."

It flapped its tail again and asked, "What brings you to our island?"

Oh dear. What would it do when it knew they were there to steal things? Isaac started, "Well, uh, we are travelers, see. But our ship is broken."

Boar asked, "The one outside?"

"No," Isaac said. "It's on the mainland, across the sea. It floats through the stars instead of over the waters."

Boar gasped. "The stars? You can do that?"

"Yes."

Boar turned his head and seemed to gaze through the cave wall at the sky. "How wonderful that must be."

"It's quite the experience."

Boar said with a hint of longing, "I can only imagine."

Isaac couldn't help it. His heart hurt a little for this giant worm, at the look in his many eyes and the sad tone in his voice.

Isaac continued, "But, in order for us to return home, we need metal. A special metal that is found here," his mouth went dry, and he struggled to say, "on your island."

The worm stared at them, becoming very still and silent.

This was it. Isaac was sure. This was about to end badly.

Then the worm said, "I will get you this metal. But only if you will take me with you."

Isaac's eyes widened. "Take you where?"

"To the stars, of course."

Well, that wasn't going to happen. There was no way that worm would fit on the ship. They hardly had room for Thipka and Annabel. Someone would be sitting on Rain's lap if they really intended to make it work—and Isaac *would* make it work. He was not about to be left behind.

A severe pain pierced Isaac's chest as if his heart was digging its way through him with a dull shovel. He struggled to breathe. The vine in his arm rippled and shifted under his skin, which made him feel even worse.

Nothe asked, "What?"

"I don't like this," said Rain. "Something's wrong."

Nothe insisted, "What did it say?"

Isaac turned to them. "It, um." Isaac placed his fingers together prayerfully, pressing his thumbs against his chin. Then he said, "Boar," he gestured to the worm, "His name is Boar. He, um, he says he'll get us the metal."

Nothe said, "That's good news."

"Right. Yeah. But—"

"But?"

"But he, um. He wants to go with us. On our spaceship."

They all shared the same *oh no* look. All of them except Thipka.

Thipka said, "Tell him okay."

Isaac wasn't sure how he felt about that. It made sense why he should say this. He'd lied many times before in his life, but he wasn't sure what the worm would do when he realized he'd been lied to. Also, to his great shock, he also found it cruel to get its hopes up. Extremely cruel.

Thipka's eyes pierced Isaac's. "Trust me."

Isaac nodded with an expression of resolution and remorse, but he turned to Boar with a smile. "It's a deal."

Boar slapped his tail against the ground. "Terrific!" He whipped his tail toward them. Everyone ducked—except Thipka. The tail flopped in front of them and, at its end, held a book. Boar laid the book in front of them, turning well-worn pages covered in pictures of monuments, oceans, forests, and rolling hills as it said, "See these? I would love to see these places."

Were these pictures of this moon-planet?

Of course they were. What other planet would it have been?

Gazing at the pictures in the book, Isaac saw that the moon they were on was very colorful and rich in its own life forms and history, especially compared to this dark and dreary volcano. No wonder this worm was desperate to leave.

"Will you take me to these places?" asked Boar.

Isaac translated this to the others, then said to Boar, "We are from another world. We don't know how to get to these places. Well, I don't. But we can help you find someone who will. I'm sure Thipka knows someone." Isaac turned to Thipka and quickly repeated himself in Theran, adding, "You know people, right?"

Thipka nodded. "I know people."

Isaac wasn't sure if he was saying that he knew someone who would show Boar around, or if he was simply stating that he did, in fact, know people.

Boar looked at Isaac. "Is it pretty on your planet?"

Isaac smiled, feeling a pang in his chest, a call back home, to the sea. He said, "Yes. It is."

Boar nodded, then turned toward the darkness of the tunnel behind him. "Follow me. But be silent. You don't want to wake my ignorant relatives."

Isaac was sure this was one-thousand percent true. "Yes, we most certainly don't want to do that." He relayed this counsel to the others.

Thipka picked up the sword Isaac had dropped and put it back in his bag. Nothe helped Rain to his feet, and he walked forward with a limp.

As they journeyed through the tunnel, they passed a pitch-black cavern where two other worms must've been having a difficult time sleeping. They were quietly discussing Boar, how he thought he was better than everyone else and above eating birds. When they were a good distance away from that room, Boar said, "My parents. Everything you heard them say is true. They'll be asleep again soon. They're probably asleep again already. They're too old to stay awake for long."

"How old are they?" Isaac asked.

"I don't know. I don't care."

Isaac raised his eyebrows. "All right then."

The tunnel branched off ahead and they followed the one to their right, which opened into a massive, boiling-hot room thick with sulfur. It was difficult to breathe. Isaac thought he might die. Was it possible to die from bad smells? *Time will soon tell.*

Elise lifted her light. It reflected off large piles of filthy, unrefined metal.

"Here it is," said Boar. "This is where we store all the metal. Take what you need but be quick about it."

Thipka gestured for Elise to bring the light closer to the nearest pile. He carefully examined each clump, tossing aside gold and silver (Isaac pocketed several small pieces; it was only fair) until he reached a fist-sized clump of silver-looking metal that, upon closer inspection, was clearly *not* silver. He placed it in his bag and dug around for more, grabbing an additional four large clumps.

A very loud scraping echoed through the tunnel outside of the room. A deep, rumbling voice growled, "What is that light?"

What Could Possibly Go Wrong?

"Oh," Boar sounded more bored and disappointed than upset, which was the opposite of how Isaac felt. "Hello, *Gooooooooar.*" Boar slid halfway into the hallway, his tail gesturing for everyone to hide in the back corner. They did as quietly as possible, tip-toeing over things and trying their best to conceal themselves behind the piles of metal.

Boar asked, "What are you doing awake?"

"I smelled a strange smell."

A strange smell? The whole place easily could've had a hundred million putrid, rotting eggs hidden within the walls. Isaac wondered how it was possible for Goar to smell anything else. He was certain that any ability to smell would burn out with constant exposure to it.

Goar asked, "What are you doing in here?" He tried to peer into the room. "What is that bright light?"

"I'm admiring the gold. What's the problem?"

"You don't admire gold," observed Goar with a tone of suspicion.

"I admire it today."

"Why today? What is so different about today?"

"Why does today have to be different for me to admire the gold?"

"Aren't you supposed to be on guard duty?"

"I'm taking a short break to admire the gold."

There was a moment of silence. Goar asked, "What is that light?"

"It is my lantern."

"Why do you have a lantern?"

"So I can admire the gold!"

"You don't need a lantern to admire the gold."

"I don't *need* it; I *want* it. The gold glistens in the light."

There was a pause. "Can I see?"

"No. Go away."

"Fine."

Goar the worm slithered away. No one moved in the silence that followed.

"He's gone," whispered Boar, immersing himself back into the room. "We must be quick now. And silent. Hurry!"

Of course, as Isaac leapt to his feet—wanting nothing more than to be as far away from this island as possible—he tripped over a pile of raw gold and sent it tumbling to the floor.

They waited, frozen.

Hearing nothing, Rain covertly sidled up to Isaac and punched him in the shoulder. It wasn't enough to topple Isaac, but it was enough to ensure he wouldn't be able to use that arm for the next ten minutes or so. And it was his vineless arm, which was upsetting. Now both arms were useless.

A scraping against the floor outside the room made Isaac's heart stop. He was sure it literally had since he could feel nothing—not his face, his pulse, or even the sweat on his brow—for a few long seconds. Goar growled at the room, "What is going on in there?"

Boar grabbed a rather large rock of unrefined gold and blocked the doorway as everyone silently rushed to hide once again. "I wanted to admire some gold at the bottom." He waved the gold at Goar.

"It smells funny in there," whined Goar.

"You smell funny."

"*I* smell funny?"

There was the sound of some large animal sniffing the air. Isaac imagined Goar sniffing himself like a dog. The giant worm made a strange, terrifying humming sound, as though wordlessly stating he was not convinced. Goar said, "You're up to something."

"*You're* up to something. What are you even doing here?"

"I—"

Boar sounded as though he'd just discovered something shocking, like runny poop right in the middle of his pristine living room rug. "You're supposed to be sleeping!"

"But I—"

"Just wait until I tell everyone."

"Tell them *what?*"

"But maybe I won't tell them if you leave right now."

There was silence. Terrible, still silence, broken only by the pulsing of blood in Isaac's ears. The vine in his arm wriggled again. He wished it would stop.

"Fine," Goar said finally. The sound of scraping against the black rock signaled his leaving.

Boar cast a quick look in Isaac's direction and muttered softly, "I can't believe that worked." He peered down the hall.

All eyes were on Isaac, wondering what Boar had said and if it was safe to breathe again, but Isaac didn't dare whisper a translation or explanation. He didn't dare move or breathe normally.

After a moment, Boar added, "You can come out now."

Isaac forced his shaking body to cooperate and move out from behind the pile of metal. He explained with a tremor in his voice, "W-we're safe, but we have to move quickly."

The worm gestured with his tail for them to follow him, and they darted from the room and down the dark hallway, passing warped, yawning entrances to black rooms. Isaac was surprised and unsettled by how fast the worm could move. He had to jog to keep up and was still falling behind, keeping on his toes and sneakily-like, as if he was running through a ward of sleeping babies.

Out of the darkness behind them rushed a giant worm, the five flaps of its mouth open and screaming *"Thieves!"* and revealing nothing but a wet pit full of hook-like teeth. Isaac cried out and jumped, twisting his ankle over a jagged rock and falling hard on his hip. The worm lunged at him, ready to swallow him whole. There was a scream, one of pure terror and rage, but it wasn't his own. He didn't have a voice to scream.

This is going to hurt.

He raised his vine-infected arm and turned his face away, an instinctive and feeble attempt to shield himself. The vine in his skin writhed and slithered and then tore from the flesh. Blinding, burning pain ripped through his body as the vine grew and spread, breaking bone and spilling over him like water thrown from a bucket and freezing into a large cage around him.

The monster worm bit down on it. The vines buckled around him at the force of its jaws. Slime dripped from its teeth onto Isaac's coat. He was overwhelmed by the putrid stench of its breath, which stank of rotting pork, mud, and swamp water. The vine grew thicker around him, the pain sending tears streaming down his face. Stars fizzled and popped in the brownish-black murk of Isaac's vision, which was when a scream filled the air around him, one that was vile, a sound he didn't know a person could make.

This was his scream.

The worm exploded. Slime rained upon Isaac as the head of the worm slid down and around his vine-cage without a body attached to it. He could look up through the vine and worm head and see the roof of the cave in the dim light. He couldn't bring himself to look at his arm, though. He was sure it was gone.

Elise screamed his name, others shushed her, and all while Boar was saying, "Oh my! This is terrible! This is all terrible!" Isaac heard everything as if he were sinking underwater.

He needed to move. He needed to get out of there, vine or no vine.

His whole body trembled as he made himself look.

His arm was still there. Mostly. It was too dark to see the full damage, but it was lumpy and bent in ways it really shouldn't have been. There were multiple stems protruding from his forearm and shoulder. He didn't have to be a medic to know that this wasn't good. He'd seen arms amputated for less.

So, the arm was there, but probably not for long. His blood rippled down strings of flesh that hung like torn fabric, splattering on the ground like raindrops from a roof.

It wasn't good at all.

"Isaac!" Elise floated above the worm head with a ball of light, her face covered with tears. Isaac couldn't get to his feet because of the weight of the vine-cage, but with a swift movement of Elise's hand—and a new stab of pain for Isaac—she broke through it. Once she reached him, she tore him free of the cage and carried him out in her arms. He was in too much pain and far too weak to protest being carried off in the arms of a woman. In fact, it was kind of nice.

She landed next to the group. Isaac's legs shook like tree saplings in a storm as he stood. He felt detached from them, from his whole body, from the puddle of blood forming at his feet. Those weren't his legs. That wasn't his blood.

No. He wasn't even there. He could almost see the snow falling, soft and gentle, touched by a breeze.

That's quite a lot of blood.

As if it were coming from another plane of existence, he thought he heard Boar say, "I've never seen anything like that before. It's all terrible. But they're terrible. Oh, I wish it hadn't come to this, though."

Boar was talking a lot. It made sense to Isaac, however. Everyone panicked in their own way.

Isaac's heart pounded in a steady, frantic beat underneath all the noise. All the screaming and talking was surely going to awaken more—

And there they were.

Worms.

Giant, screaming worms emerged from the dark rooms.

This was it. It was a way of death so frightening and terrible that, until yesterday, he hadn't even imagined it possible, yet here it was.

It's a good thing Thipka made Annabel stay at the wharf.

A bright light engulfed Isaac. He had to shield his eyes with his good arm, wincing from Rain's punch to it earlier. His gaze fell on the source, finding it to be human-shaped and made from grains of shifting sand.

No, wait. Thipka was changing his form.

No, wait. That wasn't Thipka. Thipka was over there, watching with sad eyes and wearing an almost bored expression as if he'd seen this all before.

What emerged from the light was a violet-blue, human-like monster with Rain's face but with tall, thin ears, a large chest, a long tail with a webbed, fan-like thing at the end—

And *wings*.

Of course he had wings.

Rain let out a dark, off-pitch roar, sending waves of terror through Isaac's bones. New-Rain stretched his arms out to an unnatural length, merging them with his wings. And with a gust of air, he took flight.

Nothe shouted, "Rain, *no!*"

Rain flew at the closest worm's open mouth, and it closed over him. Another worm lunged past it toward them as Nothe shot at both worms, his light-gun seeming to do nothing except make them angrier.

Isaac did the only thing his very human and powerless self knew to do. "Elise!" he shouted. "Blow them up!"

Isaac didn't understand why the terror on Elise's face seemed to grow at his words.

Boar jumped in front of his charging relative and tried to reason with him. "Stop! They're only defending themselves. If you would just listen—"

But the worm had no interest in listening. He screamed at Boar and bit him, his hook-like teeth digging into Boar's neck.

Thipka dropped his walking stick and held his hands out. With a twist and flex of his fingers, he pulled light from the darkness around them, gathering it near his chest and forming it into a ball in his hands. He flung the light at the worm attacking Boar, blowing it up into chunks and blood as Isaac, Nothe, and Elise cried out, "Whoa!"

There was a loud pop and a shower of heavy blood. The ground shook with a thud as the worm that had eaten monster-Rain collapsed on the ground with a large hole in the back of its neck. Rain climbed out of it, covered in grossness, and fell to the ground. Isaac swore the glow of his eyes had all but vanished.

"Well," said Isaac. "That's one way to do it."

Deafening, rage-filled screams echoed up the hallway from more worms. Rain struggled to his feet, his eyes, nose, and ears bleeding. He stumbled toward the army of worms, determined to destroy more of them even though he clearly wouldn't survive it.

But then the worms stopped. Their heads turned away from them, staring at something farther down the hall.

A bright light advanced up the hallway. Very bright, reminding Isaac of the stories he'd heard from people who'd nearly died and swore they'd seen Heaven. A howling emanated from it, hollow and haunting. The light washed over the worms, dividing into transparent figures that swirled around them as the howling grew louder.

The worms let out a different kind of scream then, one of pure fear. Many of them cried, "Spirits!" "They've come for us!" as all of them retreated to the safety of the nearest rooms.

Once the path before them had cleared, Isaac saw a small figure walking toward them.

Annabel.

How on Earth did she get there?

Thipka's eyes widened in horror. He grabbed his walking stick and ran toward her, scooping her up into his arms. He shouted over his shoulder—at almost the exact same time as Boar—"We have to leave, *now!*"

They followed Boar, who was bleeding from the awful bite on the back of his neck, toward a group of windows. Isaac limped only a few steps in agony before giving in and letting Elise carry him again, and Nothe half-carried Rain on his shoulder. Boar directed them toward a hot, flat rock. "Now you, sit there." Isaac sat there. "And you—no, don't sit there; you'll regret it terribly. Scoot that way. Now, I have to be in the middle here. Ugh, that pushes you too close to the edge. That won't work out well for you. Why don't you two climb on my back?"

Isaac turned to Nothe and Rain to translate and had to stop for a moment and blink. Rain's face was covered in blood. Some of it was worm blood, but there was an unsettling amount that was clearly coming from his eyes, nose, and ears. Honestly, he looked like he had some sort of terrible illness and was about to tip over and die at any second. Nothe's lips were fused together like he'd just eaten something very sour.

After Isaac had gathered his thoughts, he told them, "He wants you two to climb onto his back."

They did. It was difficult for Rain to do, but he did it. Thipka clung to Annabel, the angle stretching the neck of his shirt and revealing a strange, sunburst scar across his chest and a long necklace chain that held two rings. He complained, "This is taking entirely too long."

"What did he say?" asked Boar.

Isaac had a feeling that being a translator was going to get very old, very fast. "He said to hurry."

Boar was offended. "Tell him I can only work as fast as you guys move!"

Isaac turned to Thipka. "He says it's your fault it's taking so long."

"Now, nobody move," said Boar. Before Isaac could translate, they were thrown out of the volcanic mountain by molten lava on an absurdly massive bed of rock.

As they soared through the air, Isaac swore he saw a spaceship landing on the beach of the island. Then again, he could've been hallucinating. He was probably dying, after all.

Good News

To say that Isaac was nervous about flying across the sea on a rock propelled by lava was an understatement. He was terrified. How were they not supposed to die the moment it collided with the beach?

Oh well. It was better than being slowly digested by a giant worm. At least that part was over.

Isaac's good arm instinctively covered his head as the bed of rock landed with an explosion of sand. His body remained on the rock slab somehow with the first bounce, but when the second bounce smacked against mud and bushes, he was thrown into some tall grass, landing on his back in a soft bed of cool moss and soggy bark.

Which was lucky. He tried to savor the moment, despite the excruciating pain he was in. That kind of good fortune surely wouldn't happen again.

The moment was short-lived. His eyes burned with tears of agony. His arm felt as though it'd been snapped in multiple places over someone's knee and then ripped into strips of bacon while still attached to his body. Maybe it would hurt less if it was removed. Just taken right off.

He really didn't want to do that, though.

Oh, but it hurt so much.

His heart pounded in his chest as if it were trying to break free. But as he stared up at the clear blue sky painted with soft wisps of clouds, and inhaled the clean scent of grass and sulfur-free air, his heart calmed. It beat at an almost normal rate. His brain slowed and attempted to reflect on all that had just happened, counting how many times it had come close to death within the last two hours.

Now that all the excitement had faded, he was acutely aware that his hip and ankle were also in pain, the kind that would've consumed all his thoughts—if it wasn't for his arm. He hadn't thought such pain was possible. His vision spun as if he were being swung around in the air by his feet. He'd lost a lot of blood.

Also, Annabel had brought a bunch of ghosts to the island. That was odd.

Isaac closed his eyes and a few tears escaped. He was tempted to look at his arm in the sunlight.

He couldn't. His eyes were closed.

It was peaceful here.

Elise called his name. "Isaac? *Isaac!*"

Footsteps rushed through the tall grass.

"Maybe he's over here," Nothe said from some distance away.

Isaac wiped away the tears that had gotten away from him and mustered a deep breath. "Over here!"

The footsteps grew closer. Elise shouted, *"Isaac!"*

A gigantic, slimy rope wrapped around Isaac's waist, and, with a startled cry, he was hoisted into the air.

It was Boar. "There you are," he said, looking Isaac over. "You gave us a bit of a scare there, friend. Sorry for the rough landing. It's been a while since I last drove one of those things."

How does one drive a great big rock on lava? Isaac wondered. Also, a giant worm was holding him in the air like a doll and had just called him "friend." That was something he'd certainly never known he'd wanted to accomplish in life. "It's fine...f-friend," said Isaac.

The corners of the flaps of Boar's mouth turned upward a little as though he were smiling.

Everyone—except for Rain, who was in the distance, bleeding and looking as though he might vomit at any moment—ran toward Boar.

Boar carefully sat Isaac down. Isaac's leg buckled as he put weight on his hip and ankle, and he collapsed back to the ground, which was terribly painful.

Yes. Those were broken. Most certainly.

Elise rushed forward and knelt beside him. She looked at the others, her eyes pleading though her voice was demanding, like the old Arnaud's would've been. "We have to help him."

She took Isaac's mangled arm. With a surge of agony, he ripped his arm away from her, and it flopped onto his chest, misshapen, bruised, with strips of flesh, vine, and coat hanging from it. It was about as bad as he imagined. *"Don't touch it!"*

"Let me see your hand."

Isaac's chest constricted. "No."

"I'm going to fix it," she insisted impatiently.

He was afraid to hope. "Fix what?"

Her eyes widened with an annoyance that screamed a silent, *Really?!* "The vine in your arm. Just—" She took his wrist—what was left of it, anyway—with considerable strength, and he cried out in agony. "Give me your hand."

Could she take the vine out of his arm without making things worse or killing him? He really enjoyed having an arm, with or without a vine in it. He'd like to keep it if he could. He also enjoyed not being dead. He'd like to eat turkey and mashed potatoes one last time.

He watched as she gazed down at his mangled hand. "Are you sure it's a good idea to do this right now?"

"Shush, Isaac."

"Don't shush me."

"Isaac, *really*." She closed her eyes.

That's a terrible thing to do. You can't see anything with your eyes closed!

He was about to point this out when a searing pain in his forearm silenced him. It burned at the places where the vine touched. The fire spread up to his shoulder with the otherworldly sensation of something writhing under what remained of his flesh. Tears stung his eyes, and a scream ripped through him as the vine wriggled, tearing tissue apart as it exited his wrist, dripping with his blood.

Elise tossed the vine into the bushes. Isaac's last conscious thought was, *Wow. That hurt so much more than when she planted it.*

His eyes opened to the stars. His heart leapt with hope for a fleeting second until he realized the sky held no familiar constellations, there was a giant planet off to the right of his vision, and his mouth tasted like old blood.

Nothe's grinning face popped into view. He no longer wore his helmet or armor but was back in his strange pajama suit. "He lives!"

Isaac closed his eyes. "Oh no."

"What?" said Nothe. "I thought you'd be happy about that."

"I'm thrilled," said Isaac, and although his weary tone didn't show it, he meant it.

"I also fixed your arm," Nothe declared with pride. "Good as new."

That was good news. In fact, he would daresay that was *wonderful* news.

Isaac opened his eyes again and sat up slowly, gazing down at his arm, his coat and shirt shredded and stained with blood. It burned a little, but it was a pleasant sort of burning, not like the raging inferno of Hell he'd experienced earlier. He opened and closed his palm, rotated his shoulder. There was no pain.

He was free. He was *free*.

The dark, heavy burden he'd been carrying was lifted from the very bones in his chest and shoulders. He was overwhelmed with gratitude, with hope. His eyes filled with tears that spilled down his cheeks. He looked up at Nothe. "Thank you."

How could those words possibly convey the depth of his gratitude?

He grabbed Nothe and hugged him. Nothe froze, clearly confused, before finally patting Isaac's shoulder. Isaac let go before it could get too awkward, but he clapped his now-healed hand on Nothe's shoulder and looked him square in the eyes, hoping he could at least feel a fraction of just how much Isaac meant it when he said again, "Thank you."

Nothe's mouth fell open. He looked as though he'd never heard the phrase before. Nothe's eyes darted around a little as if he were searching the ground for words of his own before finally tossing what he'd found at Isaac. "You're welcome."

Isaac wiped his face and admired his good-as-new arm. "How'd you do it?"

Nothe shrugged. "Oh, energy and all that stuff." Subtle, black lines beneath his eyes were highlighted by dark circles. He let out an exhausted sigh.

Isaac nodded. "All right." He probably wouldn't have understood it if Nothe had explained it, so he decided he didn't have to. All Isaac had to understand was that he'd been given a gift—another chance.

He looked around for Elise. A fire burned on the beach some distance away. Boar, Gof, and Annabel, and what could've only been Thipka and Rain, were all asleep beside it. The massive crescent planet in the sky illuminated the bed of grass arrayed around Isaac.

But no Elise.

"Where's Elise?" Isaac asked.

"Well, she was here for a while, but then she got all weird for no reason and went that way." Nothe pointed toward a group of trees behind him.

"For no reason?"

"Yep." After a short pause, he blurted, "All I did was mention that— you know—that you can pretty much leave whenever you want now, and then I might've asked why she wouldn't answer your question about the party—and I was *very nice* about it, by the way—and told her that her secret would be safe with me—"

Isaac's heart tripped over itself, though he wasn't sure why. "Did she tell you?"

"Well, if she did, I wouldn't tell you because I am *the* master-secret-keeper." There was another moment of silence. "But no. She didn't tell me. She went that way." He gestured to the trees again. "And I'm just..." He put his head in his hands, rubbing his eyes with his palms. Isaac thought he felt a wave of concern and regret radiate from Nothe for a moment, but it was so brief he decided he must've imagined it. Nothe continued, "I'm so bored, and I can't sleep, and she was insisting you rest here comfortably, which is totally unsafe. I guess it's because you were so close to death or whatever. She wouldn't let anyone touch you, and we can't just leave you out here.

"So anyway, I was bored and asked her about the party and why she was getting upset—like, did it have to do with being a gross old man once? There's nothing wrong with that—and then," he sighed like he was confessing a great sin to a priest, "*that's* when she left. I guess she didn't want to talk about it. Or maybe she had to go to the bathroom or something because that was a while ago."

"So, you've been sitting here watching out for me since she left?"

"Well yeah. Someone had to."

Isaac couldn't believe his kindness. He struggled to find words to express how much it meant to him, but nothing would suffice. All he could muster was, "I'm truly in your debt."

Nothe seemed taken aback by this at first but then said matter-of-factly, "You are."

Isaac smiled. He looked at the trees Elise had allegedly fled to. "So that way, then?"

"Yeah."

Isaac got to his feet, his hip and ankle good as new.

As Isaac headed toward the trees, Nothe said, "Scream if you need anything. I'll be around."

Decisions, Decisions

Isaac had forgotten to ask for one of those flameless torches.

Oh well. They probably wouldn't have let him borrow one anyway. Well, Nothe might've.

It was all right, though, really. With planet Sam glowing down on him, lighting the night sky like early dawn, it wasn't too difficult to navigate his way. He only tripped a couple of times. Elise hadn't gone far. He followed a soft orange light and found her sitting at the base of a tree with an arm resting on her knees, rotating familiar orange gems through her fingers.

They were the same gems she'd used to hypnotize him. He stopped at the sight of them, a rage burning through his veins, shoving out any other emotions he'd had before he'd come out there. With the balling of his fists, deep breaths, and the gritting of his teeth, he managed to keep himself under control.

She appeared relieved to see him at first, but then she must've noticed the expression on his face. She looked at the gems and tucked them away into her dress, out of sight.

"What are those things, *really?*" Isaac demanded.

Elise shrugged. "I've had them since before I came to Earth. I'm not sure how they work. I just look at them, and they calm me. They show me things I want to see and make them feel real." Tears filled her eyes, and she blinked them away, forcing a smile. "They don't quite have the *exact* same effect on humans. Obviously."

With another surge of anger, Isaac reflected on how he and his crew had reacted to them. "No. Obviously not."

She looked into the shadows of the forest, unable to meet Isaac's glare. Tears streamed down her face, glistening in the planet-light. "You know, usually when a person goes off by themselves, they want to be alone."

Isaac took another deep breath and let it out slowly. She may have been horrible, but she was still a woman, and she was crying, which made him uncomfortable. He didn't know what to do, but he felt like he should do something. He folded his arms and glanced over his shoulder in the direction of the camp. "Don't you think you're overreacting a little? Nothe told me what he said, and I'm pretty sure he meant well."

She groaned. "Just stop. Talking."

He did. He stood there, looking around, listening to the chirping of what he hoped were harmless insects, like crickets.

"Don't just stand there, either!" Elise snapped, making Isaac jump.

"Well, Highness, what would you like me to do?"

"I thought when I said that I wanted to be alone, that would be clear enough."

"You didn't say that *you* wanted to be alone. You said that when people go off by themselves, *they* want to be alone—"

"Yes! Precisely!"

"Right, so you want me to leave then?"

"Yes, Isaac. Go *away!*"

"Fine!" He turned to leave, feeling stupid. What was it again, exactly, that he had been hoping for when he came out here? He really didn't know for sure, but he hated himself for whatever his hopes had been. He really didn't want Elise to be the girl from the party—the girl of his dreams. It would mean the girl of his dreams had turned out to be a murderer who'd put a vine in his arm in order to control him, and that was unforgivable. It would ruin the beautiful illusion he'd just gotten back by showing that it was simply that: an illusion.

He hated Elise for what she'd put him through, for prompting him to come out into this darkness looking for her, for bringing back the hope and pain of the memory of the girl at the party.

"Wait," she called, stopping him.

Isaac's head fell back, exasperated. He'd already made it halfway through the brush, and now he had to turn around and return to where she was sitting.

"What?" He gazed down at her, surprised to see how much her expression had fallen. Her eyes were downcast, her beautiful face weighed down with a surrender that hurt him somehow. She wrapped one arm tightly around herself and pressed a hand against her mouth as if it could help her hold back tears.

He didn't know what to think of that or of the fact that she wasn't saying anything even though she seemed to want to. He didn't know what to think of any of it, really. He asked her, "Why did you do it? Why did you let me go?"

She swallowed and turned away again as she wiped her face. "Well, you were dying, ya?" she said in an "of course" sort of way. "Which you weren't supposed to do. I didn't think the vine would ever do that. I really didn't think it would be that bad. It was just supposed to scare you. I was desperate. I'm sorry. I just needed your help. I'm so sorry." She balled her hands in her hair and buried her face in her arms.

How *dare* she put him through that? Which was worse: fake-threatening to kill him or actually threatening to kill him? He wasn't sure.

She wiped her face again, then cradled her arms. When she spoke, her voice was defeated, broken, and barely more than a whisper. "You were never mine to keep."

She leaned against the tree, closing her eyes as fresh tears streamed down her face. She whispered, "Please go away."

ISAAC FOUND NOTHE STILL AWAKE, sitting next to a sleeping Rain near the campfire and poking embers with a large stick. The light from the flames emphasized the bags under his eyes. They looked red and bloody. Worry pierced Isaac at the sight, but he kept it to himself.

Nothe looked up at Isaac. "No luck?"

"I found her," Isaac sat next to him. "She just needs some time, I think. Don't worry, I don't think it has anything to do with you."

Nothe's shoulders relaxed at this news. "So now that you're free, what are you going to do?"

He honestly didn't know what he was going to do. Should he stay, or should he run far, far away from these people?

He looked down at his vine-free arm. This whole time, his goal had been not to die. Ironically, the vine had kept him from being eaten by a giant worm—that was not lost on him. It'd saved his life in the end. It'd also destroyed his arm and probably would've killed him eventually, but still, he'd be dead for certain without it.

Now the imminent threat of death had been taken away. He was truly free. But he'd been left on a weird moon-planet that he knew absolutely nothing about. On Earth, he was familiar with the sea. He was familiar with vegetation and animals from different coasts that were good for food, for survival. But here?

Maybe he could figure it out. He'd made it this far, after all.

But did he want to stay *here*? Really? Had he come this far down the great, fabled river, to only come *this* far?

He felt that pull in his chest again, the one he hadn't wanted to look at too closely. He had to look at it now. It was clear and honest, and he couldn't look away. And it forced him to admit something he hated, so much so that it made him a little nauseous. He had to accept that, while Elise had dragged him here with these people, under threat of death, maybe he needed—even wanted—to stay with them awhile longer.

It was true. He *wanted* to stay. He was on an adventure greater than he ever could've dreamed of with a couple of folks he'd even grown to like. And while no one back home would ever know this, while his name would be forgotten among them—it didn't matter. It didn't matter at all. His life had become greater than notoriety or fame. It'd become greater than treasure. It'd become something that was exciting, that gave him hope. What started off as a tragedy had morphed into something absolutely wonderful.

Part of him hated that. Part of him loathed admitting that something that had started so horribly had led here, camping on a moon—which was far better than he ever could've dreamed.

But wasn't there something so soothing and comforting in that as well? To know that life didn't have to end at the tragedy, that something magnificent could grow from ashes?

He glanced over at Nothe. He liked Nothe. So far, he was as good as the best men he'd met on Earth and was the closest thing to an ally he had. Thipka was odd, but he was all right. He even had come to like Annabel. She could summon spirits. He needed to know more about that.

Was he really willing to give these good things up?

No. No, he wasn't.

"Well, I've made it this far," Isaac finally said with a small smile. "I think I'd like to see where this goes for a little while longer."

Nothe smiled back and clapped his shoulder. "I approve of your decision."

As Isaac laid down on his leaf-bed, he couldn't help staring at the empty spot next to him where Elise had been the night before. She was much like the vine that had been in his arm: she was horrible, had destroyed so much, had caused so much pain—however unintentionally–yet he'd be dead for certain without her. He wondered if she would return. Not that he cared anymore.

But she couldn't just fly off the planet to wherever she was headed, could she?

Maybe she could. He wouldn't be that surprised. There probably wasn't a mean old man with a shield-thing keeping her from leaving.

Unless there was. Who was to say?

Not that he cared.

WINTER WONDERLAND

The volcanic island was more like a winter scene in a painting by the time Asael was done with it. He brushed frost from his sleeves as he descended the path toward his ship. He looked over his shoulder at the black, yawning windows now lined with icicles. The cone and surrounding scorched dirt and rock were covered in snow, and the worms inside were nothing more than ice sculptures.

Yes, he definitely preferred the look of the place now.

Asael had been introduced to the worms while acting as a scout for his father. They were such self-righteous pests, and they kept popping up all over the place. He knew there was a nursery at the core of the island, and when he found it, he saw several mother-worms. They hadn't charged at him. They'd been more interested in hiding the little ones behind them. When he realized Elise wasn't there, he left them alone. Even if they were pests, it was cruel and unnecessary to hurt any of them. He'd done his service. He'd rid the planet of the worst of the hive.

And soon, none of it would matter anyway.

He reached his ship and leaned against it. Exhaustion infected each cell in his muscles and bones while anger and fear burned in his chest, making it hard to breathe. His brain burned as though it were on fire. His father had told him to go here because Elise would be here—and where was she? His stomach sank as he realized he must've just missed her. Obviously, she had to have been with those creatures and the worm on the rock.

He'd assumed the worm had been trying to eat him, just as it was about to eat all the unfortunate creatures with it on the rock. That was the only reason worms ever flew on rocks. The thought had angered him, motivating him to rid the world of the hive.

He pounded his fist against the ship, then ran both hands through his hair. He was such an idiot. Of course she was on there. He should've *known* she was on there. His pulse quickened, and his fingers trembled.

But his father had said she was on the *island*. Since Asael hadn't brought her to him earlier, his father had been right in his head, telling him where to go. Asael was expected to trust him completely, to follow his every order with perfect exactness. He couldn't assume she was leaving on a rock with a worm. That was *not* where his father had said she would be. His father would've seen this. He would've told him.

Wouldn't he?

Was his father intentionally giving him bad orders? And just bad enough to make him doubt himself and feel terrible? Why would he do that? So he had more reasons to torment him? Haunt his dreams with the worst moment of his life? Probably. He certainly enjoyed doing that. He probably also wanted to make him feel foolish, to let him know he couldn't trust himself. Likely because his father knew, more than Asael wanted to believe, that his loyalty was drifting. This was his disgusting attempt to regain his control.

Or, maybe his father's madness was finally enfeebling his mind, and he'd made a mistake.

No. None of this was right. Asael was just an idiot. He should've known.

I should've known.

But the timing...he'd told him to be there right at that exact time, and it was just enough off...he swore he was finally seeing what his father had been doing to him all these years.

Or Asael was just an idiot. That was most likely the case. Perhaps he'd missed something his father had said.

For a moment, he felt as though he were floating above the snow.

His father would be furious.

Asael leaned his back against the ship, taking deep breaths, pressing his thumb into his palm, trying to calm himself.

He would fix this mistake. He would find them. He would not return to his father empty-handed. He would find *her.*

It would be all right. He would regain his strength and go after them. She wouldn't be going anywhere off-world anytime soon; he was sure of it. Not with that human tagging along.

He really shouldn't have drained himself freezing all those worms. They really hadn't left him much of a choice. And really, they had to go. They were gross and horrible.

But he was dreading his dreams.

What Planet Do You Come From, Anyway?

Isaac awoke that morning to Thipka some distance away, singing absently about "the greatest show" while Nothe and Rain muttered to each other. He fought waking, hoping that a few more hours of sleep would prevent the pain in his head from getting worse. But they wouldn't stop talking.

"He has a scar over his chest," muttered Nothe. "Did you see?"

"The sunburst scar," said Rain, sounding awful—the audible equivalent to how Isaac felt. Not only this, but his new voice was even deeper than usual; a slightly terrifying depth that Isaac had never heard before, as if the shadows in Sister Sarah's pantry had decided to contribute to the conversation. "It's difficult to miss."

"What are your thoughts on that?"

"I don't want to think about my thoughts on that."

"Right, because he's a Hassune."

"Right."

"And that would mean he's been called back from the dead before."

"Exactly. You've stated the very things that I don't want to think about, Nothe. Well done."

"It is a gift I have."

Wait, thought Isaac, being brought further into consciousness. *Called back from the dead? What?*

Oh heavens, he was completely unrested. He had the beginnings of what was sure to turn into the worst migraine in the universe, feeling as though an ax were being pushed into the left side of his skull by a sloth—a psychotic, murderous sloth with crazy eyes, which he could picture clearly and named Hugh. Isaac had to squint through the pain in order to see because whenever he tried to view the world like a normal person, the imaginary sloth—named Hugh—drove the ax into his head with greater force.

He closed his eyes and made no attempt to move. He proposed that maybe if he remained perfectly still, he could trick Hugh into thinking he was dead. He might go away if he thought he was dead.

But they kept talking.

"I don't get what your problem is with Thipka and why you hate thinking about these things," said Nothe. He didn't sound confrontational, really. It was more like he was sincerely curious.

There was silence for a moment. Wonderful silence. Then Rain said, "I'm not sure, either. Something about him…"

He never finished that sentence.

Isaac had to ask, his tone strangled, "What do you mean, 'called back from the dead'?"

They jumped a little. Rain looked annoyed. Nothe smiled and turned to Isaac. "Hey! Good morning, Isaac." He dropped his voice again. "Well, it's when someone returns to life after being dead. It's kind of a whole ritual, where you call out to their energy in the other dimension and ask them if they want to come back."

"They usually don't," grumbled Rain.

Nothe looked away. "It's kind of hard to explain the process."

Rain raised an eyebrow. "I think you just explained it."

"Huh. I guess I did." Nothe shrugged.

Isaac focused on what he understood. "So it's raising the dead?"

Nothe considered this. "That's a…a really awkward way to put it, but I guess it is."

"I thought you two said bringing back the dead was impossible."

Nothe looked at Rain. "I don't believe we said it was impossible—"

Rain shook his head.

Nothe continued, "—it just doesn't work the way Elise wants it to work. First of all, it's not a planet, it's dimensions. And then you need things, like a body."

"That is helpful," said Rain. "It's also helpful to have a body with a heart and veins to pump blood through."

"Yeeeah, that's kind of essential, actually. And the person who's died has to want to come back. You don't want to call someone back from the dead who doesn't want to come back, or you're going to get something… else. We've seen it happen before. It's really upsetting."

Rain added, "We try really hard to avoid it."

"At all costs."

Isaac nodded. Out of the blue, his heart ached a little. He wished he'd known these guys when his mother and Captain Snow had died. He wanted to ask more questions, but his head hurt too much and talking made him want to vomit.

"Well," said Rain, changing the subject. "There is still no sign of Elise."

Wait, thought Isaac. *Elise is gone?*

Isaac wasn't sure how he felt about this. He should've been relieved. Happy, even. But he felt nothing. He attributed his lack of brain function to Hugh. If Hugh hadn't been shoving an ax into his skull, he probably would've been able to think. *Curse you, Hugh!*

"But Isaac is still here!" said Nothe cheerfully.

"A lot of good that does us," grumbled Rain.

Isaac was in too much pain to be offended by that.

"Everything will be fine, just fine," said Thipka. Isaac could hear him rummaging around, likely packing things up. "Have a little faith."

There was a loud snort and a growl. It came from somewhere much, much closer to him than Rain's voice. A small splash of something slimy dripped onto Isaac's face with a gust of fish-smelling, hot breath, like that of a large dog's that'd just eaten garbage after drinking from a moldy pond. He squinted up into the face of Gof, whose large, curious eyes stared down at him with his tooth-and-drool-filled mouth—hanging open, as usual.

Hugh or no Hugh, Isaac leaped up with a startled yell and crawled backward away from the monster, wiping the slobber from his face with disgust.

"Calm down!" shouted Annabel, placing reassuring hands on Gof's furry arm. "He's not going to hurt you. I think he likes you for some reason. He can see souls so that probably has something to do with it."

Had he heard her correctly? He couldn't have.

Nothe, who was eating what looked like a burnt chicken leg, leaned toward Annabel, his brow furrowed. "Pardon?"

Annabel explained, "He likes souls."

Isaac would've raised his eyebrows had he been able to do anything besides squint and scowl at the searing, fiery agony splitting the left side of his skull. Luckily, Rain and Nothe raised theirs for him. Nothe said, "He likes...souls?"

Annabel shrugged, petting Gof's arm. Gof continued to stare at Isaac, unblinking. Annabel said, "He thinks they're interesting. And the more interesting, the better. He doesn't like the bad ones, though. They give him a nasty taste in his mouth."

Nothe blinked, his eyes widening a little. "Does he *eat* the souls?"

Annabel gave a look that said he couldn't have asked a more absurd question. "*No.* No one can *eat* souls. They're interdimensional."

It was adorable how she said "interdimensional." It was a lengthy word even in Theran, and she couldn't pronounce the syllables quite right, reminding Isaac that, while she was obviously exceptionally intelligent and had extraordinary abilities, she was still just a little girl.

Nevertheless, Isaac had to wonder how a soul was interdimensional. How did that even work? And why would that make them inedible?

And where did Elise go?

He couldn't think. The pain... Why was the sun there? Did it absolutely *have* to exist? Probably, although he couldn't think of any good reason for it at the moment.

"But then, how does he taste them?" Nothe asked, bringing Isaac back to the present.

Annabel thought about this. "It's like when you taste a smell, I think. You don't eat the smell, but you can still taste it."

Fair enough, thought Isaac, although there were certain areas of New York and London—and most certainly at the worm volcano— where Isaac could've argued he'd eaten smells before.

His heart slowed, and, as it did, the pain in his head overwhelmed his whole body, as if Hugh the imaginary sloth had multiplied and was now attacking him with axes all over. He bent over with nausea that pulled at his ribs, and he groaned with the pain.

Nothe asked, "What's the matter with you?"

"Hugh is attacking me," said Isaac.

Rain gave him a confused scowl. "What's a Hugh?"

It was too difficult to explain. Isaac settled on saying, "It's my head, I mean. I have a migraine."

Nothe said, "Oooh, okay. I guess I didn't give you enough blood yesterday."

Isaac squinted up at him. "What?"

Nothe knelt at his side. "Blood. Here." He rolled up his sleeve.

Isaac sat upright, still squinting. "What do you mean, 'blood'?"

Nothe smiled at him as if Isaac were being downright silly. "You know. My blood. How do you think I've been healing you?"

Isaac gave him a wary look. "Not with blood."

Nothe pulled a knife from a pocket on his absurdly tight pajama sleeve and began cutting his wrist.

Isaac's eyes widened. "Whoa! Stop that! Stop! What are you doing?"

Nothe looked up at Isaac. "You're a human, right? You use blood to heal."

"No! We don't!"

"You don't?" Nothe looked surprised. "Are you sure? Because on our world, you do."

"No! Why would you—?"

"Our blood heals things."

"You're joking, right?" He was going to puke. He gagged and heaved, then put a fist to his lips as if this would keep his stomach contents on the inside. He squinted at Rain and Thipka. "He's joking."

Thipka shook his head. Both Rain and Nothe looked more confused than Isaac felt.

"Why would I be joking about this?" asked Nothe.

Right before Isaac's eyes, Nothe's wound sealed shut. Nothe looked frustrated and cut it open again.

"Stop that!" Isaac reached out to grab the knife, but his depth perception was off, and he missed, what with his migraine and all.

Nothe lifted his bleeding wrist toward Isaac's face. "Here."

Isaac leaned away, gagging, really at a loss for words. He'd been in positions like this before—well, not exactly like this, but—meeting people who ate bizarre things in their different cultures. As he had in those situations, he cautioned himself to be as polite as possible. "No. No, thank you."

"Right. You probably prefer drinking it from something." Nothe turned to Rain, "Rain, be a dear and conjure up a vial, will you?"

"No, that *really* won't be necessary—"

"Oh, so you *do* want it straight from the arm?"

Isaac's stomach lurched again, heaving. This was a nightmare. "No! I really *don't* want *any* at *all*."

Nothe seemed genuinely perplexed. "You don't want any?"

"No! How is this—?" he said the words louder as if Nothe were suddenly hard of hearing, "No. Thank you."

Nothe turned to Rain, looking shocked. "He doesn't want any."

Rain also appeared shocked. "He doesn't want any?"

Nothe said, "The *human* doesn't want any." Nothe turned back to Isaac with a small smile, "Just to be sure—you *are* human, right?"

Isaac looked from Rain to Nothe. "Dear heavens, what do you think humans *are?*"

Nothe's wound had already healed again. He turned to Rain. "Ha! You owe me sixty tulos, Rain. I told you there must be humans like this out there somewhere."

Rain said nothing. He simply studied Isaac with a look that was difficult to read. But then his expression hardened. "It's probably because the idea is foreign to him. If he knew exactly what our blood does, he'd change his mind. He'd become like every other human."

"No," argued Isaac. "I don't—nope. No." He needed to stop talking. That was what the pain in his head and his stomach were telling him. He needed shade and to stop talking.

Nothe considered Rain's words, then declared, "Let's test that!" He turned to Isaac. "Our blood heals pretty much everything. You saw how my wound healed, right?"

Isaac nodded.

"Yeah, that's because of my blood. It wouldn't have healed like that if I had just any regular ol' blood. When other creatures drink our blood or put our blood in their veins with needles or whatever, it heals them. It reverses aging, cures disease, heals neurological damage, and clears plaque from the brain—"

Clears plaque from the brain? He'd never heard of anything like that, but it sounded terrifying.

Nothe went on, "You know, whatever! Basically, if you drink our blood every day, you could live indefinitely. Sounds pretty good, am I right?"

Isaac had to think about that. He knew that some cultures drank the blood of animals. They even made sauce and soup from it. Black pudding, for example. That was a popular one. He'd always found the idea rather repulsive. Were he starving to death on his ship, of course he'd have made an exception, but had he any other options—which he usually did—he'd pass, thank you. He'd just stick with turkey and potatoes.

However, if blood could grant him eternal youth, heal any wound, cure any disease he might catch (and surely he'd catch a few, what with traveling to different worlds and such), and even relieve his migraine, could he do it?

No. Because in this case, there was a clear difference. Rain and Nothe were not animals. They were basically human—just a far superior version. The thought of drinking their blood was beyond upsetting.

But the thought of death, of growing old and frail...

He thought of his mentor, the man he'd seen as a father, Captain Snow. Captain Snow had never resented his age, only how difficult it had become to tie knots because of the pain in his fingers. But he'd always pushed through his discomfort with humor and grace. It was the wear on his body over the years that had taken him in the end.

There was a certain dignity about that, about growing old with grace. There was nothing to fear or resent. It was a natural part of life. A badge of honor, really, a feat that not everyone was able to claim. And besides, Isaac had already outlived all his friends and loved ones. He couldn't bear the thought of doing that again and again. How could anyone? Living through that level of grief again and again endlessly...

Isaac simply didn't want to die before his time—before he'd gotten to *live*. That was all he wanted.

All this thinking was making his nausea worse. He needed to stop.

Nothe said, "You know, you really look terrible—"

Isaac blurted, "I s-suppose the idea of not getting old and falling apart has some appeal. But..." Where were the words? He could only think of, "No, thank you. I take pride in being a sailor who has run out of food a time or two and never eaten any of my crew." He was attempting a joke there, but he was very serious at the same time. He patted Nothe on the shoulder. "Thanks for the offer."

"They harvest us, you know," said Rain, seemingly out of nowhere. "Back on our world. Humans have factories where they breed us just for our blood. Just so they can live forever without any physical grievances. They make us suffer so they can live in comfort and have everything they want."

This made Isaac's head hurt more. He couldn't open his eyes all the way and could hear the rush of his pulse in his ears. At the same time, there was a numbness that extended to his fingertips that had nothing to do with his agony. The thought was so horrific that it was beyond his ability to grasp, yet it made his skin crawl as if the words had touched a distant, frightening memory.

No wonder Rain had thought him a monster and a coward. Isaac opened his eyes as far as they could go—which wasn't much—and held Rain's gaze. "I am not one of them."

Both Nothe and Rain's expressions softened as though they had been looking through the remnants of a broken, abandoned house and found a priceless artifact among the rubble.

Until Rain said, "But you're not a good person, are you?" He phrased it as a question that he already knew the answer to. Nothe gave him a *why-would-you-say-that?* sort of look.

Isaac laughed a little. "I've never pretended to be, have I? But I'm better than *that*, I know. That should tell you the level of people you were hanging around with." At this, he lost his strength and lay down on the sand, fumbling for a gigantic leaf nearby and pulling it over his head.

Nothe said, "He's here, isn't he? He doesn't have to be here, and yet, there he is. That's saying something."

"Please. He's not here out of the goodness of his heart. He's here because he's a *coward*. He knows he can't get off this planet without us. Humans are vile and worthless monsters that are incapable of doing anything unless it caters to their own needs or whims. They're celyg."

Nothe turned to Isaac's veiled form to answer the question he didn't ask. "Celyg are these tiny, slimy insects that kinda look like poo and live at the bottom of ponds. They kill things by drinking their bloo—you know what? Never mind. You don't need to know."

Rain smirked. "He knows he's got no chance out there on his own."

Isaac was growing increasingly offended. "Uh, rude. I'm actually pretty good at surviving."

Thipka interrupted. "All right, all right. Enough of this. I'm in a hurry."

Nothe shook his head. "That Thipka. Always in a hurry."

Isaac really didn't feel like moving, so he didn't. Maybe he could catch up later—probably not. But Elise wasn't back yet—not that he cared, because she was horrible. Still, he should stay for a bit, so he could at least say he tried. He lifted the leaf a little to announce his plan when his gaze focused on something floating just above the surface of the ocean, something that was heading toward them at an incredible speed. As the thing drew closer, he thought he could see wings. In fact, he was certain he was looking at Elise.

He wasn't sure how he felt about that.

Nothe pointed at the ocean. "Do you guys see that?"

"See what?" asked Rain, turning to look. "Oh."

Isaac's eyes opened a little farther. "You see her, too?"

"Her?" asked Rain, confused. "I'm not sure what you're seeing, but I see a ship."

"Are you sure?"

Rain gave Isaac a funny look, which he didn't appreciate. Isaac gazed around the camp. Everyone had fallen silent. Even little Annabel watched the object approach with quiet curiosity and concern. And even the giant worm over there—

Oh. He was clearly hallucinating. There was a giant worm over there.

No, wait. That's right. The worm had come with them after the whole volcano-thing yesterday. He'd called Isaac "friend." He'd also had a terrible injury on his neck that now appeared to be completely healed.

My, his life had gotten very strange.

Gof was still staring at him, though. At least some things never changed.

The object flew over them, rustling their hair and the leaves of the trees. Isaac swore it was the same spaceship Snowman had been driving, but he couldn't be sure. He'd thought it'd been Elise only moments ago.

Isaac closed his eyes. He felt like he should be dying, but he wasn't. He would live through his migraine, and for a moment, that made him sad. The pain had no end in sight.

Nothe said, "Hey, wasn't that the same ship we saw in the portal?"

Rain looked concerned. "I believe it was."

"Hey Isaac, was that your buddy—?"

Isaac groaned. "I don't know. I don't know anything anymore."

"Oh, for heaven's sake," grumbled Thipka. He knelt beside Isaac and took his wrist. Warmth rushed up Isaac's arm to his head at Thipka's touch, filling his body with a very literal *light*. It was strange and alarming, yet he didn't pull away. There was something peaceful about the light, something wonderful that spoke of hope, that dismissed a heavy shadow from his mind and shoulders that he hadn't known was there. And in the light, the pain of his headache instantly disappeared.

It took only two or three seconds. Two or three seconds to be able to open his eyes to the blaring sun, to sit upright with perfect posture, to feel like going for a swim in the ocean, and feel optimistic again about the impending doom before them.

He blinked up at Thipka in stunned silence, feeling an overwhelming gratitude that he couldn't find words for. However, Thipka apparently didn't need to hear them. He gave Isaac a knowing smile, the ever-present-sorrow still twinkling in his kind eye, then clapped him on the shoulder, saying in a sing-song voice, "It's time, time, time to go." At that, he stood and walked away.

Rain and Nothe looked nearly as shocked as Isaac felt, which made no sense. It wasn't like they'd had a migraine that had been magically healed without the need to become a vampire.

All of them exchanged stunned blinks before Nothe rose to his feet. "Wait a minute." Nothe marched after Thipka. "Wait." He grabbed Thipka's arm, stopping him. "Wait. Okay. Just..." He appeared to be having difficulty speaking. "Wait. Okay. Wait. How did you do that?"

"I don't have time to explain it all right now," Thipka said. He turned away as he hollered, "You'll figure it out someday."

"Oh great!" said Nothe, annoyance seeping into his voice. "Right. Great. Good."

Rain stood beside him. "Very good," he said through a clenched jaw. "Right."

"Lovely answer."

Nothe threw out an arm. "Something to look forward to!"

Isaac rose to his feet, expecting to feel shaky and dizzy, but instead feeling rather exceptional, as if he'd had a great night's sleep followed by a breakfast of salted pork and biscuits. And potatoes and turkey, with turkey gravy.

My, how he missed potatoes and turkey.

Nothe asked, "So what do we do now?"

Thipka told them, "We fix my ship."

"Wait," said Isaac. "What about Elise?" He couldn't believe he'd just asked that.

Thipka marched on. He clearly wasn't worried.

Nothe and Rain exchanged a look. Rain said, "She was a tremendous help earlier."

Boar looked from Thipka—who continued walking away—to Isaac, looking as confused as a worm could look. "What are we doing, then?"

Annabel patted the worm gently, smiling up at him with compassion. She gestured at him to follow her. Gof stood protectively beside her, his gaze on the worm instead of Isaac for once. The worm slithered toward her hesitantly and then stopped, looking at Isaac.

Isaac watched Thipka with worry. He explained in Boar's language, "Well, Thipka there, wants to leave, and *is* leaving. However—"

Boar looked around. "What about the green fairy?"

Isaac shrugged. "We don't know where she is, I'm afraid."

Boar reached over and tapped Isaac's head with the end of his tail with surprising gentleness. "Don't be afraid, friend. I'll find her."

Boar slithered off toward the trees.

Annabel asked, "Where does he think he's going?"

"To find Elise, he says," explained Isaac.

Rain raised an eyebrow. "I wish him luck." He glanced in Thipka's direction. He couldn't be seen any longer for the trees. "I suppose we'll catch up with him later, then?"

"Should be easy," said Nothe. "Since we're so familiar with this planet and all."

"I know it like I know my own fist," said Rain, making a fist. But then, in all seriousness, he added, "Remind me again why we are letting him leave us? I'm having a difficult time remembering."

There was a cry. Boar appeared moments later, carrying a disheveled Elise in his tail with what could only have been a look of pride. "Found her. She was asleep in the trees over there. So silly." He sat her down.

"Thank you, Boar," Isaac said.

Annabel ran up to Boar and patted him. "Good job, Boar!" she said, grinning. Isaac swore Boar smiled at her, even though he didn't know what she said. She gestured at him to follow her, saying, "C'mon! We're being left behind! Hurry!"

Boar looked at Isaac, and Isaac said, "She wants you to follow her. I think she wants to be friends."

Boar's many eyes glittered. "She does? Really? Well, that's just so...*kind*." Was he tearing up? Before Isaac could say for sure, Boar took off, following little Annabel.

"All right," Rain said in an and-that-is-that sort of way, "let's go." He set off after Thipka with the march and speed of someone about to be stranded on the beach of an alien planet. Nothe followed shortly behind.

Elise couldn't seem to make eye contact with Isaac. She looked at his boots, squinted at the sky, and glanced at her hands as if looking at Isaac was like staring at the sun. She muttered, "Thanks for not leaving me behind. Getting to my home planet is very important to me."

Isaac nodded. "You don't say?"

They followed the others in silence.

It Would Always Be Lincoln

I saac caught on early that they weren't returning to Thipka's cave. The cave had been northwest of the wharf, and they were heading northeast. Thipka seemed to have other plans, which had something to do with fixing a ship—but not Rain and Nothe's ship.

"So, let me get this straight," Nothe had said, "just to clarify. When you said that we'd be fixing *our* ship, and we agreed to give *you* a ride, what you actually meant was, we'd be fixing *your* ship—"

Rain nodded. "That does seem right."

"—and you'd be giving *us* a ride. Is that correct?"

Rain stared at Thipka, his eyes alight with a vicious fire. "I'd hate for it to not be."

Thipka said, "That is right. My ship's bigger. It'll fit everyone."

Rain glared at him. "And we're just supposed to trust you?"

He didn't answer.

Despite the many red flags Isaac saw in the situation at the time, a strange wave of comfort had radiated from Thipka, tossing Isaac's worries out of his mind. He'd felt optimistic about the whole thing. Maybe Boar would be able to go with them after all.

But now, hours later, he grew concerned. The good feelings were gone. Why were they putting all their trust in this man?

In the sunlight, Isaac noticed something else. He couldn't stop staring at his hands and arms through his tattered sleeves. His skin was unblemished and perfect, like a hairy baby. There were no scars. None whatsoever. He checked his chest. He'd had a big one there from a fight in a tavern over who would win in a duel, Chester A. Arthur or Abraham Lincoln. The drunken debate grew heated, and Isaac wound up stabbed. He still felt he'd won that one, however. It was Lincoln. It didn't matter who he was up against; it would always be Lincoln. Yes, even against Washington.

And that was when he'd been stabbed.

He'd had so many other scars, and they all had stories. Every one of them. The piece of his finger that had been missing? Yeah, that was why you watched where you put your hands when handling the rigging.

Now, all the scars were gone. Maybe some people would be happy about losing scars. He wasn't. How was he supposed to remember all the stories now?

He understood Thipka a little better, being so desperate to remember things that he refused to heal. Thipka was a bit extreme, but still.

He supposed he'd be glad to have the scars gone from his feet; the ones he'd gotten after having frostbite removed from them when he was a child. He'd hated those reminders.

I suppose it's time for new scars, new stories.

His mind was also clearer than it had been in...he couldn't even remember when. It was as clear, bright, and optimistic as the sky above him, despite his frustration and disappointment over the missing scars. He didn't know what to do with it. It was strange not having storm clouds flowing through his brain on a constant loop. They were just gone. In fact, whatever their circumstances might've been, he felt sure things would somehow work out. It was bizarre. Was this a permanent thing?

It was going to take some getting used to.

It was a lot like the last time he'd been healed, only better. And this time, he wasn't seeing light around everything. He was grateful for that, but at the same time, he couldn't help but wonder why that was different. Perhaps this round was just an improvement on every level.

Annabel walked ahead of him, singing a song about a haunted church in what must have been her native tongue. She had a soft, sweet voice, like an angel at Christmas.

Isaac smiled. "I like your song."

She grinned, surprised. "I made it up. It's about ghosts."

"I know."

She studied him. "How do you do that?"

"Do what?"

"Speak all of these languages?"

He realized he was speaking her strange language. It was the most elegant one he'd heard so far. He admitted, "I'm not sure. Some man..."

He didn't know how to explain it. How could you explain something you didn't understand yourself? "He gave me the gift."

The idea clearly didn't make sense to her. "How did he do that?"

Isaac shrugged. "I don't know. I've wondered that myself."

She furrowed her brow, thoughtful.

"And I noticed that you speak many languages, too," Isaac said.

"Yeah, but I have to learn them the hard way." She sounded a little bitter about that.

Isaac chuckled. He had to ask, "Did you summon a bunch of ghosts to help us?"

She shrugged. "They like me." She glanced ahead at Thipka, who was still leading the march. "I got in big trouble for it. Thipka told me to *stay put*." She mimicked Thipka's tone in a way that made Isaac chuckle again.

Isaac confessed, "Well, I, for one, am glad you didn't listen to him because otherwise, we'd probably all be dead."

Annabel beamed at him.

Isaac had another question. "How in the world did you get there?"

She looked uneasy. "I didn't steal a boat if that's what you're asking. I got a ride."

"From who?"

She shrugged again. "He didn't say his name, really. He just said he was The Prophet."

Isaac stopped. "What?"

She stopped, turned toward him, and spoke louder as if she'd been told Isaac was mostly deaf. "He said he was The Prophet!"

Isaac leaned away from her as though he'd been pushed over by the wind. He nodded and said, "All right," and then they resumed their walk.

It couldn't be the same Prophet he and Elise had met on Earth who'd given him the ability to know so many languages. Could it?

No. Of course not. This was a completely different planet.

Still. There was something about those words that made his very bones feel uneasy. It didn't help that he kept having those strange dreams.

He wondered if this revelation had anything to do with Thipka's sudden and ornery death march into the woods. He did seem very angry at everything. He was currently glaring at the trees at the top of the hill ahead of them, which were apparently moving very offensively in the wind.

Isaac was sure he was reading too much into things. It couldn't possibly be the same man. Perhaps "The Prophet" was a popular title on this world.

Isaac said, "This Prophet you speak of. What did he look like?"

She shrugged. It appeared to be her favorite move. "Like you, I guess. But brown, with patches of gray hair."

"Huh." That sounded familiar.

He didn't like that at all.

Isaac asked, "Do you think he's still back at the island?" Not that he had any intention of finding him.

"Probably not. He kind of just sort of disappeared after dropping me off. It was strange. Almost like one of the ghosts. But he wasn't a ghost."

From behind them, Nothe said to Rain, "Perfectly engaging conversation, don't you think?"

Rain's eyes were still bloody, and his shoulders and wings were slumped, his tail dragging along the ground. One arm was slightly lighter in color than the other. Isaac hadn't noticed that before. Rain walked as though his feet were made of bricks. "Riveting."

"Why can't it always be like this?"

"If only it could be. I think I'd be far less angry if I never understood anything anyone said."

"Too true. It would be rather blissful, wouldn't it?"

Rain nodded and hummed in agreement.

"Not a care in the world," said Nothe.

"So much stress lifted from the shoulders."

"Yes! Those knots back there, they'd finally disappear."

Rain put a hand to his back. "I really get them in my lower back, right here, where the ribs meet the spine. They're just terrible."

"Well, if all conversations were like this, Rain, you'd never have to worry about them again."

Rain smiled wistfully, which was unsettling and sad with his eyes like that. "That would be quite lovely."

Isaac wasn't sure what to make of their conversation, but he was fairly certain they were more annoyed than serious and felt the need to tell them, "Annabel is telling me about the man who gave her a ride to the island with her ghost friends."

They both made a big to-do about this as if he'd just offered them a platter of exotic bread and butter. Nothe said, "Dear Isaac, that was just —there really wasn't a need to go *so far* out of your way to explain what's happening to little ol' us."

Rain added, "We certainly don't want to trouble you."

"No, never!"

"I was being generous, wasn't I?" said Isaac. "Since we were having a private conversation and all."

"And now you know the joy of giving!" said Nothe. He nudged Rain. "What would this man do without us?"

Rain smiled with pride. "Why, I believe we've made him a better human."

"Indeed."

Isaac sighed and looked away, rubbing his forehead.

Nothe asked Annabel in Theran, his tone muted as though he'd entered a chapel, "So what's with Thipka and his unhealthy obsession with all the 'Save Thems'?"

"I don't know," said Annabel. "He's been obsessed with that ever since my people found him and fixed him up."

Isaac nodded to this. "Huh. Where are your people now?"

"Around," she said, as though this one word made everything perfectly clear. She grinned. "They thought Thipka was crazy, but now they know better."

Isaac wondered how that was possible since they hadn't bumped into any of them. Perhaps they'd visited while he was unconscious.

Nothe clearly wasn't over the "Save Thems." He asked, "So, who is Thipka, like, *saving?*"

Isaac noticed Elise clearly eavesdropping now. It was something they were all wondering.

Annabel shrugged. "Don't know for sure. He won't talk about it. But I think I know who some of them are, and I'm pretty sure I'm right."

Silence followed this as everyone waited for her to elaborate. She didn't. Nothe prompted, "And?"

She shrugged again. "It's the same people he's trying to steal time for."

Rain looked like he might retch.

Isaac had to ask, "And who are they?"

"I can't tell you that!" she snapped. "I promised I wouldn't tell, and I *keep* my promises." She stuck her little nose in the air and scurried away.

All right then, thought Isaac, amused and annoyed at the same time.

Isaac looked back over at Elise and followed her concerned gaze toward Boar, who had stopped. They had reached the top of a hill, which gave them a heavenly view of the island out in the sea. It looked like a glistening, white mirage in the haze and colors of the rising sun, almost like it had snowed there. Boar's eyes were fixed on it.

It hit Isaac that, judging by the reactions of Boar's relatives—not to mention the deaths among them—it was very likely he would never be able to return to his home. As the seconds passed without Boar speaking or even flinching, Isaac was sure this was on his mind. Isaac's heart went out to him. He couldn't bear to imagine being unable to return home. It was a fear that slunk around in the shadows in his mind, and he preferred ignoring it.

Isaac approached Boar, hesitated, then placed a hand on his side. "Are you all right?"

Boar broke his gaze away from the distant island and looked down at him. "I am. I'm better than I've ever been. They can keep their empty treasures."

Isaac wasn't sure he believed him. There was a tremor in the worm's soothing tone.

He went on, "I just had to look back, just this once, since I know I will never look back again."

Rain and Nothe studied Boar with eyes full of sorrow as if they'd understood every word he'd said and all the unspoken things in between. Thipka had stopped and looked back at him with profound sadness. This time, they didn't need a translation. Elise studied the grass near Isaac's boots with worry.

Isaac explained, just in case, "Boar was just saying goodbye to his island." He was about to repeat this to Annabel, but she was smiling at a bizarre, misshapen butterfly-like creature the size of a dinner plate. She giggled as it touched her nose and flew away.

Nothe Has Something to Say

Nothe and Rain didn't speak much the rest of their trek. Nothe studied everyone around him and observed that nobody else did, either. A weary, thoughtful silence had fallen over the entire group.

Well, except for Thipka, who went back and forth from muttering "save them" under his breath to singing songs no one else knew. It was all very awkward.

At least it only lasted for several hours.

Elise wasn't talking to Isaac, and Isaac refused to speak to Elise, seemingly preferring to fix his attention on his tattered coat and shirt sleeves, making them shorter and more functional. Poor Boar was somewhere else in his head entirely, emitting a steady wave of mourning, confusion, doubt, fear, and feeling lost. However, when Annabel grew exhausted, Boar noticed and placed her on his back, carrying her the remainder of the way.

Gof seemed happy, though. Nothe watched him stare at Isaac with his unblinking eyes, gradually moving closer and closer to him until he could pet his hair. It was amusing and a nice break from his fuming thoughts about Rain.

Rain was growing weaker and weaker with each step. At one point, Rain had fallen far behind the group, and, right before twilight, Nothe insisted they set up camp right there in the middle of a field of monstrous flowers.

No, really. They were monstrous. They varied from the size of small vehicles to the size of large houses. Not only this, but each one of them had an eye. Yes, one large eye in the center that all the petals were attached to, and each eye had long, stem-things that stuck out like lashes. While most of them stayed still, others watched them, blinking occasionally, their gazes following them as they passed by. When Annabel assured Nothe they were harmless, he clapped his hands together and said, "Great! We're stopping here."

Thipka growled, "That will take too much time."

Nothe insisted with a cheerful-threat sort of tone, "We're stopping. Here."

Elise glanced at Rain and little Annabel and agreed. "Yes, I think that's a good idea."

If the creature powerful enough to blow them all up thought it was a good idea, then it was settled.

Did Nothe worry that the flowers might eat them in their sleep? Sure. Who wouldn't? But Thipka had been pushing them at an unrealistic pace. Annabel was clearly exhausted, refusing to walk on her own anymore. And, worst of all, Rain was pretty much fighting death.

Because he had insisted on being stupid. Again.

Nothe'd had about enough of his stupidity. He was at the end of his rope. What? Was he going to have to babysit him constantly?

It wasn't right. It wasn't fair. Didn't he know? Didn't Rain have even a *clue* of what it would do to him if he died?

Did he even care?

As everyone settled in, Rain climbed to the top of a flower to hide and be alone. Nothe stared up at it, trying to ignore the two flowers to his right that were watching him. He didn't care that Rain wanted to be alone. He wanted to climb up there and scream at him, tell him how selfish he was. Did he seriously think he could destroy himself and not take anyone else with him?

Despite the pain that swarmed in his chest like a hurricane, he knew he was being unfair. He knew what Rain was feeling. He knew it well. He'd felt it himself.

He closed his eyes. Took a deep, calming breath. It was like trying to throw a blanket over a hurricane.

He climbed to the top of the giant, pink petaled flower. It smelled like a perfect night's sleep in springtime and dehydrated seaweed from the mossiest part of the ocean, all rolled in sugar. The humongous eye in the center squinted as Nothe crossed it, then glared at them as he sat beside Rain on the edge, near the base of a petal. They sat in silence for a while as Nothe ground his teeth, trying to push through his wild emotions and find the right things to say.

At least Rain's eyes weren't bleeding anymore. His face was clean. He just looked...old.

Rain sighed. It was the sigh of a large ocean wave crashing against a sandy beach, carrying with it the weight of a troubled sea. With it was released a torrent of pain—that of a heart ripped apart by despair—and a soul-deep exhaustion. The feelings washed over Nothe, draining him so much he couldn't bear the thought of moving. Even breathing itself was tiring.

Rain spoke then, his voice almost a whisper. "Don't you ever get tired, Nothe?"

"It happens. Usually around this time of day."

Rain closed his eyes. "Tired. Of the memories. They're so heavy."

Nothe didn't like talking about the memories. He looked between the petals at the ground far below their feet. "It happens. Usually around this time of day."

Rain grimaced. "I'm being serious, Nothe."

"No, I know you are. And *I'm* being serious. It's usually around this time of day. I mean, I dread sleep. I dread it because I know what the dreams can bring."

There was silence for a moment. "I can't do it anymore."

A mixture of panic and rage gripped Nothe's stomach, twisting it, but he kept himself together. "Do what? Sleep?"

Rain sighed. "I can't escape them. The memories. How I felt then. It's always there. And then I think I'm healing, it's getting better, and then—then it comes back. Right in my chest. And I'm back there again. Hollowed out again. Everything's been taken from me again, and I'm just empty. And when you feel like that, you believe that you *are* empty. When you're treated like a monster, you believe you're a monster."

Nothe understood this perfectly. The reminder made his insides twist and burn as if they'd been doused in acid. He nodded. "You get treated like a worthless, empty, discarded punching bag and called a monster enough..."

"You find yourself slinking into the shadows. And that's what you become. You become a shadow of what you once were and all you could've been."

Nothe closed his eyes. All his anger at Rain gave way to sorrow, and he could've wept. He wanted to reach out and touch his hand, embrace him, hold him, tell him how he felt. Tell him how much he understood. That he wasn't alone. That he loved him. He needed him. He was the only light he had that kept him alive in this world of despair. Rain kept his heart beating. He needed him to *stay*. And in his heart, he pleaded with him, *please, please stay*.

He wanted to tell him everything. *Everything*.

Maybe I should.

Perhaps it would change the world the way he wanted it to—a complete revolution toward something so wonderful that he'd only recently considered it possible.

But, most likely, it wouldn't.

No. Most likely, it would destroy everything. And where would that leave Rain? Who would take care of him then? He couldn't do it. He couldn't risk it. He couldn't say a word.

His fingers trembled. He balled his hands into fists to keep them hidden. He kept his emotions under control, buried and locked away within walls of concrete and metal. Keeping his voice steady, he said, "That's why people like us need someone to shine a light. To remind us of who we are, bring us back to life. I'm not going to give up on you, Rain. Not until I've done that. I believe that—"

Rain groaned. "I'm going to stop you there. You're not allowed to go on if you're going to talk about fate or how things happen for a reason or any of that nonsense."

"Well, I won't because I don't really believe that."

"I don't believe it at all. I think it's more simple than that. Things just happen. Terrible things. With absolutely no purpose, they just —*are*."

"But they're going to change you, you know? These things that happen. Regardless of whether or not they're given a purpose by the cosmos—"

"They're not."

"Right, but they're going to change you. And maybe—maybe they make you feel like you don't have a say in how they change you, but you do. You have a say. You can *give* your pain a purpose."

Rain scoffed at this and grumbled "purpose" under his breath. He clearly didn't care for that at all. "I just want to go home, Nothe."

Nothe looked at him. Heartbreak and weariness emanated from his friend even more now. It was written in every line of Rain's tired, aging face as he continued, "But I have no home because everyone who made it a home is dead. And this *anguish*—it's everywhere I turn and I...I'm so tired of trying to carry it. I'm so tired." He closed his eyes. When he opened them again, his expression had turned to stone. "They've cornered me," he pressed his fingertips against his temple, "in my mind. There is no other way out. Dying on my own terms...that is the only freedom I have."

Nothe's heart thundered in his brain. He shook his head. "So what, then? Are you determined to die for nothing?"

Rain smirked and looked away, annoyed.

Nothe considered his next words carefully, pouring his soul into each one. "You say your one thread of freedom is to die on your own terms—that is where you are *totally* wrong. You have freedom! You have the freedom to choose how you are going to let all of this affect you— how you're going to rebuild your life, what you're going to rebuild yourself to *be*. You could change everything by just changing the way you see your life. Look," he put a hand to his forehead, thinking, "imagine you were the most powerful being in the universe—say some god-like being with all the freedom and power to do anything you wanted, and you were thrown into a world like ours, this very same universe, just like you are now. What would you do then?"

Rain answered immediately. "I would change it."

Nothe nodded, his golden eyes wild and glowing. "Yes! Exactly. And you have that power. It's just more subtle. It's like," he searched for the words, "it's like the stars shining in the black sky. But what do people do when they're surrounded by darkness, and they see those stars? They *look*. They look, and they *feel* something. Those stars," he gazed up at the sky that was shimmering with hopeful, little lights, "they are subtle and small from here, but they guide the lost back *home*—" *The way you once guided me,* he almost said. Almost. "Rain, this, *this*," he made a big, sweeping gesture over him, "it isn't you! You don't just surrender like this!"

Rain snapped, "Oh please. What do you know?"

Nothe didn't hesitate. "I know enough. I know that you have the biggest heart of anyone I've ever known; it's just broken. You need to let it heal." He quickly turned away, wrangling his emotions under control. Rain couldn't know how desperately he needed to get through to him. Nothe didn't want Rain to see that if Rain were to die, Nothe would lose *his* home.

Rain's eyes filled with tears. He rubbed his face, and they were gone. "If only it would."

"It will." Nothe's voice was firm. "Probably not without some scars, but it *will*." After a moment, he continued, "Don't think for a second that you are powerless. You have the power to rebuild yourself however you want, to *choose* who you're going to be, to change yourself, the way you see this and everything around you—and that is an amazing power. Because the moment you change that, you change the world. The moment you can disperse the darkness within yourself, that is the moment when others will see your light, and they will look, and they will follow."

He turned to face Rain, his gaze fierce. "If you want to die on your own terms, then *change* those terms. Die on your feet in the name of those you loved, in defense of those you care about, defending that light I *know* still shines within you. Not like this. Because if you die like this, the *real* monsters—they win. You deserve so much more than this. You deserve to fight for yourself, for your right to happiness, for all you ever hoped to become, for all that you love and have ever loved. So if you hate the world—the universe—so much, then *change* it. Don't let it win! Don't let it destroy you. Take control of your life and guide it away from this-this *darkness*.

"And just—know you aren't in this alone. When things get heavy, you've got me. Always. I'm here to help you. Whatever it takes."

Rain stared at Nothe for a moment, his expression impossible to read, then looked away. Nothe kneaded his forehead with his fingertips, out of things to say. Rain had never been great at hiding his emotions, but just when Nothe wanted a glimpse into what he was thinking, he could feel nothing from him.

Probably because his speech had done nothing.

Rain shook his head. "How do you do it?"

"Do what?"

"How do you...how do you carry on, and be," he made a small, sweeping gesture over Nothe, "this."

Nothe was confused. "And be little ol' me?"

"Optimistic. At all. Ever. Let alone all the time."

"I'm not optimistic all the time."

Rain scoffed.

"I'm not."

"You're a sunshine robot, Nothe."

"I am n—" He had to pause mid-sentence once that unexpected description of himself sank in. Should he be insulted? "I appreciate the compliment, but it's only because you've taken all the doom and gloom parts for yourself."

Rain snorted. "How are you not angry all the time?"

"Because it's exhausting." Nothe rubbed his face with his hands. "Rain, my whole life, I was angry. I was in a cage when I was born. Pain and anger and despair—that was all I knew. And then I—" *met you*, Nothe wanted to say. "I was set free. And I suddenly had life! The walls were gone; the chains were gone. For once, I could do *anything*. *Be* anything. I had so much to look forward to. So much that it was like I had to create a whole new blob of brain matter just to be able to fathom it all. And no one—nothing, not one thing—was going to take that away from me. No bad memories or the amount of pain they brought, nothing." His determination, desperation, and his rage at the shadows spilled into his words. "*Nothing* has permission to take this from me."

Rain straightened a little as if he'd felt Nothe's emotions for a moment. Nothe took a deep breath, getting himself under control. "I will fight to keep my freedom, to keep this *gift* that has been given to me. I will endure it all for all the things I have to look forward to."

Silence fell between them again. Nothe was drained. He wracked his brain for more words but then felt a bit ridiculous. What was he really expecting all his talking to do? He was grasping at words as if they were buckets of water to put out a fire.

Nothe glanced back over at Rain, prepared to desperately search for a few more buckets of water to throw on this fire, only to see a few age-lines fade away from his face.

Nothe smiled and looked away. He knew that, at least for now, there was nothing more he needed to say.

The Garden Is So Peaceful at Night

Isaac lay in the planet-light, refusing to sit anywhere too close to a flower. Really, he just preferred to stare at the sky and tell himself there weren't giant flowers all around him, staring at him. Watching him. He tried to force his face to look as though he were at perfect peace.

Elise approached him and, without actually looking at him—as if they were making a covert business deal—asked, "Are you all right? You look as though you've just eaten something awful at Thanksgiving dinner."

He broadened his apparently unpleasant smile. "Of course I am."

She nodded, then gazed at the sky. She spoke as if she were wondering if the postman would be stopping by that day with a delivery. "If the flowers are this big, can you imagine how big the birds must be?"

Isaac moved to the safety of a smaller, less threatening flower and collapsed onto the soft grass at the base of its stem, laying back down on his back, exhausted. Elise sat beside him, hugging her knees.

Isaac rolled onto his side and peered at the odd group sitting across the clearing. A giant worm burrowed in the dirt, a weird monster, a fuzzy little girl, and a man with a red eye, all asleep. He shook his head. "Did you ever imagine it would turn out like this?"

Elise didn't hesitate. "Not in my wildest dreams."

The thought bubbled up into his mind, and Isaac had to ask, "Have you figured out how to disguise yourself as something other than a gross old man yet?"

She glared at the flower across the clearing. "I haven't had time to work on it."

Isaac nodded. "I'm sure you'll figure it out eventually."

There was silence for a moment as Isaac pondered over something that had been bothering him since yesterday. Finally, he asked, "Why didn't you blow up all of those worms?"

She hugged her knees more tightly. "I just, I don't know how to control it—this power, I mean. I didn't want to accidentally hurt anybody else. I *don't* want to hurt anybody else."

"But you carried the boat—"

"Yes, but that's not the same. I wasn't afraid or upset when I carried the boat. When I'm upset or afraid, I don't have the same control."

Well, that was frustrating. Although, he had to admit, he appreciated how aware she now was of this shortcoming.

A thin layer of anger that had been resting firmly on his chest and shoulders faded. It surprised him a little—more than the eyeball flowers, he was proud to say.

As if letting out built-up steam, Elise blurted, "I don't think I ever told you about my father."

Isaac looked up at her. Her gaze was distant, absorbed in memory. He said, "You never told me much about yourself at all, actually."

She sighed. "I came to Earth through the portal with my people. I was only a little girl, about five-years-old, I think—if I remember right. I can barely remember it. But I remember the, uh, the gems, of course. And the softness of the blanket I carried with me. I've never been able to find anything as soft since.

"Somehow, I got separated from everyone." Her eyes filled with tears. "I couldn't find them. I don't know how long I was alone in that jungle. But I leveled part of it with my crying." She laughed a bitter sort of laugh, wiping tears away. "I cried until I was too weak to cry anymore. And then, this sweet man found me. Cared for me." She sniffed. "His name was Arnaud."

Isaac rose on an elbow at this and then sat upright next to her.

"He wasn't repulsed by my appearance, even though I clearly wasn't a human child. He didn't make a spectacle of me. He just quietly took me back to his little home in the trees. It was basically just a shack, ya? He named me Elise, but he always called me *mon petit ange.*"

Isaac recognized bits of French he'd known before meeting The Prophet: *my little angel.* He smiled at the real Arnaud's kindness, but it was a sad one. He was sure he knew how this story would end, and it filled his stomach with a cold, heavy dread. He hoped he was wrong.

She went on. "I discovered my ability to hide in plain sight around then, when people would come to visit. Someone had stopped by unexpectedly once, and their reaction to me—it frightened me. I wished

I could disappear. I honestly thought I'd remembered doing it before. But instead of disappearing, I turned into an old man."

Isaac let out a short snort of laughter. Elise shook her head, seeming amused and bitter at the same time as she said, "Always an old man. One that sort of looked like Arnaud, but not quite. He was like an amalgamation of old men I'd known," they both laughed a bit at this. "I didn't understand it. I still don't understand it. It's always felt like a curse. I hope I figure it out." She forced another laugh.

She continued, "It was around then that Arnaud changed. I think he was afraid for me, ya? I guess rumors must've been going around about me. People would hide in the trees, trying to see me. This one time, they broke into the shack and tried to take me." She looked at Isaac, a shadow falling over her eyes. "That didn't go well for them." She turned away, her expression sad. "Or the shack." She draped an arm across her chest, hugging her shoulder. "So, we moved from place to place. I practiced controlling my feelings as best as I could. We eventually ended up in France, where he was from. I was maybe seven or so."

What? He thought back to the girl at the party. Despite yet another clear connection, he kept himself composed. "France, did you say? Where did you say you were when he found you?"

She gave him a look that said he should know this. "At the entrance of the River. In India."

He gave an emphatic "of course" sort of nod, while his stomach twisted with a mixture of understanding and nerves, anger, and confusion, disappointment and excitement, and a million other things he didn't know how to label. And from this terrible knot, he said, "Oh."

Elise picked a blade of grass and then another, tossing them in front of her before saying, "I don't want to talk about this anymore."

"But you should," Isaac insisted. He could understand why she might not want to talk about it, but he really wanted her to keep talking about it. "I really think you should. It seems like this is really bothering you, and you should just—let it out."

"I don't want to."

"Why not?"

"It's none of your business!"

"*You're* the one who started talking about it! I didn't ask for your autobiogr—"

Startled cries broke the air, coming from Isaac's right. Elise leapt to her feet. The slumbering group raised their weary heads and Boar's eyes peered out from beneath his blanket of dirt. Isaac forced himself to his feet and followed Elise to see what the fuss was about.

They found Nothe and Rain at the base of a rather large flower. It glared down at them with a red, angry eye. Rain lay flat on his face in a Rain-shaped dent in the moss and mud, groaning in exhaustion and pain. Nothe rose to his feet from his Nothe-shaped dent, staggered a little, then brushed himself off. He laughed as he gazed up at the ornery flower. "I guess it got tired of us sitting on it."

Thipka and The Prophet

In the middle of that same night, a voice echoed through Thipka's dreams, calling his name from the realm between sleep and consciousness.

He awoke and looked around. Someone was there. He was sure he knew who.

Everyone around him appeared to be fast asleep. Gof was leaning against the mound of dirt Boar slept beneath, which rose and fell with a rumble like that of distant thunder. Annabel's cot was set up between Thipka and Boar. Rain, Nothe, Isaac, and Elise were all the way over there under a smaller flower, out cold.

However, the flowers were wide awake, drinking in the light from planet Sam. Many of their gazes rested on Thipka, aware of his movement. Others stared past him.

A whistle sounded behind him. Thipka turned toward it. A faint, glowing mist hovered in the shadows. It darted out of sight, deeper into the forest of flowers.

Thipka rose to his feet, heart pounding.

This was new. He couldn't remember this from before.

Glancing over his shoulder toward the slumbering group underneath the smaller flower, he supposed it made sense.

He stepped around Boar's tail and followed the fleeing mist deeper into the darkness, not noticing Rain and Nothe's bright eyes opening, watching him leave. Thipka watched the specter dart between flower stems at a strange, unnatural speed, leading him to a clearing bathed in planet-light.

Rage surged through him, biting his veins like fire. He should've known.

At the edge of the clearing stood The Prophet. Thipka counted four balls of light surrounding him this time. They were lights that only Thipka's people could see—well, them and whatever The Prophet was. He hadn't figured him out yet. Every living thing carried a glow—unless they turned bad, letting the dark scars on their souls take over, then they had darkness around them instead. Elise's glow was the brightest Thipka had ever seen. But her soul was deeply scarred, marred by shadows. She had wounds to heal.

That's what the orbs of light around The Prophet were. They were souls. Ghosts. They would whisper things to The Prophet, giving him information, like spies. The Prophet knew the future through what was told him by the lights—but there was another means by which he did this that Thipka wasn't sure of yet. Somehow, The Prophet knew multiple possible paths through Time and their outcomes.

That was not how Thipka knew the future. Some thought Thipka's knowledge of the future was powerful—he himself had thought so once—but in fact, it was very limited. The Prophet might have had to wait to know all the things he did, but there was no limit to it, and it was always knowledge that, clearly, was worth waiting for.

And then he could just show up wherever he wanted to in space and Time. Thipka still didn't know how he did that.

And Thipka couldn't see his light. There was nothing around The Prophet—no shadow, no light.

The Prophet smiled at Thipka, but it was the sort of a strained, annoyed smile a parent would give when trying to be patient with a misbehaving child. "And here we are."

"You took Annabel to the island. Why?"

"She was supposed to be there. She snuck in the boat last time, remember?"

"She *died* last time."

"Yes. You changed that—"

"And you tried to change it back."

The Prophet sighed, shaking his head very patient-parent-like, his eyes full of a compassion Thipka didn't trust. "If I'd wanted to do that, I would've brought her over sooner, and I wouldn't have told her to bring friends." His gaze drifted away, seeing something Thipka couldn't, hearing whispers from the lights around him that Thipka couldn't understand. "I like how this turns out so far. I think it could work with the big picture." He looked pointedly at Thipka. "You know, the one you refuse to look at?"

Something about that filled Thipka's bones with a deep uneasiness he couldn't explain. It wasn't necessarily a darkness, no, but a strange sort of fear. It was like standing at the edge of a rocky cliff, knowing that one good shove would send him plummeting to a painful death, and realizing that he didn't really have a say in whether the shove happened or not.

Thipka glared at him. "So. As long as you're all right with it, then it's okay."

He shrugged. "I see more than you can, so, yeah."

"Like how you gave Isaac knowledge of multiple languages."

"Yes. It made things a little less messy. You see, small parts of Time can be rewritten in order to save it. But it has to be guided—gently. Like..." He grew thoughtful, searching. "Like guiding the flow of a river. If you mess with it too much, a lake dries up, or the river dies or becomes stagnant. Rotten. Because the water can't get to where it's meant to go. But, if you reroute it here a little or there a little, not changing its course completely but just going around this rock or through that field, it stays alive. It still arrives at its destiny, where it's meant to go. So you see, Time is like a river. And you have to treat it with care."

Thipka was sickened by this. He turned to leave.

The Prophet said in an exasperated tone, "You need to stop doing this, Thipka. You know that death is not the end of the story. Please, stop torturing yourself." He sounded sincere there, but then he added, his tone pained and frustrated, "You make such a mess of things, and then I have to come around and fix it all. Why won't you—?"

Thipka whirled around. "Because!" The sadness in his eyes took over his face for a moment. He was like a lost child trying to find his way back home but didn't know how to put words to the cry of his heart. Each particle of air around him filled with unspeakable sorrow. "Because I have promises to keep. Too many sacrifices have been made—made for me, for *me*." He rubbed his lips, his wrist, and held back tears. "For me. And I have promises to keep. Life is unbearable without them, and so, so very long for *me*.

"But *I have promises to keep*. So I will fight to have both life and them or die trying, and my peace shall be great on that day, whichever one I get, because whichever one it is, I shall see them again."

The Prophet folded his arms, his eyes full of tears and his expression heavy with pain. "Not if you lose your soul."

That struck like a knife of ice to the heart. Thipka'd had enough and resumed his departure.

The Prophet stepped forward. "Make another promise, then. When you get them back, promise me you'll stop tearing apart Time."

Thipka stopped and looked over his shoulder at him, his eyes brimming with tears. "I promise." He then disappeared into the shadows back toward the camp.

The Flowers Are Watching

The next morning, after a small breakfast of berries and dried meat —which was from some sort of reptile creature but tasted like dried beef—they continued their trek to wherever this fabled ship was. Isaac was wondering how he might get Elise to tell him the rest of her story when a strange, off-pitch, and loud growl interrupted his thoughts from somewhere nearby, a growl that he didn't like at all. Before he could ask anyone about it, Annabel trotted up to him all sneaky-like, as if she were doing something she really shouldn't. She looked around as if to make sure no one was watching and stuffed a handful of things in Isaac's hand. "Here," she whispered. "Gof wants me to give you these."

He gazed down at the green objects that looked a bit like brussels sprouts. He looked up at Gof, who was watching him carefully. He must've been feeling better since his mouth was closed now, making him look like a gigantic, fuzzy fur-ball kitten. If that was how he normally looked, it was no wonder Annabel adored him.

Isaac furrowed his brow. "Why?"

She shrugged. "I don't know. He likes you for some reason."

"All right, but what do they do?" Were they poisonous? Was Gof trying to poison him?

She whispered, "They're painkillers. He wanted you to have them since you're always hurting yourself."

"Is that so?" It was true, but still hard not to feel a little insulted.

"They used them all the time in my village with like, childbirth and stuff."

He raised his eyebrows. "Well, then, they must be good."

She glanced up at the group. Thipka was giving her a look like he knew she was up to something. "Gotta go!" She darted away.

Well, he was sure they would come in handy sometime— unfortunately. As he put them in his coat pocket, he couldn't help noticing that the flowers stared at him with judgmental eyes.

Very judgmental.

And not at anyone else, just at him.

Another growl. Had it come from the flowers? He really hoped not.

As the group trudged along, the flowers' gazes followed him, growing angrier.

Elise looked at Isaac, concern taking over her expression.

Nothe said, "Boy, they sure seem mad at you for some reason."

Boar asked, "What do you suppose has upset them?"

Isaac didn't have an answer, just a horrible feeling in his stomach that said something was horribly wrong.

The flowers sprouted fangs under their eyeballs and shook their petals while making terrible hissing sounds, like the wheezing laughter of an old, wicked man, cackling at something that was more mean-spirited than funny.

The group ran, Thipka picking up Annabel with a look of surprise and panic. Thankfully, the plants were stuck to the ground, but it didn't stop them from swiping at them with their leaves or snapping at their backs.

However, one large flower pulled its roots out of the ground, throwing dirt and rocks everywhere. The roots came alive like spider legs, twitching and scurrying the flower after them. Annabel screamed. Nothe and Rain yelled profanities. Rain's arms merged with his wings and Nothe shouted, *"Don't you dare!"*

"You don't even know what I'm going to do!" Rain shouted back.

"I don't care!"

They were being chased by a flower.

They were about to be *eaten* by a flower.

Isaac was, of course, the slowest runner there. He'd be eaten first.

"Whoa!" He ducked, barely dodging the fulfillment of his own prophecy as the flower dove at him with a snap of its teeth. It was so close, Isaac could smell its wonderful, mud-after-rain, sugar, rose-petal-and-lavender breath. Boar swept him up with his tail and carried him, awkwardly, slithering from then on without the use of it, like someone trying to run away from disaster without spilling their glass of wine. Even like this, he was much faster than Isaac on his best day.

The flower exploded, splattering sap, pink muscle bits, eye jelly, and pieces of petals everywhere.

The hissing grew louder. Three more flowers pulled themselves out of the ground. Elise flew behind them. "Keep going! *Go!*"

Right. She could handle herself.

Elise's eyes glowed bright green as if lit by a flame. As the group fled, she floated upward, and with a sweep of her hand, the entire row of flowers behind them—including the three pursuing them—exploded.

The flowers stopped chasing them after that.

Thankfully, it didn't take the group long to reach a clearing. They stopped to gather themselves and catch their breath. Annabel was clearly terrified, sobbing and upset. Thipka was furious. Isaac could feel it, even though he was several feet away. He called Isaac over.

Every gaze was glued on Isaac as he approached. He was nervous. He had no idea what he'd done, but he was sure he was going to regret it. It was like being called into Sister Maria's office all over again. Or that time he was engaged.

"What did she give you?" Thipka demanded.

Isaac fumbled through his pocket and pulled out the brussels sprouts.

Thipka seemed impressed underneath his anger. "You have to really dig to find those."

Isaac's gaze darted toward Gof. There were clumps of dirt in his claws.

Annabel sobbed harder. "He's always getting hurt!"

Thipka's anger melted away. He held Annabel tightly to his chest, comforting her. "It's okay now. You're safe. We're safe."

Isaac hesitated. "What are they?"

Thipka cast him a sideways glance. "Eggs."

"Eggs?"

Elise said softly, "They were just protecting their babies." She paled, looking as though her very soul had been drained from her body.

"And you were just protecting your baby," Nothe replied, placing a hand on her shoulder, "your grown-man baby."

Isaac didn't care for that comment.

Rain said, "You were protecting *all* of us."

"They were *not* babies!" Annabel snapped. "They were *eggs*. They weren't fertilized! The fertilized ones turn pink, and then they sit on them. They lay eggs all the time in the spring. I'm not a monster! And neither is Gof! They were completely overreacting."

Boar looked very tired for a worm. His paper-like skin had lost a shade of color. He asked Isaac, "What's going on? What was that all about?"

Isaac explained the situation, and Boar hung his head a little. Then he let out a howl. Everyone covered their ears. He then told Isaac, "That's our traditional mourning cry. I felt like the situation called for it out of respect. I didn't do that for my ignorant relatives because, well, I decided that they were terrible and didn't deserve it."

Isaac patted Boar. Then, of course, he had to explain this to everyone. He turned to Annabel and put a hand on her shoulder, assuring her, "They were overreacting, though. We eat eggs all the time on my planet."

Nothe nodded. "We do, too."

Rain added, "And I completely agree. They were overreacting."

They radiated comfort, and Annabel's breathing steadied as she sniffled and wiped tears from her face.

Elise's gaze was distant, staring off somewhere as if she were lost in her mind. She said, in a tone that made Isaac question her sanity, "I'll bring them back, too. I'll bring them all back."

Isaac's chest tightened, imploding a little at those words, and he secretly wished she could do exactly that, not only for his own reasons, but for her sake. There was something in her voice, something about her tone.

Silence fell over them for a moment, then Annabel blurted, "Bring who back? What are you talking about?"

When Elise didn't answer, Annabel said more loudly—as if the volume of her voice were the problem—"What is she talking about?"

Nothe hushed her and said softly, "It's best to leave it alone."

Everyone grew quiet after that, and they continued on.

Just Remember the Plan

Meanwhile, Asael had parked his ship at a very promising site. As he'd expected, his dreams had been horrific. His father's scarred eyes had pierced him, plaguing his mind with nothing but visions of the final moments of his family, their twisted and burned bodies and tormented faces. He'd felt his father's agony as his skin and eyes melted, and his terror as his vision darkened.

It was to make sure he knew he'd failed them all.

His father had then given him instructions he couldn't ruin, a timeline he couldn't arrive late to.

He sat next to a large spaceship shaped like an elongated egg with wings and a fin. It was partly in the ground and rusting in places, with vines growing over all of it. It'd clearly been here for quite some time.

And it was where Elise would soon be.

He just had to wait.

In moments like this, sitting inside his ship, listening to his music, and left completely alone with his thoughts, he realized how much he wished he could simply leave. Flee to the other side of the universe and live a different life. Abandon the plan and his father. Maybe meet someone nice. Someone who saw more than his flaws, his mistakes—he could almost laugh at that idea, it was so absurd.

Still, he'd like to live a quiet life in a quiet village. He could be an accountant. That wouldn't be so bad. He'd always been good with numbers. Maybe he could have kids. He'd always liked kids. They were hilarious and honest. He'd never understood how anyone could hurt one, how anyone could steal even a shred of that wonder and innocence from their eyes. It made him sick to think about it. He couldn't bear it. Their lives were so fragile, and their dreams relevant and real. Who could ever dare to take that away?

If he could, he'd adopt them all and make sure none of the horrors he'd suffered ever happened to them. He'd make sure they all felt safe and secure in their little worlds and grew up to be good, happy people. They'd have family dinners, family reunions, and good lives.

But it wouldn't matter where he went. His father would find him. He'd always find him. He'd never feel safe or secure again. He'd never be able to have comforting dreams or a mind of his own.

He hated everything his father had become. The man wasn't his father anymore. Not really. At least, not the one of his childhood. He was a monster. His father's dreams had been stolen from him, and now he'd stolen them from his son, turning him into his puppet.

Asael was beginning to see his father and his precious "plan" for what it was. It was mad. It was the terrible plan of a very sick mind. And no matter how great the plan sounded, nothing could ever change what his father had become. His mother would've been devastated if she could see, if she knew. If she wasn't burned up and dead. She was better off like that—they all were—than having to see and live with the person his father had become.

No time machine could change who his father was now.

And he didn't want to be like him—like *this*.

What am I becoming?

Asael sighed and rubbed his eyes with his hand. He was exhausted. He'd been trying very hard to stay awake for the last twenty hours or so. He'd gotten out of his ship a time or two, explored a bit, looked inside the relic he was parked by. He'd watched a movie on his device and played a game against his ship's computer. It was a boring game with two people, let alone with a computer. He didn't understand why he'd done it. He could only see it as a testament to how bored he was.

Now he was back in the cockpit, listening to music. It was the only thing he still had that could bring him a sense of peace and comfort.

Soon this would be over.

He just had to remember.

His father's plan would fix everything. Everything would be made right. Maybe then he'd dare to dream again.

Maybe.

He doubted it.

Now, That's a Ship!

The woods looked almost normal now, like Earth pine trees. They even smelled a bit like them. If it wasn't for the planet-moon shining down through the twilight above him, Isaac might've thought he was home.

But then, over there to his right was a building—only it wasn't a building. It was lined with windows and shaped almost like the hull of a ship, but it didn't have sails. It was made of metal and had wings with a door on the side. It was half-buried in the dirt and covered in vines. Words slipped from Isaac's lips. "Whoa! What in the blazes is that?"

"It's my spaceship," Thipka replied.

Isaac nodded, impressed. He could accept the idea of this one being a space "ship." It might not have had spars or sails, but it didn't look like an insect. And it was actually big enough to have a bow, midship, and stern, and what seemed to clearly be a cabin, and—he saw as he peered through a filthy window—a large hold for transporting goods. It wasn't perfect, but it was far better than any "ship" he'd seen thus far.

Boar was very excited. "Ooooh! What's this, here? Is this the ship you were speaking of?" Isaac confirmed that it was, and Boar exclaimed, "How delightful!" He also peered into the dusty windows, as did Elise, Nothe, and Rain.

Annabel said, "*That* wasn't here before."

She pointed at a familiar little spaceship, partially hidden in the trees. As they approached it, Isaac noticed a familiar figure asleep inside.

It was that man, the pigeon-livered, hornswoggler Isaac had named Snowman.

Isaac frowned. "What is he doing here?"

Rain said, "And here I thought we were following him."

Nothe asked, "Do we wake him?"

Rain thought about this. "He doesn't look peaceful."

"Yes. So peaceful. Like a baby cylyg."

Isaac grimaced.

"I said he *doesn't* look peaceful. And honestly," said Rain, "I don't know if I want to deal with this right now."

"I certainly don't," said Nothe.

"We probably should wake him, though."

"Yeah. Don't want him to get the jump on us."

Without a pause, Thipka marched up to the ship and ripped open the door. Strange music filled the air as he pulled the sleeping Snowman from his seat. He wasn't wearing his coat anymore but instead was dressed head to toe in what looked like black leather sewn together in nonlinear patterns. Clearly half-conscious, Snowman swung at Thipka, who blocked one hit and then another. As swift as thought, Snowman pulled moisture from the air and slammed it into Thipka, freezing the front of his clothes to his skin and nearly knocking him to the ground.

"Whoa!" exclaimed Nothe and Rain.

Nothe said, "Did you see that?"

"How is that even possible?" Rain replied.

"I don't even understand what just happened."

Isaac stepped between Thipka and Snowman. "Whoa! Whoa! Hey!" He turned toward Snowman and stretched his hands out in front of him as if he were trying to calm a wild horse. "Hey, we don't mean you any harm. We can get along peacefully," he looked at Thipka, "can't we?"

Thipka rose to his feet and touched his frozen chest, then glared at Snowman. It didn't look promising.

Snowman had his hands up in a pose that showed he was ready for the next attack. He was looking past Isaac and Thipka to Rain and Nothe, who had their weapons drawn. His eyes darted to Elise, who stood with her arms around Annabel's small shoulders. Snowman lowered his hands a little and grumbled in English with his thick accent, "You guys sure know how to make a guest feel welcome." He looked at Isaac. "That is a rare gift."

"Yeah, well, you're really good at leaving people for dead and then stalking them when they live," said Isaac. "I can't say I've ever seen that talent before."

Snowman smiled. "That's a bit dramatic, don't you think? I didn't leave you for dead. I was notified of an emergency and had to go home. I only ever said I'd take you to the River, and that's exactly what I did. Then I had an emergency—that's none of your business, by the way—and was then sent here on an errand. I saw this shipwreck from the sky, thought it was interesting, and decided to stay here for the night. The fact that you're here is an obvious coincidence. How in the universe was I supposed to know you would be here? Huh? *How?* There is absolutely no way I could've been following you—or would even want to."

"You really expect us to believe that it's just a coincidence that—out of thousands of planets—you somehow ended up right here, exactly where we are?"

"Yes, exactly."

Isaac couldn't believe a word he said. The audacity of this man! Just how stupid did he think they all were?

Snowman asked, "Would this be more believable?" Snowman's tone grew sarcastic as he put his hands together in a pleading, prayerful way. "Oh, please, please let me babysit you wherever you go! Please let me be the one to get your useless backside out of trouble! It's all I want. *Please,* I beg of you!"

Isaac narrowed his gaze at Snowman.

Nothe muttered to Rain, "Do you have any idea what's going on?"

"I haven't a clue. I'd say that this man here is pleading with Isaac for his life, but that can't be right."

"Right? I mean, if he were talking to Elise, then maybe—"

Isaac shouted, "All right, that's *enough!*" It came out louder than he'd intended.

Silence fell over the forest. Everyone looked at Isaac in surprise—except for Snowman, who dropped his hands to his sides, looking amused. Isaac was fed up—with all of them, with all of *this.* It just kept going and going, and all he wanted was to fix this stupid, gigantic ship and take Elise to her stupid planet. And then, after at least one more grand adventure, go home and eat potatoes and turkey, and all without another single word spoken or thing going wrong.

Was that so much to ask?

Isaac knew—he *knew*—this man was up to something and that it would ruin his simple dream of eventually getting home and eating mashed potatoes and turkey. What, exactly, were they supposed to do about it?

An unsettling cracking sound made Isaac cringe. He looked over to see Thipka tearing his frozen shirt from his skin, which bled and then immediately healed. Thipka grumbled, "That's very annoying. Very annoying, indeed. I liked this shirt."

Boar, who had been quietly observing everything, asked, "This man seems to be causing trouble. Shall I eat him?"

Isaac considered it. "Let me get back to you on that. Keep an eye on him, will you?" Deep down, he knew he wouldn't let Boar eat him, but by gum, it was tempting.

"Of course!" said Boar, slithering closer to Snowman. Snowman jumped back a little, startled but ready for the fight, which made Isaac nervous.

Isaac called everyone over to him and spoke to them in Theran. "All right, so, here's what's happening. He says it's a coincidence that he's here at the same time as us—"

Nothe shook his head over-dramatically. "Coincidence! Of course! Why didn't I think of that?"

Rain nodded. "It's a perfectly reasonable explanation."

"It's the *only* thing that makes sense!"

Isaac furrowed his brow. "I...are you two...?"

Thipka grumbled, "They're not serious."

Rain mock-gasped. "How dare you?"

Nothe said, "You do not speak for us, sir."

Isaac stared at Rain. He had mock-gasped. That seemed so... different for him. He also looked younger again, somehow, which was just infuriating. How was he doing that?

Isaac moved on. "Right. Anyway, clearly, something's amiss here, and I, frankly, am not sure what to do about it. All I want to do is fix this ship and leave, and I can't help but be concerned that he is going to get in the way somehow. Boar has offered to eat him."

Nothe said, "Oooh, I like that idea. It's simple and effective."

Snowman spoke up in Theran then. "If I could just interject on my own behalf here—" Everyone glared at him, and Boar slid a little closer. "You're completely throwing out a conviction and sentence with only circumstantial evidence. For all you know, I am telling the truth."

Isaac stared at him in shock. "You speak Theran, too?"

"I speak a lot of languages. As do you, apparently."

"However, you're not being truthful, are you?" Rain didn't say it as a real question, but as a matter of fact, like a lawyer in the middle of a cross-examination or Sister Sarah when looking for the cookie thief.

"Yeah, actually, I really do speak a lot of languages." In answer to the glare that followed this, Snowman continued in a calm, amused tone, as if this debate were already won, "You can't prove that I'm not."

"Maybe not, but I can feel it and see it." Rain smiled. "You reek of exhaustion, turmoil, and fear. You're barely holding it together."

Something darted across Snowman's eyes then, stealing his smile. Panic. He recovered quickly, folding his arms and replacing any panic with a casual grin. "You can believe whatever you want. One thing I *can* prove is that I am useful. You want to fix this ship?" He gestured to the wreck in the ground. "I've got everything you could ever need in *my* ship." He looked at Thipka. "Go on. Go through it. I've got nothing to hide."

Snowman studied his black fingernails as Thipka, Nothe, and Rain went through his ship. By the looks of it, he wasn't concerned at all about what might happen to him next, even with the worm staring down at him.

Boar asked, "Am I going to eat him, then?"

Isaac finally had to admit, "Probably not, Boar. Sorry."

He looked a little disappointed. Isaac realized he was probably hungry. He was a giant worm, after all.

He also realized, having observed Snowman's powers in action, that his lack of concern was likely genuine. With how humid the forest was, Snowman could probably turn them all into ice statues with ease—even Boar. Whatever fear Rain had sensed from him, Isaac wasn't sure just how much of it had to do with this particular situation.

Which was troubling. What could frighten Snowman?

Isaac was surprised by how much they took from Snowman's ship. He didn't understand much of what he was looking at, but judging by everyone's faces, it was exciting. One of the instruments they took out looked like a massive metal arm and claw on a dial, and Thipka was delighted. When he couldn't get it to work, however, the delight turned to rage.

Snowman said simply, "Yeeeah, I'm the only one who can operate that. It'll only listen to me." He shrugged, smirking. "Told you I was useful."

Thipka approached him, a tower of muscles standing several inches above him. Snowman didn't even flinch. Thipka put a hand on his shoulder. "Better get to work, then."

There's Something in the Way

The only one in the group that knew they were being watched was Snowman—known as Asael to his father. His father sat in his large chair and made sure his son could feel his gaze upon him, ensuring he wouldn't screw this up, and all from the comfort of his living room. He could feel Asael's unease.

Good. That meant he was taking this seriously. It was about time.

Asael's father had been happy once. It was so long ago, but he remembered it like a dream, a dream that was fading in the distance of time, like a city that was so grand, wonderful, and consuming when standing within it, but diminished into nothing more than a speck of dust the farther you flew away from it.

Not that he realized it was happening, because he didn't.

There was a time that he noticed the sunlight. Not just saw its glow on the grass and on the leaves of the trees but felt its warmth on his skin. His skin had been dark with a tan in those days, because every moment he wasn't working with steel, providing for his family, he was outside with his children. His job in steelworks was tedious. He'd worked his way up to supervisor, and while the pay was better, it wasn't as satisfying as actually using his gifts in fire to create things. But it was worth it because his family was his true calling, spending evenings at home with them was his mission, and making sure they had everything they could possibly need for a safe, secure life was his passion.

He loved them more than the world. More than the stars.

While his workdays were spent immersed in the same dull scene, their faces were rich with color. While his coworkers told jokes and tales he wished he could unhear, the stories of his children enchanted him, and their laughter was music. He'd often go to work the next day pondering one of their stories and wondering how they'd become so creative. Surely it was his wife. There was no one more intelligent and creative than her. She loved to take them outside to wander through the forest, teaching them about the insects, the animals, and how the world came to be. That was her gift—she was in tune with the plants and the soil. She kept his temper in check, filling his heart with compassion and love and reminding him who he was.

Not that he really remembered these things anymore. They'd been drowned in the darkness that followed, in what he saw one day on his way home from work. Strange, celestial birds burned their way into the atmosphere, drenching the city in chemicals.

His house was on fire.

His house was on fire, and he couldn't command it to stop burning. The closer he got, the louder the fire became.

It wasn't a normal fire.

They screamed, trapped inside.

He leaped through the flames, catching on fire. The flames consumed his body, melting the fat under his skin, melting his eyes.

He tried to save them. He tried.

Asael screamed and cried just outside.

Asael, little Asael. He couldn't see his perfect, round face. Not anymore.

Asael had been playing near the lake when the house was set on fire by a passing ship. When he saw the flames, he flexed his tiny hands and used his powers to pull water and mud from the lake to smother them.

Summoning a strength beyond the ability of his tiny body, he dragged his father to the safety of the cellar. He cared for his burns with a wisdom beyond his five years, as if his mother were whispering in his ear.

But he hadn't saved anybody else. They were dead by the time he got there. He'd been too late.

Not that his father really remembered that, either. All he remembered was the pain; that his final images were the ship, his home in flames, and his family's burned bodies; and that Asael had been too late.

Maybe his father should've tried harder to hold onto the beautiful memories, the joyful images. To have reached through the shadows and saved those bright moments and remembered the bravery and intelligence of his son, how hard he'd tried, and that he'd lost them, too.

That his five-year-old had saved his life.

Perhaps he should've kept these things from drowning in the darkness. Maybe he wouldn't have lost himself if he had.

Not that he ever worried about that. At least, not anymore. Before he'd been overtaken by the rage, the regret, the darkness, and his plans, he'd occasionally notice how he was changing, how his obsessions and harsh criticisms were hurting his son. He'd sometimes notice how he was rewriting history in his mind.

He couldn't face his failure. His son shouldn't have been the one to save them. It should've been him, and he couldn't bear it. He was collapsing under the weight of that knowledge, that shame, that regret.

He couldn't control that fire. He'd tried.

But...his son had put it out. So really, it was his son's fault, wasn't it? If he'd gotten there sooner, if he hadn't panicked like a fool, pacing back and forth like an imbecile, screaming, he would've saved them all. His son needed to accept responsibility for that. He needed to *pay* for his failure.

So that worry was gone now. Instead, he made sure his son knew that this was all his fault. He *needed* to know that. He needed to feel the emptiness he'd left behind. He also needed to be reminded of how pathetic and helpless and foolish he was—this particular necessity grew every day.

And for all that he'd ruined with his failure, it wasn't enough to feel that pain for a day. He needed to feel it soul-deep, to have it written in his bones, to rot with it for eternity.

And even that wouldn't be enough.

His country's army had successfully driven the invaders from his home planet, Ethra. That's when he started truly harnessing this new sight he had, training himself to see farther and farther into the void.

And he saw the doorway to the River.

It was a bright star in the darkness deep within his planet. Getting to it was difficult, but the moment he set foot upon the riverbank, he wanted to weep. The energy there burned so bright, and he could see it all so clearly, it was as though his vision had been returned to him.

He also learned what it was: a portal to different planets, like a back door.

And he discovered that someone else had known about it, and had never told their leaders—had never told *him*. They'd known there were other inhabited worlds out there, worlds that were threats to their lives, and they'd never said a word.

He made sure they suffered for that.

Once he had command of the army, he conquered Ethra, taking them all in his grasp. To protect them, of course. He'd taken everything he needed from his people to experiment and learn how the River was built and how to harness its power. He then expanded their efforts to venture to the planet closest to them, hoping it was the one that had attacked them. It wasn't, but he destroyed it anyway, ensuring they would never rise against Ethra.

It wasn't long after that when he did find the planet that'd stolen everything from him—from them all.

Thera.

But he had a problem. His army was too pathetic to destroy Thera. When they attacked, their weakness had caused them to be decimated. His people had failed him—really, they'd failed themselves. There was hardly anyone left.

How could they let that happen? They disgusted him.

It then fell on his shoulders to come up with a new plan. And this plan was far better because it didn't require an army that could let him down. He didn't know how he hadn't thought of it before—of course, until he'd found the River, he hadn't thought it possible before.

And unlike the River, he'd only need one powerful lifeforce to fuel his machine, a machine that could move through space and time, one that would unravel all the evil that had been done. He could go back. He could destroy all of Thera, and every other world that threatened their peace before they even *dared* think of burning through the atmosphere of Ethra.

He just needed that one bright, shining star.

The lifeforce powerful enough to do this belonged to the girl who had been banished from their world by those who'd known about the River before he did.

The girl now known as Elise.

All his people's mistakes, all of Asael's mistakes—none of them mattered now. Nothing mattered, because of the plan. This plan would make everything right.

And he wasn't about to let Asael screw it up.

His Favorite Story

Isaac jumped awake in the night. In his dreams, he'd been looking for his coat. He opened a closet door, and there stood The Prophet in that bizarre room, looking out at something Isaac couldn't see. He gave Isaac an exasperated look and said, "We really need to figure out how you keep doing this," and slammed the door in his face.

Which, in Isaac's opinion, wasn't very nice.

Oh well. Since he couldn't fall back to sleep, he figured it was as good a time as any to sit near the fire and read the cherished book from his childhood. He'd been meaning to for days now, but he really hadn't had an opportunity. However, he had checked on it now and then, making sure it was still in his pocket and in one piece. It'd somehow survived everything Isaac had been through and would surely smell like worm guts, flower guts, blood, and sweat for years to come. He ignored Thipka—who was awake and muttering "save them" to himself again as he guarded a restlessly-sleeping Snowman—and sat next to the campfire.

It'd been a while since he'd read these pages. He viewed it with brand new eyes. Not only because he was now an adult, but he'd also been through the River from the story and had possibly met The Prophet.

He followed the magical tale. Prince Sky and Zhen meeting The Prophet. The Prophet leading them through the River to the fountain to save Princess Song and the queen. The ingenious queen's escape, Princess Song's strength of character, and her fighting skills as she battled a villain in a duel. And the dragons! The small dragons that ate everyone. He'd always wanted one as a pet. He wanted to sic one on Sister Maria, which he supposed wasn't very Christian, but neither was Sister Maria.

Reliving the earlier days brought with it a great sense of warmth and comfort. His mother holding him as she read. His imagination running wild in the safety of his small home. He liked himself a bit more for loving this story so much when he was little.

However, a tremendous sense of unease sank like a stone in his stomach every time The Prophet was in the scene. A drawing of him in the book looked remarkably similar. He was sure that this was the same person who'd given Isaac the ability to understand so many strange languages.

He'd seen his face vanish, like in the story. He'd seen it in those strange dreams.

But now he wondered, *were* they dreams?

"What are you doing?"

Isaac jumped at the grumble of Rain's voice, his glowing eyes studying him from across the flames. He stood there shirtless, his wings and muscles massive, looking healthy again. Honestly, Isaac swore he looked a little younger every time he saw him. What was his secret?

Isaac showed him the book. "I'm reading this story from my childhood." He made up his mind right then that if Rain asked to see the book, he couldn't hand it over to him again. He couldn't risk losing it again. He'd been foolish to hand it over the first time. Rain would have to pry it from his cold, dead fingers.

Rain asked, "Is that the one with the map of the River in it?"

Isaac nodded.

Rain hummed, his brow furrowed in thought. He rummaged through a nearby pack for some dried berries and then sat beside Isaac. "It's in English?"

Isaac nodded again. "Yeah."

Rain popped a few berries into his mouth and motioned with his fingers. "Read it to me."

So Isaac did, translating the words into Theran as he went. He was excited by how intrigued and invested Rain was by the story. As he read, he was hit by the words of The Prophet near the end, *Sometimes, it is in our moments of weakness and fear that we come to discover just how extraordinary we really are. And, I might add, sometimes that's when we also discover just how loved we are.*

He paused in his reading, rubbing his lips as tears filled his eyes. His gaze darted to Elise, then back to the book.

How had he forgotten? These very words were why his mother had read the story to him in the first place. She'd read it more frequently when she became ill. "Always remember this, Isaac," she'd said. But then the book was stolen, life became nothing but grief, and the memory faded with so many others when he was left in the snow as a boy. He certainly hadn't been extraordinary on that day.

But perhaps he'd never needed the message more than he did right then. It was as if she were speaking to him through time, through the words of a book.

He looked over at Rain, who was looking at Nothe, who was allegedly sleeping. Isaac quickly wiped tears away and continued reading.

At the end, Rain asked, "You say you've met this Prophet? And he's the one who gave you this language ability?"

Isaac confirmed that all of this was true. "He also left me with a cryptic message when he gave it to me. 'You'll do better with that,' he'd said." Isaac shrugged. "I can't imagine how horrible things would've been without it, so he was certainly right about that." Isaac laughed a little as Rain smiled and nodded in agreement.

But seriously, what would've become of Boar if Isaac hadn't been able to understand him? To know his good intentions? He couldn't bear the thought.

Isaac grew somber. "He also put this terrible vision in my head that there is so much at stake here. More than I could see." Isaac furrowed his brow, remembering. "And he said forgiveness and compassion are what separate the monsters from the men and the demons from the angels."

The words lingered in the air like the smoke from the fire. They struck him far more deeply than when he'd heard them before. And for the first time, he pondered them. Everyone—even Elise, to the threat of her sanity—knew that what had happened to Isaac, his ship, and his crew was terribly wrong. No one was out to condone it. She wasn't asking for that whatsoever.

If she was the girl from the party—and really, who was he kidding? Of course she was—she had destroyed his beautiful illusion, what he'd expected her to be. She wasn't asking for him to condone that, either. She refused to talk about it entirely.

But perhaps...perhaps that wasn't what forgiveness was ever meant to be. Perhaps forgiveness was something much more simple yet absolutely profound. Something divine. Perhaps it was liberation from suffering so life could be allowed to flow forward and evolve into something great and deep, even as a river to the sea. And perhaps it was giving someone—even oneself—permission to change, to become unstuck and grow for the better. It wasn't condoning; it was taking away the power the pain held, like breaking chains that had worn skin away. Allowing oneself to be set free and to just heal. To become better instead of bitter.

However, he wasn't sure he could ever forgive Sister Maria.

Well, maybe someday.

Probably not.

Rain's face was expressionless. "He said that?"

"Yeah," said Isaac, his mind still caught up in the words. "He did."

Rain was silent for a moment. "Fascinating. You know, we have legends of prophets on our world. It was said that they were connected to an unseen dimension and were guided by spirits. It's also said that they prophesied the uprising of my people, that they would one day destroy the Therans. And the Therans were so threatened by their prophecy that they killed them all." He looked up at Isaac and smiled bitterly. "That legend has been around for a while. Still waiting for that prophecy to happen." He straightened. "However, with everything you've experienced, it makes you wonder just how much of *this* story," he pointed to the book in Isaac's hands, "is actually real."

Nothe sat up in his spot near the fire and said, "Right? Could it be *all* of it? Even the tiger-sized dragons—whatever a tiger is?"

Isaac wasn't surprised Nothe had been eavesdropping. Did the man ever sleep?

Isaac said, "But, how could The Prophet still be alive after all this time? This story clearly took place a long time ago. The entrance to the River wasn't in the same spot as described here in the book."

Nothe considered this. "Hmm. Maybe it moved."

Rain pointed at Nothe's good point. "And if it did, then that means this Prophet has been around at *least* long enough for the entrance to move."

Isaac closed the book, rubbed his eyes, tousled his hair, then rested his chin in his hand, looking down at the cover.

What a strange turn his life had taken. Of all the people to end up in a fable, he'd never imagined it'd be him. Not in his wildest dreams.

Isaac tried to sleep again. He lay there long enough to hear Rain begin to snore and to watch the dawn break in the distance. Then he went back to the fire, reading his book again. *Sometimes, it is in our moments of weakness and fear that we come to discover just how extraordinary we really are.*

Elise appeared and sat adjacent to him near the fire. She asked him in English, "Can't sleep either?"

"I tried. A couple of times," said Isaac. He flipped the book to its back cover, then put it back in the pocket of his tattered coat. "This is still my favorite story."

"Mine, too."

Isaac studied her for a moment. "Where did you find this book anyway?"

She looked as though she'd expected this question at some point but still wasn't happy to hear it. She sighed. "Do you...do you remember the ghost in the pantry, back at the orphanage you lived in?"

Isaac's eyes widened, darting to the side briefly. "Yeah. Yeah, I remember."

She sighed again, putting her head in her hands. She looked at him. "That was me." When Isaac didn't respond, she added, "I was the ghost in the pantry, in the ceiling—"

"Under my bed."

"I wasn't there as often as you might think."

"You broke Sister Maria's statues."

"They needed to be broken. She was a horrible person. She smashed your pet spider."

"She did. I was very happy all her statues got broken."

"I stole your book. Because it talked about the River. It made me believe I could find it again. That I could go home and..." her eyes filled with tears, "and make everything right again."

He thought about getting angry. Insanely angry. He thought about throwing things and setting other things on fire. Instead, he sat there, glaring at her.

She refused to look at him as she wiped tears away. "Arnaud—the man I was telling you about earlier—he became my father. He had this incredible opportunity to move to a farm in the United States. It belonged to a relative of his that had fallen ill and they needed the extra help. It was supposed to be a good place, ya? And I know the whole thing—it wasn't easy for him. Everyone thought I was a senile, old man. Older than him. Everyone thought he was caring for his aging father. He got us this little cottage close to the farm. And then he died.

"I was broken, and so very frightened—it was a devastation that just consumed me with no relief in sight. My chest...it was like it was being crushed by an unbearable weight. Even my bones felt heavy. My heart ached with every beat. I was starving and cold. I'd heard about orphanages and that children without parents were supposed to go there. Yours was the closest one to where I lived. So I haunted it. I was there before you were, by the way.

"I would sometimes borrow books when others weren't around because I was bored, and I needed a distraction. I couldn't play with the other kids like everyone else. But Arnaud had been teaching me English for a while, ya? So I knew it well enough. But, by borrowing books and listening in on conversations—and occasionally practicing it as a gross old man that not many people were willing to talk to—I taught myself to speak it more fluently.

"So, when you moved in, I saw how much you loved that book, and I made sure to borrow it from you when you weren't around. When I realized what it was, I kept it a little longer."

Isaac's gaze narrowed. "Sure. Just eighteen years longer is all."

"Seventeen."

"Yes, I beg your pardon. Seventeen."

"I didn't understand what I was doing. I had no idea what it meant to you."

Isaac looked up at the stars in exasperation. "Right. The little boy crying himself to sleep at night wasn't a clear indication—"

"I didn't know *that* was why you were crying! Children in that orphanage cried all the time!" She folded her arms and looked away. "I was too busy being jealous that you could let yourself cry like that without blowing everything up."

He raised an eyebrow at her. But instead of prying further, he said, "Yes. I had only to fear a beating from Sister Maria."

"That was when I broke her mirror while she was looking in it. Frightened her into confession that next day."

Isaac laughed. He hadn't heard that story. It made sense that Sister Maria would've kept that one as secret as possible.

Elise asked, "Do you have any idea what a gift it is? To just cry and feel what you're feeling without fear of hurting someone?"

Isaac considered this for a moment. There was a time he'd known what that felt like, then he went to the orphanage and forgot. "I used to. And I suppose it's not so much that I'm afraid I'll hurt someone but more that I'll be destroyed by someone—in one way or another. Sister Maria made sure I toughened up. As did John One and John Two. Their methods were very, very effective."

Elise grew thoughtful and nodded. "That must be terrible. Sometimes...sometimes I wish I could just let it all out. Just scream and cry."

Isaac had to point out, "You do cry sometimes."

She smiled, but it was dark. "That's a controlled cry. It's something I've been learning how to do. When I'm feeling too much, I need to let a little out, or I'll explode."

Isaac raised his eyebrows. "That would be very bad."

She laughed a little. "Yes, it would. It would be terrible."

A slight hiss came from the shadows. "Pssst." It was Nothe speaking in Theran. "You guys are so loud."

Rain grumbled, "So loud."

"Talking in your weird, ugly language again. What have I told you about this? If you're going to keep everyone awake, you can at least give them something good to listen to."

"He's right," said Rain. "It's only fair."

Snowman joined in with, "I'd rather you just stop talking. I was actually asleep."

Nothe said, "You were asleep when we got here."

Isaac raised his hands in surrender. "Sorry. Sorry, everyone. You know, I think I might be ready to give sleep another try, so..." He shrugged. "Yeah, I'll do that."

Elise gazed at the fire for a moment. "I don't think I can sleep." She turned to Thipka, who had fallen so silent, Isaac had forgotten he was there. Eerie. "You can take a rest if you like."

Isaac didn't like that idea much. It certainly wouldn't help him sleep. Without thinking, he pressed his book against his chest a little more tightly.

Thipka studied her. "You need your rest." He pointed to his temple. "Your mind needs rest."

And that was that. She laid down on her bed of moss and leaves, as did Isaac. The moment he thought he'd never be able to sleep again, he drifted off into a somewhat restful slumber.

This Is Going Very Well

Isaac was surprised to find himself thoroughly enjoying repairing this massive spaceship. Much to everyone's awe, Elise used her abilities to pull the craft out of the dirt. She also tore down the vines and built missing and badly damaged pieces from the elements and the metal they'd stolen from the worms, following Thipka's guidance, of course. Everyone banded together to replace rot and to repair the hull, engine, wires, landing gear, and so forth. Boar would help where he could, following Isaac and Annabel around like a gigantic puppy—although, most of the time, he just played with Annabel. She liked having him around. He wasn't above tea parties.

Isaac became familiar with the different tools for the repairs of what they called "electronics." These electronics measured the status of the ship, ran the navigation systems, and controlled the engine—it was what those wires were for. He made Thipka go over, again and again, how to start and steer the ship and the importance of each contraption. He learned how the ship propelled itself through air and space and the functions of each part—all the functions except for one.

It was a thick lining along the ceiling that appeared to be made of cracked, frosted glass that bled like melted wax into the walls. An assortment of buttons connected to it near the cockpit, which buttons Thipka explicitly told Isaac not to touch.

"Why?" Isaac had asked. "What does this thing do?"

"It's broken," was all Thipka had said.

"Then what does it matter if I touch them?"

Thipka ignored this question.

"Are you going to fix it?" Isaac asked.

"I don't know how to fix it."

"Then what does it matter if I touch the buttons?"

"I don't want you to start it by accident, just in case it's not as broken as I think."

Isaac glared at him. "So what does it *do?*"

Thipka looked away, shaking his head. "Time is a strange thing. Time, time, time." Thipka's gaze drifted off into the distance as he disappeared into his head.

Later, when Thipka wasn't around, Isaac pushed all the buttons connected to the frosted glass. All of them. Nothing happened, but it was still satisfying.

The more he learned about the entire ship, the more his heart burned with an excitement and thrill he'd never really felt before. He'd experienced something like it for the ships he'd sailed at sea, but this— this was beyond that. This was more than he'd ever known possible. It was a profound longing, a call to the stars. At the end of each day, he'd step away from the ship with a sense of pride, that strange feeling having grown stronger. He never wanted to leave this machine.

They'd made remarkable progress in four days. He'd watched and helped Snowman melt, hammer, weld, and build wires and strange boxes with his bizarre claw-machine. Rain, no longer shirtless, taught Isaac about the atmosphere, gave him a rundown of how it worked, and why it was so important to make sure the hull of the ship was secure as he, Nothe, and Elise repaired it with their powers, flattening bits of metal and fitting them together perfectly against the large gashes along the outside.

Honestly, with Elise's help, the repairs were moving forward at a phenomenal rate. While the others' powers were truly remarkable in their usefulness, they'd get tired. Elise didn't. Not really. None of them could match her.

They'd be leaving here before long.

He spent time with Elise, laughing and reminiscing about the old sailing days, which felt like centuries ago. It eased a bit of the pain he felt, to talk and remember those times they'd spent together. But only a bit.

They'd also managed to put up with Snowman fairly well. He hated the name "Snowman;" he'd made that abundantly clear, but that just made everyone use it all the more—even Elise. However, Elise was nice to him overall, and Isaac caught them laughing together often—which was fine, of course. Why would that bother him? He was relieved, honestly. She could haunt somebody else for a change.

What made Isaac grow to like Snowman was how patient he was

with Annabel. One afternoon, Annabel made toys out of discarded wire, branches, and leaves and was playing near the forest with them with a ghost that held a small rock for his toy. She'd made a puddle of mud—Snowman had provided the water for her—and was sailing her twig-people toward the ghost with the rock, saying, "You don't stand a chance against us!"

Isaac had to really focus to see the ghost's form. They were always in motion and difficult to distinguish. As if a dagger had pierced his heart, he realized this little ghost looked just like her. He was a tiny child with tall ears and small antlers.

Isaac had to look away as he swallowed his tears.

Her village. She'd always talked about her village, yet she was never concerned about going back to it. Her people were "around," yet no one ever came looking for her—at least, none that he'd observed.

What had become of her village?

He closed his eyes. The answer seemed so clear now. They were always with her. They were the ghosts in the trees, following her everywhere she went.

Annabel cried out. She'd gotten so carried away in the battle between the rock and her twig-men that she stumbled backward just as Snowman walked past her. She stomped as she caught her balance and splashed mud all over his clothes.

The whole world seemed to freeze, waiting. The ghost dashed back into the trees as if worried it was in trouble. Isaac prepared to intervene. He would call Boar for backup if he had to.

Snowman cursed under his breath in French and sighed. He looked at Annabel. "It's all right. I suppose we can't have a battle without some casualties, am I right?"

Annabel gave him a wary smile.

Snowman crouched down to her level. He pointed to the twig men. "What are their names?"

She glanced down at her toys. She lifted one up, followed by the other. "This is Sira, and this is Ed."

Snowman grew thoughtful. "You know what Sira and Ed need is a boat. They're swimming across these mighty waters," he gestured to the puddle, "they must be so tired by the time they reach the—what's your friend's name?" He pointed to the rock that had been abandoned by the ghost.

She shrugged. "You'll have to ask Ver. He's hiding." She turned to the trees and yelled, "Like a coward!" She looked at Snowman. "He used to be older than me. Now I'm older than him, and you can tell. He acts like a baby."

Isaac laughed a little. Leave it to Annabel to call a ghost a coward and a baby.

Snowman rubbed his chin, thinking. "Perhaps Ver would feel more prepared for battle if his rock-friend had a spaceship."

Annabel's eyes lit up. "Yeah!"

Isaac thought he saw a flash of ghost-light in the trees, drawing closer.

"Perfect!" declared Snowman, determined. "All right, we need a boat for Sira and Ed and a plane for the rock-man. Let's go!"

He then took a break from fixing the ship to help her find supplies and carved her a boat out of wood. He showed her how to tie branches together to make a little spaceship. She told him all about the ghosts and her adventures, much of which Isaac missed due to being inside the actual ship, putting things together.

Isaac would've maybe genuinely liked Snowman after that, but it was obvious he was still up to something. There was no way he was telling the truth about why he was there, and he'd often catch him studying Isaac, looking away quickly once he was caught.

Snowman slept less and less each night. Anytime Isaac awoke from a nightmare or to relieve himself, there was Snowman, eyes wide open, sitting not too far from the fire, music playing lightly from his ship. By day five, dark circles were well-formed under his eyes.

It was disturbing. Something was very wrong with that man.

Isaac didn't find it as disturbing as discovering "Save Them" written in dried blood all over a large rock near the campfire one day—which activity was apparently a fun pastime for Thipka at night—nor as disturbing as Thipka's request on day five. Two days before, Thipka had said, "I have music stuck in my head." He groaned. "I can't help it." He rubbed his eyes. "I can't. It must be done."

No one knew what he was talking about. But he immediately abandoned the repairs to build crude instruments out of wood, all while singing quietly to himself about "the greatest show." When asked why he was doing this, Thipka said, "Because I have songs stuck in my head. I need to get them out."

On day five, he explained that the instruments were for a musical, and he would be dragging any willing victim into singing it with him. Isaac thought the whole concept of musicals and operas was downright silly. No one burst into song in real life. And if they did, they'd wind up shot, and everyone in the street would applaud the gunman for getting rid of a public nuisance.

Nothe said, "I like to sing. I didn't know I liked to sing until recently, but I do."

Isaac said, "I don't sing."

Elise cast him a look. "Liar."

Thipka handed Elise and Isaac a strange tablet—which he'd claimed he had kept in his battered ship—with a glowing face and words on it. He also handed one to Nothe and Rain and another to Snowman and Annabel. Isaac politely declined the invitation to participate with a "No, thank you," and excused himself.

Nothe taunted him. "You're missing out."

The whole thing was bizarre. Why this moment? Of all times, why was Thipka doing this *now* when they were so close to leaving? No, Isaac would much rather continue cleaning and polishing the ship. Even Snowman would occasionally take breaks from the madness and help him clean, though he wasn't great company since he rarely said anything.

Isaac was happiest when he was working on the ship. Despite how uncertain the future was, despite all the pain, all the heartache, and crushing disappointment he'd experienced in his life, when he was working on that ship he somehow knew he was exactly where he was meant to be. It gave him hope that somehow, everything could be made right, and the future ahead of him would truly be far better than anything he'd left behind or dared dream of.

Isaac could hear them rehearsing. *Oh!* This *is what Thipka's been singing.* The music was a bit odd, but their singing wasn't bad. The melodies were catchy. It was easy to see how Thipka could get them stuck in his head.

There was a tap-tap-tap on the hull. He looked out the open door to

Boar. "Beg your pardon, but I'm bored. I can't understand a thing they're saying over there. I think they're either in pain or singing, but I've never heard singing like that before."

Isaac smiled. "Yeah. They're singing."

"My goodness," said Boar, peering over the hull of the ship at the group. "Don't tell them I said this but they sound awful. For a moment, I thought they'd all fallen terribly ill."

Isaac laughed. "Your secret is safe with me."

Boar spent the rest of the day with Isaac, telling Isaac his thoughts on things—mostly on the singing—and sleeping more than helping, not that there was much he could do. He couldn't really squeeze inside and help him clean. In fact, Isaac was worried there'd be no way for him to fit in the hold at all, ever. It was a large one, but Boar was only a fraction smaller. He was sure Boar knew this, and yet, he stayed around them all anyway, spending his nights buried in the dirt.

Isaac's heart went out to him. He had no one. He'd left everything behind to take a chance on their word. How could they just abandon him? Isaac had grown even more fond of Boar than he'd ever been of his pet spider. He kept hoping a solution would present itself.

Perhaps that was what Boar was hoping for, too.

Another day passed. It was clear their focus on musical theatre was changing the energy in the whole forest. It brought the ghosts, who danced and joined in singing the songs, their forms going from balls of light to distinguishable, faint outlines of creatures stomping their feet and spinning around each other in time with the music. They played the instruments. Their voices were hollow when they sang, like the echo of a choir. It made the scene a bit eerie, really.

Elise attempted to use this as an opportunity to speak to the ghosts and gather more information about the planet of the dead. They were dead, after all. Surely, they'd know something. However, this would always end with the spirit giving Elise a sad smile and disappearing—with no hard feelings, apparently, as they always came back, and everyone continued to get along.

Later that afternoon, as Isaac searched for something to snack on, he noticed a knife lying on a tree stump. It was massive, recently sharpened, and decorated in swirling blue veins, clearly belonging to Rain.

It'd been so long since he'd thrown a knife. He'd once been pretty good at it, if he said so himself. He'd perfected the craft during long days at sea. He was unbeatable among the men on his ship. The only one who ever got close was Arnaud.

He was filled with an uncontrollable urge to test himself, see if he'd lost any of his skill during this adventure.

The knife was just *right there.*

Who left their knives out like this anyway? They might as well have left a note that read, *Test yourself, Isaac...*

Seeing as Rain was busy with all his singing and whatnot, Isaac thought he might not mind if he borrowed it for a moment, just to see. Glancing around, Isaac picked up the knife and slipped into the trees. He jumped when Boar said, "Oooh, you're taking Rain's knife, are you?"

Isaac shushed him. "I'm just *borrowing* it. Just for a moment."

Boar spoke softer. "I see. Of course. Don't worry, I won't tell."

Boar stuck around to watch him, making it rather obvious to everyone where Isaac had gone since there was no real hiding Boar when he wasn't burrowed in the ground.

Isaac examined a tree. After double-checking to make sure it didn't have eyes and wasn't likely to come out of the ground after him, he carved a small X into the trunk. He focused on his shot, took aim, and threw the knife. It stuck right in the center of the X, leaving a thin gash in the bark.

Now Isaac's goal was to strike the exact same spot. He steadied himself with a deep breath and took aim.

He hit the mark precisely.

"Well done!" cheered Boar, slapping his tail against the ground.

"Bet you can't do that again," said a deep, rumbling voice.

Rain.

Oh dear.

Isaac squished his lips together sheepishly and turned toward him. Rain stood close to Boar with his arms folded.

"Why hello, Rain! Didn't see you there," said Boar. Boar then said to Isaac, "Sorry, I would've said something, but I didn't see him there. He was very quiet. And so small."

Rain was the opposite of small, but he supposed everyone here was small compared to Boar.

Rain raised his eyebrows at Isaac. "Well, go on. Let's see if you can do that again."

Isaac's nerves twisted his stomach as he pulled the knife out of the trunk. It was like he'd been caught stealing cookies out of the pantry and had been dared to eat another one.

Isaac steadied himself, took aim.

He hit the mark with even greater exactness than he had before.

Rain stared with wide eyes then shook his head. He ripped the knife from the trunk and aimed.

He missed. Just barely, but he did. He missed it. Isaac tried not to show his delight.

"What's all the hubbub?" asked Nothe, entering the trees while eating a handful of dried berries. "Hi, Boar!"

Isaac informed Boar that Nothe had said hello.

Boar said with delight, "Hello!" and patted Nothe on the head with his tail.

Rain grumbled, "Turns out Isaac is pretty good at throwing knives."

"Oh!" Nothe raised his eyebrows. "You mean, he actually has talent?" He grinned at Isaac.

Isaac was more than happy to show him.

Nothe inhaled the remainder of the berries as he said, "Let me try, let me try."

He almost hit it.

It became a contest. Elise joined in, adding laughter to the game as she heckled them all, at one moment saying, "Ah, c'mon, ya foozler! What a rubbish shot. My grandmother could do better than that while blindfolded," to which Nothe responded with sincerity, "Wow, really?"

Snowman and Thipka found them shortly after and with a general sense of unease, they agreed to let Snowman join in. He hit the mark on the first try. Elise cheered while Isaac, Nothe, and Rain let out a shocked, "Ohhh!" Snowman raised his arms in a taunting, I'm-simply-the-best sort of way.

But Snowman missed on the second attempt.

Nothe and Rain proved they could, actually, hit the mark, much to the cheers of everyone and an "About time!" from Elise. Snowman was exact in his attempts most of the time, but it was Elise and Isaac who tied for first rank, neither of them missing a single shot.

The game left a warm light in Isaac's chest. Not just because he was having fun or that he kept beating Rain and Nothe—but because, for that moment, he was among friends again.

As another day went by, Boar complained about the music less. Rain got even younger, now looking to be in his forties, and had morphed back into his human-like form. And Elise's face started to exude happiness.

And the ship looked gorgeous. Even Thipka said it hadn't looked that good when he got it.

Ships were something Isaac understood. Their demands were reasonable. He somehow knew now—really knew—despite the moments of darkness and horrible detours on the path, he was where he was meant to be.

MEMORIES

Isaac discovered a lake not too far from their camp the next evening, after he'd run out of things to fix and clean.

He knew what to do the moment he saw it.

No, not jump in it, although it was tempting since it'd been far too long since he'd bathed, and his growing facial hair was itchy. But this was an unknown moon-planet, and he had no idea what was in that water. For all he knew, it was something horrible that would melt his skin. He'd heard of lakes like that.

Instead, he took off his boot, his worn-out sock—his foot, though beautiful and scar-free, smelling like moldy, old cheese left out in the sun and humid air—and dipped a single toe into the surface. When his skin didn't melt, he dipped in a few more toes. When nothing else terrible happened, he took off his other boot and sock, sat on the beach, and stuck both of his feet in the water. It was cool, crisp, and completely rejuvenating. All his concerns were washed away.

He started singing.

It was a song from home, one he missed. He was getting the words wrong, he knew it. He didn't care. He was quiet, barely more than a whisper. No one would hear him.

A voice behind him sang in harmony. He jumped as Elise belted the rest of the lyrics at him. She laughed. "I thought you didn't sing."

"I don't."

"You sing well! You always have."

"I didn't say I *couldn't* sing—look, it was just stuck in my head."

"I'm not judging."

She sat beside him, placing her feet in the water. She closed her eyes. "Ah. That is nice, isn't it?"

"It's the little things you miss—like sticking your dirty, sweaty feet in water."

"Yes, indeed."

"I still don't dare get all the way in. I don't know what's out there."

She gave an emphatic nod of agreement. "That's smart thinking, right there. I feel like what we're doing right now is a bit dangerous, ya?"

"Well, as you know, I do like to live a dangerous lifestyle, throw all caution to the sea."

She laughed. "That is certainly true." She pushed her toes into the mud. He hadn't noticed this before, but even her feet were perfect. She said, "Thipka thinks we should put on a performance for the ghosts."

Isaac grimaced. "Wow. He's really getting into this, isn't he?"

Elise shrugged. "It's fun. You should come watch. He's got Rain singing the part of a character called The Bearded Lady."

Isaac smiled. "That fits him perfectly."

Elise laughed. He'd grown fond of her laugh.

Isaac said, "You sing well."

She looked at him, surprised. "Thank you. I meant it when I said you do, too." She nudged him and teased, "You shouldn't hide that under a bushel."

"Ah, but it brings the bushel such joy. Wouldn't want to steal it from...from the bushel..." He'd tried to make a joke, but it didn't work, and he couldn't remember what the joke was really supposed to be anymore.

She laughed again, which he was grateful for. After a moment, she said, "We'll probably be leaving the day after tomorrow."

"That's good news. I'm sure you're ready to go back home. Find your family."

She gave an emphatic nod. "Yes. Yes, I'm *so* ready." After a moment, she added, "I can't tell you how sorry I am for everything I've put you through. I know sorry is not enough. I know there aren't any words that can possibly make any of it right. But I need you to know that I am. I am so, so very sorry. I should've known better, but I didn't. I didn't."

She took a deep breath as if bracing herself to jump from a cliff into deep water. "I've been wanting to tell you something."

Isaac's heart skipped a little. Maybe this was it. Maybe she was about to confess and say, *I was at the party*. Of course, he'd hate that confession. Part of him was glad she'd never said it. And why would she say that right now? That'd be stupid.

She swallowed. "I haven't really wanted to tell you, I don't want to tell anyone—yet I do because I want you to understand. Not that it can possibly make anything right. It'll probably make things worse, but you already hate me," she let out an airy, more-ironic-than-real sort of laugh, resting her forehead in her hand, "so what does it matter?"

An awful dread spread its way through his limbs like cold dead hands. He probably didn't want to know what she was about to say.

She wiped her face, then looked resolutely at the setting sky. "I was a little girl, ya? And it had been such a long move to the United States. It'd taken us so long to get to Maine and get settled. I was tired of ships—if you can believe it. Tired of carriages. Tired of the way people treated me and of my shoes being too small. The house smelled like manure, and the weeds made my face itch. On top of this, I caught some sort of sickness, and I kept having these horrible, *horrible* nightmares about being left behind, and I was just miserable.

"And one night," she pulled her knees to her chest, "I woke up. I'd dreamed I was *deliberately* left behind, and my whole family— imaginary, dream family, but they felt real, ya?—they all told me that I was a monster and that they hated me. Even Arnaud, in the dream. He said it, too. And I woke up screaming." Tears welled up in her eyes. "There was this sound. Crashing, breaking, splattering sound. It was so loud. But I thought it was part of my dream.

"I opened my eyes, and...it was so dark. I kept screaming and crying, waiting for Arnaud to come and comfort me, but he never did. I was wondering why I was lying on the dirt, why there were stars and no roof, why it was so cold."

Isaac reeled, looking away as if he'd been slapped, his eyes burning with a layer of tears.

Tears streamed down her face and she wiped them away, her gaze drifting, darkening, going somewhere Isaac couldn't see. "I called for Arnaud, but he never came to me. Then the sun rose, and I saw...I saw what I'd done. The house was gone. There was only stone, splinters, and blood. Blood *everywhere*. I destroyed a lot more things in that moment, but I didn't mean to. I was just in so much *pain*."

Agony tore through his chest for her as though he'd been hollowed out with a dull knife. He couldn't even bear to imagine what that little Elise had seen, what she'd felt.

She pressed her hands against her face. "I didn't mean to, I didn't mean to."

He knew the look in her eyes. He'd seen it in many a sailor before—even in Elise, when she'd been Arnaud, when they'd once encountered a lost little boy crying out for his mother. It was a look that remained on Arnaud's face even after the little boy had been found by his family. Her stare was vacant; she was going back to the wreckage of the farm in her mind. Isaac put a hand on her shoulder and shook her gently as though trying to wake a sleeping child, massaging her arm. She blinked, coming back a little. "I remembered a story told back home—that there was a place where the souls of the dead go. A world." More tears spilled down her face, and she quickly wiped them away and sniffed, trying to regain her composure. "And I just kept dreaming of being able to go there. And then I found your book, and—"

Isaac squeezed her shoulder. "It's okay, it's okay. I understand why you took it."

She sniffed and wiped her face as a sob escaped her. "I'm so sorry. I'm so sorry for all of it. I didn't mean to. I didn't mean to."

He wrapped an arm around her shoulders. After a moment of not knowing what to say—because what could he say? What words could possibly ease her pain?—he said, "Well, there's certainly no need to apologize for breaking Sister Maria's statues or her mirror. Those were things that needed to be done."

He wasn't sure about his timing with that comment, but he had to try.

Elise chuckled a little and wiped her face. "They did. That needed to happen."

He held her tightly there for a while as her breathing steadied, watching the stars emerge from their hiding places.

If Only Sleeping Were So Easy

That next morning, Isaac noticed that the bags under Snowman's eyes were worse than ever. He'd clearly lost weight, his cheeks sallow and his eyes sunken, and they'd only been there for nine days. It wasn't like they didn't have food. Rain and Nothe were actually very good hunters. Had Snowman eaten anything since they'd shown up? He was tempted to grab some dried meat and annoy him until he ate it.

Snowman stood away from everyone, staring off into the trees, his gaze fixed on the shadows. Isaac thought there might've been a ghost out there, but he didn't see one. He approached Snowman, his boots snapping twigs, but Snowman didn't even flinch. It was as if he couldn't hear him drawing near. The closer Isaac got to him, the more details he could see. Snowman's black eyes were frozen open in an expression of terror, bloodshot and unblinking. Isaac couldn't tell if he was breathing. It was like he was dead on his feet. Isaac reached out, placing his hand on his shoulder, "Hey—"

Snowman grabbed his hand, twisting it. He let it go and seized Isaac's collar, his wide, inflamed eyes fixed on his. *"Do you see him? Do you see him?"*

Snowman's grip on Isaac's clothes was tight like Isaac was the only thing there keeping him from drowning.

"See who?"

Snowman pulled Isaac closer, his gaze darting wildly to the trees. "He's there! He's *right there!* We need to run. We need to get out of here. He's here. *You can see him!*"

Isaac looked toward the trees, searching the shadows. There was nothing. Not a ghost, not an animal, nothing. "I can't. I can't see—"

"He's *there!*"

This poor, terrifying man. Isaac placed his hands on Snowman's wrists as if he were trying to comfort a delusional, elderly man waking from a nightmare. "Asael—" He thought using his real name would be more appropriate for this situation.

"Don't call me that!" hissed Snowman.

Isaac's heart was pounding now. Was anyone else seeing this? Anyone? Could someone rescue him? Please?

Isaac kept his head. "All right, Snowman." He squeezed his wrists gently, then placed a reassuring hand on his shoulder. He imagined himself as a child, waking from a horrible dream at the orphanage. What did he wish had been said to him? "It's all right. You're safe. You're not alone. What are you seeing?" Isaac asked. "Tell me. Help me see."

Snowman looked back into the trees. Isaac watched as a bit of the madness lifted from his face, replaced by tears. "He—he was there." His grip on Isaac's clothing loosened. "He was there, just now. He..." Snowman let him go, wandering toward the trees. Isaac stumbled after him, knowing it wasn't a good idea for the man to be alone right now.

Snowman turned to him. "You didn't see him?"

"Who was I supposed to see?"

Snowman blinked as if he'd just woken somewhere completely unfamiliar and strange. His forehead glistened with sweat. He began to tremble, and he collapsed to a knee, burying his face in his hands.

Isaac stood there, feeling awkward and not knowing what to do. Should he leave? No, that would be terrible.

With the carefulness of someone approaching a wounded bear, Isaac kneeled beside him and placed a hand on his shoulder. Snowman looked away, seeming embarrassed. "You must think I'm mad."

"Nooo." But then on second thought, "Well..."

"I saw him," Snowman insisted, not looking anywhere in particular. "He was there."

Isaac squeezed his shoulder. Snowman had certainly seen something that frightened him. That was very clear. Whether or not that thing actually existed—who was Isaac to dispute that? It would only upset him further. "I'm sure." Isaac added, "You know what I think you need? Some sleep."

"No."

"Some good sleep."

"I can't sleep."

"I think you'd be surprised."

"You don't understand. I see him. In my sleep, he's there. Those eyes..."

Isaac's stomach seized up at those words. "What eyes?"

"His eyes. They're always, *always* watching. And—and the things he shows me," he fought to hold back tears, "the things he won't let me forget."

Isaac considered asking, *Are they melted eyes, perhaps?* but couldn't form the words. He opened his mouth to try, and he just *couldn't*. Because he didn't want to know. He just wanted to pack up their beautiful spaceship and leave. If he acknowledged the possibility that the eyes he'd seen and the eyes haunting Snowman were the same, he'd be acknowledging that all the fears he'd had about someone interfering in his wonderful plans might have merit.

He just really couldn't handle that right now.

He patted Snowman's shoulder. "Well, then, we must feed you. I know things always seem a little better for me when I have a full stomach."

Snowman snorted and rubbed his eyes. He looked away, wiping a few tears from his face. "Yeah, all right."

"All right?"

He nodded.

"On your feet, then." Isaac helped him up. "And you get to do your performance for the ghosts tonight." That was something Isaac never thought he'd say. "That'll surely help."

Snowman nodded again and smiled a little, but there was profound pain behind it. "Yeah. That'll be good."

Isaac patted his back. "C'mon." He started back toward the camp and stopped. Snowman hadn't moved.

Snowman shifted his feet. "I'm sure you're going to tell everyone about this."

Isaac fixed his gaze on him. "Of course not. It's nobody's business." He meant it. He thought of crewmen who'd gone mad at sea and reflected on his fit at the beach after Elise blew up his ship. "Besides, we all have our moments."

Once There Was a Snowman

Snowman sat at the camp near the embers of the fire. Isaac was making him eat dried, nasty meat and drink water because he believed he was dehydrated. He was probably right. About everything. Dehydrated, starving, sleep-deprived. Isaac even draped a blanket over his shoulders. It was an old, moldy one that'd been left in the ship for who knew how long, but still. Snowman was in awe at Isaac's thoughtfulness. He'd never seen that in a human before. Isaac was a rare gift, one that made his heart feel alive and wonderful, a warm feeling that was unexpected and grew with each day and every act of kindness.

He'd grown rather fond of Isaac.

Thanks for making my job even harder, Isaac.

He wondered if everything he felt—all the guilt, conflict, fear, and pain—was visible on his face.

Probably not. If it were, they'd have left him for dead already—or at least have tried. There was no way any of them could overpower him. Not even Elise, he was sure of it. He'd mastered his abilities, had perfect control. This was a matter of fact.

He wasn't sure how proud of that he should be. Yes, he could kill anyone and anything. *Good for you, Snowman. Your mother would be so proud.*

His mother had been genuinely kind. He remembered her smiling face, the comfort of her embrace, the songs she'd sing as he fell asleep. He remembered how his older brother made him laugh, the teasing of his oldest brother, and the glow-bugs he'd caught for his little sister and put in a jar. They brought her comfort at night when the shadows distorted the furniture and welcomed out the fabled beasts that hid in the closet.

In its own absurd way, the week he'd spent with these people reminded him of those days. They were the best times of his life. The images were a little blurry in his mind now, but he remembered the feeling perfectly. The comfort, the safety, the joy.

Snowman. He'd really hated that name at first. He didn't anymore. He liked the image it brought—of creating something fun out of the cold, something that brought joy on a sunny winter day. It stirred within him feelings of longing and pain, a pain he didn't hate. It was a wish for something that could never be, but he enjoyed dreaming about it when he was awake.

A new beginning. A change in direction. A chance to be someone different—the creature he'd always wanted to be. A chance at a happy life.

What was so bad about that?

He liked being around these creatures. He didn't like that Thipka guy much, but he didn't hate him. He didn't hate any of them, which was a relief to his mind since he hated most creatures. He liked listening to them talk and watching them work. He liked making Elise laugh. She had a wonderful laugh. She had a kind light in her eyes and fought for the impossible with so much hope. Even though he knew that wouldn't end well for her, he cherished her hope for its purity and envied it.

And then there was Annabel. She was a sweetheart. Creative. A bit mischievous. When she'd asked him to show her how his ship worked, she successfully switched it on and made him think she was going to take off in it. She had the self-respect not to let anyone treat her poorly, yet was willing to learn. She had the potential of a compassionate, intelligent leader. He'd decided this when he saw how she took good care of her pet, Gof. If he could ever be lucky enough to have children of his own, he hoped he'd be a good enough father to raise a youngster like that.

There weren't supposed to be children among these people.

Annabel deserved better. She deserved to feel—and know—that she was safe. She deserved to embrace the bright future ahead of her.

Honestly, they all deserved better. Even the worm was all right, and that took a lot for Snowman to admit—he truly hated those things.

No one could tell him that his father's righteous, almighty "plan" to build a time machine would make everything right, that bringing it to pass would make what his father wanted *right*. Some things couldn't ever truly be made right.

Some wounds were soul-deep and would follow him like his shadow, no matter where in time he was. They'd always be there somewhere.

The same for his father, whose very soul had changed. The father he'd once loved was dead, the kind of dead that truly lasted forever. He'd wanted to believe, but, in that moment, he saw everything with more clarity than ever before—he saw all the things he'd been trying to ignore.

Snowman's mind was broken with regret. He'd failed. He'd fallen. He hadn't been able to save his family.

But he'd *tried*.

He'd been too late.

They'd burned so fast.

He thought his mother would've been proud of him for how hard he'd tried, for the people he *did* save—because he'd saved his neighbors, he'd saved *some*. He'd had a nanny that had told him that. And he swore his mother had told him these things in a dream once. She'd said she loved him, she knew how hard he'd tried, and how she was so proud of him. That'd been a long time ago. He'd seen her and hugged her and his siblings. They didn't blame him, they'd said. It'd felt so real. He liked to believe it was.

Oh, it would be wonderful if the plan would make it all clean again, if it could bring them back, make everything right, just like his father wanted—like he, himself, wanted.

But deep down, Snowman had always known it wouldn't happen— not the way his father wanted to use it. It would make everything worse. So many innocent people would suffer, would die, would never be born. People who had nothing to do with the tragedy that had befallen his world—his family.

Snowman wouldn't survive it. He was barely surviving now.

Even though Snowman adored the thought of having his family back, of erasing this agonizing timeline and returning his soul to a moment of peace, love, and a bright, wonderfully-boring future—where he could seek life advice from a sane father—he knew that wish was dead. And even with a time machine, it always would be. His father wouldn't magically return to the man he had once been. No, he'd go back and begin his work of death on innocent worlds before he even married his mother, before any of Snowman's siblings were born.

Even if Snowman were to somehow leap into the time machine first and set things back the way he wanted, it wouldn't work. All of these wounds were soul-deep. And besides, how would he close the loop?

More importantly, it simply couldn't be allowed to exist. There was more than one madman out there in the universe and if any of them got a hold of such a powerful machine...

No. He couldn't let it happen. These good, innocent people who surrounded him now, they would all die to give power to a man who wanted to spread terror. It was worse than dying for nothing.

A severe pain pierced his chest as if someone had stabbed him clear through with a thin blade. He struggled to steady his breathing.

He caught Rain staring at him then. He'd recently shifted back to his human form, looking much younger than when they'd first met. He studied Snowman with his brow furrowed with curiosity and concern as he sipped from a wooden mug. He and Nothe would both do that when he had an inner meltdown near them, as if they somehow *knew* what he was feeling. Rain cast him a look of sympathy, of understanding, and walked away.

Snowman hated that look. He hated that he just walked away. If only Rain would kill him. If only he and Nothe could. If only he'd die here. Right here. From this pain. If only his heart would just *stop*.

Annabel had already lost so much. She'd told Snowman that the ghost that followed her closely, Ver, was her brother. She'd lost him, along with her parents and her entire village, to a mudslide. It had been spring-cleaning time when it happened. She'd lost against her brother in a game not unlike drawing straws and had been tasked with the unwanted chore of cleaning the chimney. The rocky flue had protected her, so she'd been spared. She was small enough to climb out of the top when it was over.

Just like that, everyone she loved was dead.

Except for Thipka. He'd been back at his ship and missed it. He was weeping when he found her and kept saying, "This wasn't supposed to happen. I changed it, I changed it."

Annabel seemed to think he knew the future, or at least parts of it. He kept trying to change the parts he didn't like, but Time had a way of fighting back. Snowman wasn't sure he believed that was possible, but there were times when he considered asking Thipka if he knew how his fate would turn out and how to escape it.

But Snowman thought he already knew the answer. His dreams told him his father was aware of the answer as well and was losing faith in him.

He grimaced as he took another chewy, rough bite of his food. This dried meat was terrible. What was he eating? He gulped moss-tasting water to wash it down.

His full stomach let him know just how exhausted he was. Fatigue flooded his body. He fought to keep his eyes open.

HE WAS PLAYING near the lake, a five-year-old boy with round cheeks testing his abilities as he held a ball of water in the air with pudgy, tiny fingers. He turned it to ice, then plopped it back into the lake to watch it float away. He'd made so many of them. They were floating across the surface in front of him. The crisp air smelled of grass and spring flowers, and a light breeze kissed his face.

There was a strange sound, like a distant explosion. He turned. Waves of red and orange flames rippled through the clouds as though sky had been set on fire.

Giant black bugs fell from the clouds and glided through the air. One headed straight for him. It darted toward the row of homes down the lake, dropping blue light on top of them. The houses burst into flames with a deafening roar, filling the air with the smell of smoke.

His house was one of them.

He blinked, his ears ringing, his little heart thundering in his chest. Tears filled his eyes. He didn't know what to do. What was he supposed to do?

A dark voice said, *You just stood there. Worthless. Useless. You just stood there!*

He ran toward his family, his home. The scent of campfire smoke and burned meat overwhelmed him, reminding him of the wooc steak his mother would make. He'd never been able to eat it since.

His chest hurt so much. With each breath he took, he felt it might burst. He couldn't get enough air.

He screamed as his father leapt into his burning home. He couldn't stop screaming. He paced, tears streaming down his face as he pulled his hair. What was he supposed to do? What could he do? They were dying!

Pathetic. The voice said. *You just stood there. Useless.*

He ran toward the lake. He had no idea where the strength came from, but with his tiny hands, he caused the lake, with its muddy banks, to gush up into the sky, a massive mountain of mud and water soaring over his little body, pouring out onto the houses and drowning the flames.

You took too long.

Once the fire was out, he ran toward his house, the sound of water dripping from the roof echoing in his ears.

It's your fault.

You were too late.

He was too late.

It was only by the sizes of their blackened bodies that he could tell who they were. Their hair and clothing were melted, their eye sockets empty, their bodies twisted in agony.

It's your fault.

You were too LATE!

HE JUMPED AWAKE, stumbling as he leapt to his feet, nearly falling into the embers.

"Whoa! Whoa!" Isaac said, catching him.

Snowman's hands shook. He was there. He was back *there.*

No. No, he wasn't. He was on Lolaar. The moon planet. The sky was clear and bright without ships. He was with Isaac and other people who weren't dead or terrible.

It didn't feel that way. It was like he was viewing this place through a screen. He wasn't actually there. His mind was at his ruined house, small and helpless, seeing the remains of the only people who had ever loved him. It wasn't until he felt tears fall from his chin that he realized he was crying.

He quickly wiped his face, which was numb. He glanced at Isaac. His brown eyes full of worry. Isaac would say they were dull eyes, but they weren't, really. They were soulful. They just didn't glow like everyone else's.

Isaac squeezed his shoulders, bringing him back a little, reassuring him as he said, "It's all right. You're safe. Right now, you're safe."

He was. At least in *this* moment, he was safe. Snowman composed himself, his gaze darting around, searching to see if anyone else had witnessed him make a fool of himself just now. No one else was there. He could hear them singing and laughing on the other side of the ship. "How long was I out for?"

Isaac said, "You weren't. At least, I thought you weren't. I had no idea you'd fallen asleep at all. I'd just walked over there for a moment."

Snowman nodded, and Isaac dropped his hands to his sides. Snowman rubbed his face. Something gripped him then. Perhaps it was because he was being shattered again and again and now stood in the presence of someone who made him feel a sense of safety he hadn't experienced in years. Perhaps it was the sleep deprivation. Really, it was probably all of it. But he blurted something to Isaac that he'd never told anyone. "He blames me. My family was murdered when I was five, and I couldn't save them. I tried, though. I really tried."

Isaac looked shocked. His expression filled with empathy and a sorrow that reached his eyes. "Who blames you for it?"

Snowman couldn't meet his gaze, and he didn't answer. He shouldn't have said anything in the first place.

Isaac placed his hands back on his shoulders. "Snowman, listen. This is very important—you were five. I don't need to have been there to know you did everything your five-year-old self could. The only ones who are guilty are those who committed that heinous crime. No child should ever go through what you've been through. No child should ever shoulder that burden."

Snowman bit his lips, holding back more tears. Isaac might as well have been talking to that little five-year-old boy standing in the middle of the charred remains of his family.

That little boy could've used some kindness.

He shouldn't have saved his father. He should've let him burn.

Isaac hesitated; then, resting his arms at his sides, he forced a smile. "You know, er," he pointed his thumb at the singing group, "I can't believe I'm saying this, but, if you can't sleep, then I think some singing and dancing would do you some good. You need to go have some fun. Take your mind off things. Most definitely."

Snowman successfully fought the tears away. "I think you're right." He cleared his throat and wiped his face again, plastering on a smile. "How do I look?"

Isaac clearly considered his words. "Like you need some singing and dancing. And maybe a drink."

Snowman was confused. "I actually had a lot of water a moment ago but thank you."

"Not that kind of drink."

He caught on and grinned. "Ah. I see. I probably could use one."

"But nobody here has what I'm talking about, so never mind. Just—go enjoy yourself."

And he did. At least, as best as he could with those eyes watching him through the shadows.

Cards From Disneyland, and There's a Musical

It was their last day on the planet, and Isaac couldn't have been more thrilled. The atmosphere around the camp grew happier and happier as the day wore on. Snowman even laughed from time to time and seemed to be having fun, which was a massive improvement from his terrifying episodes the day before, which Isaac now completely understood. How could anyone fully recover from such a past? He'd worked with many men on his voyages who were fleeing to the sea from their own stories; several had succumbed to madness for far less than what Snowman had lived through. Sure, the man was up to something, but Isaac couldn't help it—he was glad he was getting some relief from his memories.

Isaac was still concerned about poor Boar. He spent most of the day with him since neither of them was involved in the play. Gof would usually hang around also, petting Isaac's head occasionally and combing his hair with his bear-like paws as if Isaac were a puppy. He just let it happen. It was kind of hilarious, honestly.

Isaac had found a deck of strange cards in the ship while cleaning it —there were many odd treasures in there. These cards looked a bit like cards he'd seen before, but they were brightly colored and had a skeleton dressed in a red outfit, sitting on a carved pumpkin. It read *The Nightmare Before Christmas* in the mouth of what looked like a monstrous wreath and *The Haunted Mansion* in the corner. In English, no less. It was all very strange.

Still, he knew a few games he could play with these cards, and he taught them to Boar, who was quite cheerful, considering his uncertain future.

That evening, the two of them gathered with a multitude of glowing, ghostly orbs to watch the play. The music was better than the overall story. Isaac had known of the man whom the story claimed to be based on—the *actual* P.T. Barnum—and it was well known among his friends that he was a crook. An entertaining crook, but a crook, and not likely the halfway-decent fellow portrayed in the play. Isaac wondered if P.T. had been behind writing it.

Also, how *did* Thipka know this musical about P.T. Barnum? He made a mental note to ask him about this when he had the chance. Thipka would probably respond with, "Time is a strange, strange thing," or something.

He suspended his annoyance at these details and had to admit that each person in the play was doing a good job. He enjoyed it more than he thought. Rain's performance was particularly moving. As he sang, it was as if a wall had crumbled around him. Emotions of unbearable pain and indestructible hope washed over everyone, even bringing the ghosts around him to tears. Something inside of Rain had healed through music, a wound that had been thought to be beyond repair. Isaac knew this because he felt it. Even Boar, who didn't like any of their singing, wiped tears from his many eyes.

Every performer was thoroughly entertaining, and he liked them all a little better by the end, having seen a side of them he hadn't known was there. Elise was beautiful. Or, rather, her voice was beautiful. And she was beautiful. She had a perfect face and perfect curves and was lovely, like a work of art. And a very good dancer. Who would've thought?

Yes, he did enjoy the play overall. If you left out all the ghosts playing back-up characters, it almost felt as though he were back home on Earth. But he was still grateful when the show was over—just like he'd been with the two operas Alice had dragged him to years ago. Maybe a little more so, especially after hearing the ghosts applaud and cheer, which was similar to hearing hundreds of people screaming in a dark room when you thought you were alone.

He hugged Rain after—he couldn't help himself. Rain looked shocked. He also, somehow, looked like he was about his own age now, and the light in his eyes had brightened.

Maybe Isaac should've been in the musical. Perhaps he would've come out younger.

Then Isaac hugged Snowman, which he also couldn't seem to help. It turned out awkward, and Snowman didn't seem to know what to think of it, but Isaac felt like he really needed a hug. After wordlessly patting him on the back, he then turned to Elise and pulled her aside, telling her, "You know, you were wonderful up there."

She beamed at him. "Thank you." Tears filled her eyes. "Thank you. I think it was the most fun I've ever had."

Isaac was a bit offended by that. "More fun than that time we stole back our supplies from the machete-wielding drunks in Bali?"

She laughed. "Ah yes. That will always hold a special place in my heart. All right, all right, this has been *some* of the most fun I've ever had. Better?"

"Yes, thank you."

She grinned and shook her head a little. "You know, this week has just been *amazing*. There were times when I almost forgot all the awful things. I don't want it to end. I don't—I mean, I just wish I could hold onto these days forever, ya? Keep them in a jar." She chuckled, then sniffed and wiped her face.

He thought he could understand. He'd found his calling, working on that spaceship. However, he didn't know if he'd ever be able to live it out. The future would certainly shatter this new dream somehow.

If only he could keep it in a jar...and then proceed to live in that jar.

Isaac nodded. "If only all hope and happy memories could be so perfectly preserved and stored, to be savored again when we need them most."

"Ha. Hear, hear, Isaac. Who knew you could be so poetic?"

"I believe this week has brought the genius out of me."

Elise laughed—he was glad he could make her laugh. "Indeed!"

THAT NIGHT IN HIS DREAMS, Isaac found the room with The Prophet again. The Prophet was so annoyed this time that he didn't even bother to look at him. "Whatever," he said. "I guess you can see what I've been working on. Might be a bad idea, but maybe you'll have some helpful insight."

Before Isaac could take a look, he was ripped awake by a terrible scream, one that pierced his heart and flooded his veins with horror. It was the sound of a man being attacked by a wild cat, whose last breath was only seconds away.

Isaac jumped up, scurrying away from the sound, his eyes searching the shadows around him for the danger. Nothe and Rain rushed through the darkness toward Snowman, whose eyes were frozen open. "Enough!" He screamed into the darkness at nothing. "*Enough!*"

In the flicker of a thought, Snowman gathered water from the humid air and shot it toward the trees, narrowly missing Thipka and turning the trees and foliage to ice.

Gof rose with an indignant growl, putting a protective arm around a startled Annabel. Rain grabbed Snowman's wrist and he visibly relaxed, his body collapsing forward till his head rested on his knees. "I fell asleep," Snowman muttered. "I fell asleep."

It wasn't until that moment that Isaac was sure there was no real danger—not right now, anyway. However, he did make a mental note to always sleep somewhere outside of Snowman's line of vision.

The ground rumbled. Boar emerged from the dirt, bleary and still waking, "What's going on? Who do I need to eat?"

Isaac explained that Snowman had had a nightmare and froze the trees. Together, they watched as Rain rubbed Snowman's shoulder, his tone comforting. "It's over."

"Yeah," added Nothe, "It's all right."

"You're safe."

Boar said, "Oh. Well, if that's all, I'll just go back to sleep then, if you don't mind." Boar slithered away.

Snowman shook his head. "No, no, no. No one's safe."

"Sure we are," insisted Nothe. "Look, it's just us—"

"No." Snowman sat upright. "I need you to listen to me. All of you. *Listen to me.*" Sweat glistened off Snowman's face, his expression panicked and wild. He had everyone's attention. "You were right not to trust me. I was sent here for the sole purpose of making sure you," he looked at Elise, "made it back to Ethra."

Elise looked at him, confused. "That was unnecessary. I'm pretty determined to get there myself."

Isaac nodded in a very matter-of-fact way. "That is true."

Snowman said, "Well, I did bring my machine to repair your ship. And took out the ornery tree-man for you and guided you to the River, so...yeah."

That was also true.

"I do what he wants—or I used to. He definitely doesn't want me to do what I'm doing right now."

"What are you doing right now?" asked Rain.

"Wait a minute, wait a minute," said Nothe, "I think a better question is, who is this *he* that you speak of?"

Rain narrowed his gaze at Nothe. "That is a good question, but I don't think it's a better question."

Snowman's expression fell, wracked with anger and sorrow. "My father." He turned to Elise. "He was well aware of you before you were left on Earth. You were taken there before he knew of the River. You were on Ethra one day, gone the next. He was delighted when he found you again through his sight." His gaze fixed on Elise through the darkness. "He knows just how powerful you are. I'm telling you, do not go back to Ethra. Just leave it alone. Whatever you're hoping to gain by going back, just—don't. You'll only be disappointed. Go back to your precious Earth." He looked at Isaac. "Go back to your canvas sails and your turkey and potatoes—I mean, you don't stop talking about those, Isaac. So just go. Go to them."

Somehow, that didn't have the same appeal it had just a few days ago. He might like to go back eventually, but only after he flew to a few new places in that ship.

Elise scrutinized him. "Why?"

"Why do you want to go back to Ethra?"

"I have things to make right."

"She has people to bring back," explained Nothe.

Snowman smiled, but it wasn't from amusement. He chuckled. "Ah, don't we all?" He shook his head. "You can't bring them back, Elise. It doesn't work like that."

Nothe muttered, "That's what we tried to say—"

Rain swatted Nothe's shoulder. "But like the intelligent creatures we are, we dropped the matter, didn't we, Nothe?"

Snowman said, "She's the one who needs to drop it."

Isaac asked, "What are you talking about? Why? Why does your father want her there, and why is it so important that she not go there?"

Snowman looked at his black fingernails. "Well, my father knows how the River was built, and how it works."

Silence fell over the group. Thipka looked unsurprised, bored even, distracted by the scars on his hand as if he'd known this all along.

Snowman continued, "So now, with what he's learned from studying the River and from all his experiments, he thinks he can build a time machine." He pointed at Elise. "But he needs *you* to power it."

The Truth

"Wait a minute, wait a minute," said Nothe, his face scrunched up as he rubbed his forehead. He squinted at Snowman as if he'd shrunk to a size so small he was difficult to see. "What?"

"To which part?" Snowman asked.

Rain leaned toward him, giving him a very similar look. He tapped his palm with his finger as if taking notes on it. "Your father...built the River."

"No, actually. He likes to tell people he built it, and for the longest time I believed he did. But I learned later that he didn't. He discovered it and took credit for it, and killed almost everyone who knew better. Then he studied it with his..." he made gestures with his hands as if trying to summon something, seeming to search for a word, "*abilities* to figure out how it was built and how it works. He killed a *lot* of people in the process. A lot."

Rain said, "So, wait—he didn't build it?"

Nothe replied, "Did you fall asleep in the middle of his explanation?"

"Maybe."

"He just said he didn't build it."

Rain gestured toward Snowman. "He said that his father said he built it."

"But he also said his father was *lying*."

"But allegedly, his father knows how it was built, and how it works. Those seem to be things you'd need in order to build it."

"He found it and figured it out later. He just wanted credit for building it so people would think he was all-knowing and all-powerful," Nothe looked at Snowman, "Am I right?"

Snowman squished his lips together in a look that wordlessly said, *Pretty much,* and nodded.

"That's dumb," concluded Rain. "Then who built it?"

Rain and Nothe looked at Snowman. Snowman shrugged. "I don't know. No one does."

Rain didn't seem convinced. "Right. So, if your father knows all this, and wants Elise to come to her home planet—which is your planet, apparently—why did the River attack us when we tried to actually—"

Nothe finished the question for him, "Enter your world."

"Right."

Snowman seemed genuinely surprised and perplexed. "It did that?"

Rain nodded. "Yeah."

Nothe demonstrated with his arm. "A big ol' wall of-of faces."

"It was terrifying," added Isaac.

Elise didn't contribute to the group testimony. She'd apparently become very interested in a small rock near her foot.

Snowman rubbed his chin, thoughtful. "Huh. That's odd." He concluded, "All I can figure is, they've somehow learned about my father's machine and don't want him to build it."

Isaac furrowed his brow. "*They?*"

"Why not?" Annabel suddenly chimed. Isaac hadn't realized she'd been listening, but it made sense. It'd be hard to go back to sleep after all the commotion. Snowman's scream probably even woke the nearby bears—or whatever monsters lived in that forest.

He couldn't think about that too much.

Annabel went on, "What would be so bad about a time machine? I think it's a good idea."

"Well," said Snowman, "it's not. Especially when people have to die to build it; people that are here, among us," he gestured to Elise, "and it might not even work—"

Annabel said, "Couldn't you just use the time machine to bring them back after they're dead?"

Isaac raised his eyebrows at this. She was quite the little conspirator. "The non-human sacrifice you're speaking of is sitting right here."

Annabel waved this away. "I just mean, like, if it wasn't Elise, but someone else."

Nothe said, "If you go back in time and save them, then the way it was built wouldn't exist anymore, and then the time machine wouldn't exist, and it would probably all cancel itself out somehow, right? Revert back to the original timeline?"

Rain considered this. "Or perhaps Time would break somehow."

"Or maybe it'd all turn out exactly the way you want it, with a new timeline and no machine."

Rain brightened. "Maybe."

"Probably not, though."

Rain's shoulders slumped a little. "Right. When does anything turn out well?"

"The play went well."

Rain smiled. "It did, didn't it?"

Snowman shook his head. "In my father's mind, he'd be trading certain innocent creatures' lives for others. I mean, it's devastating, yes, to lose those you love more than..." He swallowed, as if he suddenly had a very bitter taste in his mouth. "Anyone. But how does taking an innocent life—or thousands of them—for another, make it right? It just digs the hole deeper. Poisons you. Creates catastrophe.

"And now, bringing back the people he lost—it's not even about that anymore. Now it's about destroying everyone else, anyone that could possibly hurt him or humiliate him. Whole worlds—that's what he wants to do. He wants them destroyed, and long before any of them can hurt us. Or most importantly, *him*. He believes this is what will finally bring our planet peace. It's the only way to peace—universal peace, even. That's what he tells himself, anyway. People are peaceful when they're all dead, they can't hurt anyone."

Isaac raised his eyebrows. That statement chilled him to his bones, like falling into the frozen sea.

"That's his mindset, apparently," continued Snowman. "Pretty hypocritical of him if you think about it.

"But in reality, it's all about power and control. No one else's peace really matters. If he has all the control, then *he'll* have peace."

The words sat heavy in the air like a thick fog. No one took a breath.

Rain broke the silence. "Not really, though. People like that, there's never enough power. And true peace, it's always just out of reach for them."

Snowman pressed his hands prayerfully to his lips, seeming to ponder this. "That's his own fault." His gaze darted to the frozen trees, piercing them with a fierce glare. "I won't let him ruin anybody else."

Silence followed these words. Isaac was about to ask what the new plan was and maybe suggest they all take a long vacation and explore other planets that *weren't* Elise's when Annabel said, "Okay, but, what if you go back in time, fix what you wanted to fix, and *then* save the people from being killed to make the time machine, and then it didn't exist anymore, and then it couldn't be used for hurting anyone else."

Apparently, she wasn't over figuring out how to properly use the time machine.

Nothe looked at Rain. "Isn't that basically what I said a minute ago?"

Elise then said, her voice tense, "But then, that would just unravel everything that was done, ya?"

"How?" said Annabel. "It was already done!"

"How could it be done if there was no way to go back and fix it in the first place?"

Nothe nodded. "You'd probably need to complete the loop, right?"

Snowman's response to this was a sigh. A deep, exhausted, I've-considered-all-of-this-before-and-I'm-tired-of-arguing-and-of-life-in-general sort of sigh.

Rain said, "Wait—just, stop for a moment. Everything this man is saying," he gestured to Snowman, "we are not discussing this seriously, are we? This is complete madness!"

"Well, he is telling the truth," said Nothe.

"That's not the issue. This man is severely sleep-deprived. We all know what that does to the mind."

Isaac had been thinking about it all seriously. He thought Snowman was probably sane—sleep-deprived, yes, and maybe dehydrated, but sane. For example, how did he know how to navigate the River so well when so many seemed to not even know of its existence? It wasn't like the River was a busy highway. It was massive and dumbfounding and absolutely did *not* exist in the normal universe.

And how had he found them when he hadn't even seen where they'd gone? They'd been swallowed by the River and tossed onto a random world.

And did this mean it was his father who blamed him for the death of his family—tormenting the poor man since he was a small child?

Isaac had seen many lunatics, swindlers, and liars in his day. Unlike the first day he'd met him and the day he'd shown up at the ship, there was nothing in Snowman's demeanor now that said he was lying. Rather, he looked repentant, like a child apologizing to a friend, and—most of all—utterly defeated. He didn't even seem to care if anyone believed him. He was finished. His final act was to tell the truth and warn of impending disaster.

Then there were Isaac's former visions of the eyes. Snowman had said he'd seen eyes.

Isaac approached Snowman while Nothe and Rain continued to argue, speaking softly. "You said you saw eyes. Were they...did they look burned?"

Snowman's gaze fixed on Isaac's. Slowly he nodded. "How do you know that?"

"I've seen them before. In my sleep."

"Those are my father's eyes. He has these psychic abilities. He can see everything. It's how he found the River, and Elise, and knew where to send me to find you. He told me to bring my machine to make sure that ship was repaired—he knew what Thipka's plan was. He's been watching you."

Well, Isaac hated that. "But he can't see the future, it seems?"

"No. That's one positive, I guess."

Rain and Nothe had stopped arguing and started listening.

Isaac asked, "What does—"

Snowman's eyes widened in terror. "He's coming." His hands trembled, but his voice was calm. "He knows what I've done, and he's on his way." He rose to his feet and told Thipka, "Take Annabel. Take her, and—no. No. Never mind. We need to leave. He'll destroy this planet looking for us if we stay."

Nothe looked shocked. "Whoa, what?"

"He'll set the whole thing on fire trying to get to Elise. We need to leave Annabel and Thipka and whoever else wants to stay, and take Elise, and just go. Somewhere. Draw him away from here."

Isaac's heart stopped beating for a moment. "Wait-wait-wait-wait, w-wouldn't he just destroy any other planet we go to? Where are we supposed to go, exactly?"

Nothe and Rain exchanged a look. Rain asked Isaac, "Are you seriously worried?"

"Yes!" As quickly as he could, he listed all the reasons why he thought Snowman's story was legitimate.

Nothe looked at Rain and shrugged. "Those are fair points."

Rain grumbled, "I guess there's no harm in playing it safe. We were planning on leaving anyway."

Elise rose to her feet. "Why don't we just go home, then? Fight him on his own ground. He won't burn down his own planet, will he?"

Snowman raised an eyebrow, saying nothing.

Isaac finally asked the question he'd started earlier. "What does this have to do with Elise? How is she supposed to power his machine?"

Snowman glanced away. "Basically, the machine needs to operate outside of this realm—this known world, or whatever—in order for it to send someone across time. So, it needs something interdimensional, something from outside of this dimension to power it and allow it to cross planes of existence. Follow?"

Isaac wasn't sure he did, but he was trying.

Snowman continued, "He needs her spirit, her life force, to power the machine. No little soul will do. For example, you human souls—it would take thousands of you to power a machine like that. I mean, once you're dead, all you can do is mess with lights or jangle door handles, *oooh!* But someone like her—she is the most powerful being anyone on my planet has ever encountered. The energy she has..." He threw up a hand. "I don't know how he figured out how to use living energy to power his machine. All I know is that the outcome of this is going to be devastating. I have enough regrets. I can't be a part of it." He glanced at the sky. "And we're running out of time."

Elise stepped toward him, her gaze piercing and her eyes glowing in the darkness. "I won't let that happen. I will fight him. And I will win."

Snowman shrugged, surrendering, his expression weary and full of sorrow. "I really hope you do."

Thipka picked up Annabel and hurried toward the ship. Snowman grabbed his shoulder. "What are you doing? You can't take her."

"I'm not leaving her here."

"Are you mad? I told you to stay here. You *both* stay here where it's *safe!*"

Thipka ignored him.

"Thipka," Annabel said, her tone gentle. "Stop."

She climbed down from his arms, then tugged on his shirt until he knelt in front of her. She cradled his face in her tiny hands. "My family is here. You need to go find yours."

Thipka shook his head. "No. I can't leave you alone."

She gave him a sad smile. "I am not alone."

All around them, one by one, the shadows in the trees were chased away by hundreds of brilliant lights. Each one took a shape. Isaac could see their beautiful individuality, some short, some tall. Some with massive antlers and some with none. Some held hands. But their expressions were kind and warm.

The final lights illuminated around Annabel—a couple, a man with antlers, an arm wrapped around his wife. A small boy appeared next to her, placing his hand on Annabel's shoulder.

Tears streamed down Thipka's face, and he hung his head. Annabel, with a grace and wisdom beyond her years, lifted his chin. "We'll see each other again. You need to go find your family."

He nodded at the ghosts, who smiled and nodded in return. He embraced Annabel tightly and had a difficult time letting her go.

Gof had a hard time letting Isaac go. He wrapped his big, furry arms around him and patted his head, growling sadly as if he were trying to say goodbye. Isaac felt as though his heart were being crushed, and he couldn't help but hug Gof back tightly in return. He sure hoped he'd see him and Annabel again someday.

Once Thipka had turned away, Snowman handed Annabel a tiny, rectangular box with buttons on it. He gestured to his ship. "Take care of it for me, will you?"

Isaac followed Thipka onto the ship, flipping the appropriate dials and switches at his direction. The massive ship hummed to life. Lights came on—flameless ones. It was outstanding, and despite his panic, a thrill of delight ran through him. Thipka flipped a few more switches and the back of the hull opened. Thipka said to Isaac, "Go get Boar."

With a happiness that surprised him, Isaac dashed out of the ship and hollered into the hole in the ground where Boar was sleeping, "Boar! Get up! We're leaving!"

Boar rushed to the surface, eyes bright. "Really?" Once the big worm saw open hull and that he could fit inside, he wept from every one of his eyes. "I just knew you wouldn't leave me."

It was a tight squeeze for him. Boar did his best to make himself smaller and was clearly uncomfortable. "I do hope this is a short trip."

After Isaac saw to it that no part of Boar's tail would get shut in the cargo hold door, he boarded the ship through the cabin and entered the flight deck where Rain, Nothe, Elise and Snowman sat in the seats behind Thipka, leaving the co-pilot chair empty. Thipka gestured for Isaac to sit there, saying, "You've got to learn the ropes sometime, Captain. I know you'll remember everything I taught you."

Isaac's whole heart danced with such excitement and gratitude that he could've wept. He didn't know why Thipka was being so generous, but he was glad for it. He was also extremely grateful to be surrounded by experienced pilots who would correct him before he could do something too foolish.

As they darted toward the sea, Isaac said to Snowman, "I hope you didn't want anything from your ship."

Snowman replied, his tone tired and indifferent, "I suppose some music would've been nice."

They flew over a small city and the wreckage of Rain and Nothe's ship, then dove into the sea. Isaac switched on a light that shone through the front of the ship, illuminating the darkness ahead as they moved deeper and deeper into the ocean toward the monstrous mouth of a cave.

The ship darted this way and that, up then down, before leveling out again–back in the River. Once again, Isaac forgot how to breathe. The River simply had that power over him. The details had faded a little in his memory since he'd left it, and they pierced his mind again with all their stunning glory. It was like he'd slipped into a vivid dream, rich with color yet with a dark and starlit sky and the green and blue moon-planet of Lolaar looming behind them. Boar peered through the windows and said with reverence, "My, isn't that something? This is much better than looking at pictures in a book."

Isaac had to agree. It was more spectacular than he ever could've imagined possible.

The River rose in front of them like a wall. Thousands of yawning faces with hollow eyes, arms outstretched to catch them.

Snowman's eyes widened, and he cursed.

Thipka darted to the left, throwing everyone over, to which poor Boar said, "Oh my!" Isaac muttered a prayer of gratitude for the roomy seat that he was belted into, unlike when he'd first flown through this nightmare with Rain.

Thipka pulled down on a lever, and the ship bolted forward, moving faster than Isaac thought possible and filling his stomach with butterflies. Isaac could clearly see the tormented faces outside his window as they passed them—young faces and old, hands outstretched, eye sockets empty. The wall lurched after them as Thipka darted right. Isaac threw his arms up to shield his face as they dove into a branch of the river.

Onward to Ethra

They slammed into a beach, spewing mud, sand, and water over the nose of the ship. As everyone groaned and struggled to recover, Thipka announced, "We're here."

"Here where?" asked Isaac.

Elise gazed out the front window, her eyes wide as if awaking to a memory, her voice full of reverence. "My village."

They'd crashed at the beach of her village? Isaac looked through the front window through bits of mud and saw dark green trees and tall, colorful buildings. He turned to Thipka and stammered, "H-how did you know where it was?"

Thipka ignored Isaac and went about his business with a sorrowful frown and slow, deliberate movements, as if he were trying to ignore ghosts while prepping a body for burial.

Isaac thought about asking him how he knew about P.T. Barnum then since he'd forgotten to do so after the show, but it was clearly a bad time.

After the group unwedged Boar from the inside of the ship, they stumbled out after him. They stopped in their tracks on the beach by a row of gawking faces.

Isaac had never seen such a diverse group of people in all his life.

A plump, old man rose from a nest of moss, appearing quite groggy, as though he'd been rudely awakened from a very deep sleep. A sad, withering tree grew from his back, and he could've been the brother to the tree-man in the cave.

That cave felt like years ago.

People with fuzzy, green, moss-like skin gathered behind him. Others were blue like water or red-orange like fire, while others seemed to be carved from stone. Some had wings, others fins. And yet, they all had human-like faces, five fingers, hair of varying textures, and were clearly of the same race of beings, despite their differences. They whispered to each other as they pointed in the intruder's direction, some at the giant worm, others at Snowman, but mostly—at Elise.

It was fascinating watching them, really. Isaac was quite boring in comparison with his simple, almost monochromatic appearance. Why were humans so dull?

One other feature they all had in common: none of them looked happy to see them.

A voice rose like the howling of the wind through a canyon. "Go away!"

A man in long yellow robes approached from the midst of the crowd. He carried an elegantly carved, heavy-looking staff and had a spiky white beard, eyebrows, and hair. His faded blue eyes were almost white and shockingly cold, like snow glistening in the moonlight. He looked like a much older version of Snowman, which Isaac didn't like at all.

Snowman himself, however, stood slightly in front of Isaac, a little closer than Isaac would've preferred, but given the situation and the fact that he had no special abilities, he decided he was okay with it.

The man in the yellow robes said again, "Go away! Turn back! You are not welcome here." His horrible eyes were fixed on Elise.

Elise stepped forward. "Please, you're all in danger—"

"We certainly are," said the man, "now that you're here."

A rustle surged through the crowd as every onlooker took a defensive stance as though preparing to attack. Nothe blurted, "Whoa!" as Isaac and his comrades took a step back—all except Snowman, who raised his hands as though preparing to turn them all into ice statues.

Isaac's heart leapt so far into his throat he could chew on it. He had to swallow it again. If these people were as powerful as Elise, their little group didn't stand a chance. Well, maybe Snowman and Elise did.

The man glared at Snowman, visibly upset. "Why have you brought her here? What torment has your father planned for us now?"

Elise held out a calming hand and said softly, "Please. My name is—"

"We know who you are," said the man. "We've been protecting this world from you for years."

Elise furrowed her brow, her gaze darting around at everyone as if to silently ask if she'd heard him right. "From *me*?"

"Go away!" he snarled. "Leave us in peace!"

Isaac watched Elise search the faces of the crowd, desperately looking for one person—just one—with any light of compassion for her. He searched, too.

There were none.

Elise forced a smile. "You must be mistaken. I was left—accidentally—on Earth when I was a child. I—"

The man smirked. "Accidentally? You were banished there."

"Banished? No, you're mistaken. I—"

The man advanced, his eyes growing colder with each step. "It was the only place for a monster like you. No one—*no one*—should have your kind of power. When you didn't get your favorite doll right when you wanted it..."

Elise and Isaac stepped back as he drew closer. Snowman stood his ground.

"...you blew up three people. When you didn't get your nap, you blew up a house with everyone inside."

Elise shook her head and whispered, "No."

"Your favorite toy trolley was snatched by a little boy—"

Isaac's heart sank into his stomach. He was going to be sick.

Elise took another step back, saying more forcefully, "No!"

"You made sure that wouldn't happen again."

She covered her ears. "*No!*"

This was not good. Air pricked Isaac's his skin as if lightning were about to strike.

"And when your mother—"

"No, no, no—*NO!*"

She threw out her fists. A gust of wind pushed the man back a step. He gazed up, startled. Some of the crowd began to advance.

Tears poured from Elise's eyes, but she spoke as though she weren't weeping at all. "I can bring them back. I can. I just need the wise man to tell me where the planet is. The planet of the dead."

A light of empathy flickered through the man's eyes. He raised a hand to stop the advancing people. He shook his head, his gaze fixed on Elise. "I *am* the wise man. There is no planet of the dead. That was a fairytale your mother told you to make you feel better."

Clouds formed above them. Lightning cracked across the sky.

Elise shook her head. "No. No, that's not true. That's not *true!*"

His empathy turned to anger. "There is no planet of the dead."

"I need to bring them back!"

"No one can bring them *back*."

Elise pressed her hands to her chest. She gasped for air as though she were drowning. "You're lying. You're *LYING!*"

A strong wind picked the man up and threw him several feet through the air, slamming his spine against the ground. Blood oozed from his face and hands onto his torn robes. A few of the people rushed to him, the rest prepared to mobilize. One lit fire in his hands. Snowman pulled a ball of water from the sea.

This was very bad, and they hadn't even met Snowman's father yet.

Isaac grabbed Elise's shoulders. "Elise, stop!"

Her frantic, lost eyes met his. She broke free of him and flew away.

He cried after her, "Elise!"

She was gone.

He watched her soar over the trees, landing with an explosion in the distance. Rocks and smoke billowed into the air as though someone had just lit off several sticks of dynamite.

As the debris settled, the crowd turned to Isaac and the crew. Isaac threw up his hands. "We surrender!"

Hoping for a Miracle

Snowman gave Isaac a look that said, quite clearly, *Really?* He didn't drop his ball of water, as if to silently add, *Well, maybe you surrender...*

And perhaps on another day, Rain, Nothe, and Thipka would've given him a hard time for surrendering, but this day they didn't. In fact, Rain and Nothe didn't seem to hate the idea at all. They kept glancing toward the massive explosion. Thipka, on the other hand, looked sad and bored, as if he couldn't possibly care less about any of it.

Isaac tried to think of a strategy to get all of them out of there in one piece. As eight burly soldiers approached them, their terrified-yet-brave faces fixed on Snowman, Isaac said, "Look. I know you guys don't want us here. And frankly, we don't want to be here. We'd love to get out of your hair," Isaac turned to the others and said to them, quickly, in Theran, "You men would like to get out of their hair, fly away as soon as possible, wouldn't you?"

Nothe nodded emphatically. "Yes, love it."

Rain also nodded. "Love it. Adore it."

Isaac turned back to the people. "See? We all *really* want to leave. And I know you most certainly don't want Elise here. We all know that none of you stand a chance against her, or Asael here." Isaac wasn't so sure about that, but they were clearly frightened, and he hoped he could use this to his advantage. Without flinching or blinking and with absolute conviction, he said, "You don't. So," his heart pounded in his chest, "let me go get her. Let me talk to her. She'll talk to me. Let me get her to the ship, and we'll put your planet to our engines and never return."

The wise man was sitting now. There were multiple gashes on his face and panic in his eyes. He looked at Snowman for confirmation of Isaac's words, but he remained stoic and unmoving. The wise man consulted with the weird man with the withered tree on his back and a few others. He studied Snowman warily, clearly not trusting his presence and doubting that this would work out so simply, but when Snowman didn't say or do anything, he fixed his gaze on Isaac. "Very well. But you must never return. If you do, we will be prepared for you, and you will not leave alive." He turned his stern expression onto Snowman as if daring him to challenge this threat.

Isaac considered bursting with gratitude but decided against it. He didn't want them to see how much this meant to him; he couldn't give them that upper hand. He kept his head high like he knew he was their only hope, oozing confidence and composure while desperation wreaked havoc within.

After informing Rain, Nothe, Boar, and Thipka of the plan, Isaac was accompanied into the forest by Snowman and two men who looked like marble statues. None of them said a word, which was fine with him. He didn't feel like talking. He felt sick. Miserable sick. His stomach twisted in an unbearable pain, and his face prickled like it was going numb.

He couldn't stop imagining what it must be like.

A little girl. An innocent child born just like any other, but with an extraordinary gift. A gift tied to her emotions.

He hadn't met a single child who didn't throw a fit when they were tired, hungry, or upset. No child ever meant to hurt anyone in those tantrums, they simply felt things deeply—pain, discomfort, exhaustion, heartache; it didn't take a genius to know it was all new and frightening for them, and they didn't know what to do with such big emotions.

He remembered how his mother would comfort him, how her soothing tone and tight embrace could make him feel safe and soothe those overwhelming feelings. How she helped him understand them so they didn't seem so alien. That was what a child needed. To accidentally destroy everyone and everything you adore instead, leaving yourself all alone, without any comfort or understanding, as a lost, little child...

The pain she must feel. It's more than anyone should ever bear.

It wasn't right. It wasn't fair. It wasn't fair at all.

How could he possibly help her?

The air changed as though he were walking into a room full of static. The hair on his arms and on the back of his neck stood up, and he was overwhelmed with the smell of dirt and sap. The guards stopped, looking at each other with expressions of terror. One said to him, "You're on your own."

Oh good. He hadn't wanted them there in the first place.

Isaac and Snowman crept through the foliage of the forest, the only sound the crunching of twigs and leaves underneath their feet and the occasional rumble of thunder. The scent of strange flowers, sawdust, and rain filled his lungs, and the sensation—that of electrified air—grew with each step. Small leaves and rocks floated motionless around him. He tapped a leaf, and it spun, weightless.

Then the trees ended, opening into a large clearing that had been created by broken and uprooted trees, bushes, and rocks, all of which floated around the woman lying in the center. Her was back to him, wings lifeless, knees to her chest, her body shook with sobs.

Isaac's eyes filled with tears. She must've been in so much pain. He had no experience with this level of grief and regret. He had no idea what to do.

He turned to Snowman. "Wait here."

Snowman grabbed his shoulder. "No. You shouldn't go alone."

"No, trust me. She—I *need* to do this alone." There was no reason for Snowman to trust him. He had no idea what he was doing. For all he knew, he'd be turned to a puddle of blood in the next few minutes.

Yet he knew that going alone would be less upsetting for her. It would make her feel less like some spectacle at P.T. Barnum's circus to be gawked at and misunderstood. He had to get to her. He had to help her.

He had to try.

He moved carefully toward her as though approaching a wounded lion. The feeling of static grew more intense. Lightning shook the ground nearby like a threat, warning him not to take another step. He froze, his heart frantic in its rhythm. Warm raindrops fell here and there, landing on his face, his shoulder.

The pull in his chest was so strong. If he turned away, something within him would break. He couldn't leave her, no matter how much she wanted him to.

He continued forward, his legs trembling. More raindrops fell as he knelt in front of her. The ground quaked.

This would be the end of him. She was going to blow him up right then and there.

It didn't matter. He had to try to reach her, to help in some way.

He touched her shoulder, but she hid her face in her arms. The ground shook again, and rain poured down. It wasn't raining anywhere else, just on them. Snowman was dry, studying them with his arms folded.

Isaac didn't explode.

Elise lowered her arms and looked at him. His whole body went numb. He knew that if anyone tried to harm Elise now, she would let them. He knew the look in her eyes, the vacancy, as though her soul were no longer really housing her mind but dwelling somewhere far away—and not just for a moment. This was fresh sorrow and darkness mixed with old, rotting wounds, infecting whatever hope had remained and leaving emptiness in its place. It was an agony without visible marks that lingered without relief. He'd seen it in the face of a sailor once. And one day, Isaac woke to find that the sailor was gone, having cast himself into the sea.

He lifted her from the ground. She resisted for a moment, swatting him with a wing and a hand, causing more tremors through the planet. After a moment, she lowered her wings, letting him wrap his arms around her. He held her tightly as she wept, clinging to him like he was the lifeline keeping her head above the raging sea. Tears streamed down his face for her.

Words had no place in that moment. It was too full of pain, too sacred. Words would've left in ruins all that was spoken through tears and an embrace.

All at once, the rain stopped, and the debris fell from the air.

In the Falling Snow

Isaac didn't know how long they were there. It could've been a few minutes or a few hours. It didn't matter. In that moment, they were somewhere outside of time.

He could almost see the snow falling, dancing softly, carried in a breeze.

It'd started to snow after Isaac had fled from the orphanage as a child, after the worm incident all those years ago. He hadn't been worried about it at the time. His only focus had been on getting as far away from that Hell as possible.

But then he grew hungry, and the sun began to set. His feet had turned to bricks made from solid pain. And it was cold. Really cold. He had no money to buy food. Any building he stepped into to warm himself, he was shooed away. In his mind, he'd surrendered. He was ready to go back to the orphanage. At least there were blankets there, and even if he were to be beaten and have food withheld from him for a time, he could find a way to steal cookies from the pantry again. But, most importantly, he'd have blankets. Maybe he could steal an extra blanket from the cupboard, too, after he got his cookies.

But he couldn't get back to the orphanage because he was lost.

He tried. He thought he was going in the right direction, but all the buildings were unfamiliar. He might as well have stumbled into a foreign country.

Isaac limped; his feet hurt so much. The sky grew darker, and the air grew colder. The snow fell, tumbling to the ground. His coat was thin, meant for fall, not winter. This was the first snow. It'd been raining earlier; how had it started snowing?

He couldn't stop shivering. He couldn't stop crying.

One by one, the lights went out in the buildings, leaving him in a frozen darkness. He wandered down an alley, seeking shelter in a door frame. He curled up, pulling his knees tightly to his chest. His tear-filled eyes looked up at the sky. The snow looked so cheerful in its graceful descent.

So cheerful.

He couldn't stop shaking. His toes were numb.

After a few hours, he fell asleep. Somehow, the shaking had stopped. For a while, he thought he could see and feel a light, like the warmth of a small fire. He thought he saw someone there—a little girl. The ghost from the orphanage, maybe. But he couldn't keep his eyes open long enough to see. His mind danced between consciousness and sleep, and he couldn't tell what was real anymore.

The light faded, and the world became dark. A thin blanket of snow had buried him. A strange warmth spread through him, almost boiling, although he couldn't feel his toes or fingers. He considered taking off his shoes, but he was too tired. His fingertips were purple. He kept them under his armpits, but it wasn't doing anything to help anymore.

An old man screamed, "Help! Help! There's a little boy down here!" His voice was frantic. "There's a little boy! He's dying! He's *dying!* Please, help! *Help!*"

Isaac couldn't open his eyes.

Someone shook his shoulders. Patted his cheek. "Hey, boy. *Boy.*"

His eyes rolled open to the outline of a not-old man with a thick, black beard. Someone said to the man with surprise, "He's alive! How is he alive?"

The man said, "Quick! We need to get him to the fire."

Snow fell from Isaac as he was carried away by the bearded man. He took off Isaac's frozen coat and shirt, replacing them with a massive, man-sized coat and shirt. He sat him right next to the fireplace, covered him in blankets, and made him drink hot tea. He didn't leave Isaac's side until he was brought back from death.

That man had been Captain Benjamin Snow.

And now, as Isaac sat on a strange planet with a broken woman in his arms, he thought he knew who the old man had been. He'd been the ghost who had brought him a light in that cold darkness, the one that'd broken Sister Maria's mirror and figurines.

And she was most certainly the girl from the party.

Now, he understood. Now, he held her a little tighter. Her crying subsided, and her breathing steadied.

He thought up some words. He wasn't going to say them at first, but then he did. "We're broken. Life is like sharp stones that we're pushed onto, and we just break. But broken is not the same as bad. I think sometimes, it's from the rubble of broken dreams that we pluck the stones we use to build better ones.

"And," he hesitated, "and maybe we're not meant to really know much about the afterlife—other than it's there—because we're supposed to be focusing on this one. This life. And doing the best we can with it. Maybe."

He winced at his stupid words. He knew it was little consolation, and he probably shouldn't have said it. He thought this even more when she started sobbing again. Once she composed herself, she whispered, "You should leave me. Let them come for me. Let me die."

He shook his head. "I can't do that."

"I shouldn't exist. I was never meant to exist."

"I don't believe that. You can beat this. You can learn to control your abilities. If that wasn't so, then I'd be dead right now." He shrugged. "Listen, I know that what I'm about to say—it can't remove your pain. But I want you to see what I see now, after our time together. What happened—it's not your fault."

She let out a sob.

He continued, "It's not. You need to free yourself from all the 'should-haves.' You know? The 'I should've done this,' or 'I should've done that.' Perhaps, yes, there was something that could've been done differently, but you didn't know that at the time. All those times, you didn't know. You didn't know how to do things differently.

"But now, you're at this higher level. You know more now. But that doesn't give you the right to punish yourself for what you didn't know then. It's not fair. You simply readjust your sails, chart a new, better course. A-and I believe...I believe you are meant to do something great with these abilities. There's so much good you can do. You need to give yourself another chance. Build new dreams from the broken ones."

The ground rumbled. Isaac thought he could smell smoke. He blurted an apology, "I'm so sorry, I am not good with words. I—"

She sat upright, placing a hand on his shoulder, looking exhausted. "No. This isn't me."

They turned toward the hilltop. The trees were on fire.

Footsteps moved swiftly toward them. It was Snowman. His gaze was fixed on the fire. "That's him," he said. "He's found us."

NOTHING'S WRONG HERE

"Oh my! The trees are on fire!" said Boar.

Of course, no one around him understood a word. They could piece things together, however, since the fire was very noticeable, and Boar seemed to be looking at it. Rather than sending anyone to put the fire out, the people from Elise's village frantically gathered their favorite belongings and fled in ships. They weren't even guarding Nothe, Rain, Thipka, or Boar anymore. It was as if they'd forgotten they were there.

"Huh," Rain said to Nothe. "Well, this can't be good."

"Maybe they've just collectively decided to go on vacation," said Nothe. "All of them. Together."

"I hear those can really bring people closer."

Nothe nodded. "Yes, exactly."

Rain also nodded. "Bring a real unity."

"Right. What better way to unite a village than to take a luxury cruise together?"

"Why, I don't think there *is* a better way."

"What we hear as screams of panic are really squeals of joy. Like, 'Hooray! A vacation! I've really needed one of those!'"

"Precisely. Definitely not, 'Oh no! A huge fire that's coming toward our village at an alarming speed! That we could probably put out but would rather let our town burn because something really bad is about to happen!'"

"Yeah," agreed Nothe. "Definitely not that."

"Yeah. I'm sure we'll be fine."

"Yeah. Right, Thipka?"

They looked over at Thipka, who still looked bored and sad, even as he watched the fire spread toward them.

Nothe looked back at Rain. "I think that's a good sign."

Rain nodded. "I think it's a definite 'yes.'"

"Yeah. We'll be fine."

After a moment, Rain asked hesitantly, "Do you, uh, do you think we ought to go look for the others?"

"Probably. Yeah. Just in case they didn't notice the huge fire."

"Best to be safe."

As they started in that direction, a deep, loud growl shook the ground beneath their feet. Rocks broke and trees cracked as if a large boulder were tumbling down the mountainside. A beast the size of a large house barreled through multiple buildings, shattering them. It was the ugliest thing either of them had ever seen, with a long, jowly neck that shook with the turn of its head. It had three sagging, humanoid faces and large, lopsided eyes with bulging, red veins running through them, and broken, jagged teeth. Its body had the appearance of a melted candle, with long, skinny arms and bony fingers, and a slug-like tail instead of legs; its skin was the color of vomit after a spicy meal.

Boar hissed at it.

Nothe's heart hid somewhere in his abdomen. "Well, I hate that thing."

Rain grinned at him. "Come now, Nothe. I'm sure it's just misunderstood."

Nothe glared at him.

Hundreds of smaller versions of this monster pooled around it. They stood about to Nothe's knees, scurrying around and climbing over each other until he couldn't see the ground at all. They swarmed toward an unfortunate trio carrying too much luggage as they headed to the ships, looking as if they'd attempted to take everything but their house with them. People on the ships screamed as the boats pulled away from the dock, unable to do anything but watch as the slowest of the three was snatched up by the long, bony arm of the massive monster and devoured, chewed up by three mouths like crunchy candy. The remaining two dropped their things and sprinted toward the fleeing ships.

Nothe's mind froze, his skin prickling as though covered in dull needles, knowing what was about to happen. He and Rain moved toward the couple, his heart pulling him to their rescue, but they were a half a mile down the beach. It was too late.

The people turned, pulling up sand, dirt, and rocks and throwing it all at the oncoming hoard. The monsters swarmed them, cutting off their screams and leaving nothing but blood on the sand.

The little monsters' focus shifted, their direction changing like smoke, heading toward Rain, Thipka, Boar, and Nothe.

Nothe and Rain armed themselves. Nothe shot the monsters that got to them first, bursting them into blobs of red and green slime. Rain hacked a few in two with his ax, splattering blood and slime over his armor. Nothe took aim at a group of them heading toward Boar, who, thankfully, was being guarded by a bored Thipka and the sword he'd been hiding in his walking stick.

Three of the massive monster's lopsided eyes rolled around, drool dripping from its mouth, until the front face focused on the group. Nothe and Rain made their way closer to Boar and Thipka as a second, bigger wave of mini-monsters approached, followed by the lumbering, massive creature.

Boar said, "Friends, I think I have an idea."

But of course, they didn't understand anything he said, so they had no idea why he tunneled into the ground behind them and disappeared.

Nothe looked at Rain. "I guess he's had enough of this."

Rain shrugged. "I can't say I blame him."

They looked over at Thipka, wondering if he was also about to flee. But instead, with his sad and bored expression unflinching, he dropped his sword and pulled light from the air, forming it into a ball. He chucked it at the monsters, turning several of the smaller ones into puddles and leaving a massive open wound in the abdomen of the gigantic—and now very angry—monster.

Another wave of mini-monsters swept toward them. Nothe's stomach twisted, sending panic through him like a bolt of lightning. He couldn't let any of them get close.

He couldn't let them get to Rain.

Maybe they should follow Boar through the tunnel.

Boom.

Boom.

The giant drew nearer, the slap of its hands against the ground shaking the planet. The monsters picked up speed.

Boom-boom.

Boom-boom.

The horde of little monsters was unending. Rain cried out as one leaped onto his arm. He ripped it off him and chucked it. A shock of pain shot up Nothe's leg. One of them had wrapped itself around his calf, its teeth breaking through his armor. Its side face looked up at him with wide, lopsided eyes and hissed.

That was more terrifying than the fact it was eating him.

He tried to pry it off him. The front face let go of his leg, and the hissing side face bit his hand. "*Eeeugh!* I hate these things!"

Thipka sent another ball of light through the swarm, leaving another wound in the giant, which towered above them now. Rain crouched, clearly ready to do something stupid.

Boar burst through the ground underneath the monster, shoving it through the air onto its back. With a fierce roar, he jumped on top of it and clamped down on its left side face with his jaws. The flood of minions turned their attention away from Nothe, Rain, and Thipka and rushed toward Boar. Nothe shot the mini-monster off his leg and ran to Boar's rescue.

The monster wrapped its hands around Boar's torso. When it ripped him away, the top of its left face was gone—nothing more than empty, bloody eye sockets and a slimy mess. It threw Boar toward the sea, where he landed hard on the beach. His side popped open in a large, mean gash, spilling slime and blood across the sand. His body curled up.

"*NO!*" cried Rain.

The little monsters shifted their pursuit like leaves carried in the wind, following the body of the worm. Rain and Nothe ran after them.

Thipka stayed, looking more sad than bored now as he watched them run to Boar. The fire had reached the village—what was left of it, anyway—and was spreading to the surrounding trees.

Thipka just stood there, turning his head toward other distant screams.

The monster rolled back onto its stomach, shrieking from its remaining faces.

Why did they think they had to fight Snowman's dad again? What was the reason? They needed to get to the ship. It wasn't far from where they stood—perhaps one hundred feet, just over there.

But Boar wasn't moving. His insides might all fall out if he did. Nothe needed to heal him first.

It would take a miracle.

Nothe shot round after round at the mini-monsters. *Where's*

Snowman when you need him? Where's Elise? He said to Rain, "We could sure use some magical powers right now, don't you think?"

"I'd even take non-magical back up at this point," said Rain, covered with guts and out of breath from the near-constant swinging of his axe.

Nothe shouted at Thipka, "More of those light balls would be much appreciated, thank you!"

Or he thought he was shouting at Thipka. But Thipka was gone.

He was *gone*.

Time to Run

S nowman said, "I need to get closer to the water."

Isaac tried not to panic as he nodded and helped Elise up. He thought of the village below and looked at Snowman. "Perhaps Elise can make it rain or something like she did earlier, but bigger. That'll help keep the fire from spreading, right?"

Snowman nodded.

Isaac put a hand on Elise's shoulder. "Elise?"

Her eyes were vacant as if her mind had fallen asleep and she was dreaming while awake.

He tried again. "Elise?" Isaac placed a hand on her cheek, then cradled her face in his hands, trying to bring her back. She closed her eyes, tears streaming down her face as she pressed her head into his palm.

Snowman's eyes widened. "Isaac." He pointed toward the hilltop. The fire had drawn significantly closer in just a few seconds.

Isaac tried again. "Elise, please. We need you."

Snowman grabbed her shoulders and shook her, a bit more violently than expected. "*Elise!*"

There was no response. It was like she was dead on her feet. But Isaac knew the look on her face. She was gone, lost inside her head.

"We don't have time for this," stated Snowman. "We need to move. Now."

Isaac was surrounded by disaster. First, there was the fire, which approached at an unbelievable rate—and something about the way it moved was odd as if it were connected to someone running through the trees. Second, with the fire suddenly so close, the air was growing too dry, and Snowman was too far away from a good source of water for his ability to be of sufficient use against the man coming their way. Finally, Elise was only half-there. As they sprinted toward the beach, Isaac had to lead her by the hand through the forest while she floated along, as though he were dragging a balloon; otherwise, she would've collided with every single tree.

He really didn't like that fire.

The ground rumbled beneath them.

Snowman asked, "Is she doing that?" The look on his face said he already knew the answer but hoped he was wrong.

Trees fell around them, revealing a massive slug-man with three faces. It exceeded Isaac's original understanding of the word "grotesque." The faces were hideous beyond reason, with long, matted hair, jagged, broken teeth, and jaws that hung open, seeming to pour drool from them like one might pour cream into tea. A giant, skeletal hand reached for them as hundreds of smaller versions of it skittered in their direction.

Isaac had never screamed like that before. He didn't know he could make that sound.

He picked up speed, dragging Elise along by the wrist while blurting every expletive he could think of. It took him a moment to remember Snowman. Isaac slowed his pace to search for him, relieved to see he was still alive, though far behind him with one of the little monsters on his arm, looking like a lumpy, nasty growth. He was trying to tear it off, but its face was hooked onto his shoulder.

Isaac stopped, trying to think. He ripped a branch from a nearby tree and ran toward Snowman, swinging it with a cry and splattering the small slug-monster as its body flew toward the oncoming hoard. Its head was still attached to Snowman's shoulder, the side faces looking shocked. Snowman winced as he pried it off and chucked it into the woods, blood pouring down his arm as they took off running again. Isaac grabbed Elise's wrist along the way.

"Thanks," Snowman said.

Isaac had never seen himself as an every-man-for-himself sort of person. He was better than that—or at least he'd always thought so. Instinct had completely taken over when they'd first fled from these things, leaving Snowman in the dust. A sick sort of shame gnawed at his stomach at the thought. He vowed to himself he wouldn't let it happen again.

"What are these things?" Isaac shouted at Snowman.

"Demvarkil," Snowman shouted back.

It sounded like a medicine for dysentery.

Snowman continued, "My father brought them. He's here somewhere."

Isaac tried to picture how someone would keep these things penned up, preserving them for a rainy day—the sort of day where your son decides that killing someone to build a time machine so you can kill billions more isn't a good idea. He couldn't imagine it'd be like keeping cattle.

Or maybe it would be. Who was he to say?

Water glimmered just ahead through a break in the trees, and waves crashed gently against the shore.

Snowman sped past Isaac, stopping just short of the beach. He reached his hands out, flexing his fingers and letting out a cry of rage as he pulled the water into the air. Isaac watched in awe as it soared over their heads like a massive watery bridge and fell on top of the swarming monsters, freezing in an instant and turning about a hundred of them into ice statues. Those that remained screamed and ran back into the trees.

Where was the big one?

Isaac's mouth was dry. What he wouldn't have given for that water to be drinkable. The flames were near. The smoke drained moisture from his eyes and made it difficult to breathe.

Through the crunching, falling trees appeared the massive silhouette of the giant monster in the smoke, slowly crawling toward them, shaking the ground with each thunderous slap of its hands against it. It appeared through the haze with a man standing in front of it. He was dressed in black and yellow leather, the yellow wrapped tightly from his shoulder to his waist, almost like the robes worn by Roman emperors, but nice and form-fitting. His head was covered in a black hood, and his face was scarred. He took the hood down to reveal his melted eyes. They stared straight forward, blind yet seeing everything.

Isaac knew those eyes.

Snowman's brow was laced with sweat, his face etched with fury and terror.

And there was Elise, standing next to Isaac, her expression

completely empty. She wasn't even there. Maybe her body was, but *she* was gone. Long gone.

This was bad.

Where were Rain, Nothe, and Thipka when you needed them?

Take It Down

"You must be *joking?!*" shouted Rain at no one in particular—the universe, perhaps. "He left us!"

"Maybe he was eaten?" Nothe suggested.

"I think we would've noticed." Rain's rage-fueled pulse cut through him as if each blood cell wielded a tiny knife. With several livid huffs, he exploded into a rage, yelling and shouting as he ran at the little monsters and chopped them to pieces. He kicked one and then another, sending them flying and hissing through the air. One leaped on his shoulder and snapped at his face. Rain grabbed it and crushed it in his hand.

"Rain!" Nothe cried out.

Rain could hear Nothe's gun as he shot at monsters behind him, trying to follow.

Rain focused on the gigantic monster ahead of them, half of its one face gone and the others agape with a mixture of confusion, fear, and anger.

He wasn't going to let Nothe and Boar die. Maybe Thipka had fled like a coward, leaving them all for dead. But Rain—he wasn't going anywhere.

His heart pounded in his chest, letting him know he was alive—alive for *this* moment—to save them.

He ran.

"*Rain!*" Nothe shouted, panic in his tone.

Rain hacked his way through the monsters, sheathing his ax as he got close to the big one. It reached out to grab him, but Rain dodged it, leaping onto the monster's arm and climbing up to its neck. It tried to catch him but missed. It tried to shrug him off its shoulder, but he grabbed its hair and hung on.

Little monsters were climbing up it now, racing toward him. He needed to hurry. He used the hair as a rope and steadied himself, finding his footing. He focused on the cells of the monster's neck. He could see each one, all through its spinal column and near the front of its throat.

He could use his powers to heal, to bring cells back together, to make them right again.

He could also use them to tear cells apart.

Rain raised his hand like a sword and then brought it down. A gash opened diagonally across the back of the monster's neck. Blood spurted as the head fell forward, hanging from the neck by the front flesh. Still holding onto the hair, Rain was thrown into the sand. The ground shook as the body collapsed, its blood a river flowing into the sea.

The little monsters' screams rent the air as they fled, a few of them tipping over and dying of fright.

Rain's muscles ached. His stomach swirled with nausea and exhaustion. He could taste blood in his throat. He didn't want to move—not even his pinky toe. He just wanted to lay there and sleep.

That was what using his powers like this did to him. It made him want to sleep for a solid seventy-two hours straight, if not more. More would be better.

Footsteps in the sand rushed toward him, skidding to a stop and kneeling next to his shoulder. "What is wrong with you?!" Nothe yelled at him.

Rain forced his eyes open as he muttered, "It's dead, isn't it? And I'm alive, and you're alive, and Boar's..." He peered over at Boar, who hadn't moved at all. "Something. Everybody wins." He pushed himself upright to show Nothe he was fine. Everything was fine. This may have looked like another suicide attempt, but it wasn't.

He looked at the dead monsters, the village engulfed in flames. His heart filled with anguish at the sight, at the memory of those who hadn't made it onto the boats—who'd had a thousand possible reasons for trying to carry so much with them. He tried not to imagine them weeping as they struggled to gather every possible treasure, each one representing a memory.

Not everyone had won.

He caught a glimpse of something from the corner of his eye.

Water from the sea, flying up through the air. Just down the beach.

"Huh," he said, "must be Snowman."

Trees fell over there, and the large silhouette of another big monster headed toward the figures standing along the shore. In front of it stood a man in a black hood. It didn't attack the man. It simply stood as if waiting for a command.

Rain waited for Elise to destroy them both. It would be so satisfying to watch.

She didn't.

Nothe asked, "Do you think these monsters... Do you think they..."

A few little monsters gathered around the man in the hood, waiting.

Realization filled Rain with a cold darkness and bitter rage. "He brought them."

This man had destroyed an entire village—his own people.

Rain went numb, like he was floating, watching the scene from somewhere else.

The leader of Thera was exactly like this man. Two people who ruled two different worlds, but the story was the same. It wasn't about the people they ruled. The people didn't matter. They were allowed to exist for one purpose only—to make the ruler feel powerful. The more pain and fear they caused, the more power they had.

Nothe stood. "Something's wrong. We need to help them."

Rain couldn't move. He couldn't speak. Tears filled his eyes as he rubbed his wrists. The chains were gone—they were *gone*. The sand ground uncomfortably into his pores. He studied the trees, the fire, the sky and inhaled the salty sea air. He wasn't there. He wasn't in his cage, in the cold darkness in chains.

But he felt like he was. His mind was *convinced* he was there.

Nothe knelt, removing the armor from his hands and cradling Rain's face. "Look at me. Look at me, Rain. Come back to me."

Nothe's eyes glowed bright, like the sun setting over the sea just after a storm. Warmth spread through Rain at his touch, calming his mind and his heart, bringing him back to the present.

Rain swallowed, his blood burning with rage as cruel, grinning human faces from his past ripped through his mind. He struggled to gain his composure. He could only whisper. "I hate them."

The phrase was almost out of place. He could've meant anyone. But of course, Nothe seemed to know exactly what place he'd fallen to in his head and knew exactly what people he meant. "You can't hate them. You just can't. Look at this!" Nothe gestured to the gore around them, to the village in flames. "Look at what hate has done. This is all hate, Rain.

All it does is destroy *everything*. It destroys you first and then everything around you. You have to let it go. And I'm not saying it has to be right now, but you just do. You can't let it beat you. If it does that, then *they* win because you've let them poison you over time until you're nothing more than a dried-out, withered, ugly version of yourself. Not on the outside, but on the inside. You got that? Hating them doesn't change them. It changes you. All hate does is destroy the good that might've been."

Nothe seemed to glow brighter as he spoke, like he had that night on the flower. And just as his words had on that night, they pierced Rain. He could feel their sincerity, their truth. Rain swallowed his hate, his pain, his tears. How was he supposed to let these things go when they refused to let him? When the memories kept coming back, again and again?

But he knew Nothe was right, and he hated him for it.

But really, he loved him. He was his rock, his anchor, a light in the darkness. Rain was broken with the sort of wounds that, at times, felt beyond repair. He had nothing to offer. Yet Nothe set out to rescue him anyway. Nothe was someone who understood him and refused to give up on him—his dear friend.

"Now get up," Nothe said, rising to his feet and reaching down to him. "They need our help."

A loud, inhuman scream came from the trees, followed by an explosion, and another rush of little monsters ran away, little monsters they hadn't known were there. They looked down the beach toward Isaac, Elise, and Snowman. No one had moved.

Was there another monster on the way?

Nothe was right. They needed to get everyone out of there *now*.

Try

"So, it's come to this," said the man with the black hood.

Several little monsters gathered at his feet.

Isaac second-guessed all his life choices. *Perhaps I should've just named the ship Arnaud.* The very idea still made him feel sick all over. But now, he understood—they'd both wanted the same thing. *She'd just wanted to name it after her father, the one she'd been going home to save.*

Snowman stepped forward, putting himself in front of Isaac.

The man said, "You've let your family down yet again. It seems to be the only thing you can do."

Snowman's hands balled into fists. They stood in silence for a moment. Isaac looked at Elise, wondering if she'd started caring about their situation.

She hadn't. She was still gone.

He hoped she was at least somewhere sunny and monster-less, with a cool breeze and glass of clean water.

Snowman brought his hands forward, pulling more water from the sea and holding it in the air in front of him. The man in the hood raised his arms, his hands turned upward as if offering a gift. Fire erupted in his palms.

That explains a lot.

"And here I thought I couldn't be any more disappointed in you," said the man with the black hood. "I suppose it's time for you to know how your mother—the love of my *life*—" he said the last word with a hiss before continuing, "—and how your brothers and your sister felt when you let them down that day—especially your poor little sister. Her helplessness. Her *fear*."

Isaac's heart sank for Snowman, for this nightmare in front of them, for the nightmare of his past. *So it is his father who blames him.*

He threw a steady stream of flames at Snowman. Snowman created a thick shield of ice, bending a knee to hold back the force of the fire. He shouted at Isaac, "Run!"

Isaac dragged Elise several feet away, searching for an exit. The ship was down the beach. He could see it, surrounded by fire. He thought he could see Nothe and Rain. Rain was collapsed on the ground near a river of blood and what looked like a curled up and very dead Boar.

Something in his heart shattered into a thousand rotting pieces.

Tears filled his eyes, and rage lit up his veins. He looked at the flames and the frozen monsters, at Snowman battling his *horrible* father, at Elise with her vacant eyes. His mind grew still, and he saw everything with clarity, like looking through a telescope after the glass had been cleaned.

This was why he was here.

He wasn't going to run for the ship. No.

He had so little to offer, no great earth-bending powers. But he had enough to *try*. To try to make things right, to try and save his friends.

Snowman leapt out of the way of the fire, throwing knives of ice at his father. One fell on the ground and slid toward Isaac's feet. Another struck the hooded man, sticking in his shoulder, putting an end to the flames for a moment. His father gripped the bloody ice, melting it until there was nothing but an open, bleeding wound.

Between deep, exhausted breaths, Snowman said to his father, "No." His voice was steady. "You let us down. I was *five*. I did everything I could to save them. It was all I wanted. And I *saved* you. I saved your life, and you destroyed me. You saved *nobody*. You're a coward who's pathetic enough to break your only living child for your mistakes."

The man in the hood didn't flinch. He didn't even bat a melted eye. There was only a whisper. It seemed to come from everywhere and echoed through the trees. The words spoken were unintelligible to Isaac, but whatever was said, it made Snowman raise his hands, readying himself to fight again, his expression resigned like he knew this was his final moment. His eyes, lined with shadows and red from smoke and exhaustion, filled with tears—as if his mind had been flooded with all the joy that once was and all the things that might've been. "You were my hero. I loved you once."

Isaac wondered what those words might do. His gaze darted toward the hooded man, who didn't move. His expression was stoic and unreadable. But the air around them, the silence...it was all so heavy. Something was wrong.

No. This wasn't going to end well. The hooded man was almost exactly like Sister Maria, and you couldn't just walk away after confronting Sister Maria. Even if she was completely wrong, she'd kill you to stop you from saying it and then go back to convincing herself she was right. If you brought the Bible to her, with the scripture ready to read, and told her she was wrong for beating you until you bled from your eye because Jesus said it was better for people who hurt children to be thrown into the sea than meet God in the afterlife, then she'd kill your pet spider.

Isaac did the only thing he could think to do.

With a steadying breath and a prayer, he picked up the ice-knife that had fallen at his feet and flung it. The knife flew end over end, hitting the hooded man in the face. Teeth burst from his mouth, and blood spurted from the gash on his cheek. Isaac picked up a rock and lobbed it, hitting the man in the temple, toppling him to a knee.

Isaac went for another rock and was hit by a stream of fire that threw him through the air and into the sea. He thought he heard screaming, but it couldn't have been him because he couldn't scream. The fire had consumed his lungs as he inhaled, melting him from the inside. His body was in a pain more excruciating than he ever imagined possible as his skin and eyes sizzled and melted. It filled his every thought until he hit the water.

He saw a light, though he no longer had eyes to see. The pain was replaced by a peace that he had never experienced before. He was dancing with the girl at the party, laughing as they stumbled over each other and pretended to have grace. Grundy smiled and nodded to him from across the room. The far-end wall opened into a glorious garden in the spring. The colors of the trees were more vibrant than anything he'd ever seen. In fact, he was certain they were colors that didn't exist on any known world. Captain Snow stood behind his mother. They were both young again, healthy and radiant. She reached out to him, smiling.

He bid the girl farewell, and her eyes filled with tears. As the world around him trembled, he took his mother's hand.

Don't Go

Rain and Nothe were running toward the others when fire shot from the hooded man's hand, throwing Isaac's burning body into the sea. Snowman's fight, Isaac's knife throwing, the whole battle—it had happened so fast.

Rain froze.

It was just another human, wasn't it? The universe was better off.

Rain's hands trembled.

No.

It wasn't. The universe was worse now. Much worse. Isaac had been good, genuine. The best, no, but...well, Rain couldn't think of one who was better. He'd been a dim yet shining star in a sea of darkness. A light —a much-needed light—had gone out.

Snowman screamed, *"NO!"* He pulled massive chunks of ice out of the sea and threw them at the hooded man, hitting him several times before he leapt out of the way, returning fire. Finally, he poured a mountain of water on the man, a mountain he couldn't escape. As the water froze, the giant monster behind him reached out to seize Snowman.

There was another scream.

It rose in its intensity until Rain and Nothe had to cover their ears. The freezing deluge of water fell as Snowman covered his ears as well, and the weakened, hooded man hid in a ball of fire. The massive monster stiffened, its rolls jiggling, its eyes wide in terror. It burst with a pop, along with all the surrounding monsters, like water balloons filled too full. The trees splintered into nothing.

Snowman ran toward them, shouting, "Get back! Get back!"

The three of them fled, looking over their shoulders.

Rain was sure they couldn't get far enough away fast enough.

Elise's body splintered. Blinding light broke through the cracks as if she were made of porcelain. The light grew brighter, the cracks grew in number, and her scream grew louder until she exploded. A wave of light washed over them, knocking them to the ground.

Rain took a breath. Then another. Was he dead?

When he opened his eyes, he thought he might be. There was nothing around him for about a half mile but splinters of wood, blood, slime, and pieces of dead things. No trees, vegetation, rocks, or corpses.

Where was Nothe?

With a stab of panic, he sat up, feeling instant relief when he saw Nothe, Snowman, Boar, and the ship. The man in the hood was gone, and Elise—

Elise floated high above the ground, her form brilliant, indefinite and difficult to see, like looking at the sun. With a gesture of her hand, she lifted Isaac's body from the water and placed him on the shore in front of her. Her voice roared across the beach, commanding and yet somehow pleading. "Save him."

Rain pondered her request—not because of his doubts about doing what she asked, but because of how sad he thought it was. This creature, with seemingly unlimited power, couldn't heal the one person she loved. She was at their mercy.

Thipka, covered in blood, appeared from behind the ship, carrying tubes and a small bag. His eyes were red and swollen. Blood streamed from them and from his nose like tears.

What convenient timing. What had he been doing? How did he have equipment immediately at the ready? Rain decided he'd kill him later, but of course, now was not the time. Bringing Isaac back from the dead would take all three of them—that was assuming it was possible at all.

The closer they got to Isaac's body, the more the air changed. The pain was consuming, as if a hand of darkness and despair had reached into his chest and crushed his heart, leaving only a piece still beating, rotting the remainder of the cavity away. The feeling spread through his arms, making them heavy. He fought to breathe as though he were drowning in the rot. Tears streamed down his face without him realizing it.

He knew this feeling. He knew it well.

Part of the feeling came from Snowman, but most overwhelmingly, it poured from Elise.

Nothe, Rain, and Thipka wiped away tears as they knelt around Isaac. His body was barely recognizable, with only a few tufts of hair on the backside of his head and a few portions of clothing remaining. The charred and soggy remnants of his book stuck out from the remains of his coat.

Snowman turned away, his expression fallen, his eyes bereft of hope. Rain could feel the suffering radiating from him like the cold of a frozen lake at night. It was more than his grief for Isaac. It was the accumulation of betrayal, hurt, and despair that had built up over time, rotting away his soul like rust. It was the agony of a childhood stolen. All of it had finally crashed upon him in a single moment, and it was more than he could bear.

Rain knew this sort of pain.

He ached, knowing Elise and Snowman were experiencing such anguish.

Thipka looked at Elise and Snowman. "It will be all right. You'll see."

Rain thought this was a hefty promise, given the condition of Isaac's body. They needed a heart that could beat and veins they could put blood through. Also, he had to *want* to come back. Otherwise, there was no hope of saving him.

Frankly, it didn't look good.

Rain asked Nothe, "Does he want to come back?" Nothe had a gift for knowing these things. He'd touched death several times but never fully crossed over. It'd left him with a sensitivity to the other dimensions that few had.

Nothe closed his eyes, searching. He looked at Rain. "He's okay either way. If we open the doors, he'll come back. He really wants turkey and potatoes. The real question is, is it—" he glanced at Elise, nervous, his voice turning to a whisper—as if that would keep her from hearing his question, "—is it possible?"

Thipka bowed over Isaac's head, his hands over Isaac's charred face, his eyes closed. Searching. Finally, he nodded. "His heart is intact. Damaged. But it's there." He rolled Isaac over and pointed to a spot of burn-free skin on his back. "Here."

Thipka opened the small bag he had carried. He pulled out two needles, which he attached to each end of a medical tube.

Rain leapt at the opportunity. "Give it here." He took the tube. He plugged one end into a vein he found in Isaac's back and the other into his own arm. Thipka put a hand over Isaac's heart, forcing it to beat. Rain guided his blood and the cells, healing layer after layer of tissue. He gave his blood and worked with his energy until he could taste blood, and his head spun, and he was sure he was about to puke.

Nothe shooed him away before he died, replacing the needles and tube with fresh ones and taking over. Then it was Thipka with Rain triggering the heartbeat. Together they worked, watching Isaac's tissues return to perfection, leaving his clothes tattered since he didn't need them to live and most of his hair missing—but the follicles were repaired, so it'd grow back. The whole process was exhausting. A Hassune could die while raising the dead if they pushed themselves too far.

Once his body was whole, Nothe knelt at Isaac's head, both hands over his temples. Thipka kept his hand over his heart.

After a moment of meditative silence, a pink sunburst burn settled across Isaac's chest. Isaac took a deep breath and fell into a coughing fit, his eyes fluttering open, then shutting as he lost consciousness. Thipka assured Elise and Snowman that this was all perfectly normal.

Elise's iridescent form took on a solid shape, becoming a glowing version of her old self as she landed on the sand. She ran toward Isaac, falling to the ground and pulling him into her arms, cradling his face as she sobbed. No word or phrase was adequate for the joy that overwhelmed the air. It had no name. It was the joy of a song sung by a happy child, reaching beyond anything worldly but perhaps could occupy Heaven. The sort of joy Rain had never experienced himself, but in that moment, he knew there was nothing he wanted more, and perhaps the pursuit of it was something worth living for.

"Thank you," Elise whispered. "Thank you."

There was a sniffle and a whisper so soft, he was sure no one else heard it. It came with a tangled web of joy, relief, and indescribable sorrow. "Thank you."

It was Snowman.

A roar echoed from a far distance. The man in the black hood had apparently survived Elise's fit and was sending more monsters, though Rain couldn't imagine why. It made zero sense. He was obviously beat. There was no trapping Elise and whatever she had become.

But clearly, he was also insane.

Elise looked at them, her eyes alight as though on fire. "You should leave."

She picked up Isaac as if he were nothing more than a life-sized doll and leapt into the sky. With the brilliance of a falling star, she parted the sea before her and disappeared.

"Huh," said Nothe, "I didn't see that coming." He looked at Thipka. "Did *you* see that coming?"

Thipka stood. "We need to get Boar onto the ship."

Nothe turned to Rain. "I think he saw it coming."

Rain remembered he had plans to murder Thipka and rose to his feet. After overcoming his dizzy spell, he chased after him. "*Hey!*" He was beyond weak and nauseated, his legs shaking so much he could barely stand, but he managed to trot alongside him. "What is the matter with you? Leaving creatures for dead—how can you live with yourself?"

Thipka didn't answer. They were almost to Boar, whose skin had paled. The sight made Rain angrier. He shouted, "I'm talking to you—!" and gave him a hard shove.

As he touched Thipka, a vision ripped through his mind: a strange, rain-soaked street in the dead of night; Nothe's eyes bleeding as he sat, dead; a little girl with blond hair, playing with dinosaurs; Rain's brother in a long, black coat, his smile off; Rain curled up in pain, consumed with a grief unlike anything he'd ever felt before, it's brief touch on his mind making him wish for death, and—

A time machine.

Rain stopped breathing. He was sure his heart had stopped as well. He was floating, no longer feeling connected to his body.

What had he just seen? Was that the future? *Please, no. No.* He prayed to a God he'd heard of but didn't believe in. *No. Please, don't let that be the future.*

Thipka looked at him, his eyes watering and full of sorrow. "I knew you wouldn't die." He turned and continued his march toward Boar.

"They're here," Snowman shouted.

Amid splinters and broken rocks, the ground in the distance appeared to move with the waves of so many little monsters, all of them heading toward the ship.

When he turned back to Boar, Thipka had already healed his

massive wound. He wasn't sure how he did that without dying, but he did. He wiped blood from his nose as he stepped away, his legs visibly shaking, but he didn't seem to care about the blood pouring from his eyes and ears.

Boar let out a groan and struggled to move. Nothe gave him a shove. "C'mon, buddy. We've got to go."

The monsters drew closer. The ground rumbled.

Boom-boom. Boom-boom.

Three massive monsters raced toward them.

Why was Boar moving so slow?

Boom-boom. Boom-boom.

Their gigantic, disgusting bodies flopped along, drawing closer.

Nothe, Thipka, and Rain pushed and shoved, helping poor Boar into the back of the ship.

Boom-boom. Boom-boom.

The ship rumbled to life, and they buckled themselves into their seats. Little monsters flooded around the outside of the ship, crawling over the metal.

Thipka and Rain flipped the appropriate switches, and Thipka pushed a lever. The ship rose into the air. A massive monster reached out, grabbing the tail, tossing the crew, and making poor Boar let out a groan of complaint.

Thipka flipped more switches. The engines whined and roared. The ship slipped from the monster's grip and dove into the sea.

To the Ends of the Earth

They emerged into the River, relief falling over Rain's mind like a warm blanket. He knew it was too soon to celebrate, but the farther they got from that planet, the better he would feel.

Thipka seemed to feel the same way. He pushed the ship forward at an alarming speed.

"So," said Nothe, as if they'd just finished dropping something off at grandma's house, "where are we going now?"

"Earth," said Thipka.

Nothe sounded pleasantly surprised. "Oh!" He looked at Rain. "Isn't that where Isaac said he was from?"

Rain nodded. "Yes, I think so." He didn't really like the thought of going to Earth. But perhaps, if there were more humans like Isaac there, maybe it wouldn't be so bad.

He wasn't super optimistic.

Snowman announced, "We're being followed."

They looked at the monitor and peered through the windows. A black ship that looked like a spike from a weed followed close behind them, so much so that someone could jump from their ship onto the front of it.

A crash, like a bolt of lightning, slammed into them and the whole ship shuddered.

They'd been shot.

Thipka hung his head, his face twisted in despair. Rain panicked, his stomach turning to cold lead. "What? What is it?"

"We have guns!" Nothe leapt from his seat and opened a hatch in the floor where the outer guns of the ship were located. He fired back at their attacker. The ship spun and dodged, shooting and hitting them again.

Thipka commanded Rain, "Drive."

Rain took over the main controls as Thipka left, Snowman jumping into the co-pilot seat. Rain shouted, "W-wait! Which one's Earth?"

Thipka pointed ahead. "The little blue one. Next exit."

"Next exit?"

But Thipka had already grabbed a massive gun from a compartment and opened a hatch in the roof of the ship, pulling himself through it and closing it behind him.

Rain had to assume he meant the next branch of the River. It was an exit from the main system, right?

Thipka fired from the roof with the gigantic gun. The ship couldn't dodge him *and* Nothe. They got in a couple of good shots, but it didn't do anything to the pursuer's ship.

So Thipka ran and jumped on it. With a flick of his fingers, he broke a hole into the cockpit and reached inside.

A light raced toward them from behind, growing brighter and brighter like an approaching star. Rain watched it through the monitor, his brow lined with sweat and his heart racing. He could make out a form.

It was Elise.

She flew up to the back of the pursuer's black ship, grabbing the tail. Light ripped through the surface, cracking it like a ceramic bowl until it shattered, throwing Thipka and the pilot—the man in the black hood—into the River.

Snowman said in a good-riddance sort of way, "Well, that was effective."

Rain gave a small shrug. "I approve."

"We should go back for Thipka."

Rain was fine with leaving him there. "Must we?"

Elise put her hand in the River. Light spread through the purple water like lightning.

Nothe shouted, *"What is she doing?!"*

Snowman leaned toward the monitor, shocked. Nothe jumped up from the gun deck.

They all knew.

She was about to destroy the River.

They all cursed, talking over each other and pointing toward the branch. "Right there! Right there!"

"I know! I know! I'm trying!"

"We're almost there!"

"Shut up!"

"Hurry!"

"Will you just let me drive?"

"*Go! Go! Go!*"

As Rain turned toward the branch, the River rose in front of them—the faces ghastly and hollow with lightning running through them—and swallowed them. It tossed them out in a dark cave. The ship dropped several feet, sending Rain's stomach into a somersault. It slammed into the cave floor then into a wall as he fought to gain control.

A small light illuminated the cavern behind them, flickering as though from a flame. Rain looked in the monitor.

It was Snowman's father, holding fire in his outstretched hands. His hood was down, his clothes soaked in River water. His face was split open on one side, leaving behind a wide, bleeding smile. Blood streamed over his melted eyes from gashes in his head—melted eyes that stared through the blood at them.

"*What?*" exclaimed Rain, his heart leaping into his throat.

In a flash of light, Elise grabbed Snowman's father, her hands gripping his face and chest, and pulled him back into the darkness.

An explosion rocked the cave, the impact deafening. It filled the cavern with light and threw their ship into stalagmites. Rocks fell from the ceiling and pounded against the hull.

The cave was collapsing.

Rain struggled to regain control, shouting at Snowman to find the switch that brightened the lights so he could see better in the darkness. He darted through the unfamiliar tunnels, racing against the clock, smacking into walls. He ignored the yelling and the cursing of his name and poor Boar's bemoaning groans. He just needed to get them out alive. That was his focus.

They were spat out of the ocean. He didn't even know how many miles they were thrown or in what direction, but they were moving fast. Rain again fought to regain control of the ship as they soared across land and sea. He took deep breaths, wanting to calm himself before he tried to land. The ship had endured tremendous damage; he didn't trust it to handle a crash.

They landed not-so-smoothly in a place where it was early morning. The area was covered with dry trees, rocks, and dirt. A river meandered nearby, but it was more like a creek and didn't appear to be doing much good. There might've been a farm over there, but it was hard to say. Rain had hit his head, and he was having a difficult time focusing.

Groans of pain filled the ship. Nothe said, "Nice landing, Rain."

"Shut up, Nothe," growled Rain. "I'd like to see you do better."

"I would've done better."

Snowman swatted Rain's shoulder and pointed.

A small group of humans approached, their steps slow and cautious —three males, he counted. The two biggest ones held guns that looked like they'd been made two thousand years ago. One of the humans was small, holding a shovel. Farthest away was a woman in a light blue dress, wearing a funny hat tied around her chin, standing in front of a tiny girl in a purple dress with flowers on it. Each of these humans held varying degrees of light, and they were all brighter than any Theran.

Nothe asked, "What do you think the threat level is?"

Rain looked at the humans and their ancient weapons, then at Snowman. The three of them laughed.

Rain thought he might understand why they were armed. A strange ship had just fallen from the sky, and they had a family to protect. "We'll go visibly unarmed, see what happens."

Just before leaving the ship, Snowman changed his form. He had sandy-blond hair, blue eyes, and wore funny clothes similar to what the other people were wearing. He smiled at Rain and Nothe. "What? It's my disguise." With a swipe of his hand, it disappeared, and he was back to his old self. He swiped again, and it reappeared.

If only it were that easy for Nothe and himself. They were stuck in their clearly foreign and smelly suits.

Snowman's smile turned to one of concern as he cautioned, "You... both might want to clean up a bit. You're covered in blood."

They found rags in a compartment and did their best to do just that. Before leaving, Rain put a hand on Boar's face. He could feel his fear, his exhaustion, his pain. He sent a wave of comfort through him. "Hang in there, friend. It's almost over." He knew he couldn't understand his words, but he sensed he could feel them. He could feel Boar's relief.

The humans raised their guns as they approached but didn't point them. Seeing the redness around Nothe's eyes and remnants of dried blood around his nose, he imagined they both looked diseased and terrible. Still, knowing the people were ready to attempt to kill them if threatened made Rain's skin crawl.

The oldest male said something that sounded like a question.

"That sounds like Isaac's ugly language," Nothe said. "What did he call it?"

Rain thought for a moment. "English."

Nothe pointed at his correct word. "It's English." Nothe leaned toward the humans, saying one of the two English words they both knew. "No," he gestured to himself and Rain. Not knowing the word for "speaking," he gestured in a sweeping motion over his throat and mouth as if mimicking words coming out, "English."

The people seemed confused. "No English?" Repeated the older one. He moved in closer and spoke louder, as if they were simply hard of hearing.

Snowman grinned, clearly amused.

Rain, however, was confused. "They're talking louder. Why are they talking louder?"

"I don't know."

"Did you tell them we're deaf?"

"No! You heard me, I said, 'No English!' What else could that possibly mean?"

"Well, apparently, it means, 'We can't hear you, please speak louder.'"

"Why would it mean that? That makes no sense! I'm so confused."

"Clearly, so are they!"

Snowman stepped forward, speaking English.

That's right. Rain remembered him and Isaac talking that one time. Snowman could speak English—but had just sat there the whole time, smiling.

Snowman had the humans laughing. Though their laughter was nervous, Rain hoped it was a good sign. Snowman turned to them and explained that the humans had wanted to know where they were from and what their purpose was and that he had told them they were from a small country in Europe—whatever Europe was—and had tried to create a device that could fly. Clearly, since it'd crashed, it couldn't do that very well.

Seeing that the humans didn't appear to want any sort of battle, Rain took a deep breath. He focused on his own energy, allowing himself to step a little closer to the people, and pressed light and comfort from himself. The humans visibly relaxed. The woman even invited them in for food and water.

Rain and Snowman went inside, keeping the humans distracted, while Nothe let Boar out of the ship to burrow into the ground near the river before it got any hotter outside. Inside the house they discovered these people had a very young child who was ill and lying in a bed in the corner of the tiny cabin, his skin pale and wet from sweat. He couldn't have been more than three years old. The tiny boy offered them a weak smile, his little brown eyes full of light and radiating curiosity and kindness.

The child haunted Rain throughout the remainder of the day. He couldn't get his face out of his mind.

Early the next morning, while the other humans were either out tending to their strange animals and working on their property or sneaking around the wreckage (they thought they were being very sneaky indeed, but everyone knew what they were doing, they just didn't care), Rain snuck into the house and healed the little boy. Seeing the smiling child dance and play and feeling the happiness his mother and father felt at his miraculous turn filled Rain's heart with a light that was wonderful and radiant. They'd clearly thought he would die, and their pure, heavenly joy at his renewed life brought them both to tears. Rain's happiness at this was something he hadn't thought he'd ever feel again.

Perhaps Nothe had been right. Perhaps it was possible to change things for the better.

SNOWMAN FELL silent a few days later, hardly speaking a word and clearly lost inside his head. A few days after that, he disappeared. With the ship.

Rain stated the obvious on the morning of this discovery, sitting next to Nothe on a hot rock and wearing the hot, human clothes the humble farmers had given them. "Well, looks like Snowman took the ship and left us here."

Nothe wiped his brow. It was early morning and already hot—not unlike how most of Thera was several months out of the year. "That's upsetting. I guess we weren't really planning on leaving anytime soon, but now we're definitely not."

Rain showed Nothe what Snowman had given Boar. "At least he left us this book. It appears to be a list of English words and what they mean. Written in English."

Nothe's lips squished into an unamused line. "Well that's very helpful."

"I certainly thought so."

"It's kind of hilarious, though, if you think about it."

Rain dropped the book onto the ground and then kicked dirt on it.

Silence fell between them for a moment. Nothe sighed. "There are a lot of good people here, I think. At least these people are, and Isaac was. That's already more than what was on Thera. There's probably a lot of bad ones, too."

Rain raised an eyebrow at him. "What are we going to do about it?" It was a sincere question.

Nothe grew thoughtful. "I think it's a lot like gardening, Rain."

Rain smiled. "Gardening, huh?"

"I've been doing that a lot lately."

"Yes, you have."

"Pulling out weeds so there's more room for flowers to grow—in the world *and* in the mind, see. Mostly in the mind, of course, because that's where the real change happens." He tapped his head. "Then you nourish and water those flowers until they grow and fill the garden. You know, gardening."

Rain nodded, his smile growing. "Gardening."

"Yeah. Gardening."

"We've got a lot of good work to do, Nothe."

Nothe grinned. "That we do, my friend. That we do." He grew thoughtful, then fixed his gaze on Rain's. "Promise me you'll keep doing good work, Rain. Promise me you'll never give up again."

Rain grimaced, looking away. "I don't know how to promise that."

"You just do it. And you do it because there will always be good work to do and good things to look forward to. Just over the horizon, there."

Rain held his gaze, then gave a small smile, surrendering. "All right, Nothe. I promise."

"Good." Nothe grinned at the sunrise. "I guess we'd better get to work, then."

Epilogue: What Actually Happened to Isaac Moore

Near a small star, a new planet had been put together. It was small, a lot of it built from stolen pieces of other planets, but it was perfect. It had gravity, oxygen, clouds, seas, rain, and seasons. And time, well, people didn't age there like they did everywhere else.

It was safe.

There was plenty of water. Rivers, lakes, and seas. Lush greenery and ideal temperatures, and a mansion on the top of a mountain so high, it almost touched the stars.

There were only two occupants on the entire planet. Well, now three. Elise had flown across the stars to Earth and stolen Boar. She could do that now. Earth wasn't far from this new world, but also, she just *could*, creating pockets that allowed her to slip through space and time with little more than a thought and a wave of the hand.

Boar was okay with living there on this new world. It was beautiful. The air was moist, not like that wretched place he'd ended up on before, with the dry trees, hot sun, and dirt. Elise made sure he had plenty of books. And he was with someone who would understand what he was saying—at least if he ever woke up.

Elise sat at Isaac's bedside as he slept in the mansion, the fading, sunburst scar on his chest a reminder of all she'd gotten back and all that would never be stolen from her again. Boar was downstairs in the library, trying to teach himself new languages. Elise stared out a great window at the moonlight, watching the clouds drift across the sky, as she did nearly every night these days.

Isaac stirred. She turned toward him as his eyes fluttered open. She held her breath, waiting to see what happened next. Would he drift back to sleep again? Or would this time be different?

Isaac gave the ceiling above him a confused look as if it'd just said it loved to eat penguins. "I feel like I've been asleep for days," he said, his voice rough, unused. "How is it night?" He looked around. "Where am I?"

Elise's eyes filled with tears. Relief and joy etched on her face, though she didn't move from where she stood. "You're safe. Nothing can hurt you here. You're safe."

Isaac sat up, the hair on his head about the length of the hair on his face, the confusion growing in his expression. "I am?" He looked down at his hands, his clothes, the strange scar across his chest. He blinked again and again as if trying to summon something to the forefront of his mind. The confusion on his face bled into terror. "I, um. This is probably going to sound like a ridiculous question, but *who* am I, again?"

Tears spilled down Elise's face. "What?"

"Who, er," he swallowed, clearly not liking the terror reflected in her eyes. "What's my name again?"

"Isaac Moore. You're Captain Isaac Moore."

He smiled, but it was forced. "Yes, yes. Of course. That sounds right. I think I remember that now." He swallowed. "You look familiar. You are...?"

"Elise."

"Right, of course. I knew that." He clearly hadn't known that. "Beautiful name, by the way."

She was caught off guard. He'd never said such a thing before. "What else do you remember?"

He ran shaking fingers through his exceptionally short hair. He rubbed his head, looking alarmed. "I remember having longer hair than this." He grew thoughtful, clearly trying so hard to recall his life and what happened. "I remember ships. I believe I liked them. Did I like ships?"

"Yes. Yes, you liked ships."

"And the smell of the ocean, and the feel of the sea against my skin. And turkey and potatoes, I remember that. I *lived* for turkey and potatoes."

Elise laughed. She couldn't help it. He smiled at her. It was a smile that had always filled her heart with warmth, light, and butterflies, like jumping into the sea on a summer morning.

Isaac continued, "And I remember a ship that could sail through the air." He furrowed his brow as if the words sounded ridiculous.

"That's all true," she assured him.

He looked encouraged by this. He went on, "And a river. There was a purple river made up of a sort of living water. It was terrifying but amazing and beautiful. That feels more like a dream, though. Was it a dream?"

"That was real." She was less panicked now as her hope for his memories grew. This was surely a temporary thing.

After a moment, he said, "I remember a girl. At a party. She looked like you, I think."

She smiled and placed a hand to her face as more tears flowed. Her stomach fluttered as if she were falling through the floor. "You remember that?"

"I do. Was that you? I feel like I've wanted to ask you that for a long time; I don't know why."

"Yes," she finally confessed. "Yes, that was me."

He studied her, a smile growing on his face. "I uh, I remember really liking you."

For Isaac, the smile Elise gave him at that moment—there weren't words for it. It was magic. It filled her whole face with light. He didn't need to remember everything in his life to know it was the most beautiful smile he had ever seen.

ACKNOWLEDGMENTS

I almost didn't write this book. It started off as a dream I had several years ago—back when I was less stressed out and my dreams would tell me stories. I dreamt about a sailor in the late 1800s who was offered treasure by an old man. The old man said all he had to do for this treasure was take him somewhere and name the ship after him. The sailor said, "I will gladly accept your treasure, but I will not name the ship after you. I will name it after...me!"

And of course, the old man wasn't having that. He blew up the ship and the sailor's crew, revealing his true form—a goddess. She had been watching the sailor and had fallen in love with him, but was furious that he refused to name the ship after her. The sailor floated in the water, clinging to debris, sinking into despair as he realized how much trouble he was in, and wondering how he was going to get out of his situation.

That was where the dream ended. I woke up—it was still dark outside—and wrote until the sun came up. I didn't know who this woman was, though. I wasn't going to go through the list of many folklore gods and goddesses to pick which one she might be. I wanted her to be different. Her own thing.

Then one day, my oldest son, who was probably around five at the time, was playing with a camping lantern. He told me that his pet space storm lived inside it, and that she was so cute. "My cute little space storm!" he said.

This light inside the lantern, Canon told me, was his (and these are his exact words, which he said in a sweet, little voice as if he were talking to a puppy), "Cute, little space storm." She (yes, she) was his pet, which he kept in this lantern. Yes. A space storm.

And if you asked his little brother, Dexter about it, he discussed it very matter-of-factly, "Yeah. Canon's pet space storm. It's downstairs."

My imagination immediately went wild with this. The idea that a space storm was a living thing that my son kept in his lantern was one of the most magnificent things that I had ever heard. And my mind kept coming back to it.

What if this goddess wasn't a goddess at all, but a living space storm? And if she was, how did she get to that point? How did she earn that title?

I knew I needed to uncover her story, and how her and Isaac Moore's paths crossed.

I wrote the first few chapters, but after a series of awful events, I ended up shelving the book. Eventually, I gave up on finishing it altogether.

But Isaac and the Space Storm, Elise, continued to haunt me. And when I had to cut a couple of scenes from *The Very Real World of Emily Adams*, I knew I needed to put them somewhere. And it was then that I realized, "I need to write another book." So I took this book from my mental shelf, dusted it off, and got to work. Those scenes I had to cut ended up in this book, right where they were always meant to be.

I'm so grateful things fell into place the way they have, and for the opportunity I've had to excavate this story and get to know who these characters truly are. I still haven't uncovered all the answers to the questions I had about Elise the Space Storm, but that just gives me something exciting to look forward to.

Canon's so much older now. I can't believe how fast time has gone by. But I'm so grateful to him for being so supportive of this story, and for wanting me to write it. I'm so grateful to his brothers, Dexter and Oliver, for their wonderful support and encouragement. I'm so grateful for these boys, for always, *always* giving me something to look forward to, for giving life meaning and helping me rediscover the magic of each day, for being a light among the shadows.

My many thanks will always go out to Holli Anderson because she changed my life. I'd *wanted* to be an author since before I could write words, but I didn't know I could actually *be* one until I met her. I'm so grateful to her for seeing this story as something worth telling, and for all her work on it. And many thanks to my editor, Lindsay Flanagan, for her awesome patience and hard work. For reading this thing over and over, and for making it SO much better—for helping me make it everything I wanted it to be. And I must extend my thanks to Staci Olsen, for putting the book together and making it pretty. And I'm so grateful to Rebecca Barney for her fun, wonderful cover!

I also must say thank you to all those who read the early, trash-drafts of this book and helped me make it what I wanted it to be: Susan Stradiotto, Nikki B., and Decillis. And especially thank you to Richard Odey for his thought-provoking feedback, it truly helped me get to know my own characters and story better. And thank you so much to Lisa White, for reading the ARC and catching needed edits that I'd missed! And of course, I have to thank the wonderful Kaci Morgan for her endless support and for her feedback. She made me believe there was really something in this story, and that it was worth seeing through to the end. Whenever I was doubting myself, I thought of the kind things she said about it, and found the strength to keep trying. She is the kind of person everyone with a writing buddy should strive to be!

Thank you to Mom and Dad for their endless support and for helping me so much with this crazy writing dream. So much wouldn't be possible without them. Thank you to KrisAnn, Corey, Kenny, Brook, Jeff, Katie, April, Karen, and Diana, for being there for me and supporting me, for reading my weird books and believing in me. I truly have the most wonderful family in the whole world! And thank you so much to my dear friend, Rachael Christensen, for always, always being there for me, for helping me through some of the worst moments of my life. I've said it before, and I'll say it again: I'd be lost without you.

And thank you so much to Paul, for letting me keep my Jack Skellington animatronic up all year. For making my writing possible and believing in me. For being there when the monsters of the past claw their way to the surface of my mind, and for helping me fight them away. For being my best friend, my teammate, my confidant, and for making me laugh. For knowing my skeletons in the closet and loving me anyway. And of course, I'm so grateful to God for all of these wonderful people I've encountered in my life, for the magic and light that make life meaningful, for guiding my feet and my words. This book, as well as me, personally, would not be here without Him. That's just the way it is.

These folks just prove that kindness goes a long way. It can save dreams, and it can save lives. Never underestimate the power of loving kindness.

About the Author

Samantha J. Rose is a forever-student at Utah State University who will one day have her Masters Degree in Psychology, and is the author of the award-winning novel, *The Very Real World of Emily Adams*. She wrote her first novel in permanent marker on her sister's vanity chair when she was three years old. It wasn't well received.

She currently resides in the mountains of Utah in a little house full of toys, where she's enjoying her happily ever after with her Prince Charming and three adorable little bears.

This has been an
Immortal Production